The ...ters

Amanda Mitchison

D1633577

The Wolf Hunters
© Amanda Mitchison 2021

Cover illustration: Graeme Clarke
Wolf mask: Lucy Vooght, Whispering Woodcrafts

Published by:

Fledgling Press Ltd.
1 Milton Rd West
Edinburgh
EH15 1LA

www.fledglingpress.co.uk

ISBN 978-1-912280-46-9

Printed and bound by:

Print on Demand Worldwide, Peterborough

To my happy lockdown family: Neil, Aideen, Jeremy, Donnchadh, Naomi, Ruairi, Eóghain and Catrìona.

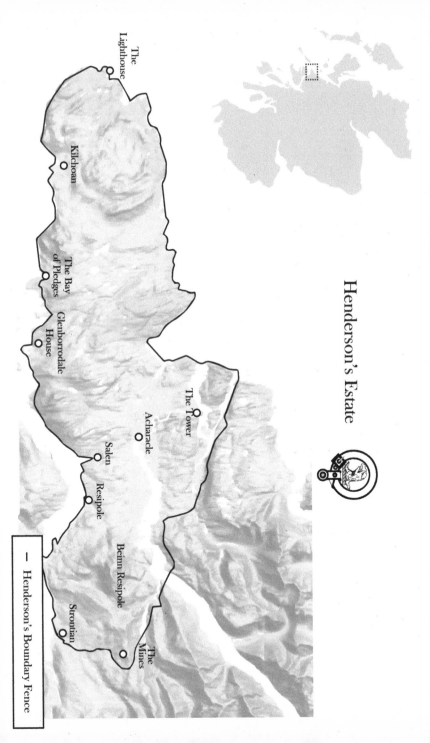

Henderson's Estate

The Lighthouse

Kilchoan

The Bay of Pledges

Glenborrodale House

The Tower

Acharacle

Salen

Resipole

Beinn Resipole

Strontian

The Mines

— Henderson's Boundary Fence

PROLOGUE

Passport control at the Carter Bar border crossing on a bright December morning. A long grey frill of breezeblock four metres high and topped with razor wire runs along the humps of the Cheviots, like the crest on a lizard. An old billboard proclaims: Welcome to Scotland, *Fàilte gu Alba.*

On the English side a bus draws up. The doors wheeze open and out spill a bevy of Scottish migrant workers in hi-vis jackets. Last off the bus is a woman in her thirties: black jeans, grey jacket, grey face. Rhona Ballantyne is clearly not a shabby migrant worker. She is tall and very thin, with shoulder length brown hair. She has regular features, faint lines at the side of her mouth. It's a neutral face which is thoroughly forgettable – this has been useful in the past.

Technically, Rhona is completely shit-faced, having downed all six of the grappa gift miniatures she'd brought for her friend Cat. But she still manages to hoick her bag over her shoulder, and walk directly up to the wall and join the queue a few metres from the border checkpoint.

Rhona waits, holding her vaccination certificate and her passport with the obligatory 1,000 American dollars, which she will have to change into the local Merks using the extortionate official rate. She rummages in her pocket, finds a tube of mints and takes one. Will they still have mints in Scotland?

She looks up; nailed to a pillar of the gate is a severed

human foot. A practical joke? But when she looks closer there's something very familiar about how the toenails are prising themselves away from the cuticles – in the police you do learn about death, and what time does to flesh and bone and blood.

The queue moves closer to the passport gate, closer to the foot. Behind it, pasted to the pillars of the gates, are the Peace and Stability Ordinances. A paragraph has been circled in red with an arrow pointing to the foot.

She shuffles forward, and notes that the foot is glazed, like the top of a French tart; they've used yacht varnish.

On the Scottish side of the border, Cat is waiting for her. Just for a moment, Rhona sees her friend as a stranger would see her: a pretty, snub-nosed woman, mid thirties, dressed in leggings and a long, flecked cardigan, a chopstick holding her hair up. Not really changed, Rhona thinks. Some women (like Cat) soften and glow with age, others (like herself) look as if some giant, red-eyed vampire spider sucked them dry in the night.

And then Cat sees her and holds out her arms.

'Roo!' Cat gives her a great, enveloping hug while Rhona stands stock still.

'I thought nobody touches these days.'

'*I* do!' Cat draws back, 'Let me look at you! You're so *thin*!'

'You mean old and racoon-eyed.'

'That's not what I said. I said, "thin".'

'Mmmm. Well, you look great too,' says Rhona tonelessly. 'I don't know how you do it.'

'I eat, Roo. I eat.' Cat takes Rhona's bag from her. 'Is this all then?'

Rhona nods.

'I thought this was you coming home.'

'It is. I've brought some nice underwear. And a funeral outfit. You always need a funeral outfit.'

'That'll do for church then,' says Cat.

Rhona looks at her askance.

'Didn't you read my letters? You have to go every Sunday now. The Holy Willies keep registers.'

'I'm not going.'

'Believe me, you will be,' Cat weighs the bag in her hand, 'You forgot the gearbox, didn't you?'

'Sorry.' Rhona flinches. 'I mean it, I'm sorry.'

Cat gives her a weary smile.

They walk across the car park to Cat's van which is being watched over by two pointy-faced boys with cropped hair and long sticks. Cat hands them each a five merk coin and they slope off.

Cat and Rhona climb up into the van and then Cat pushes down the snib to relock the doors. Here in the cabin, they're perched high above the ground. The seats have brightly coloured hand-knitted covers, and a pine tree air freshener hangs from the rearview mirror. Cat always was a homemaker. When they were children, she'd sewn little cushions for their den. The three of them, Cat and Rhona and her twin sister, Maggie, all bunched up together with their piles of sweets and their candle stubs and their secret pacts sealed in blood from a compass point. Together-forever-and-ever. Perhaps that is still true, even if there are only the two of them now.

Rhona sinks back into the woolly seat.

'You all right?' Cat starts up the engine.

'They've put a dead foot up at the crossing point. They've even covered it in varnish.'

'That'll be to preserve it.'

'But it's medieval!'

'Left foot? Or right?' Cat edges the van out of the parking bay, skirting round a flurry of crows.

'Left. And someone young. Christ, does it matter?'

'The right foot controls the accelerator so that's what they take for repeated speeding offences. The left foot is for the clutch. That'll be joyriding.'

'I hope I don't have to enforce this.'

'You could be lenient and just chop off toes instead,' Cat glances at her. 'Sorry, that was a joke.'

One of the car park boys runs into the crows, swinging his stick. The birds fly up in a rush of black. But the boy has hit home. Now he bends over to smash in the bird's head.

Cat toots her horn. When the boy glances over at the van, she sticks up her thumb and he gives her a little yellow smile.

'Don't encourage him!' says Rhona.

'That's his supper.'

Rhona shuts her eyes. Her teeth ache, her eyeballs ache, muscles in her scalp, that she didn't know she had, ache.

The road sweeps round the brow of a hill and down into a valley. There are no trees any more. They pass a pair of roadside shacks with roofs of corrugated iron and uncountable small filthy children wading in puddles. The gardens grow a forest of oil drums, and rolls of rusty chicken wire. On the washing line hangs a pair of lonely jogging bottoms. Two cardboard signs: 'The Lord Hath Mercy' and 'Jesus Coming Soon!'

'This is worse than Catania,' says Rhona.

'It's better than it was,' replies Cat tightly. 'If you'd only flown into Edinburgh, then you wouldn't have had to see all this horrible stuff. At the airport they cater for tourists. They've got a piper in the arrivals lounge, and girls in mini kilts with trays of welcome whisky.'

'That's a great idea!'

Rhona opens the glove compartment hoping for a bottle of welcome whisky. Instead, she finds a welcome gun. She picks it up: an old Colt 33, clean, oiled, loaded.

'What the hell!' she says. 'I thought you made handicrafts.'

'I do. But everyone carries a gun now.'

'I'm going to have my work cut out.'

'Oh, you are,' says Cat. 'But the crime isn't what really gets to you. The worst thing is the double speak, the hypocrisy of it all. So everyone trots off to church and opens their Reading of the Day App and pretends life is still okay.'

'Did you say, Reading of the Day?'

'Yep. It'll pop up on your mobile every morning. Apps are part of the Kirk's outreach programme. Sometimes they become ear worms – you just can't get them out of your head.'

'You wrote that the Holy Willies have been praying for Dad.'

'How is he?' says Cat. 'The hospital will only talk to next of kin.'

'I don't really know. He had another operation yesterday. He's still in ICU.'

'So?' Cat tilts her head to one side.

'So why am I coming home? It's time, isn't it? I can't run away forever.'

'But why *now*?'

'I suppose I thought the prospect of death might soften him up a bit. Make him more forgiving.'

Cat says, 'You may be pleasantly surprised. He's lonely. He's always saying that he has no one to look after him. You can mop his brow.'

It's an absurd idea. They look at each other and smile.

Cat is quiet for a moment. Then, cautiously, she says, 'And Maggie?'

'She's there in my mind all the time,' Rhona is pleased that her voice has stayed steady. 'Any other persecutingly intimate questions you want to ask me?'

Cat just nods and keeps her eyes on the road.

At the foothills of the Eildons, the van struggles. Cat screeches down through the gears, eyes flicking reproachfully at Rhona. Finally the engine gets some traction and the van judders forward.

As they zigzag up the hillside, Rhona watches a buzzard circle high above them. It stops and hovers, wings tilting, its gaze fixed, no doubt, on one microscopic mousehole. That was the answer to life, wasn't it? Think of just one thing only.

'I need a pee,' says Cat.

Near the summit they pull into a lay-by. While Cat goes behind a rock, Rhona gets out of the car and stands looking down on the valley below. She follows the glide of the river past the clumps of gorse, the crumbling walls, the little hamlet of houses with dented roofs, the churchyard with its tree stumps.

Seven years ago, she left in pursuit of Sergio Verviani, her sister's killer. In Italy she finally managed to do what she had failed to accomplish back home; she got Verviani and several other members of his criminal network put behind bars.

But in the meantime, Scotland has changed. Of course it has – only she hadn't expected things to be quite so desperate. Yet it's still home. It's still the land that has made her who she is and where, despite everything, she still belongs.

Down in the valley, shadows already rim the little buildings. Rhona thinks how meanly winter light is apportioned here. It'll be growing dark by the time they reach home.

They head on northwest, past the old slag heaps of Lanark, loop round the south of Glasgow and come into Paisley under the dead-eyed tower blocks where the rusty metal sidings are sheering away from the concrete. In the car park below, scores of skinny children are playing among the incineration bins; the boys kicking footballs, the girls huddling on the benches, some holding babies wrapped in blankets.

'It'll be different when we get up north.' Cat has both hands on the steering wheel, chin tilted up, her glasses halfway down her perfect ski jump of a nose.

'Will it?'

'Well, it'll be wilder.'

'What kind of wild? Wild as in mountains and forests? Or wild as in Wild West?'

'Both. There's even bears up there now. And wolves. The Ardnamurchan peninsula has become a game reserve. It's still got loads of trees. They say that if you stop your car in a lay-by there, the bears will come out of the forest and pry open the boot. They'll kill for a chicken sandwich.'

'So would I,' says Rhona.

At the Erskine Bridge Cat pays the 70 merk toll and they come out onto the A82 which, Cat tells her, is now designated a 'signature road' by the Scottish Executive and is duly fitted out with birch saplings along the verges and hideous modern statues at every roundabout.

Cat is driving faster now, talking easily and going over seven years of local news – which is mostly who got the virus and how they died. Rhona pours out cups of dark brown tea from a thermos.

They cross Rannoch Moor, the land rolling out flat and

raw in the winter light. Eventually, the road swerves to the west and they enter the great, desolate scoop of Glencoe. They're in the Highlands now, nearly on the home straight.

But at the first car park Cat pulls over. 'I've just got a wee delivery.'

'*Here?*'

'It's just for some friends.'

Cat takes two holdalls from the back of the van and sets off briskly along a track across the glen. Rhona, head down, trails behind. Cat, she knows, always has some money-making scheme underway.

Cat waits for her on a small footbridge. When Rhona catches up, she says, 'What's wrong?'

'Nothing,' says Rhona. 'But if a wild dog was chewing my leg off you'd say, "I'm just finishing off this macramé plant holder."'

They come to the foot of the mountains. Behind a large rock stands a metal pillar with pulley wheels at the top and a loop of steel rope that disappears up the slope. From the rope hang two green plastic baskets.

Cat puts the holdalls in the baskets, opens a small metal flap on the side of the pillar and presses a switch. The baskets wobble away up the mountainside.

'Good, isn't it?' says Cat. 'It's solar-powered. I had it made.'

'What's in the bags?'

'Epoxy resin, Vaseline, tampons, paracetamol and two months' worth of insulin.'

Rhona frowns.

'You'll see.'

Cat leads the way up a path in a cleft of the mountain. After a steep climb they come out onto a narrow ridge. On the far side the ground dips down into a small hidden valley, cupped between the two mountains of the ridge.

Rhona sees before her a small, squalid settlement surrounded by piles of old tin cans and plastic casing and broken machinery. In the middle are low stone byres with black plastic sheeting on the roofs, and holes for windows. The nearest byre has a white metal door that once belonged to a fridge. And everywhere there are goats: goats in corrugated iron enclosures, goats tethered to rocks, goats tied to posts in the ground.

Standing at a slight distance is a much larger building with a corrugated iron roof. Two women in brown tabards are waiting outside, holding Cat's bags. They have hard, dark faces and hair in long plaits.

Near the entrance to the building, a hubcap filled with liquid has been set into the ground. Cat dips both her trainers in the little pool and walks towards the women. Rhona dips her feet in too and follows.

The women lead them through plastic seal flaps and into a hot, noisy workshop smelling of epoxy resin and burnt hair. At the nearest long table small boys are sawing deer antlers into fingerlength sections, and two bigger boys, one with a squint, the other with a starburst of warts around his neck, are gluing the bits together to form hands. At the next table are trays of completed antler hands onto which women and girls are gluing tiny gold balls, seed pearls, crystals, lapis lazuli, and little squares of tartan cloth.

Cat picks up a hand, 'They're Highland ring holders. What do you think?'

'Creepy *and* hideous! Next you'll be making lampshades from human skin.'

'I've learnt what sells,' Cat surveys the table. 'Think of the most bad taste thing that you can. Then – and this is the real secret – you go that one step further. You add the glitz and the tartan.'

'I didn't know you were quite that cynical!' says Rhona.

But Cat seems distracted. She scans the room. 'We're short-staffed today. Some of these orders are going to be late.'

She says something in a foreign language to one of the women.

The woman replies at some length and then turns her head away.

Cat looks worried.

'What's up?' says Rhona.

'They've lost a couple of young girls. And a boy.'

'How? What happened?'

'We don't know. They were all good kids – not the sort to join gangs.' She takes a breath, 'Maybe they got sick and went off to die on their own. People do. They skulk off like dogs.'

'But I thought Scotland didn't get the flux? That was the one thing it had going for it.'

'Don't you believe it.'

'Wasn't that the whole point?' says Rhona in a strangled voice. 'Wasn't that why you closed the borders?'

'Of course it was. And they're still pretending we've been virus-free.'

'You never mentioned it in your letters.'

Cat gives a scornful snort, 'What do you expect? It's a state secret. And there are still little pockets of disease. Nobody here will have been vaccinated. They are not *officially* here. They're off the record. They'd be turned away at the hospitals.'

Some of the women have put down their glue and tweezers. They're watching.

'What happens when they get sick?' asks Rhona.

'Either they get better. Or they don't.'

'And school?'

'I can't get anything in their language. They're Moldavians. I have to speak Russian to them.'

'Do you speak any Russian that isn't in the imperative?'

'What do you mean by that?'

'You said they were "friends".'

'They are. We get on well.'

'They're your *staff*, Cat.'

'I pay them a good wage.'

'I'm out of here. I've had enough.' Rhona walks quickly to the exit and plunges back through the plastic seals. Outside, she finds a rock, checks it for goat droppings, and sits down. She eats a mint, but a drink is what she really needs.

Someone is watching her. Quickly she turns, but nobody's there. Then she sees a billy goat looking at her with the same mournful, heavy-lidded eyes as Cat's workers.

Cat comes out and joins her. 'What's the problem?' she says.

'I didn't know you kept slaves.'

'That's not fair! I'm helping them.'

'Helping them? You said you hated doublespeak. How can you do this?'

'They need the money.'

'Doesn't look like you pay them much.'

'It's better than what they'd get from anyone else. And I put the pulley in and the workshop.'

'But that was for *you,* for your business,' says Rhona.

'You don't get it, do you? This is what they need. It's better than charity. It means I can pay them *and* bring in medical supplies.'

Cat picks up a stone, flicks it high into the air and catches it again. 'I wonder if they traded them.'

'Sold their own children! You're joking!'

'Take a look at the kids here, they all have something wrong with them. But the three that have gone were perfect. They had good teeth, straight limbs, no groin rot. Sorry, Roo. That's just how things are these days.'

Rhona feels a sudden weariness wash over her. She says, 'Take me home, Cat.'

'You sure about that? I thought you'd stay with us. At least at the beginning, till you found yourself somewhere.'

'No. I want to go home.'

'But the house…'

'It's still standing, isn't it? Or is that another horrible thing you've just been waiting to tell me?'

'The house is there all right.'

'So, what's the problem?'

'Just, you know…' Cat says delicately. 'Nobody has been living there. You might feel…'

'I might feel *what?* Ghosts?'

'Yeah.'

'I won't be going into her room. Please Cat, take me home. Just take me home.'

And Cat takes her home

SIX MONTHS LATER

A BEAUTIFUL DAY TO DIE

Reading of the Day
'Jesus answered and said unto him, Verily, verily, I say
unto thee, Except a man be born again, he cannot see the
kingdom of God.'
John 3.3

On a morning in June, Rhona is the duty officer and takes the first call of the day. She dresses quickly and drives straight through Fort William. She takes the public road through the scalped hills of Lochaber, past the tinker settlements and the quarry and on down to the coast.

The road ends when she reaches the boundary of Henderson's wild game reserve. In front of her is the great steel mesh boundary fence which cuts off the Sunart and Ardnamurchan peninsula from the mainland. A coat of arms has been wrought into the metalwork of the gate; the crest shows an eagle head in profile.

On the far side of the fence Rhona can see the green woods of the estate and, just by the gate, a transparent, egg-shaped cabin. The glass or plastic of the cabin is clean and unscratched. And sitting inside is a guard wearing a green fleece. He has a semi-automatic rifle resting at his feet and he nods to Rhona while making a circling motion with his hand. She winds up her window, smiling at the idea that a sheet of glass would really save her from a wild bear. The gates open and she enters the reserve

She drives fast between columns of trees, occasionally

passing neatly boarded-up houses. The road is smooth and beautifully cambered, the tarmac shiny. Yet it is also wild here. At the luxury, foreign currency hotels she is used to stage set woods that are only two or three trees thick. But this is different. These are real forests that reach up into mountains. Miraculously, nothing here has been destroyed.

What is the price?

When the road divides she heads inland. She winds the window down again. It is the freshest, dampest, cleanest morning of the world. Later, it will be hot – the first day of summer. Tiny yellow blossoms of tormentil shine in the grass and when she drives through the wood, the car plunges into pale green light from the beech trees vaulting high overhead.

A beautiful day to die.

In a lay-by up ahead she sees a Land Rover and she parks behind it.

Matt Simpson, the gamekeeper, is waiting for her. He too is dressed in a green fleece with a small gold embroidered eagle head. His tweed cap is crunched deferentially in his hand, folded tarpaulins lie at his feet.

'You must be the new lady inspector,' says Matt.

'I'm not that new. I've been here six months.' She looks at the tarpaulins. 'Leave them. The men will do all of that when they get here.'

She's made it sound as if they are on their way, but she hasn't even called the procurator fiscal's office yet. She always puts that off. She knows that the more people around the less you sense where you are, and what has happened.

She walks along the verge for a better view down into the dell. The clearing in the woods is about seventy metres wide, with a round, brown pond in the middle and a small shed off to one side. Near to the pond lies the body of a young man. He is naked, lying on his front, his arms loosely at his side, one leg slightly bent and with the foot facing inwards. There's no sign of any injury, except a couple of brown smudges on his back. You might even have thought he was taking the sun. But who would sunbathe here?

And, as always, there's that terrible, emptied out stillness.

'It's nobody local,' says Matt. 'No one from the reserve.'

'So who is he then?' she says.

'I don't know.'

There's just the faintest quiver in Matt's voice.

Rhona thinks: *his first lie.*

'But you have some record of who comes onto the reserve, no?'

'Mr Henderson keeps a register of car number plates. But I haven't checked at the Big House.'

'And you're certain it was a bear?'

'They're all satellite tagged. Wilber was here at 2 a.m.'

'*Wilber?* Isn't it a wild animal?'

'That's his name. Short for Wilberforce.'

'So we know the killer, but not the victim. That's most unusual.'

Matt blinks slowly and doesn't reply. He's a coarse-featured man, his forehead and nose pitted by the flux. An ugly face, an honest face – or so you'd have thought.

'How did you find out about the body?'

'We had a tip-off.'

'Who gave you that?'

'A man. He didn't leave a name.' *That's his second lie.*

'And you don't know who it was?'

Matt shakes his head.

'Matt. You don't mind if I call you Matt, do you? This is a reserve, right?'

'Yes.'

3

'So, I presume not many people live here?'

'Twenty-eight adults.'

'Exactly. And the land is surrounded by a five metre electric fence?'

'Four metres. And only electrified over the sections on dry ground.'

'Whatever. But the number of people likely to have seen the body is small. And you know them all.'

'You'd be surprised who creeps in. We get a lot of tip-offs. People call up with sightings of the peregrines and sea eagles all the time.'

'It's nice to know there are people still interested in wildlife. But this isn't about a roosting bird, is it? This is a little bit different, no?' She gives him a quick, devastating smile.

Matt looks at his boots.

They walk down the bank to the dell, through buttercups and dog's mercury. At the foot of the slope the ground is boggy, moss and hummocks of marsh grass, a buzz of bluebottles and the smell of standing water. Through an opening in the trees she can see the shore and the huge seaweed-covered boulders hunkered into the sand. The green mesh boundary fence traverses the shallows of the beach. Beyond lies the sea with the thin line of Coll on the horizon.

Matt introduces his son, Gordon, who is sitting very still on a rock, a few feet from the body. The boy is thirteen, maybe fourteen and with a lumpy nose – his father's son. His face is set and stolid, and he holds a shotgun across his knees. He'll remember this morning for the rest of his life.

She takes a step closer. The grass and moss are scuffed up. There is a circle of brown blood – it must have spurted out. And scattered across the ground are shreds of flesh, crawling with bluebottles. Yet the corpse, at least the man's

4

back, looks untouched. She's never seen a body quite like this.

The air suddenly feels thicker. It's getter warmer now, the flies and fluff from bog cotton and dandelion seeds are everywhere. She watches a cloud of gnats circle slowly upwards, as if climbing an invisible spiral stair. Even after all these years, she still has to quell a heave in her stomach.

She brings out her mobile and turns on the camera. At least when she is taking photos she looks at her phone, not at the terrible thing itself. She starts with the surrounding area. The pond. Click. The surface is brown and lumpy with reeds; nobody could swim in that.

Around the body, the marsh grass is broken and bent. Click. But there are no footprints. Moss springs back immediately – how many crimes in Scotland remain unsolved thanks to moss? Ah! Some pieces of bloodied string. Click. The string has a blue thread running through it – so partly synthetic and probably imported. What's it doing here?

She clicks on the muddy feet. Then she works her way up: the calves, the thighs, the heartbreaking fuzz of pale hair on his buttocks. Click. Click. Click. And then his hands. Soft and clerical. The nails are whitish; *he didn't fight back*.

There is an old scar – a pink, knobbly indent – in the small of his back. A tiny tattoo of a swallow under his ear. He's spotty round the shoulders. And at the back of his neck, he has a tan patch where he's caught the sun, and a tiny pink birthmark is just creeping up into the hairline. She likes necks. They are the most childlike and intimate part of a man. Down below it's all thrust and shove and show. But the nape of the neck…

She feels Matt's eyes on her. She stands back to get a proper overview of the corpse. Brown wavy hair cut very

5

short at the sides, long on top. His face is in the tall grass so she can't, thank God, see much. Nearly six foot? A big lump of a bloke: BMI 30? 35? Not an athlete, so probably tender meat. But the back is almost untouched, save for the smudges of blood round his waist. So why these shreds of flesh? Why the string? And why, she wonders, had the young man taken off his clothes? It can't have been in order to swim – Henderson's fence blocks access to the sea and the pond is full of hornwort. So why strip off? Was it a bet? A dare? He must have been on something.

'Are his clothes here?' she asks.

Matt indicates with a jerk of his head. Behind Rhona, tucked in among the trees, is a small stone shed with a blue door. On the doorstep stand a pair of Wellingtons and a pile of men's clothes: jeans, a pink shirt, and boxers, all neatly folded and the socks paired into a ball. On top of the clothes lies a red azalea blossom and, tucked down into the trumpet of one of the flowers, is a very tightly folded playing card. Before Matt comes over she quickly places the card in her pocket.

'Did you fold up his clothes?'

Matt shakes his head.

She turns to Gordon and he shakes his head too.

'Who wears pink shirts these days?' she asks.

Matt shrugs.

'He might be one of Will's friends,' says Gordon. She sees Matt take a breath.

'Who's that?' she asks.

'Mr Henderson's son. He has friends staying at the tower down the road.'

'Why didn't you tell me that before?'

Matt's eyes narrow. 'I wasn't sure. I don't see them that much.'

'And you're quite sure it was a bear? Couldn't it have been the wolves?'

'I know it was Wilber,' says Matt. 'And the wolves would have left nothing. They'd have taken some of the bones away with them too. They like marrow.'

He pauses. 'Bears are different. Bears start with the belly.'

It's time now. She puts on her vinyl gloves and squats by the corpse. She clenches her jaw – not that that will make any difference.

She lifts and tilts back the dead man's shoulder. She glances at the face, all askew and muddy. The eyes are shut, but the mouth – large-lipped and loose – is open, a froth of saliva in one corner. The throat has been clawed open – that'll be what killed him. But this still doesn't account for the shredded flesh on the ground.

She lifts the shoulder further up so that the man's torso is clear of the ground. His chest is covered in blood, and there's a gash down his middle – a great open red zip. It seems to swell and then something glistening slithers out. Gaining momentum, his guts slop onto the ground.

She rests the body back down again. And as she does so, she hears something. Gordon springs to his feet. He is pointing the shotgun towards the trees.

She turns her head to look, but the wood is silent. All she can see is the light slanting down between the trunks of the alders.

A pale green beech leaf floats in through the open window of the car. She puts out her hand and it lands light as air on her palm: a blessing.

She takes another gulp from the hip flask, wipes her mouth on the back of her sleeve and opens the folded playing card. A Queen of Spades, with nothing written on it, no message, a small pale blob of some kind of residue still sticking to the bottom of it. The card has been folded and folded again and then scrunched up very tightly. She takes off her gloves, wraps them round the card and tucks the bundle into the side pocket of the driver's door.

Rhona brings out a tube of mints and the tablet from her briefcase. She uncoils the foil wrapping of the mints and, as she turns on the tablet, puts several sweets in her mouth and crunches through them. The internet connection is astonishingly good; she overrides registration details by putting in the police code and turns on Google Maps. The road and the dell with its little pond appear on the screen. She zooms out a little and notices a U-shaped building tucked in the woods nearby. She'll get Sergeant Boyd to have a good look round there.

She zooms back further, until she can see the whole of the Ardnamurchan peninsula, a long tongue of mountain and forest jutting out into the Atlantic. The Google photography was done some time ago – before Henderson's fence was erected – but it is so detailed that she can see the white of the waves where the cliffs drop away into the water and the tips of the trees in the forests. Up on the mountain plateau there are deep black lochans and the rock faces are grey and creviced like the hide of a rhino.

Her mobile rings. It's Chief Superintendent Travers, who everyone in the Fort William office refers to as 'The Bassett' because of the bags under his eyes and his lugubrious drooping jowls.

'Rhona? Where are you?'

'I'm still on the reserve, sir.'

'Who's with you?"

'The wolves, the killer bear, a few red deer.'

'You shouldn't be there on your own. Why didn't you take Boyd?'

'Boyd wasn't in yet. He was at his helicopter training.'

'Cummings, then. Why not Cummings?'

She doesn't answer.

'Are your windows up? Is the car locked?'

'Sir, they told me all of that at the checkpoint. And yes, I'm armed.'

'Get the bear killed. Do you know who the victim is yet?'

'No. It's a young man. Caucasian. Someone properly fed, properly clothed.'

'Not a scally, then?'

'Not a scally. I'm sure he'll be registered.' She pauses, 'And we should treat the site as a crime scene.'

'What!'

'I'm serious. This was no accident.'

'A man gets killed by a bear. How is that *not* an accident?'

'There's something going on. There's string and bits of animal meat – I think pork or bacon – all around the body. It just doesn't make sense.'

'So what happened then? Did the bear not kill him?'

'I think the bear *did* kill him. His heart was certainly pumping when he was attacked. He was alive alright.'

'Go on.'

'Well, it must have been a very polite bear.'

'What are you getting at?'

'The bear didn't eat much of him, which is unusual.'

'How did it kill him?'

'Ripped his throat and slit his stomach open.'

'That's not very polite.'

'Sir, it's all a bit odd.'

She can see her boss, dressed in his maroon cardigan, slippers on under his desk. He'll be leaning back in his chair, torturing the springs.

The Bassett says, 'Don't tell me you're claiming

9

culpable homicide? What'll you ask in the interview room? "Mr Bear, where were you on the night of the 14th June?" "Grrr." "We will need to look at your bank details." "Grr. I don't have an account…"'

'You do a good bear, sir. You could give up the day job.'

'I'll have to if you go on like this. Why is it worrying you so much? All you've got is some unaccounted-for string and bits of bacon.'

'There's more to it. When wild animals kill they make a huge mess. But this bear ate almost nothing.'

'Did it get frightened away? Never discount the simple explanation.'

'The body was flipped over onto its front. You know, kind of tidied up – like when people put their knife and fork together at the end of a meal. Why would a bear do that if he was being chased away?'

'Maybe this fellow didn't taste right?'

'Yeah, but I never thought bears were that fussy. And…'

'And?' he asks quickly. She can tell he's interested now, despite himself.

'The victim's clothes were all folded in a neat little pile nearby.'

'Maybe he was a tidy man. Where exactly did it happen? Are you down in the woods beyond Acharacle. Is he by that pool?'

'Yes,' says Rhona. Of course, he knows the area. The Bassett has a holiday cottage out at Kilchoan, near the end of the peninsula.

'Then the simple explanation is that he'll have got stripped off to go for a swim. You know, some men are house-trained – they can fold. Think of Cummings.'

'But on top of the clothes was a flower.'

'Did you find anything else? What was in the shed down there?'

She's surprised. He really *does* know the estate well. He must know the landlord, Archie Henderson. He probably knows Matt too. Probably knew the bear as well.

'There's nothing there,' she says. 'The door was unlocked, but there were cobwebs across the entrance.'

She hasn't mentioned the playing card. He'd laugh at her if she said it had been scrumpled up too tightly and was worrying her.

'It's most probably nothing,' he says. 'Just a midnight bathe that went wrong.'

'It doesn't *feel* like that. There's more to it.'

'You and your feelings,' sighs The Bassett.

'I've been right before. You read the report from Signor Petroni.'

'And you've been wrong before.'

'I've been *not proven* before.'

'Same thing,' he snorts. 'And what are you up to now?'

'Archie Henderson is my next port of call.'

'Well, you'll find him interesting. He's a man of many parts.'

'What do you mean?'

'He can talk about anything. He's educated, reads books. Remember books? He plays the oboe, speaks German and Russian. He got a rowing blue at Cambridge. The oar is in his hallway.'

'Thanks,' she says flatly. 'That's a real help.'

'Take the road slowly. You don't want to bump into another bear.'

'Yes, sir.'

'And don't stay away too long. The summer bludgeonings have begun in Lochgoilhead.' He takes a breath, 'One more thing, Rhona.'

'Sir?'

'Make an effort. Try and be nice.'

GLENBORRODALE CASTLE

Rhona drives further into the peninsula, weaving through green tunnels of trees and at times coming out onto the banks of Loch Sunart. All the way, Henderson's fence keeps her company and she sees the loch through a green mesh.

And everything feels almost smirkingly neat: the fence posts are all upright, the gates freshly painted, the boarded-up houses have gutters and roofs still intact. She is not used to this. Where are the button-eyed children in rags? The dented hen coops? The piles of old animal bones?

She turns in at the entrance to the castle, presses the buzzer and waits. Eventually the great metal gates open.

The drive is lined with towering conifers and blossoming azaleas and rhododendrons in every shade of yellow, red and purple. She passes a tennis court and a walled garden. Then the drive climbs on up the hill and ends in a car park at the back of a very large, red stone Victorian country house.

Rhona parks the car and sits for a moment taking stock. In the wing mirror her own bloodless face looks back at her. She should have eaten some breakfast, should at least keep some muesli bars in the glove compartment. But who is she kidding? Cat is right; she runs on ethanol and sugar, not food. If they cut her open they won't find blood. She'll just leak a thin, sour lemonade.

She gets out of the car. A pump thrums somewhere in the woods behind her and there's a smell of moss and mulch.

She catches a glimpse of a woman's face at a downstairs window. That'll be the mad housekeeper; these houses always have a mad housekeeper. But nobody comes out.

They buzzed her in, didn't they? Isn't anyone coming?

She examines the building. It's a great brute of a house: five or six storeys of Victorian gothic, turrets sprouting at the corners, crowstepped gables, heavy iron balconies. But the aspect is wonderful. The house is perched high above the road. And Henderson, thanks to an expensive ha-ha, will be the one inhabitant of his estate whose view is uninterrupted by the fence.

She walks under a stone arch and round to the front door. Ahead of her, beyond the flagpole and the shining loch, lie the grey and green folds of the mountains of Appin.

Henderson, dressed in yellow corduroys and an old linen shirt, stands waiting for her on his front steps. With him are three straggly Irish wolfhounds with long red tongues and two with testicles that bloom out at the back. Like his dogs, Henderson is tall and thin. But his pelt is superior: he has a full head of grey hair swept back over craggy features and huge eyebrows. A handsome man – if you like your men beaky.

But there's a dark, stretched look of fatigue round his eyes. She does a quick calculation; he'll have got the news three to four hours ago.

'Good morning, I'm Inspector Rhona Ballantyne.'

'Archie Henderson.' There's not a trace of Scots in his accent. Probably an English prep school, she thinks. Then Eton, or Rugby.

He puts out his hand and she shakes it. His skin is cool and dry and surprisingly pleasant, like holding a snake.

'You must be Roddie Ballantyne's girl,' he says.

'Yes, I'm his surviving daughter. But I'm not a girl.'

'You're not a girl?' He gives her a mocking smile, 'You certainly look like a girl.'

She takes a breath, smiles glassily at him and says: 'I'm a female graduate in my mid thirties. I am fluent in French and Italian and I can ride a horse and skipper a boat up to 40 feet long. I have a licence to bear arms and a great fat folder's worth of other qualifications, but if you still want to go on calling me "Roddie Ballantyne's girl", please be my guest.'

'You still look awfully young to be an inspector.'

'We get younger every year, Mr Henderson. That's what police do.'

The bitch, greying round the muzzle, lopes up to Rhona and snuffles at her groin.

Henderson clicks his tongue and the dog backs away. 'Sorry about that,' he says, rewarding the creature with a scratch under the ear. 'Zezou always likes to check everyone out.'

'It's okay,' says Rhona wearily. 'I grew up with dogs.'

'So you did. I used to shoot with your father. I'm sorry about what's happened to him.'

She nods and then waits to see if he'll ask more. But he doesn't.

How can he know Dad and not know about Maggie?

Henderson thrusts his hands into his trouser pockets. 'Do you know who it was yet?' he asks. 'Matt told me it definitely wasn't William.'

'It's a young man – in his twenties, I'd guess. Just over six foot. Does that ring a bell?'

Henderson's gaze is fixed on the loch. 'It's probably one of my son's friends,' he says in a drained voice. 'They're staying up at the tower. It's only half a mile from the dell.' He pauses. Then he asks, almost hopefully, 'Was he balding?'

14

'No. He had a full head of hair.'

'Did you say the body was fat?'

'No, I didn't.'

'A bit plump, though?'

'Well, yes.'

He sits down abruptly on the stone step. 'It'll be Johnnie then.'

'Who?' Rhona sits down beside him.

'Johnnie. He's the Fergusson boy. You know the Fergussons?'

'No.'

'They're a big confectionary family from Ayrshire. Father is in the army. I think the mother is a Stephens. One of the Aberdonian Stephens. They're related to the Frasers of Lovat.' Henderson takes another breath. 'Johnnie was a nice lad, but a bit lost. Oh Christ! I said "*was*"! Have you...?' He looks at her cautiously. 'Have you any photographs? Then I'd know for sure.'

'I'm sorry. I can't do that. And I don't have any images of his face.'

'And I suppose there's not too much left to see anyway,' he adds gloomily.

She doesn't put him right.

He combs his hand through his hair, but it still flops forwards.

'Mr Henderson, you do know that the bear will have to be destroyed.'

Henderson's chin jerks up, 'Wilber? Wilber has to be killed? That's ridiculous! He's my best bear. He was a major investment.'

'I don't doubt he was. I'm going out with Matt Simpson this afternoon to dispatch the animal.'

'Matt *agreed*? Why was I not consulted?'

'You're most welcome to come,' she gives him another

15

little smile. 'And if you don't want your gamekeeper to carry out the shooting, we'll send a police sniper.'

Boyd, she knows, would enjoy that job. He'd probably mount the bear's head and paws in his living room. It would certainly look better than the scrofulous little pine marten he has on his old piano.

Henderson drops his voice, 'These kind of bears are rare now. Very rare. Do you have any idea how much an animal like this costs?'

Rhona shakes her head.

'About one and a half million Canadian dollars. He had to be air-freighted from Vancouver. He took up nine seats in a passenger airline. Nine seats! We had to have a specialist handler with him and a high spec crate. The insurance premium was phenomenal. And now,' he wipes the hair back from his face again, 'you're just going to kill him!'

'It's the law. A man has died.'

Henderson's jaw moves. He's chewing on a thought. She waits.

Eventually, he says, 'Are you sure it was the bear? Couldn't the boy just have had a heart attack or something – and then the bear came scavenging. They do that, you know.'

She thinks back to the dell. Arterial blood had pumped out across the ground. 'The victim, I'm afraid, was very much alive when he was mauled. I can't go into the details now.'

'I still don't understand.' He sounds petulant now. 'I tramp these woods and mountains every day. The bears always slink away. They're timid.'

'I've never thought of grizzlies as timid.'

'Young lady, that just shows what you don't know. Something must have happened. Bears aren't like people

– they don't go mad without a reason. The boy must have done something incredibly stupid.'

She sits and waits. *Always wait.* When it's difficult, you wait. When it's awkward – especially when it's awkward – you wait.

But Henderson doesn't answer. He gets to his feet and dusts himself off. 'I think we need a drink. Inspector, will you join me?'

It has been a long dry morning – for nearly two hours Rhona has not had a drop to drink. She looks up at Henderson and grins.

They go inside, the dogs padding behind them. The hallway is a magnificent panelled room smelling of damp stone, old leather, and a faint undertow of fried kipper. Up on the wall, attached with metal staples, is Henderson's oar from Cambridge. The surnames and initials of the crew are painted on the paddle.

They climb side by side up the grand staircase. The newel posts are as wide as a giant's thigh. Henderson swings open the door to a drawing room with a bay window looking out over Loch Sunart.

Rhona sits down in an armchair by the fireplace and surveys the room with quick covert glances. The walls are lined with leatherbound books: Homer, Virgil, Caesar's Wars, a slim little volume of dirty verse by Catullus. There are also the never opened, non books: theological tracts and old farming manuals. Everything is stored in cupboards with wire mesh fronts, as if the books were cheese in an old larder.

As Henderson pours out two whiskies, she says hopefully, 'It's been a long morning.'

He hands her a full glass with a teardrop of air in the bottom. She sniffs the rim. Peaty, probably an Islay malt –

at least two shots worth. She tips the drink back, her throat is instantly and deliciously hot as a stovepipe.

Henderson stands with one arm leaning on the mantelpiece and his dogs curled on the floor, three hairy commas at his feet. It is, she supposes, the proper pose for a laird.

'I should call William,' he says. 'But reception at the tower is terrible and he never has his phone on anyway.'

That's good news; she will be able to get to the students before he has primed them.

Henderson continues, 'You know I could lose my licence over this.'

'Your licence?' She is faintly surprised that anyone has to have a licence for anything these days.

'From The National Trust for Scotland. Don't you know anything?'

'Does that let you off tax?'

'Not quite, but it exempts me from kirk feus. *And* I don't have to be at the beck and call of the Inspectorate of Elders.'

'I see.' She doesn't see. She still doesn't understand how the country really works now. But she will probably need his cooperation. She adds slyly, 'I might be able to write a report for you.'

'Thanks.'

'But we *are* dealing with a fatality.'

'I know. And of course all this is terrible. But the whole future of the estate could be jeopardised. Everything I have struggled to create here. It has been my life's work.' He says it again softly: 'My life's work!'

Why is it only men who talk of a 'life's work'?

She takes out her notebook, 'I just need a bit of background information. Can you tell me when you inherited the estate?'

'September 2005. The death duties nearly killed us. I had to sell off our London house.'

'And then what happened?'

'Well, what do you do with 500,000 acres of unfarmable land? Make a paintball arena? Turn it into a giant golf course for the Japanese?' He gives a bitter bark of laughter. 'I'm not quite *that* vulgar. I wanted to do something worthwhile. I wanted the land to be true to itself.'

'That's a curious phrase. What do you mean exactly?'

'The land needs to be properly wild. The estate was completely degraded when I took over. There was Sitka bloody spruce everywhere. Half the birds of prey had been poisoned and there were sheep all over the high ground, and hordes of red deer were stripping the trees. The estate was nearly bankrupt – it was all spend, spend, spend. We'd just about got ourselves back on our feet when the shutdown came. Everything went to pot. We'd been offering deer stalking at 1,000 dollars a day, and suddenly, of course, we had no takers.'

'How does the estate pay for itself now?'

'We do very high-end hunting. People come from all over the world to stalk our wolves.'

'When you say "we", are you a company? Or does it mean you and your family?'

Henderson sits down, legs unattractively akimbo. He picks a thread off the knee of his corduroys, smoothing down the material as it were a beloved fourth dog. 'Well, not quite. I suppose my "we" is more generic.'

'You mean "we" as in "the Scottish people"?' *God, he has a nerve.*

'The estate, the Highlands, Scotland…' he smiles vaguely.

'And what about your own family?'

'They're not too involved in the estate. Marissa hates the

cold, poor love. She spends most of her time in Morocco. She's a painter – likes the light there. And our daughter, Lucy, is training for the bar in London. Only William is up here in Scotland. He, at least, has a feel for the wild. He's a good shot too. Well, he *was* a good shot, I'm not so sure now.'

'Why not any longer? Does he not shoot?'

'It's not his style these days. He's interested in books and art, and those kind of things.' Henderson waves a dismissive hand.

'Once you're gone, will he continue your work?'

Henderson shakes his head, 'I can't say.'

He drains his glass and fondles the ear of the lankiest of his lanky dogs. 'You know what's going to happen, don't you? They'll say I should have gone for black bears. Black bears are much more timid. They never attack humans.'

'You didn't consider it, then?'

'Of course not! Black bears aren't indigenous to Scotland. Nobody, I sometimes feel, really understands what I am trying to do here. I don't just introduce animals for the hell of it. But I suppose that's beyond the comprehension of the Scottish Executive, and of those blasted Elders.'

He rolls his eyes to the ceiling. She looks up too and notes the elaborate cornices: the plaster vine leaves and eagle heads in every corner. The heads are picked out in gold paint, the tongues are red. A logo-encrusted ceiling. *Cat would love it.*

'I don't understand why we are still crawling with bureaucracy. We've had the shutdown and the crash and a pandemic, but it doesn't seem to have killed off any of our institutions. The National Trust is still up in its offices in Edinburgh and they seem to think I've got *rivers* of money. And then there are their poisonous little friends at Historic Scotland. Give them half a chance and they'd want my backside harled in authentic limestone mortar applied by a craftsman in a handmade smock. And there's the Forestry Commission – they haven't got any trees now but they still spend their time inventing new diseases and bullying me to look for symptoms. As if I had all the time in the world.'

She watches him walk over to the window. One of the dogs opens a Smaug-like eye, and closes it again.

Henderson picks angrily at a spot of loose paintwork on the sill. 'They're all little paperclip men and Holy Willies. The country goes to rack and ruin, frackers are destroying the water table, the people starve, children go shoeless and there are bandits everywhere. But do they ever see the bigger picture? They're all mired in detail and every one of them is a second-rater. They have never taken on real responsibilities or followed their passions. They've never lived.'

'And you've lived?'

'Well, I have now!' he harrumphs.

'What makes you think that you have lived any more than an Edinburgh lawyer?' she asks. His hair is over his face again. *He needs a hairband.*

'Because an Edinburgh lawyer has never experienced real danger. He has never put himself on the line.' He concedes a quick smile: 'Or *herself*, of course.'

He doesn't take women seriously, but she wonders if this might be to her advantage.

Now Henderson changes tack. 'Have you ever hunted?' he asks. 'Ever gone deerstalking?'

'No, never.'

He turns towards her, his gaze fixed on his dogs, 'You spend your day crawling through the undergrowth. You creep up on a herd and you raise your gun and you're just about to shoot when a twig snaps or the wind suddenly changes and the herd will be off. Then you'll have to start all over again – and that can happen a hundred times. But just wait. There'll come the day when the wind is still and you're just getting ready to fire, and suddenly the hind you've picked senses something and turns and looks at you. It's a moment of complete, beautiful silence. The deer has realised it's the victim... That's when you have the connection. You breathe together and you are one. Time stands still and you make the kill. Honestly, it's just exquisite.'

Rhona takes a gulp of air.

The mood is broken. Henderson looks at her and gives a tired laugh, 'You must think I'm a nutcase.'

'Not at all.'

'Let me take you up Ben Resipole one day. Then you'll understand why I do what I do.'

MRS COLLINS

Before Rhona leaves she asks Henderson not to visit his son for a few hours and explains that there'll be a police cordon on the road until the early afternoon. Henderson seems to buy this story.

He offers to walk Rhona back to her car, but she insists on going alone and leaves him with his dogs on the front steps.

In the car park she scrunches as noisily as she can on the gravel and stops in full view of the back windows while she pretends to look for something in her handbag.

She has never been able to fake fainting. Instead she has to do it the hard way, for real. So now she holds her breath and starts to count. It's such a cheap trick, and she's done it countless times before. The oxygen deprivation has no doubt knocked a few points off her IQ. But then intelligence is something she's never lacked, and never really rated.

She goes on looking in her bag, counting the seconds while the trapped breath stacks up in her lungs, and pushes for release. Her heart beats faster, louder. She thinks, I have control over so little in my life, except this. She reaches 110…111…112… She doesn't feel her head swirl, or her knees buckle. She just goes down.

When she comes to, she's sitting on the gravel, a hand holding her head down between her legs.

'Breathe in! Take it easy!' says a woman with a local accent.

Rhona breathes in. She looks up at a round face, thick glasses over bulgy blue eyes, a halo of overly brown, tightly permed curls.

The woman, who introduces herself as Marie Collins, is in her fifties: big-bosomed and fat-backed, strong as an ox. She hauls Rhona to her feet, 'Come into the house and have a sit down.'

It's an order, not an offer. But Rhona doesn't mind. She wants to be fussed over, given a drink, chatted to, *told things*.

One hand on Mrs Collins' arm, she totters into a huge, low-ceilinged kitchen where two short-haired, skinny little boys, one a blond and the other a freckly redhead, are kneeling on chairs at a table.

This is the type of kitchen Rhona knows so well from childhood: worn, well-heated, a bit squalid. The floor is covered in flagstones and old rag rugs, the walls and lampshades are yellowing with age, speckled with fly spots.

She flops into a sagging settee by the stove. The seat is still warm. A cushion perched oddly on the other end of the sofa catches her attention. A loose gold embroidery thread trails out from underneath it.

On the far side of the room are the two boys. They look about nine or ten, and are dressed like old-fashioned prep school pupils in white shirts and corduroy shorts. They glance at her but quickly return to their board game. As they move their plastic pieces across the board, they munch messily on butterfly cakes. Beside the game there is also a plate of Bourbon biscuits. So, cake *and* biscuits. Mrs Collins, Rhona concludes, must be a feeder.

'How long was I out?' she asks.

'Just a minute or two,' replies Mrs Collins. 'What can I get you? Tea? Aspirin? Alka Seltzer? Bicarbonate of soda?'

'A whisky, please.'

'*Another* drink?' Mrs Collins' forehead narrows.

'Just a nip, thank you.'

'Ye aren't expecting?'

'Me? No!' Rhona can hear how overly casual her voice sounds. 'I've just got low blood pressure.'

Mrs Collins brings out a bottle of sherry and pours her a very small glass.

'Thanks,' says Rhona dully.

'Ballantyne? Don't I know that name?'

'I'm new to the area.'

'You should have something to eat. I was just about to make myself a potato scone. Would you care for one?'

'That would be lovely,' says Rhona. There is nothing she wants less than a potato scone, but it will keep her here in the kitchen for longer. And people usually talk more when their hands are busy.

While Mrs Collins toasts the scones, she gives Rhona a potted history of her life. She is, she says, a local girl and was born in Culgoven, just north of Fort William. She only went to Glasgow for the first time in her life when she was 17 and burst her appendix. Then there was no stopping her. She moved to Edinburgh and worked for a dressmaker on Leith Walk and then for an exclusive furrier in George Street. Those were her salad days. Later, she returned north to look after her aged parents. Once she'd tucked them into their graves, she got a job looking after the old laird. When he died, Henderson inherited her, along with the mahogany furniture and the bad roads.

'I put my hand to everything now,' she says. 'I clean, I cook, I mend the curtains. I've even started doing French polishing. I look after everything and everyone.'

She glances at the boys. 'Tom, Eddie. Out you go now.'

The boys, who have demolished the cakes and biscuits,

look up from their game. Mrs Collins tilts her head coyly to one side and puts her hand in the pocket of her tabard. The boys immediately jump down from their chairs and, as they run towards her, she brings out a white paper bag and holds it open for them.

'Hold your horses! One at a time!'

Each boy reaches in and takes a yellow sweet from the bag.

'Now, what do I get?' She bends over, folding at the waist like a jointed doll.

Each boy kisses her quickly on the cheek and runs outside. Mrs Collins smiles indulgently after them.

'Who are they?' asks Rhona.

'Mr Henderson's wards. They're good lads and it's nice to have young people around.' Mrs Collins crosses the kitchen and stands in the doorway watching the boys disappear into the walled garden. 'They won't be here long, more's the pity.'

Then she closes the door, walks back to the kitchen units and turns her gaze to Rhona.

'Terrible news. I gather it's one of Will's friends?' Mrs Collins flips the scones out of the toaster. She butters both sides, scores the top of each scone with the knife and presses more butter into the cuts. Rhona has to look away.

'Probably,' says Rhona. 'But it's not official yet.'

'Is that all we know?' Mrs Collins hands her a small plate with the scone.

'Go on,' Mrs Collins is watching her intently. 'You need fattening up.'

Rhona takes a bite. The scone is awful – a coaster-shaped starch base swimming in warm fat. She swallows quickly and then swirls the last of the sherry round her mouth.

Mrs Collins consumes her own scone in small mouthfuls dabbing the butter from her lips with a piece of paper towel.

'Those bears!' says Mrs Collins. 'They're dangerous animals, aren't they? We'd be fools to trust them. Mr Henderson always says they are more frightened of us than we are of them, but I've never been so sure.'

'Everyone's always wise after the event,' counters Rhona.

With her pinkie Mrs Collins wipes the last drops of butter from her plate. 'Since he brought those first wolves in – that'll be six years ago at least – I've been waiting. And every time I go near the woods the hairs rise on the back of my neck. What if you were driving at night and your car broke down? They'd come for you, wouldn't they? They'd smash the windscreen and eat you up like a pork chop.'

'Do you mean the bears, or the wolves?'

'Both, really. And the wild boar are bad too, *and* they don't just stick to the woods. Jimmy Macfarlane from Ardnacarrick was charged by a boar last September. He had just stopped by the roadside to relieve himself and it came skiting out from among the trees and went for him.'

'What did he do?'

'He threw his mobile at it. He missed it but the boar ran off. And he smashed his screen. I never take my car out at night. And I always, *always* carry a spare mobile when I'm driving…'

'So you can have a second hit at the wild boar?'

Mrs Collins doesn't smile, 'It's all very well for Mr Henderson. He has money and a flat in London. During the shutdown he and Will were here, and then we did at least have enough to eat – though a diet of meat can be very binding.'

Her finger still lingers on the plate. She adds, 'The winters are long here. And Mrs Henderson doesn't ever seem to come up. And when they do…'

Mrs Collins stops.

'When they do?' prompts Rhona.

Mrs Collins frowns, 'I've never understood moneyed folk. They seem to have a talent for making themselves miserable. Mrs Henderson never smiles, and I've never seen her finish a meal. Miss Lucy, you could blow her away too. And that Will. Well!'

'Well?'

'He's clever all right... A wonderful piano player. But so quiet. And he *looks* at you.'

'Why doesn't he stay here at the Big House?'

'The Henderson children never do. Will brings his student friends with him and they stay up in the tower. So usually there's only Mr Henderson here and those dogs of his.'

A resentful pause follows. Rhona waits.

'I wanted to import a Pekinese.'

That fits.

Mrs Collins shakes her head, 'But I don't trust his dogs. They would rip it to shreds.'

She reaches into an overhead cupboard and brings out a Tupperware box. Inside looms a yellow block of cake.

'I've a lemon drizzle here. I'll just cut you a slice.'

'I'm fine, honestly.'

But Mrs Collins has already got out the knife.

'It's nice and moist,' she prises out a slab.

Rhona has to accept. It turns out to be a dose of food colouring and sugar, bound together with trans fat. She takes a mouthful and feels it coalesce on her tongue.

'Thank you,' she says thickly.

Mrs Collins rubs her eyes under her glasses. 'I'm glad I sleep upstairs. Nowhere is safe here nowadays. Nowhere.'

Rhona shifts in her seat as if the sofa weren't quite

comfortable. This allows her to pick up the cushion on the seat next to her.

Underneath lies a round embroidery frame with the threaded needle stuck in the fabric. And in the middle of the frame is a tiny round piece of very finely executed embroidery – a portrait of a girl's face: long brown hair, big almond-shaped eyes set at a slant, and a small, neat chin. The embroidery is only about two inches across but the work is extraordinarily detailed: a pinkish thread has been used on the cheeks, and there is even a tiny dimple stitched in the chin. The work is very nearly complete – only the corona of gold chain stitch around the outside needs finishing.

Rhona holds the needlework up to the lamp, 'This is beautiful! Is it some sort of badge?'

'Oh, that's nothing!' Mrs Collins' eyes widen in alarm, 'Keeps my fingers busy. Just a hobby of mine. I should have finished it ages ago.'

She steps quickly over, takes the embroidery from Rhona, and retreats back to the safety of the kitchen units where she stuffs the needlework in a drawer.

'Do you work from life? Or from a photograph?'

'No, no. It's just from my head. Something I dreamt up.' Mrs Collins turns her face to the window.

'It looks like a real girl,' persists Rhona.

At first Mrs Collins doesn't answer. Then she murmurs, 'I was always top of the class in art. I had a talent. I could have taken it further.'

Rhona scrambles around for something to say, 'Do you always use silk filament?'

'Yes, I like the sheen,' Mrs Collins brightens, 'Do you embroider?'

'No,' says Rhona, sensing that her turn has come to be evasive.

'But you know about it?'

'My sister did a lot of embroidery.'

'That's nice! And what did she use?'

'Wool, sometimes cotton. Her work was much cruder. She just did kits: kittens, lambs and shepherdesses in fields. That kind of thing.'

'And she doesn't do it any longer? That's a shame!'

'She passed away.' Rhona looks at the stove. 'Passed away' was such a euphemism; as if death were just some painless turnstile.

'Oh! That's very sad!' Mrs Collins is waiting for more.

Rhona keeps her gaze on the stove. She can feel Mrs Collins' eyes on her. The pause lengthens. The atmosphere has somehow changed between them and Rhona knows she can now ask a proper question.

'So, what do you believe happened here?' she asks. 'Why did this man die?'

'I don't know,' replies Mrs Collins. 'But he must have been up to something.'

'Up to what?'

Mrs Collins laughs, 'You're green as grass, my girl. There are always plenty of things to do in the woods.'

'Such as?'

Mrs Collins' eyes slide sideways. 'You tell me, girl,' she murmurs.

'But what happens there?' Rhona asks. 'Why is anyone going to the woods?'

'But that's it, isn't it?' replies Mrs Collins. 'Nobody goes there. These are places where no one will look for you or for whatever it is you are hiding.'

She pauses. Rhona looks at the stove.

Go on!

'And there're the old lead mines up there,' Mrs Collins looks flushed. She takes her glasses off, blows on the lenses, wipes them on her tabard. She blinks repeatedly, the way spectacle-wearers do when their faces are suddenly naked. Rhona can see that it's not much of a life, stuck here in the kitchen. Just her and the boys and the ghost of a yearned-for Pekinese.

Mrs Collins sits down. 'Don't expect me to know anything more. It's not my place. And I never leave this kitchen.'

From the pocket of her tabard she takes out the creased paper bag.

'Would you like one? They're sherbet lemons.'

Rhona shakes her head.

Mrs Collins takes a sweet and places it in her mouth. She closes her eyes and sits very still, one plump hand on the bosom of her tabard.

'I'm waiting for the sherbet to come through,' she whispers. 'Ah! There! It's... it's a rush of light in your mouth. Like the Holy Spirit moving across the water.'

Rhona looks at her queasily. 'I think I should be heading back.'

THE GOLDEN BEAR

They meet by a barn on the road between the dell and Acharacle. Matt is huddled miserably against the gate, his cap tilted down over his eyes. In one hand he holds his rifle, broken open.

'Isn't the master coming?' he asks.

'No. And your lad? I thought he'd be with you.'

'One of your men took him home.'

'Who was that?'

'A big blond fellow.'

'That'll be Cummings,' she says. Anyone would have been better than Pinkie Cummings. He has children of his own, yet she knows that he won't have found out anything useful from the boy.

There is a putrid smell in the air. She looks around but can't locate the source. She notes that the barn is new and has freshly painted slatted sides. The oak doors are fitted with sturdy brass handles and hinges which must have been imported.

'That's quite a barn you've got.'

'Mr Henderson likes quality.' Matt takes a cloth from the pocket of his jacket and wipes the gun stock. 'I can't believe I'm doing this,' he murmurs.

'I'll shoot him if you want.'

Matt shakes his head.

'Where's the bear?'

Matt picks up a small black tracking device resting on the bonnet of the Land Rover.

'376 metres away.' He points up the hillside. 'You can carry the tracker if you want. The path's a bit of a scramble. Will you be okay?'

'I'll be fine.'

But it turns out there's no path at all, and they're soon climbing up between mossy rocks and oak trees growing miraculously out of fissures in the stone. The light is dappled and the air inhabited by little white butterflies and miniscule bloodthirsty insects. Rhona soon has a flaming ring of bites around her neck.

Matt walks fast, agile on the rough terrain. Rhona follows behind holding the tracker. On her screen the bear is a pulsing red dot.

'In the old days we'd have walked for hours,' says Matt. 'We'd have looked for scat and followed stoved-in ant hills, and broken branches. Now the skill in it's all gone.'

'And in those days Wilber would have had a chance to get away?'

'Aye, it's too easy now.'

High above them a bird squeals. The tone reminds Rhona of the plumbing in her father's house.

'What was that?' she asks.

'A dunnock. It was an alarm call. I haven't heard one for days. Nowadays I just seem to sit in the office phoning suppliers and watching the monitors.'

'Monitors?' She's alert now. 'You've got cameras in the woods?'

'Mr Henderson would never allow that. It's the animals that are tagged. Except the wild cats. He's always regretted that he never tagged them when they arrived. Now we can't find them. I've seen their tracks down in the sands at Kentra. But they always vanish. They're smart.'

'Why does Henderson want the animals tracked?'

'It's for the hunters. That's how the estate makes its

money. We're a rich man's playground – everything here is for the hunters.'

'So when the hunters come here, do they use the hand trackers too?'

'I don't know,' says Matt stonily.

'But aren't you the gamekeeper?'

'I'm a game*keeper*. Not a killer. I'm off duty for the wolf hunts. That's when I get my days off.'

'I suppose it's no fun seeing the animals you look after getting killed.'

He doesn't answer.

After a while the land levels out and they come to an area of birch trees. Matt stops suddenly, splaying his hand out behind him. Rhona looks at the screen on the tracker. The red dot of the bear is only metres away and moving towards them.

She first sees Wilber in silhouette. The bear comes over the brow of a hillock: the head and the ridiculously cute ears, then the great lumbering shoulders.

Matt lifts the rifle, raising the sight to his eye. There's a tiny slub of sound as he pulls back the safety catch.

Rhona stays his arm. He turns and she shakes her head.

'Don't shoot. I want to see him, get a sense of him,' she whispers.

Matt lowers the gun.

The bear lollops forward. He's so soft footed that barely a twig snaps. And he's huge. If he reared up on his hind legs he'd be as tall and wide as a garage – a garage covered in a rug of pale, tawny fur.

'He's blond!' She hisses.

'Honey-coloured,' Matt hisses back. 'Wilberforce came from Alaska. He might be a polar cross.'

As if responding to his name, the bear lowers his head. The snout and eyes are far too small, just tiny cake decorations in the great furry roundel that is his head. Now he is looking their way and walking slowly towards them, swaying from side to side.

The bear stops, raises his snout and rocks slightly on his forepaws.

'Do you think he's smelt us?' she whispers. 'We're downwind of him, aren't we?'

'Of course he's smelt you, miss. He's a *bear.'*

'But...'

'Bears are half deaf but they can smell you if you passed along the path two days ago.'

That's quite a claim.

But she says nothing and just nods.

'He can smell me – who he knows and who has never caused him any trouble. And you, who he doesn't know from Adam.'

'How old is he?'

'Only four.'

'He could do with a wash.'

Matt's eyes are fixed on Wilber, 'He's definitely a bit peaky.'

'How on earth can you tell?'

'He's swaying too much. And he should have his hackles up. He must be unwell.'

'Or maybe human doesn't just agree with him.'

Matt looks at her reproachfully, 'You've got a "sense" of him now? Are you happy?'

She nods.

Matt quickly puts the gun to his shoulder and fires. A moment of silence follows. Wilber's back legs suddenly sag, and he slowly folds to the ground.

Matt walks over to the bear and, as Rhona follows him, she slips the tracker into her jacket pocket.

She watches blood seep out from the hole in the animal's

chest. Now she is close enough to smell the brackish stink of bear and see the crawling mankiness of his fur. The claws are dark brown, narrowly fluted, the tips yellow and microbe rich. *How long till his fleas jump ship?*

She takes a step back. The bear's eye – the one she can see – is closed. What if Wilber is just waiting, about to bound to his paws and slice them open? Yet Matt drops his gun and crouches by the bear's head. He reaches into the great furry neck, feeling for a pulse. He shakes his head, closes his eyes, runs a hand down Wilber's back.

'I haven't touched him since he was a cub.'

She watches, quite unable to empathise.

'He didn't like water much,' says Matt fondly. 'He wasn't one of those bears that's always out catching fish.'

'Then what was he doing down by the pond?'

'I don't know.'

'Where's the chip?'

'In his neck.' He shows her where. Rhona burrows her hand down into his fur, where the bear is still horribly warm. She feels a nub of scar tissue and presses down on a tiny hard shard inside. It wobbles under her finger.

Now's the time to break the bad news.

'We'll take the body to Fort William,' she says.

'What?'

'To the forensics lab. I want to check Wilber out. It's a standard procedure.'

'But he's an animal!'

'All the same, he's committed a murder. I want to know what happened.'

'But we were going to bury him here! Where he lived, where he played as a cub.' Matt's eyes are brimming.

'You can do that when Forensics have finished with him.'

Matt rubs his eyes with the back of his hand.

'He was a good bear.' She realises he can't look at her now. 'I just don't know what got into him.'

'Do you think he could have been drugged?'

'Possibly...' says Matt guardedly.

'Why else do you think he'd do it? Boredom?'

Matt stares at her aghast, 'Animals don't kill out of boredom.'

'How do you know? People do. I've seen it happen.'

'I've spent years watching over this bear. Even if Wilber never saw me, he knew my smell. He knew I was his keeper. And I know that he wasn't *bored.*'

She takes out her mobile, finds the GPS coordinates and quickly texts the procurator's office, asking for a pick up. She fills in the online form and, Wilber being enormous, requests the bariatric patients' hoist.

'Then maybe he was lonely?' she says. 'Lone males always spell trouble.'

'Bears are solitary animals.'

The office texts her back: pick up in 45 minutes. Rhona smiles – she had called them from Glenborrodale and asked them to be on standby, but this is astonishingly efficient.

'There has to be some other explanation for why the bear attacked that young man.'

Matt hesitates.

'Well?' she says.

'It's so out of character. He'd have to have been intentionally provoked. Goaded by somebody. But why would anyone do that? You'd have to be a madman.'

'So bears aren't killers?'

'I know an animal that kills humans when I see one. I'd never fancy getting on the wrong side of the wolf pack up at Kentra. But Wilber wasn't a killer. He just wasn't like that. He was a very steady bear. He was special.'

'Special?'

Matt bows his head and says in a crushed voice, 'He was my golden bear.'

WILL AND HIS FRIENDS

The procurator's men, Sandy and Alex, don't have a body bag big enough for Wilber, and the hoist, with its little metal wheels, keeps getting stuck on the rough ground. Rhona goes ahead, pushing back brambles and finding a navigable route through the woods. Gradually, with Matt's help, they manoeuvre the hoist down the hillside, with the bear swaying like a giant woolly fruit.

When Wilber is finally packed away in the van, Sandy and Alex extract themselves from their overalls. Matt, his cap held over his chest, stands looking at the mound of bear in the back of the van.

'That nearly broke my back,' says Sandy.

Rhona says, 'Just tell Doctor Rabina to treat it like a standard autopsy. I'll need bloods, stomach contents, any signs of bruising and cuts.'

'That'll be tricky with all the fur,' says Sandy.

'Yep, God probably made us hairless just to help pathologists.'

'What do ye want with that animal, anyway?'

She just shrugs. Start explaining your hunches and you're lost.

'We won't have a great drive back. It's got quite a smell to it,' adds Sandy.

'It's a "him". Wilber, that's his name. I put it on the form.'

Her mobile rings – it's Jeanette from the office in Fort William. Rhona tells her that the bear has been killed and asks her to call Henderson's estate office and demand a 24 hour lockdown on the reserve. She doesn't want anyone running off.

Rhona drives back down the road past the dell. Boyd's patrol car is parked in the lay-by and bright yellow, fluttery plastic tape is strung along the roadside. Are he and Cummings duly combing the woods for evidence? It's unlikely – Boyd's boot is open and his fishing rods are leaning against the car.

Half a mile further on, the road ends on the banks of Loch Moidart and here Rhona leaves the car in a graveled parking area shaded by pine trees. Nearby is a stylish but battered green convertible.

She comes down to the water's edge. The beach is empty, except for a pair of oyster catchers dabbing in the mud, their legs and beaks the only touch of red on the foreshore.

In front of her stands the tower, a spectacular ruin perched on its own small island at the end of a causeway. Henderson has spared no expense and has incorporated the tower into his reserve, so the green fence, with its posts sticking out of the water, loops out into the loch and round the island and comes back in further down the shore.

The tide is still pulling out. She walks across the causeway, where the wet sand is strewn with the corpses of tiny, bleached crabs.

The entrance to the tower is round the back of the island. She climbs a short muddy path, passes under a stone arch and into a walled courtyard, shady and smelling of drains. In a wooden shed a generator hums and a stone-flagged path leads through nettles to the huge iron-studded front door of the tower. The windows above are mere slits, deeply embedded in the walls.

She tirls the iron ring on the latch.

A slender, unshaven man in a blue velvet jacket and jogging bottoms opens the door. He is older than she expects – probably in his mid thirties – and balding, with a high, pale dome of a forehead. The rest of his features are squashed under a low brow.

Rhona shows him her police badge. 'Good morning. I'm Inspector Ballantyne.'

She's expecting the moment of blank-eyed shock with which people normally greet police on their doorstep. But he just gives a slight jerk of his chin.

'You'd better come in.' He takes a step back, pulls aside a heavy velvet curtain and leads the way into a square, poorly lit room where four young people, two men and two women, are sitting on old sofas and armchairs.

The air smells of whisky and fry ups. Rhona takes a minute to gaze round the room and at the five pale, underslept faces. They look a fright: clothes crumpled, matted hair, post-operative complexions. Only one woman – petite, and with sharp features – is neatly turned out. Her mousy-coloured bob has been brushed and she's wearing carefully applied makeup. She is holding a balled-up handkerchief to her mouth.

Rhona repeats her name and rank. The balding man, who looks older than the others, introduces himself as Arthur. The small, neatly turned out woman says her name is Zoë. The other young woman, puffy-eyed and with a curtain of long dark hair that half covers her face, is Rachel. A freckly, ginger-haired young man, looking desperately pale and hungover, waves a greeting across the room. This is Ray.

Lastly, there is the smallest and most remarkable-looking person. He's small – barely bigger than a boy – with high cheekbones, a long, thin-lipped mouth, and a hedge of unbrushed brown hair. He wears black, heavy-rimmed spectacles and his eyes, made bigger by the lenses in his glasses, are dark blue. His jeans are skin tight over spindly legs and he's wearing an ancient Arran sweater, many sizes too big and elaborately frayed at the neck and cuffs. He has a certain watchful presence.

When she says, 'And you must be William Henderson.' He nods. "I'm Will.'

'Can we help you, Inspector?' says Arthur.

'Are you all here?'

'All but one,' says Zoë. She has small, sharp teeth like a cat.

'Who's missing?'

'Johnnie,' replies Zoë.

'Johnnie Fergusson,' adds Arthur.

They know already.

'I'm afraid a body has been found in the woods near the shore.'

'Oh God!' mutters Arthur. Rachel puts her head in her hands and Zoë snuffles into her handkerchief. Will's face remains deadpan.

'Do you have a picture of your friend?' asks Rhona.

Arthur flicks through his iPhone and, his face expressionless, hands her the device. The photograph is of a group selfie taken in a cafe or pub. In the middle sits Will, smiling wanly, and on either side of him are the young women and Ray. Behind, with his arms outstretched and grinning sloppily, is a familiar plump young man with dark, curly hair and a sallow complexion.

'I'm afraid that looks like him,' says Rhona.

Zoë gives a little groan. The others remain silent.

Rhona sits down. Normally at this point somebody would ask what had happened and how had he died. What is the matter with them?

She glances at Arthur. His pupils look normal.

41

'He was killed by a bear,' says Rhona.

Again, there's silence. Zoë gives a slow blink.

'I realise this must be a shock,' says Rhona, thinking how very unshocked they all seem. 'Later I'll take formal statements and names and addresses. But we have some things we need to discuss first.'

Still nobody says anything. Rhona looks pointedly at a small makeshift kitchen in the turret, 'Would one of you like to make some coffee?'

Both the women start up from their seats, but Ray beats them to it and quickly goes to the kitchen.

'Can you tell me what happened last night?' asks Rhona. 'Did you have an argument? Some sort of falling out?'

'No, we didn't,' says Arthur. 'Why are you asking?'

'I'm just curious. What sort of mood was Johnnie in?'

'Does that really make any difference now?' says Arthur. His tone is disbelieving, as if this was the stupidest of questions.

'He was much the same as usual,' adds Zoë. 'He was like cool, chilled, just hanging out.' She has a lowland accent. Edinburgh? It's slightly clipped, but certainly not posh.

'So, tell me how the evening went,' says Rhona.

There's another long, drifting pause.

She waits to see who will talk first. And again it's Arthur, 'We had supper and a few whiskies. Then we went for a midnight walk. And after that, we came home.'

He's overdoing the bored tone.

'All of you?'

'Yes,' says Arthur. 'All of us. Johnnie came too.'

'You know this is a reserve for wild animals. It's not that sensible to wander around here at night.'

'We thought there'd be safety in numbers,' says Arthur.

'And Cassiopeia was very bright,' says Will. He has a

clear, high voice, as English as his father's. On the phone you'd mistake him for a woman. 'We could just see Arcturus.'

'And then? After the stargazing?'

'We came home and went to bed,' says Arthur. He thrums the fingers of one hand against his trousers. The young women nod in agreement.

Rhona sighs. *Liars, every one of them.*

Arthur is watching her. He concedes, 'We did stay up a bit and have a nightcap – like we usually do.'

'So what time would that be?'

'I don't know. Maybe we turned in at about one thirty,' says Arthur.

'Or two,' Zoë examines her split ends.

Ray returns, carrying a mug for Rhona. He passes it to her, a slight tremor in his hand.

'So,' she takes a sip. It's real coffee. No dandelion roots, no potato peel.

'It was only when we got up that we realised he wasn't here,' continues Arthur.

'That was when, roughly?'

'We didn't all get up at once,' says Zoë. 'Maybe lunchtime. Or two-ish.'

'And we didn't immediately realise he wasn't here,' adds Arthur.

'You see, we called him,' says Zoë. 'And he didn't come. And then, when we went upstairs, his bed was empty.'

'Was it warm? Had it been slept in?'

'He wasn't there,' says Arthur.

'Did you check? Did someone feel the bed?'

Arthur shakes his head dismissively.

'Did you go looking for him?'

Rhona catches a pleading look from Rachel to Arthur. The young woman still hasn't said a word.

'We checked everywhere,' says Arthur. 'We even went up on the roof.'

'You didn't go out? If I were looking for someone, someone who might have drunk a lot, I think I'd have gone outside.'

'As I said, we looked out from the roof. There was no sign of him,' persisted Arthur.

'We were going to set out quite soon to look for him,' says Zoë.

'Really?' Rhona gives her a broad smile. Then she turns to Arthur. 'When you were up on the roof, was the tide in or out?' She sucks the top of her pen.

'I don't remember,' says Arthur. He looks at her coldly.

'Did you see any footprints?'

'It's too far away to see from up there,' he says. She nods: *at least he's tried.* She glances at the old ship's clock on the wall – it is 4.45 p.m. The tide was moving out when she crossed. High tide would probably have been at about one or two o'clock in the afternoon. So, when Arthur supposedly looked out from the roof, there would have been no chance of footprints as the causeway would have been covered in water – which is something he'd have noticed. But he didn't notice because he never did go onto the roof. Why would he? *He already knew that Johnnie was dead.*

She gives Arthur a long look. He's annoyed and nibbles at his moustache.

'Just to recap…' She'll give them one last chance to fess up. 'You all went on the midnight walk together. And all of you returned. Then you all went to bed. Is that right?'

The women and Ray nod.

'Yes,' says Arthur firmly.

Will remains very still.

She notes the long dents in the sofas, the flattened

cushions, the dirty plates and mugs and glasses everywhere. They have been here all night, sprawled everywhere like puppies; drinking, eating, drinking some more, trying to work out what to do.

And what else have they taken? It won't be hard to find out.

With a sudden flick of her hand, she spills the remains of her coffee over her trousers and onto the flagstones.

'I'm so sorry! I'll get a cloth.' She springs up from her chair and goes into the turret kitchen. Frying pans and dirty crockery are stacked in the sink, and a small table nearby is heaped with splayed-open pizza boxes. The make is Dutch, and must have been bought from a foreign currency outlet. She hasn't eaten all day, hasn't touched a half decent pizza in six months. She grabs a piece of crust, but thinks of Johnnie lying down in the dell, and puts it back.

On the cooker lies a used cake tin. They went to the trouble of baking brownies, yet they ate ready-made pizza? She dabs her finger in the cake crumbs – the brownie has a bitter aftertaste. What was in it? Something you couldn't smoke or take in pill form. Magic mushrooms, most likely.

Rhona opens the top drawer: cutlery. The second drawer: at the back, bound neatly, lie a couple of coils of that same string with the blue thread.

She nearly forgets the wet cloth.

When she returns to the sitting room, there's still a cowed, nervy silence. She asks, 'So where did you get the pizzas?'

'There's a freezer in the generator shed,' says Zoë.

'Where's that?'

'The shed in the courtyard. We've got enough in there to feed an army.'

Rhona crouches down on the flagstones, and wipes up

the coffee. She glances under the sofa where an empty bottle of vodka has been forgotten.

'Tell me a bit about Johnnie. What sort of person was he?' She scrubs at the flagstones.

'Johnnie was great,' says Rachel, speaking for the first time. *English boarding school.* 'He was really warm and kind. And funny. He'd do anything for you.'

'What did he do for a living?'

'He was a student,' says Rachel.

'What was he studying?'

'French with Italian.'

'Where?'

'St Andrews. We're all at St Andrews,' Rachel looks over at Arthur. 'Except Arthur.'

'And I *was* there,' he says wearily.

'What do you do now?' Rhona walks towards the kitchen and lobs the dishcloth into the sink.

'Mostly, I'm an editor,' replies Arthur. 'I work for a small imprint in Edinburgh.'

Of course he's in high end publishing – what else would a man in a velvet smoking jacket do for a living?

'There're still publishing houses there?'

'We mostly work on clan monographs for the American market. Have you any more questions?'

Isn't she meant to be the one doing the asking?

'Did Johnnie have any brothers or sisters?'

'He had a sister,' says Rachel, her face half behind her hair again. 'She's much older. And they weren't close – he was away at boarding school. His father was in the army.'

'So he had spent time abroad?'

'That was why he was so good at languages,' adds Ray.

'Could I see his bedroom?'

Arthur nods to Ray, who immediately gets up from

his armchair. She wonders if they all meekly do Arthur's bidding. Perhaps not Will.

Ray leads her up a spiral staircase of narrow, uneven steps. The first floor has been divided into two bedrooms; the floors are covered in old, cracking linoleum, the walls have fading floral wallpaper. Unlike the rest of the estate, the tower is evidently not on show.

'That's Will's bedroom,' says Ray. 'And that's Arthur's. I sleep in the turret off Arthur's room.'

Will has a few concessions to luxury: a double bed, a down duvet and a sheepskin rug by the bed. In the other rooms the bedding is just blankets and sleeping bags.

'Do you keep each other warm at night?'

'What's that supposed to mean?' Ray's eyes shine.

'Are you all single?'

'We are all mostly on our own, except Arthur and Will.' He stops. 'Maybe I shouldn't have said that.'

'Don't worry. I have nothing to do with the kirk.'

They climb on up the steps to the second floor. Zoë and Rachel share the bigger room above Will's. Johnnie's room is smaller. There's an orange sleeping bag on the bed, a pair of sheepskin moccasins and a small pile of French novels in cream dust covers on the bedside table. His suitcase is splayed open on top of a chest of drawers, his clothes all jumbled up in the suitcase.

If Johnnie was a tidy soul, he'd have put his clothes in the drawers.

Who folded his clothes down in the dell?

'Remind me, how long have you all been here?'

'A week.'

'You don't have a cleaner, do you?'

'I wish we did.'

'Did Johnnie leave anything like a letter behind?' she asks innocently.

Ray shakes his big freckly head.

'Nothing?'

'No.'

Then, finally, Ray catches on, 'It was an accident, you know.'

'You're sure?'

'Of course!' He tries to look her square in the face but his eyes quickly veer away.

Arthur has missed a trick. He should have come upstairs himself and not delegated the job to this nice young halfwit. Or – and this is what really puzzles her – do they simply not care what she thinks?

When they return to the stairs she says, 'I'd like to see the roof. I'll go on my own. I need a bit of air.'

Ray smiles, relieved to be let off.

She climbs the stairs and comes to a small landing with large striped cushions piled to one side and some old Tilley lamps. She puts her shoulder to a low metal door and pushes. The door opens with a screech of hinges and she comes out onto a paved rooftop with a low wall of battlements around the sides.

She steps out into a world of sky and treetops and mountains. Below her the loch shines like a wet pelt. This, she thinks, is what a bird of prey flying high overhead would see.

Something moving over in the woods catches her eye; a small blue van is speeding down a driveway, making its way to the road by the dell.

Did Jeanette not get that curfew order through?

There is, most conveniently, a telescope concreted into the battlements. She peers through the eye piece and quickly trains the sights on the van. It's a smart-looking vehicle, not one of the usual cobbled together affairs. She writes down the registration number in her notepad.

Even after the van has disappeared, she goes on staring at the little driveway. She cannot get her thoughts straight. The students – and that spooky overgrown student, Arthur – are obviously lying. *But, why?*

She doesn't understand them – they seem a throwback to an earlier age, a cliché of what students used to be in the 1970s, or even earlier. What binds them all together? The small neat woman is from a completely different background to the rest. And why is Arthur hanging out with people who are ten years younger than him?

What are they hiding? Did Johnnie go out on a *second* night walk and never come back? No, they're a group, a pack. They stick together. They'll have been there when the bear attacked. Then they came home. So, of course they haven't been able to sleep.

And what of the blue string? Was this some sort of dare that went wrong? An elaborate form of suicide? A death wish? If you wanted to top yourself, why not just come up here and throw yourself over the battlements?

After all, the stone wall in front of her is only knee high. You could just jump. One push and over you'd go. You'd probably stove your head open on the rocks below. Or maybe your head and shoulders would burrow down into the sand. She remembers a suicide off the Dean Bridge in Edinburgh where the body landed head first on the river bank. All the police could see was the legs sticking up out of the mud like a giant lugworm.

There's a slight movement behind her and Rhona turns round sharply. It's Will, wrapped in a blanket.

'You gave me a fright!' she says.

Will comes and stands next to her, surprisingly close. She's glad his arms are tucked into the blanket – though

49

it does seem odd that he's bundled up like this when the day is so warm. For a moment, only a moment, she muses whether he might be hiding something in his blanket. A firearm? A sword? That wouldn't be out of keeping.

Will looks out west towards the islands.

His hair, very thick and wiry, is pulled back off his forehead and she sees a neat little ear and the indentations of his cranium. He's as fine boned as a bird.

'Are you Roderick Ballantyne's daughter?' he asks suddenly.

'I am.' *How does he know?*

'I met your father when I was a child.' He points over to the western skyline, 'Look at Rhum. It's really the shape of a crouching dragon. Can you see it?'

'M-hmm.' She can't see any dragon.

He says dreamily, 'Scotland was once inhabited by giants. By the Fiann. They're buried over in Glencoe. They had eyes of basalt and stood tall as houses. Their greyhounds were the size of horses. And the glacial boulders in Rannoch Moor are their widows' tears.'

Why has he searched her out?

'Tell me about Johnnie,' she says.

'I'm not really surprised he's gone,' replies Will.

'No?'

'You know in the autumn when the leaves are turning?' His mouth twitches slightly. 'There are some trees where you only have to touch a leaf, just breathe on it, and it falls to the ground. Johnnie was like that. He was ready, he was waiting to fall.'

'So what really happened, Will?'

But he just shuts his eyes and turns away.

CAT

In the sitting room, Rhona writes down the students' names and contact details slowly and laboriously. She is playing for time. The atmosphere is muted – the students behave like earthquake survivors, hugging their knees and staring into space. She hopes against the odds that one of them, maybe sniffly little Zoë, might burst into tears and tell all. But nobody cracks.

From the roof, where mobile reception is better, she calls the office, gives Jeanette the contact details for Johnnie's parents and asks her to liaise with the Aberdeen police for a home visit to break the news to them. She also reads out the registration number of the blue van – could Cummings please see to that?

Then Jeanette, in a knowing undertone, tells her that the staff nurse from her father's new ward has called. Rhona thanks her and rings off.

Roderick Ballantyne is being moved from Inverness back to the small Fort William hospital. This either means they think he'll soon be well enough to come home, or that there's not much more they can do and he is being farmed out to die. For a moment she imagines both of these terrible scenarios: her father back at home, sharing the house with her, or her father dead. She can't decide which would be the worst and she can't face asking them; she'll call the hospital later.

By the time Rhona eventually leaves the tower, it's after 6 o'clock and the causeway is broad, with the sea coming near to low tide. Matt told her that the wolves lived mostly on the far end of the peninsula, but she still walks briskly to the car. Once inside, she locks the doors and drives as fast as she can down the winding road to Acharacle. She toots the horn at every bend. Repeatedly she asks herself: why are the students lying? What do they know?

When she eventually reaches the main entrance to the reserve, the guard sitting in his fibreglass egg opens the gates and she is at last out and free. Glad to get away, she belts down the coast road.

At Ardgour, the ferry is docked. She drives directly up the pontoon, turns off the engine, and feels in the glove pocket for the hip flask. But it hasn't magically refilled itself.

Rhona doesn't get out of the car. As the ferry chugs out across Loch Linnhe she rests her eyes on a section of broken metal balustrade. The iron has turned brown, and as it has disintegrated, the rust has formed layers of decay. It looks curiously organic, as if it were wood. The hull is no doubt just the same.

She takes out her mobile and dials the hospital.

Memories of their last terrible row rise up in her mind: her father's hand slamming down on the kitchen table. Maggie's death was her fault, he'd said. He'd called her a selfish bitch.

If he's awake she might have to talk to him. She can't do this now. Not now. She hangs up, sinks back into the headrest and thinks over the day's events. What had happened with the bear? Why the folded clothes? The flower? The playing card? In the card game that she played a thousand times as a child, the Black Maria was the Queen of Spades. End up with the black queen and you lose – just as Johnnie Fergusson lost.

Why hadn't she seen the connection earlier? She is, she

realises, out of practice. It has been a while since she's had to *think*.

When she first arrived, back in the bitter days of December, The Bassett had sat her down in his office for a briefing. He said, 'The Highlanders are great drinkers and great brawlers. And in their own way, they're quite heroic. They've no money now, no jobs, and no hope. But give them half a bottle of Bells and a length of 2 by 2 with a nail in the end and they're Robert the Bruce.'

He glanced down at her CV lying on his desk. 'You won't be needing your smart psychology degree here. Or your good brain. There won't be clever plots and alibis. Who was that fella that used to be here? The Italian. What was he called again?'

'Sergio Verviani.' She says the name cold and clear. She's amazed that The Bassett could have forgotten.

'There's no one like that now. Our people here don't think beyond their next drink. And usually,' he looked up at her over the yardarm of his glasses, 'it'll be so obvious you'll want to cry.'

And The Bassett was proved right. Verviani had been so smart, so professional. He kept his head down and his syndicate, like any effective parasite, never overburdened its hosts. Instead, he skimmed small amounts of money from absolutely everybody: every West Highland corner shop, every garage, every hotel or pub paid their weekly dues to his 'charities'.

His men, always a card machine in their pocket, were everywhere: 'I'm Sergio's brother, I'm Sergio's cousin, I'm Sergio's mother's cousin, I'm Sergio's mother's cousin's cousin...' They had an Italian sense of family; defy them and they wouldn't just break your legs, they'd break your cousin's legs too, and your cousin's cousin's legs. But the next time they'd be round with apple turnovers for the grandmother, lollipops for the children. They'd even draw cartoons on your plaster casts.

Rhona knew them all. She'd spent endless nights with the car parked in darkened side streets and her hunkered down in the front seat with a baseball cap on, writing down number plates. She had tracked Verviani's charities and his amorphous holding companies in Lichtenstein and the Isle of Man.

She'd unleashed a forensic accountant on him, but in the blink of an eye the Orphans of the Holy Cross would shapeshift into the St Adolphus Mission Hospital which would then dissolve into a spray of small accounts in the Cayman Islands. A day later, up would spring The Little Sisters of Spina Bifida (he did sometimes overegg the pudding).

In comparison, the crims of today are a poor substitute. Usually Rhona can rely on finding her murderer within a twenty metre radius of the body, and the culprits are normally comatose with drink, or high on a magic mushroom concoction they called 'sniv'. Often they'd still have the victim's wallet in their pockets. Some were trophy hunters and cut off ears or fingers, (or worse…) And as for eliciting a confession, in most cases that was as simple as taking a toy from a baby.

But this time things are different; the answer will not be so headbangingly easy.

On the drive home she decides to call in on Cat. A couple of miles before Kinlochleven, she stops by Cat's big electric gates. She sees the old white wooden post with the rusty hook and she smiles to herself. Scotland is so different now, but some things remain: for example, this white post. When they were children, Cat's father ran the smokery in

54

a shed in the garden. When he had kippers to sell, there'd be a wooden fish dangling from the post.

Cat buzzes her in and she parks by the house, where the lights are all off. She heads up to Cat's studio which is a wooden cabin, up the slope from the house.

Cat meets her at the door. She's dressed in her old chambray apron. She has two paint brushes in her hand and little silver commas swing from her ears. Her left wrist is bandaged.

'Heeeeello!' Cat takes a quick glance at Rhona's pale face. 'What on earth is the matter? Did you forget to eat?'

Rhona smiles wearily and looks at her friend's arm. 'What happened?'

'It's just a sprain. I fell down by the stream.'

'How about a drink?' says Rhona.

Cat just looks at her, eyes dark.

'Nothing wrong with a drink.' Rhona flushes.

'Roo, how about a *sandwich*?'

'I'm fine.' Rhona sits down on one of Cat's revolving stools and spins round.

'You'll keel over if I don't get something into you.' Cat disappears into the little kitchen at the back of the cabin.

Rhona twirls round again on the stool. Cat's workplace normally smells of varnish, but today it has a new mulchy freshness and there's a trestle table covered in tiny green figures of golfers, some in mid swing, others standing with their clubs. Rhona picks up one of the little men. He is light, made of moss and chicken wire. His club is a stalk of tightly rolled paper.

Cat returns carrying a plate with three meat sandwiches.

'Why would I want a little green man?'

'A little green *golfer,*' says Cat. 'Good, aren't they? And you can bend them into shape. They're for the Gleneagles Hotel. They've got a convention of insurance salesmen from Delaware on the 4th. Every member of the senior round table is to be given a personalised golf ball display holder.'

'But why the moss?'

'Moss is in at the moment. Felt is out, tweed is out, heather gemstones are out. Taxidermy is in. And moss is in – which is very good news for me. All my people need to do is step outside for supplies.'

Rhona notes the proprietorial 'my people'. She says, 'Why are you're working so late?'

'I've got to take the prototypes over to Perthshire tomorrow. I'm so short-staffed I have to do it all myself and I haven't even started on the novelty ornaments for the kids. I'll be at this all night.' Cat looks down at the tray, 'You still haven't eaten anything.'

'What about that drink? says Rhona.

'Only once you've eaten.'

Rhona bites into a sandwich. The meat is peppery, with an aftertaste of blood. She shudders and quickly swallows.

'Is this some sort of experiment?' she asks.

'Sorry. It's Highland cattle pastrami. Sheila Galbraith's new startup.'

'It's disgusting.'

'You should try the smoked vension. That's even worse.'

'*Now* can I have a drink?'

'That's what you always say. We'll have to write it on your tombstone.'

Cat returns to the little kitchen. Rhona hears the fridge crank open and then comes a happy clink of ice cubes. Cat returns with two glasses of gin and tonic.

'So tell us about your new case,' she says.

'How did you know?'

'You've got that knickers-in-a-twist-look again.'

'You're wasted on handicrafts,' says Rhona.

Cat, she knows, has always had a nose for people, even in childhood. She'd moved in next door and joined school in the second term of P1 – a neat little figure in white lacey socks and patent leather shoes. From the very first day Cat could tell Rhona and Maggie apart. Rhona once asked her how she'd done it. 'Easy peasy,' said Cat. 'Maggie had the rounder face, and she liked the Wendy house. You had the scowl and the pointier chin, and you liked the stickle bricks. In fact, Rhona, you *are* a stickle brick.'

Rhona finishes her gin and tonic, picks out the lemon and chews it.

'Another?' she asks.

'Make your own. And remember, there's meant to be some tonic in it.' Cat picks up a small scroll of chicken wire, takes a wedge of moss from a black plastic bag and sticks it onto the wire, deftly gluing it into place. 'So,' she says, 'what's happened?'

Rhona pours herself a long, fragrant gin and adds a splash of tonic. She takes a gulp. Then a second. Of all the spirits, gin is the cleanest – like drinking perfume. But she still prefers whisky.

She tells Cat about Johnnie's death and how the evidence doesn't stack up. She describes the bear and Archie Henderson and his housekeeper, and Will and his friends. 'Nobody's coming clean,' she says. 'Everybody seems to have secrets – even the bear.'

'I still don't see why that bear worries you so much. Bears are wild animals. Of course they're killers.'

'But apparently not *this* bear.'

'How do you know? Are you some sort of bear whisperer? Pass me those clippers.'

'Matt the gamekeeper is. And he says the behaviour was out of character. He loved that bear. He'd clearly watched

57

it for hours. He knew Wilber. He can see stuff that you and I can't.'

'That's interesting.' Cat tears off another lump of moss. 'What was it Maggie used to say? "Love teaches you".'

'Yeah,' says Rhona uncomfortably.

'She was right though, wasn't she? Love *does* teach you.'

'My sister could be so sappy at times.'

A moment of silence. Then, in a brighter voice, Rhona says, 'Think about that bear. You know those old books from the Raj about man-eating tigers? The tigers that went for people were always the old, cranky ones with poor teeth. They resort to humans because they're desperate. Human is a *last option*. But Wilber was in his prime and the reserve is stuffed with red deer.'

Cat shrugs, 'Maybe it was just some drugged-up midnight walk that went badly wrong.'

'Then why aren't the students fessing up?' says Rhona. 'And why the folded clothes, and the flower with the playing card?'

'But it's the bear that killed him, no? So the students can't be guilty, can they?'

'They *know* something. And they're not even trying to disguise it. Their lies are so elementary, so pathetic, really. It's as if it hasn't occurred to them that the police might take an interest.'

'They'll have other things on their mind. It must be drugs, mustn't it? And what about the big chief? What's Henderson like?'

'He's a snob. A bit mad, too. And a bully, I think. But probably not a totally bad man. I quite like the fact that he has a dream – you know, this rewilding project of his.'

'That's just a natural consequence of having money,' says Cat. 'You and I, we can't afford to have dreams. We just survive.' Cat presses more moss into the chicken wire frame, and snips off the loose ends. 'And what is it with that son of his? I saw him at the outpatients in Fort William when I went for my X ray.'

'How did you know it was him?'

'They called his name. I think it was him. He's tiny, isn't he? Lots of unbrushed brown hair? He was in there with this older, Sweeney Todd-like guy.'

'Balding? Squished features?'

Cat nods.

'That'll be his boyfriend, Arthur.'

'What a couple! Have you noticed William Henderson's eyes? Next time you see him, have a good look. They're *really* strange. He's a mutant. One of them is white and the other one is yellow.'

'Oh, come on!'

Cat continues, 'I mean it – the whites of his eyes are different. One eye is white and the other is a kind of yellowy colour. I thought he might have been in a fight. Then I wondered if it was genetic. You can get those cats with long white fur and one blue eye and the other one brown. And they're stone deaf.'

'You're having me on.'

'No, honest. I knew a family in Dunblane that had one. It used to walk up and down the piano at night. It liked the vibrations. The sound was really spooky.'

'So, you're telling me Will Henderson is a mutant alien?'

Cat grins and the silver commas in her ears jangle, 'Well, kind of. And that friend of his probably landed with him.'

'Or do you think he's got some disease? Jaundice or something?'

'Jaundice down one side of the body? That sounds likely. I'd go with the alien theory,' says Cat.

'I should visit those students again.'

Cat gives her a worried look, 'Other detectives work with a partner, don't they? You always seem to be out on your own.'

'I have a partner,' says Rhona gloomily.

'You do?'

'Pinkie Cummings. He's just rubbish.'

'Why don't you take me? I could come along as, I dunno, your dog.'

'And what breed would you be?'

'An Afghan hound.'

'But they're so stupid!'

'They're thin, though. And they've got lovely hair.'

The chicken wire tube is now completely covered in moss. Cat rotates it, checking for holes.

Rhona says, 'Since I came back, I've seen plenty of those yellow dogs – the wild scavengey ones that hang out in packs. But I haven't seen any fancy breeds. No Afghan hounds, or pugs, or poodles. Henderson has some horrible hunting hounds, but that's about it.'

'The fancy dogs all got eaten after the crash,' says Cat. 'After we'd finished the sheep we moved on to dogs.'

'You're joking!'

'Maybe not *all*. Some border terriers got away – but they're like cockroaches. They can fend for themselves. Otherwise the pets all went west.'

'You ate *dog!*'

'Of course I ate dog. I ate Pedro.'

'But Pedro was a lovely dog!' protests Rhona.

'He was very tasty too. Glenn shot him. We made him into stews, mince, more stews, more mince. There's a surprising amount of meat, even on quite a small dog. He kept us going for a couple of months.'

'You sound pretty blasé about it.'

Cat puts down the tube of moss, 'What do you want me

to say? There was no food. There were no shops open. No internet. No gas supply. No electricity. You were in Italy munching pizza. We had a trade blockade and *absolutely nothing to eat!* Of course we killed our pets. We killed everything that had a pulse. We scoured the shore for seaweed and cockles. We ate birch bark. And catkins. I don't know how people in the big cities managed. Actually, I *do* know.'

'How *did* they manage?'

Cat shakes her head.

'But the blockade was only six months. You've got a smokehouse. Couldn't you grow a few potatoes?'

'Six months with no food is a long time. And there were gangs out at night digging everything up.'

'*Potato* bandits?'

'Don't give me that Miss Sneery look. You weren't here. You never saw how it was. You'd just buggered off. I lost my brother, and I never even got to see his body. He probably just got hurled into one of those pits in Kelvingrove.'

'You're not being fair. I couldn't get back. Remember. It was a blockade.'

'I bet you didn't even try!'

Cat bends the moss tube once, twice, three times. In her fury she bends it too vigorously. She takes a breath and goes back over the bends, smoothing them down.

'Sorry, Cat,' says Rhona.

You are always saying sorry to Cat.

'Hold this, will you?' Cat's voice is still sharp.

Rhona holds the tube while Cat narrows one end to a point with pliers and snips off the extra moss.

'What is it anyway? A snake?'

'Of course not. It's a Loch Ness monster. It still needs eyeballs and a mouth.' Cat gives a puzzled frown. 'Where did I put that box of wee tam o' shanters?'

THE AUTOPSY

Reading of the Day
'But ask now the beasts, and they shall teach thee; and the fowls of the air, and they shall tell thee.'
Job 12.7

'There's a present for you in the back car park.' The Bassett, his cheeks folded into angry creases, shuffles the papers on his desk. 'It's from Forensics – a bear.'

'Really?' She stands, legs apart and hands behind her back, braced for the argument.

'Yes. A. Bear. Dr Rabina wasn't at all pleased. She phoned me herself. She said you hadn't mentioned it was a bear. You'd just put "Age: 4" and "Name: Wilberforce" on the form. Anyway, what kind of name is that for a bear?'

He looks up at her. She smiles flatly back at him but doesn't reply.

'They haven't touched it. She said it wouldn't have fitted into the CT scanner anyway, and Sandy Elsworth nearly broke his back trying to lift it. For heaven's sake, will you sit down?'

Rhona sits down, 'They've had heavier corpses. That fence, Jason Burt. He must have weighed at least 25 stone.'

'Yes, but he was *human*. Dr Rabina is a forensic pathologist for *humans!*'

Rhona nods noncommittally.

'For God's sake, Rhona. Why didn't you ask me beforehand?'

'Because you'd have said no, sir.'

'Right you are. I would have. It's a crazy idea, and a waste of time. We know the cause of death. You shot it, didn't you?'

'It wasn't me. It was Matt Simpson.'

The Bassett waves this detail away as if it were a cloud of midges, as if *she* were a midge.

'I just wanted to know what Wilber had eaten, that's all.'

He doesn't reply.

'I'll cut him open myself,' she blurts.

'*How?*'

'I'll use a Stanley knife.'

'You'll need galoshes. That bear'll be runny.'

'And I'll need plastic sheeting and bags. The stores are out of nearly everything, sir. We don't have any evidence bags or vinyl gloves. We can't go on like this.'

'Ask Jeanette.'

'Jeanette says we have to wait for the next accounting year. That means next April, which is ten months away. That's ten months with no evidence bags.'

'Improvise, then. And be grateful that I prioritised salaries over equipment.'

'*Some* salaries,' she glances to the side. Outside the Bassett's smeary glass box cubicle lies the main office with its swathes of empty desks.

The Bassett doesn't reply. He hunkers further into his cardigan.

'And how can I do a proper job without gloves and bags?' she persists.

'You're not doing a proper job as it is. You seem to be investigating bears.'

'So what am I going to use?' She fixes her eyes on an inlaid mother of pearl box on his desk. 'That's a nice box you've got there. I'll need something for the stomach contents.'

The Bassett clamps a fat hand over the box and gives her a baleful look.

'And I'll need to take bloods too. You got any spare pipettes? Any decanters?'

'What on earth do you want bloods for?'

'I've got a hunch, sir.'

'God spare us!'

'You know I'm usually right.'

The Bassett sighs, 'I was hoping to get off early. I need to fit in some work on the range.'

'I didn't think golf was work, sir.'

'You need to get out more. Then you'd be a bit less crabbit.' He pauses, 'Are you really going to cut up that bear?'

'Of course.'

'Then get Boyd and Cummings to give you a hand. And you should always work with Cummings – he is your partner and that's official. And I certainly don't want you wandering round Henderson's land again on your own.'

'Please, not Cummings!'

'You give me a bear in my car park. I'll give you Cummings. That's a fair exchange.'

'Couldn't I have O'Malley? Or even Laidlaw?'

'Cummings will stand between you and any wild animal.'

'He'll stand between me and any rational thought.'

'For heaven's sake, do what you need to do, Rhona. But use the pressure spray when you've finished. I don't want to skid on bear guts.'

He pauses, 'One more thing. Would you call in on the seminary up in Glen Righ? My poor nephew Joel began his crypting yesterday. Just see that he's okay.'

64

Crypting, the final rite of passage for all seminarians, means three days and nights interred in a stone coffin. She has never been to a crypting, and can't think of anything she'd like to do less.

'That's a horrible task. While I'm there, would you like me to strangle some kittens as well?'

'It needs a woman's touch.'

This is the line he always uses when there's a disagreeable task to offload on her.

'They hate women. Wouldn't it be more appropriate if you went, sir?'

'I can't possibly go. It would look like interference.'

She gives him a long sideways look. The Bassett has always been very careful to watch his back, especially with the kirk. 'So what exactly do you want me to do? What am I to say to the Willies?'

'Say whatever you like, but make it clear I didn't send you. You are there in a private capacity. Just check he's still alive and can breathe.'

'Thanks,' she says stonily.

At least he'll owe me for this.

'We all do things for family,' he says heavily. 'Family is important. And by the way, Jeanette says the hospital called again this morning about your father. Apparently he's already down here. You should visit.'

'I'll get onto it,' she says.

She removes several pairs of vinyl gloves from the secret store in her desk. Then, with her usual sense of dread, she opens the office equipment cupboard. It's almost empty; a few rubber bands in a plastic bag, a box with some batteries, some pointless rusty G clamps and blunt chisels. There's no Stanley knife and no electric saw, though the spare blades for one are still there. One shelf has a pile of used overalls and a couple of packets of wet wipes. At the bottom of the cupboard she finds the box she filched a few months ago from Forensics: there are still some green hypodermic syringes and a few small glass vials with rubber stoppers.

She takes one of the chisels, a packet of wet wipes, a syringe, three glass vials and the least dirty overalls and puts everything in a sports holdall. From the kitchenette she removes the First Aid box, a sharp knife and a couple of cereal bowls. On the way out she passes Cummings' desk. It is, as usual, very tidy: a neat pile of expenses, his twitcher's notebook, a framed photograph of his wife and two children. Everyone in the Cummings family is pink-skinned and slightly podgy. Cummings junior is a clone of his father; the same gammon complexion and gap-toothed smile, the same slather of blond hair across his forehead.

They are God-fearing, thrifty folk, regular in all things. Cummings records his weekly mileage, and his wife makes her own jams. Rhona can tell the day of the week by his sandwiches.

She opens his top drawer. And there's his lunch box. She removes his sandwich and juice bottle and puts the Tupperware box in her handbag.

She needs more stuff. That bear will have a hide as tough as roofing felt and she'll need a good bone saw, tarpaulins, a mask.

She heads down the stairs into the public reception area. Jeanette is ensconced behind the counter. Rhona likes Jeanette, who is clever, underoccupied, always thirsty for gossip.

So, just for a minute, Rhona stops.

Jeanette slides back the grill. 'Hello, stranger. Your bear is round the back of the car park.'

'I know, I know.'

'The Bassett is not happy.'

'Tell me about it.'

'And Angie MacIntyre called again from the hospital.'

'Yeah.'

'She wasn't sure you'd got her last message.'

'You told her I was busy?'

'Up to your eyebrows. But I said you'd be over today.'

'Thanks,' says Rhona. 'What's the news? Did you ask?'

'It's not my place. They'll only give out medical details to next of kin.'

'So you *did* ask?'

Jeanette raises her hands in the air and gives an exaggerated shrug.

'Off the record, you'll be pleased to hear his pulse and blood pressure are just about okay. And this morning he opened his bowels.'

'That's more than I needed to know.'

'Forwarned is forearmed,' Jeanette raises her eyebrows theatrically and pulls back the grill.

Rhona could call the hospital from the car, but she doesn't. She thinks, I'll go tonight. I'll give myself one last day of freedom.

She drives down the lochside, passes Cat's gates, and turns in by the next set of gates which leads, along an avenue of tree stumps, to a big square stone house which is her family home. She opens the front door to the familiar smell of camphor and old furnishings. Rhona doesn't really live in the house – she tells herself she merely lodges here, rat running her way between the kitchen, bathroom and bedroom. Real possession was long ago consigned to the mice and moths and silverfish.

She opens the door to the drawing room and, even though there's nobody here, she creeps in. This is where all the family mementos live and above the mantelpiece is a terrible portrait of her mother as a bonnie young woman. She is dressed in a white cotton dress, bluebells in her hand as she leans against – of all things – a Doric column. Rhona has always suspected that the painting is posthumous: all her mother's skin tones are hypersaturated, her bosom marbled with blue as if she were already dead.

Rhona plunges her hand into the vase on the fireplace and finds the key.

The gun room is at the back of the house, north-facing and fossilised with damp and disuse. She unlocks the door and enters. There are two low armchairs, a deal kitchen table, and some very solid wooden cupboards along the length of one wall. In the corner stands a formica unit with a sink and kettle.

She doesn't know the room. As a child, she was never allowed in and only ever saw inside by peeping through the window. Her father would sit there, still in his shooting clothes, a drink in one hand; in the other armchair would be one of his hunting friends, most of whom were not considered suitable for the drawing room.

She knows there will be a bone saw somewhere in here, and some good knives. She opens the drawers. One drawer has fishing flies, and coils of line, another is all neat boxes of cartridges, yet another has falconry jesses and metal couplings and tiny little leather hoods. There are no masks, but the tools, it turns out, are in the bigger drawers at the bottom of the cupboard. Here she finds two good Stanley knives, a drill, several sections of tarpaulin, and an electric hand saw. She plugs in the battery for the saw and puts everything else in a couple of metal pails from under the sink.

She opens the wardrobe section – maybe she'll find some handy gear in here. The cupboard breathes out mustiness while she flicks through the hangers: ancient Barbours, gardening coats, leather waistcoats with many pockets, waterproof fishing jackets, tweed shooting jackets.

Why do men need so much kit?

At the far end of the cupboard she comes upon two small leather jerkins. Surprised, she pulls one out of the cupboard. It is a stiff, old thing, padded front and back, with holes for the arms and small metal loops attached to the sides and back – these must have worked as fastenings. The leather is stained in places, and the straps and buckles tie up at the back, so the wearer was strapped into the garment. And it is *so* small. Only a child could wear this. She has no memory of wearing anything like this. And the purpose seems obscure: it's too carefully crafted and expensive to be fancy dress. She takes out the other jerkin. It is considerably smaller. She and Maggie couldn't have worn these, at least not at the same time. She puts the hangers back.

She finds herself still holding the corner of a jerkin. She sniffs the stained padding, but all she smells is age and old leather.

She takes the saw, the pails and the tarpaulins, and locks the room up again. She calls Cat.

'How do you dissect a bear?'

'It's dead easy,' says Cat. 'Just like opening a banana. You find a crease in the middle, run your nail along it and then press gently on either side and a crack will appear. You then remove the innards in one piece.'

'Very funny.'

'For God's sake, how do you expect me to know?'

'Well, you've cut up a dog before now.'

There's a pause, then Cat says, 'Tell you what, though, I know a man who can.'

'Yeah?'

'Jim McCreal.'

'Who?'

'He's a funny, grubby little fellow. But he has clever fingers. Knows his way around every dead animal. There'll be a price though. He'll want the mountings.'

'Mountings?'

'The head and paws. And definitely the gallbladder, as well.'

'Jesus!'

'Business is business. I'll pull over in a minute and call him for you.'

A few minutes later Cat rings back to tell her that McCreal will be at the station in an hour. 'He'll meet you in the car park. He doesn't want to go inside. Probably scared of Jeanette.'

In the car park the tarmac still shines with rain. McCreal is late. Meanwhile, the bear, lying sideways on a plastic sheet, is being watched over by Cummings, the grizzled desk sergeant, Boyd, and three small, whey-faced boys. They're brothers, or cousins – for they are all wearing anoraks made from the same shower curtain. They have cropped, greasy brown hair. Seen from above, they'd be three shiny, little voles.

Were they seven years old? Eight? *Probably older but stunted.*

Rhona puts down the pails and the holdall and turns to Boyd.

'How did they get in?'

'Over the wall, they often hang around the bins.'

She looks at the boys, 'Shouldnae yous be at school?'

They don't answer. The biggest boy gives a long, scornful sniff. He prods at Wilber with a length of garden cane.

'Careful!' says Rhona.

'He's deid!' says the boy.

'He's sleepen,' says Boyd.

The smallest, scabbiest boy looks worried.

Rhona remembers her own childhood. Long afternoons with Cat and Maggie, lingering outside the Kinlochleven butcher's waiting for chicken claws. You could pull the ligament and the claw would jerk closed around your finger. There was no better, creepier toy.

She climbs into the overalls and puts on some vinyl gloves. She wishes she had found a mask.

As she starts up the electric saw, everyone else stands back.

It's only meat, she thinks, and she slices through Wilberforce's right hind paw. She presses down on the joint. A nauseating scorching smell rises up from the blade as she drives into the bone. Just as she has predicted, bear juice sprays up into her face.

Slicing the paw into sections proves fiddly – again there's that horrible ease as she slices through flesh and then a hot grinding as she drills through knuckle bones. But soon she has three roughly same-sized claws, each attached to a lump of gore.

She hands a claw to each of the boys.

'Thanks, Miss!' they chorus.

'She's "Inspector" to you,' says Boyd.

'Thanks, inspecta!'

'Now get out of here,' she says.

And they leave.

'They'll get tetanus.' Cummings looks disgusted.

'They won't. They'll be just fine,' she replies. 'And if they do, at least they'll die happy.'

She's still holding the dripping saw when she sees a small, plump man with pebble glasses. He's walking on the balls of his feet, wheeling a small suitcase towards them. He has the earnest look of a curate.

The man stops, eyes Rhona, then the bear. His face falls.

'Mr McCreal? You can park in here, you know?' she says. Cat was right – he *is* grubby. His fingernails are black and under his shirt she can see a yellowing larval vest.

'It'll be safer in the compound,' adds Cummings.

McCreal's eyes stay fixed on the bear, 'What happened to the paw?'

'It's gone west,' says Rhona. 'The bear was a joyrider.'

Boyd grins and Cummings manages a smile, but McCreal's face remains deadpan. 'The four paws would have made a nice set.'

'Like dining room chairs?'

There's a pause. Boyd grins his grin again and she wonders how often she's made herself enemies just for the pleasure of a quick quip.

'But you're welcome to the head,' she adds. 'This bear is a most unusual colour.'

'I know,' says McCreal. 'Which parts do you require?'

'The entire digestive canal.'

'There will be quite a bit of him.'

'And I'll need to take some bloods.'

'I'll get the gases out first.'

Rhona nods. She hadn't thought of the gases.

McCreal kneels by the body. From a side pocket of the suitcase he takes out a wooden-handled awl and plunges it into the side of the bear. The bad air hisses out.

Cummings holds his handkerchief to his nose. 'I wish I was back on Traffic.'

'We'll leave you to it, Mr McCreal,' says Rhona.

McCreal works quickly. Twenty minutes later, when Rhona and her men return, McCreal and the bear's head and paws have all vanished. Now there's just a furry mound of headless, gutted bear lying on its side and split down the middle. Beside it lies one of Rhona's pails, heaped with small intestine. The stomach has been laid in the smaller pail, an upturned hub cap contains a lumpy length of lower bowel.

'Not so much as a thank you,' says Rhona.

'But a tidy worker,' says Boyd. 'You always get what you ask for from Jim McCreal.'

'Didn't know you knew him.'

'Everyone knows everyone these days,' says Boyd. Cummings nods in agreement.

Rhona takes the syringe from the holdall and crouches by the bear. Boyd pulls the pelt back and she ducks her head down into the red room of the carcass. Blobs of curd-like fat hang down from the ribs and, at the back of the cavity, lie two long dark organs, one of which has to be the liver.

Boyd peers into the carcass and points to a length of tubing near the spine. 'There's a nice fat vein for you, ma'am,' he says comfortingly.

She presses the needle in, pulls back the plunger and the syringe fills with dark red blood.

She comes out for air, picks up one of the sample vials, squirts the blood in and pushes the rubber stopper down.

She takes another breath and reaches back into the bear again. Up near the lungs, she takes a sample of brighter blood. The plunger seems to stick and it takes her longer this time. When she pulls her head out, her diaphragm twitches and she burps into her mouth. She squirts the red blood into a second vial and presses down the stopper.

Boyd closes the slit in the bear and runs a knowing hand over its rump. He takes the tweezers from the First Aid bag, removes a gob of flesh stuck to the hood of Rhona's overall and flicks it away.

'What are you checking for?' he says.

'You know me. I never know what I'm looking for.'

'So what next?' he asks.

She looks over at the wet, shiny innards.

Boyd picks the stomach out of the pail. It is pale, bulbous, wet-looking. He weighs it in his hand, and she knows that look. He's weighing her up too, wondering why he has to take orders from a skinny little chit of a girl.

'It's nice and full,' he says. 'Do you want to open it up? Or shall I?'

If she lets him take over, all the office will know by lunchtime.

'Wait a minute.' She turns to Cummings. 'My car keys are in my bag. Can you get the hip flask from the glove compartment?'

'It's ten o'clock in the morning.'

'That was an order, Cummings.'

'Yes, ma'am.'

Rhona and Boyd drink the whisky – Cummings refuses a drink and waits for them to finish. Occasionally he wipes the corners of his mouth with his handkerchief.

Finally, it is time.

Holding her breath, she crouches by the pail and slices the stomach open down the middle as if it were a haggis. A rich smell of vomit rises into the air.

Boyd peers over her shoulder and prods at the contents with a spoon.

'See this?' He flips over a glaucous nodule, 'That's muscle. That'll be *him.*' He prods the stomach contents thoughtfully with his spoon, 'The bear ate quite a bit. But bears are *gorgers.* They hold an animal down with their paws and tear off bits of muscle while it's still alive. Then they go into the innards. So here you'd expect to find great strips of gristle and half-chewed muscle. They prefer older meat to totally fresh stuff. And they love innards, but there's no liver in here.'

'You know a lot about bears.'

'You know me. I take an interest in the wild.'

'But you didn't see the body, did you?'

'Forensics got there first. We were unavoidably delayed.'

Fishing rods.

'Maybe the bear was disturbed,' she says.

'Or maybe he was a picky eater,' says Boyd with a shrug.

'Does he *look* like a picky eater?'

Rhona and Boyd stare at the furry vastness of the bear and Boyd snickers. Cummings, meanwhile, looks up at the sky.

Boyd peels off his gloves and gets to his feet.

'We're not done yet,' she says. 'We're going to cut the whole intestine open.'

'I've got a flying lesson. I'll be late,' says Boyd.

'Be late then.'

'It's important. The test is next week.'

'What is it with you? Today is a working day. You're meant to be here. You're not paid to drive helicopters, or make your own fishing flies.'

Boyd's lips tighten.

'Get a grip!' she says. 'You don't go into a house and just search the living room, do you?'

She sends Cummings back to the office to look for more wet wipes. This, she hopes, will take him some time. And while Boyd calls on his mobile to postpone his lesson, Rhona makes a quick incision in Wilber's neck and pockets the bear's tracking chip.

Cummings returns with the plastic sheeting and the wet

wipes. He says, 'You can smell that bear from the far end of the car park.'

Rhona stretches out the first sausage-like bit of small intestine on the sheeting. While Boyd holds the section taut, she runs the Stanley knife along its squirming, sliding length. Inside there is nothing but liquid excreta.

There are over a dozen meters of intestine and they get into a rhythm, Boyd whistling tunelessly as they work. Now she is no longer nauseous and feels light and fluttery from the whisky.

After they've processed all the small intestine, Rhona sits up and stretches her back. She notices a tiny red flash in the sky above them. It's a drone, hovering about twenty metres overhead. You'd never normally see a drone here. The police don't have them, and the car park is just by a public road.

'It's been there for ages,' says Cummings. 'I think we're being watched.'

How could she have missed this? She keeps her face completely rigid. *Never show fear in front of men.*

'Sergeant, shoot it,' she mutters.

'You can't be serious,' says Boyd. 'Those drones can cost thousands.'

'I don't care. Quickly, just do it.' She doesn't even look at him. She keeps her eye on the flashing light.

By the time Boyd gets his gun out – he fumbles with the holster – the drone is moving away and picking up speed. Boyd's shot cracks through the air and the drone gives a quiver but keeps on going, its flight juddery now, legs askew.

'I thought you were meant to be a good shot!' she says.

'I did wing it!'

She turns to Cummings, 'How long was it there for?'

'Ever since you started on the bear, ma'am,' he replies stolidly.

'And you didn't think to tell us? Or are you just a wet wipe dispenser?'

Cummings blinks back at her. He has very long, pale eyelashes. In fact, he blinks beautifully. It is the only thing she has seen him do well.

Rhona turns back to the bear's innards. She cuts open the colon, which reveals a crinkly mass of soft, shit-filled ridges. She turns a section of it inside out.

'You never know what you'll find here,' says Boyd. 'All sorts of stuff gets stuck in the folds. Before the shutdown I went on holiday to Bali and had a colonic. I got back a marble I'd swallowed when I was seven. It was still shiny.'

'Bears don't play marbles,' she says. He's getting on her nerves.

She comes to a corner in the colon. Here the ridges are tucked together, tight as a closed accordion. She removes some lumps of shit and then runs her forefinger along the inside of the crevices. She feels something small and round, scoops it out with her finger and scrapes it onto the palm of her gloved hand. She spits on it and rubs.

A kidney stone? No, kidney stones came out through the bladder. Maybe bears eat grit.

But when the dirt comes off she sees that the bead is smooth and shiny.

It's a pearl.

With a jolt, she looks up to check the sky. But there's nothing, just a scattering of clouds. She rolls the pearl across her palm and sees two tiny holes.

'What have you got there?' says Boyd.

'A pearl. A little seed pearl.'

'He must have been eating mussels,' says Cummings. 'I've never cared for shellfish myself.'

'It's from a necklace or a bracelet,' says Rhona.

Boyd leans over her and inspects the pearl. He swears under his breath.

'Johnnie Fergusson wasn't the type to wear pearls,' says Rhona. She sits back on the tarpaulin.

She closes her eyes as if having a quick rest. Really she's thinking. Pearls are old-fashioned; they're very pre-shutdown. And seed pearls don't tend to be worn by women. They're what nice young girls wear.

Boyd rolls up a cigarette of raspberry leaves.

'That pearl could have been in there for years,' he says.

Rhona doesn't reply. She bends over again and turns the rest of the colon inside out. The skin is delicate as silk and heavy with shit. It flops between her fingers. She lays it out on the tarpaulin and runs her forefinger along every ridge. There are more tiny balls and two shards of something hard with glints of bright red. She collects the bits in the palm of her left hand. Again, she spits into her hand and washes off the shit.

More pearls.

The shards are two fragments of fingernail, red with nail varnish.

She looks up at the men's shocked faces. Cummings is no longer pink-skinned.

Rhona folds the pearls and the bits of fingernail into a wad of wet wipes. She takes out the Tupperware box from her bag and places the bundle of wet wipes inside.

'That's my lunch box!' says Cummings.

'Sorry, I needed something airtight.' She gives him a quick smile and slips the box closed. 'I'll send these to Forensics,' she says.

She leaves her men to dispose of the bear.

A MURDER OF CROWS

Rhona gets out of her overalls and takes a shower. She washes her hair and scrubs at her nails and, afterwards, she sprays herself with lavender water. She puts on a long black shift dress which she keeps in her locker for formal occasions. It'll do for the seminary and for the meeting with Johnnie Fergusson's parents at 4 p.m.

She checks in the mirror. She has that haunted look again: tiny folds round her eyes, thin little lines bracketing each side of her mouth. Youth, she feels, is like being a new car. For a surprisingly long time you zip around oblivious, looking new, smelling new. And then overnight your bodywork turns tatty and chipped. You turn into the wreck you really are.

Rhona dabs on some tinted moisturiser and rubs it into her face. She lifts her chin and rubs it into her neck too. She never wears necklaces – the idea of something metallic so close to her windpipe is unbearable.

The seed pearls. You'd never see them on any of the working girls on the public roads out of Fort William. Bar staff? Receptionists? No, they wear chunky stuff.

She refills the hip flask, climbs the stairs to the office and sits down, puts her elbows on her desk, and her head in her hands. Pale yellow Post-its have settled all over her computer screen, and the message light on the phone is flashing '8'. She presses the button and half listens; a couple of beaten up pensioners, three larder break-ins at the Fasnacloich Spa where the manager doesn't know the score and still isn't putting out enough food in the car park, more yachts burned out at Oban, and that young fool, the thirtieth Cameron of Lochiel, has had his llamas stolen yet again.

So there's nothing urgent: no homicides, no mobs gathering, no informers reporting on planned raids. Rhona still cannot get over how badly organised the Highland criminals seem to be. If they only grouped together they could run kidnapping squads, or take over the hard currency hotels. But instead the crime is all so small scale, so random and feeble. The Scots are too demoralised, too limp-wristed, too sodden with drink. Proper white collar fraud seems beyond them; they are lousy at scams, and their dark web networks are pathetically easy to penetrate. Even the sniv dealers are amateurs and lack class.

It's this mass ineptitude, rather than any of the extreme measures by the Scottish Executive or the looming presence of the Church, which keeps up the thin pretence of civilised society. Scotland, in effect, runs by default.

Rhona turns on the computer and checks the missing persons' file, even though she knows she'll probably find nothing. She starts four years ago, when Wilberforce arrived in Scotland, and from there she scrolls forwards. Mugshots of sad, scraggy men stare back at her. A few bedraggled sex workers are in there too.

But none of the women or girls, she finds, are still actually missing. All the entries are accounted for and photographs of the corpses have even been added. Many of the faces have a characteristic hard stare. These are what the office calls 'blinds'. When a body rolls into the morgue, The Bassett will send someone down with a camera and then Boyd will photoshop open eyes onto the head shots and register the corpses in the missing file retrospectively. This boosts Fort William's clear-up rate.

Rhona leans back in her chair and rubs her eyes. Boyd comes in.

'Have you cleared up?' she says.

He grins.

'Did you and Cummings find anything in that wood yesterday? You did trawl the area, didn't you?'

'There was nothing.'

'Nothing belonging to Johnnie?'

'Nothing,' says Boyd. 'Just woods and some old outbuildings full of junk.'

'What kind of junk?'

'Old farm machinery, bags of cement powder, some sharp sand, a couple of paraffin canisters, a bit of fishing gear.'

'Rich pickings then?'

He winks at her.

Fassolich seminary, a grey stone barrack of a building with an adjoining church, stands in the middle of a glen probably selected for its elemental bleakness. There is nothing else here, except a couple of bent hawthorn trees and a few drystone walls marking the boundary. In every direction the enclosure is cupped by mountains – God's heathery paw holding the Holy Willies up to the wide skies and a perpetual cold wind.

The road is full of potholes and Rhona drives slowly. Up ahead, by the front gate to the church, stands a small bearded figure in black, his cassock billowing in the wind. She mutters an oath and stops the car abruptly. She had hoped, hoped against hope, that there'd be nobody here – just the poor lads in their tombs. The last thing she needs is a Holy Willie.

The minister is looking her way. She shuts her eyes. That won't make him vanish, but it'll give her a moment to prepare. She fumbles in the glove pocket, finds the hip flask, ducks her head below the dashboard and takes three gulps. She lifts her head and tries to slow down her breathing. No, she needs more. She ducks down a second time and takes a long swig at the flask. She shuts her eyes and waits a moment for the whisky to work its magic. She still hasn't drunk enough for a meeting with a minister, but all the same that raggedy, jangling nearness of the world has softened slightly.

When she sits up, the minister is still looking in her direction. And further off, in the doorway to the seminary, she sees two dark figures who turn towards her for a minute and then return inside.

Sucking on a mint, she starts the engine up, stalls and starts again and takes the car slowly down the last section of the drive and parks on the hard standing. She locks the car – you never know, even here – and takes the stony little path up to the churchyard.

She repeats to herself her old catechism: mind your tongue, bite your lip, stare at your shoes, don't let him get to you. But churchmen always *do* get to her.

The drystone wall is low, so she can see into the graveyard, where, scattered among the graves, lie a dozen old stone sarcophagi. Most are very plain, the inscriptions chipped away – just some moss or a creep of pale lichen. They are all different and have been raided from various churches across Scotland and brought here for the seminarians' last spiritual test.

In each tomb, ventilation holes have been drilled into the stone on the sides and lid. No sound at all comes from these stone coffins. The silence is unnerving; she'd have preferred screaming.

As she approaches, the Willie inclines forward slightly as if leaning into the wind.

She tries to work out his age. Thirties? He's not yet greying. The beard and moustache are wiry as pubic hair. There are blackheads on his nose and his nostrils and eyes are red – it's a tough life.

'Good morning,' she says.

The minister nods his head gravely.

'I'm Rhona Ballantyne. I have come to visit Joel Travers. I work for his uncle, Chief Superintendent Travers.'

'The police have no jurisdiction on hallowed ground.' The Willie has a little sideways mouth, like a flounder.

'I'm here in a private capacity.'

'We don't recognise temporal authorities here. We are a place of God.'

No, you're not, she thinks. She looks down at the ground. By the minister's sandalled feet there's a bucket of paraffin and, propped beside it, lies a long stick with a cloutie of rags wrapped around one end. He'll be here all night with his flaming brand, like one of the cherubim of the apocalypse. But how do you make small talk to a cherub?

'It must be cold in the tombs,' she says.

'Aye, it's cold.'

'So you were crypted in your time?'

'Mine was a November crypting, in the snow. We're doing this cohort in summer, which is a kindness. They are each given a winding sheet to wrap up in, too, and we took out the mortal remains beforehand. And the woodlice.'

'How nice!' She flashes a smile at him.

He eyes her warily, 'It strengthens faith. Our great founder, John Knox, took refuge in a crypt.'

'And bodily functions?' she asks lightly.

'They make do.'

'They could die in there, couldn't they?'

'If they pass, they do so in a state of grace.'

83

'So that's okay, is it?'

Stop! You have enough enemies.

His nostrils flare, 'What's the purpose of your visit?'

'I'm just here to check he's okay.'

He gives her a heavy-lidded look. 'I suppose that's allowed. It's still only Friday.'

'Where is he?'

The minister points to a tomb near the perimeter wall. 'You can have a minute. Only a minute. He is here to be in communion with God.'

'Thank you, pastor.'

She is just turning to leave when he says, 'What's the problem with the car? Is it the alternator? Or the crankshaft sensor?'

She suppresses the urge to giggle and looks him straight in the eye and says, 'It's just the ignition. It keeps cutting out.'

'Ah,' he nods his head again. 'Thanks be to God.'

Rhona walks across the graveyard on a path of trodden grass that passes two other sarcophagi. She comes to Joel's tomb.

She can't imagine the total darkness, the utter cold and silence. Maybe a little light comes in through the ventilation holes? Perhaps he has a buzzing fly in there with him – at least that would be company. The poor lad. She's seen a picture of him on the Bassett's desk. He was a young boy then: pigeon-chested, nerdy-looking, glasses. All attributes of impending ministry. So he didn't stand a chance against The Bassett and his big brother. It's a canny move, though: these days many families hedge their bets and feed a spare son to the Church. And the Holy Willies are really creatures of prey, a breed of big black crows. A murder of crows.

She casts a glance back at the gate. The Willie is watching.

She walks round to the far side of the tomb, away from Holy Beady Eyes. She kneels down like a penitent by the ventilation holes. She thinks, you could have done anything, Joel. Anything would have been better than this. You could even have joined the police.

She puts her mouth to the cold stone.

'Joel!' she says in a stage whisper.

Silence.

She tries again: still nothing.

This time she shouts, 'Are you okay?'

A tiny, young voice comes back from the tomb: '*Yes.*'

THE FERGUSSONS

When Rhona arrives back at the office, she calls Cat who hears the hitch in her voice and immediately says, 'What's up?'

'It was unbelievably horrible. Those lads are just kids, really. How can they do it to them?'

'You mean the crypting? I heard you were up there today. Is the Travers' boy okay?'

'He's still alive. But it shouldn't be allowed.'

'It's meant to bring them closer to God,' says Cat matter-of-factly. 'And they need the experience to get those mad, staring eyes.'

'There was this awful Willie guarding them at the gate. He had a face on him like a slapped arse. Why don't they ever smile?'

'You don't smile much either. And there's no smiling in the Bible. Absolutely no jokes there. You can open the good book anywhere you want and you won't find a verse that begins, "A pigeon walked into a bar…"'

'True enough.'

'But that's not why you called, is it?'

'No. It's about the bear.'

'Did Jim McCreal come and do his stuff?'

'Yep, and he took away the head and paws. God, it was gory. But tell me one thing. Those Moldavians of yours – the ones up in Glencoe. Did the missing teenagers ever show up?'

There's a pause. Cat's voice is slower now, 'No. Why do you ask?'

Rhona looks across the office. Just Boyd here, but Jeanette does like to listen in too.

'We found the ainsrem fo a 'irlg, a 'ngyou 'irlg, in that 'rbea.'

'Sorry? It's years since we did this. I'm rusty.'

Rhona slowly repeats what she just said.

'Christ! What remains?'

'Erfing ilsna, and some earlsp,' Rhona smiles hard at Cummings who has just come in and is staring at her.

'Pearls? Real or fake?' says Cat.

'Real.'

'My girls have pearls. Little ones. We use them on the jewellery holders. I know they make themselves little bits of jewellery on the sly. But I turn a blind eye to it.'

'Dre ilna ishvarn?'

'Yes, they like to make themselves look nice – it's only natural. I've brought them sets of nail varnishes and they love them. But… But how could they have ended up in Ardnamuchan? It's miles away.'

'I don't know.'

Cat makes a soft sucking sound. 'Be careful,' she says. 'Be *very* careful. You don't know what you're getting into.'

'I'm in already.'

Rhona puts the phone down, and then turns to Cummings, 'I meant to ask you earlier. You know Gordon Simpson, the gamekeeper's son.'

'What about him, ma'am?'

'You gave him a lift home yesterday, didn't you? Did he say anything interesting? Did he tell you about the estate? Or Henderson?'

'No, we discussed his Higher Certificate options. And openings in the fishing industry.'

'And that number plate?'

'I'm working on it.'

'Thank you, Cummings. I know I can always rely on you to do your work promptly and efficiently,' she says sourly.

'Any time, Inspector.' Then he adds, 'Excuse me for asking, but what language were you speaking.'

Rhona narrows her eyes at him, 'Finnish.'

Jeanette calls to say that Colonel and Mrs Fergusson have arrived and that she has installed them in the Beaufort Suite. This is the police 'hospitality room' and is decked out in muted colours, with thick wool carpets, and soft engulfing armchairs, framed photographs of police awards' ceremonies and a two-way mirror discreetly framed in silver. Nobody has ever had a nice experience in the Beaufort Suite. It is set aside for cases that require delicate handling – children in abuse cases, rape victims, the partners and relatives of the violently departed. So the room is essentially dishonest; a pastel, absorbent antechamber to torture and ruin.

First, Rhona visits the observation room and looks in the two-way mirror. The couple are sitting very still and upright. He is rugged and leathery. She is immaculate: silver hair, a touch of makeup, her gloves lying obediently on the lid of her handbag. Her eyes are stricken.

What are the words of a stranger worth? There is no point, Rhona knows, in trying to comfort them, and no point in pretending that the body might not belong to their son. She must just go slowly, and remember they will only have half their minds on what she is telling them.

She knocks, pauses and then opens the door. As she does so, the couple get to their feet. She puts out her hand. Mrs Fergusson takes it, but the colonel merely nods.

Keep it simple.

Rhona introduces herself and says, 'I'm sorry for your loss.'

'Thank you, Inspector.' Mrs Fergusson gives her a pained smile. And the general nods again.

'Do we have a time of death?' he asks a little too loudly.

'We think between two and three in the morning, sir.'

'But what was he doing out at that time?'

'I'm afraid we don't know. We have spoken to William Henderson and your son's other friends, but they claimed he must have gone out after they all went to bed.'

'You said *"claimed"*. Are they under some kind of suspicion?'

'No, they're not. Not at all.' He's sharp. She makes a mental note to be careful.

Mrs Fergusson smiles at her conspiratorially, the way the wives of difficult men do.

'When can we see the body?' he asks.

'The car is coming now,' replies Rhona. He hasn't said 'Johnnie' or 'my son'. Just 'the body'.

Cummings brings the car round to the front.

The colonel, who has a bad leg, promptly ensconces himself in the front. Mrs Fergusson and Rhona take the back seats.

The Highland Forensics' office is also in Fort William and happens to be only a few minutes' walk away. But they will still need a car: there is the usual motley crowd outside the police gates hitching onto the internet signal, and afterwards they'd have to brave the beggars and touts on the High Street.

Cummings embarks on the long loop round the one way system. When they stop at the first set of lights, Rhona watches a wobbly one-legged pigeon pecking at a crack in the pavement.

Meanwhile, Mrs Fergusson has sunk back into her seat and shut her eyes.

'Madam, are you all right?'

Mrs Fergusson, her eyes still closed, nods.

They drive on. Rhona looks straight ahead at Colonel Fergusson's brutally short haircut and at the red back of his neck which has two deep, lateral folds. He will have a desk job these days and that can't suit him.

The neck moves. 'He'd never have made it!' says the colonel.

'Alan!' Mrs Fergusson's eyes open. Her fingers press on her clutch bag. Her nails are broad and flat, just like Johnnie's.

'Well it's true! If the bear hadn't got him, the wolves would have. Or something else. He was natural prey.'

'You don't know that,' says his wife wearily.

'How did he let himself get into such a stupid situation? What was he up to? That's what I want to know.'

That's what we all want to know.

'He had his whole life in front of him,' says Mrs Fergusson. 'He was so talented.'

She turns to Rhona. 'We were fine with him going to St Andrews – every young man has to have his moment in the sun. But, of course, the understanding was always that he'd enlist afterwards.'

Rhona shifts stickily on the plastic upholstery.

Mrs Fergusson continues, 'But Johnnie wasn't happy about that. He wanted to go on and do a doctorate. It would have made him 26 or 27 before he went in.'

'That would have been too late,' says the colonel. 'He would have been *far* too old.'

'I think more recently he'd given up on the army,' adds Mrs Fergusson dreamily. 'The last time – that very last time that I spoke to him – he seemed to have lost interest in the idea. He said it no longer mattered.'

'When was that?'

'Only a few days ago. He was in Fort William with Arthur and Will on some hospital visit. He said he was having a good time here. He said it was all "very special".'

'You can say that again!' mutters the colonel.

Mrs Fergusson looks out the window.

There's a moment of silence. Then the colonel speaks, 'I blame Will Henderson for this.'

He turns in his seat, his cheeks two angry pink cliffs, 'Johnnie was fine when he was younger. Absolutely *fine*. He was a great athlete, a real team player. He loved his outward bound and had a great future ahead of him. And then he fell in with Will. He gave it all up and started to put on weight. He no longer cared.'

The colonel shakes his head in disgust. 'And he got into *poetry*.'

He says it like a dirty word.

Johnnie Fergusson is laid out under a sheet on a gurney. It's a bare, chilly room and Rhona thinks they could at least have stretched to a couple of chairs and a water urn. But at least he isn't in a refrigeration drawer, and the heavily made-up assistant who ushers them in is respectfully taciturn.

Mrs Fergusson holds her fist against her mouth.

'Are you ready?' asks the assistant. The kohl round her eyes is turquoise, as if she were a gannet.

'Yes,' says the colonel, and he holds his wife's arm while the assistant slowly peels back the sheet as far as Johnnie's shoulders. How tactful. If the job had gone to Dimitri, the chief technician, he'd have whipped the whole sheet off in one theatrical flourish.

91

Rhona considers the body. Some people make better corpses than others, just as some faces do the early morning better. The young, if they're not too wasted on sniv, usually fare pretty well. They've done quite a good job on Johnnie. He looks a bit shiny and yellow, and strangely puffed up around the nose and mouth. But things could have been far, far worse.

Mrs Fergusson gives a little cry.

'It's Johnnie, isn't it?' says Rhona.

'Yes,' she says. 'It's him. But it's not him.'

Johnnie's hair, so curly and luxuriant, has been combed back revealing the little swallow tattoo just under his left ear.

The colonel strokes his son's cheek with the back of his hand. 'Nothing matters now,' his voice is breaking. 'Not even that bloody bird.'

Rhona leaves them there with their son. She takes the stairs up to the labs.

Outside Dimitri's room she stops to brace herself; he's a man you only want to meet when your last meal is well settled. But Dimitri Belyakov opens the door on her before she has even knocked.

'Senorita! My favourite lady!' He makes a mock bow and ushers her in.

Belyakov beckons her to the seat opposite his desk. He sits down in his swivel chair and reorganises his paunch in relation to his trousers.

'Dr Rabina is not happy. Not happy at all. Next time you come to Uncle Dimitri. He *loves* bears!'

'That couldn't be helped,' she says. 'You prepped Johnnie Fergusson, didn't you? You did a nice job.'

'You know me. My bodies must look happy. No more chewed-on-wasp expressions! You see, the bloo...'

She puts up her hand to signal him to stop. But he

continues regardless, '…the blood, it makes a little pond in the back of the cranium. So the nose comes sharp. The lips go thin, thin, thin – like an old auntie. He is a young man. *Was* a young man. So I put a little cotton wool in his mouth, just above the gum line. For the nose I have a special trick!'

'Spare me the details!'

'Polyurethane crack filler. I get it from the builders' merchant in Caol. 127 Merks for one tube and it lasts and lasts. It swells in the nostrils, fills them out. And it's a good yellow colour. No one sees it.'

'Just don't tell the colonel and his wife. They won't want to know their son has been repointed like a dodgy wall.'

'Squeamy squeamy! I always say, Rhona, you chose the wrong job. Wrong job.'

'No, Dimitri. I choose the wrong mortuary technician.'

'Ha! Ha! And how are his parents?'

'She's desperately sad. He's furious. What do you expect? Military families are all primed for battlefield deaths and helicopter crashes. But not for this.' She pauses. 'What was the BAC?'

'0.23.'

Rhona nods. At 0.23 Blood Alcohol Concentration Johnnie Fergusson would have been stumbly, sloppy drunk. But not entirely legless. Any hallucinations would have been down to the mushrooms.

'He certainly made a night of it,' she says. 'And the fingernails?'

Dimitri's shoulders go up and then down again in a slow shrug. 'The nails are not strong – maybe not a good diet? Maybe the bear's colon was not the best storage facility! Ha ha! The nails are small. Maybe belong to a young person. Maybe 11, 12 years old? We think the right hand.

Not a smoker. We think nervous – they're very chewed at the ends.'

'You're sure the nails aren't just damaged?'

'Chewed. I'm sure. Chewed.'

'It's not much to go on, is it?'

'You don't give us much! What do you want? Brown hair, 28-year-old, 173 centimetres, appendectomy, early orthodontic work? Is that right? You gave me two little chips of fingernail!'

'Okay. Keep your hair on.'

'A DNA profile is possible. The nails are good – better than old bones. We get five months of life in a nail. We can find genetic inheritance, drug use, pathology, diet, location history.'

His voice trails away, but his eyes look at her hopefully.

'Go ahead then,' she says. 'What's the problem?'

Dimitri rubs his forefinger and thumb together, 'It's very expensive. Electron microscopy work goes to St Petersburg – I have a colleague there. But we need an outsourcing form, crime reference, invoice number, costing code.'

'I can do you The Basset's signature.'

He gives her a steady look, 'And if he discovers?'

'It'll be my head on the block, not yours,' she replies. 'Did you find out anything about the varnish?'

He gives a disgusted little puff, 'Cheap stuff. No UV filters. I'd say Eastern bloc. Their make-up is terrible. They always take short cuts, always. So maybe this is a cheap brand, maybe something cooked up in a garage in Belarus.'

'You are harsh on your own people.'

'No, I'm a realist.'

'Can you find out more? Is it a brand? Can you wing it without the paperwork?'

He leers at her, 'You want more favours from Uncle Dmitri?'

'Exactly.'

'So this is a murder investigation?' he leans forward, elbows on the desk, smiling, waiting. Rhona smiles back. She's known him for years – from long before she went to Italy. Even if Dimitri is a ghoul, he's a clever and inquiring ghoul, and he can be very helpful at times. He must, she is sure, get bored of cutting open old drunks with livers the size of shoeboxes. So if he wants to know what's going on, then Rhona owes it to him. This is the price for his help.

'Don't get your hopes up,' she says. 'At the moment Johnnie Fergusson is not even a manslaughter investigation. There won't even be an open verdict. It'll be an accidental death.'

'Unless you find another body?'

'Yes. And they'll want more than fingernails.'

'So where can it be? There will be bones, no? Bears don't eat bones.'

'The remains could be anywhere on Henderson's land and that'll be 100 square miles at least. We can't arrest him. We don't have a body. And we don't have a reported crime. Nobody will give us a warrant.'

'You have no one reported missing?'

'In the records there are no missing girls or women. Not in the North West, or the entire Highland region. Everyone that vanishes has most disobligingly turned up as a corpse.' She doesn't mention The Basset's 'blinds'.

'Missing hands, then?' ventures Dimitri. 'Maybe a little scally puttan with no right hand?'

She gives him a dark look.

But Dimitri beams at her. 'It's hard to do a job one-handed, eh? Like a deaf violin player? Or a blind taxi driver? Ha! Ha!'

'Shut up, Dimitri!'

'If he eats one girl, maybe he eats more.'

'We need to keep this quiet at the moment,' says Rhona. 'I hope you haven't told anyone. Or does the whole of Russia know about our bear?'

'Nobody knows! Nobody!' protests Dimitri. But she sees the old liar flinch.

ARTHUR

Outside the Highland Forensics building she sees Will Henderson's friend, Arthur, standing with his hands in his greatcoat pockets. Wisps of his comb-over are sticking up vertically as if he were standing over a hot vent.

She crosses the road. *Did he follow the police car?*

'Is it me you want?' she asks.

He nods.

'You been waiting long?'

'Only half an hour. They're in there, aren't they?'

'Johnnie's parents? No, they've gone back to their hotel,' she lies effortlessly.

'Can I go in? Can I see him?'

She shakes her head.

'I need to talk to you about something,' he says.

They are just metres from the Ben Nevis bar. She pushes open the swing door and leads the way into its murky interior. The bar is busy; street traders are already drinking their way into the weekend, and three bare-legged sex workers in micro skirts are bent over the betting terminal. A hawker is going from table to table with little doses of something in plastic bags. He slips quietly out the side exit.

Rhona chooses a booth with padded seating which wheezes as they sit down. Mackay, the barman, strokes a cloth across their table but leaves them the full spittoon. He returns with two double whiskies.

Rhona swigs hers back. Arthur takes sips and she watches him lick his lips with his small, spatula-shaped tongue. He really is a remarkably ugly man. Misshapen features, terrible skin, grubby crevices: a face that looks as if it has been let out to students.

'I have a special request,' he says.

'What's that?' she replies. She notes a Paisley silk scarf wrapped around his neck. It's warm in the bar, too warm for a greatcoat. She wonders what he has on underneath. A vest? Maybe nothing.

'We'd like Johnnie buried in Ardnamurchan.'

'That's really not up to me. And who is "*we*"?'

'Me, Will, the girls.'

Someone is missing from this list. The big red-haired student. It takes her a moment to remember his name.

'And Ray?' she asks.

'He's gone home. I've just dropped him at the station.'

'I said none of you were to leave without contacting me. You've just disobeyed a police order.'

'Sorry. I'll text him and tell him to call you.'

'Why did he leave?'

'I think he panicked,' Arthur takes out his e-cigarette holder, pushes in a refill and takes a draw. 'He suddenly came up with this essay he had to redo – which is distinctly odd as his term is over.'

'Why would he panic?'

'I think he had a change of heart, or a loss of nerve, if you like. And I suppose he always was a bit on the periphery of things.'

'How do you mean?'

He says wryly, 'I suppose he didn't really share our poetics.'

'Your *poetics?* God Almighty!'

'I was joking, really.'

'All the same, this has made my job harder. You shouldn't have let him go.'

His face breaks into a surprisingly warm smile. 'I'm sorry,' he says. 'I didn't realise it was important.'

For a moment, she feels disarmed. He does have charm, she can see that now.

'I'm aware we got off to a bad start.' He looks down and jiggles his glass. 'And I'm sorry if I was a bit thin-skinned when we met before. You see, I've not always had great experiences with the police. And I do feel quite protective of Will.'

She leans back in her seat, 'How long have you known him?'

'For years. I taught him when he was a boy. He was in my class.'

'I thought you were in publishing?'

'I am *now*, but I used to be a teacher at Fettes in Edinburgh.'

'Ha! It must have been cold in those cloisters in the winter!' She is beginning to feel cheered by the whisky.

'You know the school?'

'I know that godawful building. It looms over the Lothian police headquarters.' Of course Henderson chose Fettes for his son: how could he resist a public school with gargoyles?

Arthur smiles a little sadly, 'My father was a housemaster there in his time, and his father was before him too. It was what we did.'

'Why did you give up teaching?'

'It gave me up really. I just wasn't cut out for it.' He adds wearily, 'And there were a few misunderstandings.'

That fits.

'You had to leave because of Will?'

He shakes his head.

'So when did you and Will become so close?'

'Only much later – after he'd gone up to St Andrews.

I met him again at a friend's house party in Perthshire. I recognized him instantly. He hadn't changed at all.'

'Was he your star pupil?'

'Will has *always* been exceptional.'

Arthur pulls out his mobile and starts scrolling through his images. 'Look, here's the place we want for Johnnie.' He passes her his phone, open at a photograph of a small, steep-sided bay. Henderson's fence crosses the land high up on the hillside, below lies the beach and a strip of land with a small graveyard and an avenue of tall trees.

'That's very beautiful,' she says.

'The morning sun would shine on his grave,' says Arthur. 'He'd have the seals for company. And the wind and the ceaseless sea.'

Rhona looks up at him, his eyes shiny and beseeching under that great tuberous forehead.

'Ceaseless sea,' he says. 'That's Ezra Pound.'

She hands him back his mobile.

'His grave would be outside the fence too,' he adds. 'That would be cleaner, purer. Don't you think? And he wouldn't get dug up by the wolves.'

'Did Johnnie say he wanted to be buried there?'

'Not in so many words. But he liked the bay. We all do.'

'But I can't help you with this. It's up to the Fergussons. It's their decision.'

Arthur's voice drops, 'But can't you still ask them?'

'You should ask them. You should go and see them anyway. They're staying at the Marriott in Torcastle – as you probably know. And they won't listen to me. I'm just the police. It's none of my business.'

'But it's none of *their* business either!' he exclaims. 'Johnnie was a stranger to his parents, especially his father. I don't see why crude biological imperatives should rule here.'

Where was this going?

'Don't you see? Those are just ties of blood,' his voice becomes more lispy as he grows insistent. 'But there are deeper connections of spirit and soul. They're surely more important.'

'Not in the eyes of the law, they're not. You're not family.'

'But we *are* family in a way, you know. Our little group, that's what we were, what we are.' He clasps his hands together, fingers clenched, filthy nails pressing down. 'Alive and dead. Present and past. We're linked, we're together.'

Foreverandever. Rhona remembers the old Anderson shelter in her father's garden. Cat and Maggie and her, in there together.

Arthur's eyes are downcast, 'It's been very special this time that we've had. Very special. And after Johnnie, I feel as if we're... well, it's bound us together.'

He takes in another breath of vapour and adds coyly, 'You could say we have made our own personal pontoon into the River Styx.'

Any discussion of the afterlife, Rhona feels, requires another drink. She beckons to Mackay and he comes over and refills their glasses. For a moment she shuts her eyes and listens to the sound of the whisky gurgling into the two glasses. It's sweeter than birdsong.

She gulps her whisky down.

Arthur sips dreamily, 'You know, in the scheme of things a life is such a small thing. And Johnnie just let go of it. That was his right.'

'That's a very odd thing to say. Johnnie was 21. He had his best years ahead of him.'

'I'm not sure that's true. By the time you're in your mid-twenties, it's usually all done and dusted. You no longer have an original thought left in you. Mundane things take over: work and mortgages and, in Johnnie's case, there was the army calling. So, you're already dying inside, really. I'd call it a sort of emotional anaemia. I am 34 now and I certainly don't see and feel the way I did when I was sixteen. Nothing's the same.'

Arthur sucks at his e-cigarette. Under the boiled sweet smell of vapour she catches a whiff of mould and staleness; the greatcoat must have come from a dressing up box.

He continues, 'Sometimes, when I walk somewhere, particularly in a graveyard, but even in the streets of a city, I am so aware of all those legions of dead under our feet. They all know something that we don't. Even a child of two or three who has died understands more than you or I do about what really matters. Even an idiot or a small child who has died has touched the divine. For they've experienced the most mysterious, and the most important event of any life.'

'You mean their own deaths?' She thinks, how very young he is. Bald, a bit past it, but still so *young*.

'It is the ultimate big secret, isn't it?' he says.

'But how can you put so little store by life?' she counters.

'I thought you would understand,' he replies.

'What have you heard about me?' she says sharply.

'Nothing.' He gives her a wary look. 'Nothing at all.'

She looks away.

He continues, 'I like to think that there is a small, exclusive band of people who are fighting the deadening of the soul. That is what Ardnamurchan is all about.'

'You mean you and your friends?'

'Not only us. In his own way, old Henderson is fighting that battle too.'

'In what way?'

'That call of the wild thing he has. All those bears

and wolves, the hunting, all of that.' Arthur casts her a measured look. 'Mind you, I wouldn't want to cross him. He can be a right piece of work.'

'You think so?' She sits glacially still. *Is this the real reason for his visit?*

'He doesn't approve of me,' says Arthur. 'He thinks I've led Will astray.'

'Why would that be?'

'He thinks it's my fault that Will doesn't love dogs and doesn't hunt and shoot. He thinks I've put him off. As if! Will's hated all that stuff for years. And it's probably all Henderson's doing.'

'Is there a rift between Henderson and his son? Is that why you don't all stay up at Glenborrodale?'

'Who'd want to stay in the Big House? Would *you* want to? It's got stuffed animals everywhere. They're even in the toilet. If you go for a piss, there's a boar's head above the cistern goggling at your manhood.'

His guard is down now. She thinks of the playing card. He'd deny all knowledge of it. She tries a softer tack: 'Arthur, why were you so nervy when I came to the tower?'

He gives her a hooded look. 'Mmm. I think I've already told you more than I should.'

'People don't get charged over drugs these days. You saw that sniv dealer when we came in. I didn't exactly go running after him, did I?'

'True enough.' He inspects his empty glass and won't be drawn.

Rhona glances over at Mackay and makes a little tipping gesture with her hand. The barman brings the bottle over and again refills their glasses. She swallows her dram and feels fire run like a river down into her belly. But it's her mind that needs to burn brighter. *Every unsolved crime is a failure of imagination.*

She says, 'I'm missing something.'

'What?' His hand is tucked round his glass, as if guarding it.

'I don't know. But there is some connection I am not getting.'

'That's interesting,' he says with a slight smile. 'I never thought of police work as very cerebral.'

She looks at him wearily. She's sick of his condescending manner and his sixth form intensity, and the fact that he's not had a proper wash in a hundred years. She knows too that she'll get nothing more from him. She shakes her glass and downs the last few droplets. 'Well, you thought wrong.' She wipes her mouth with the back of her hand. 'And never underestimate us.'

When they leave the bar Arthur offers her a lift back to the station – he says his car is in a guarded car park down by the waterfront. She refuses. She wants to walk and it will give her a chance to see if anything new is being touted on the High Street.

She watches him retreat down one of the wynds leading to the shore. His back is stooped, his shabby greatcoat swings round his legs. From behind, where you can't see that silk cravat, you might take him for just another scally.

THE HOSPITAL

Rhona stops at the petrol station and sprays a few two merk pieces at the gauntlet of beggars outside the shop. She buys a dozen tubes of peppermints for the glove compartment, a bunch of marguerites, a box of fudge, a half of Famous Grouse and a bottle of Irn Bru. Then she drives up the road to the hospital. In the car park, with her back to the security camera, she empties the orange fizz out of the Irn Bru bottle and pours in the whisky. The whisky isn't quite the same vivid orange. But it'll have to do. And hopefully it will sweeten the visit.

There is no one about and the hospital has a deserted pall. In the lift, she presses the button for the fourth floor, but the elevator doors open onto the public ward on the second floor. She sees a grey-faced girl of about ten lying on her side on a wooden bench with a wash bucket and an old plastic bag by her side.

The metal doors close again and the lift glides on up to the fourth floor. Here, Rhona steps out into a hallway with a polished parquet floor and armchairs. The air is hushed and clean and smells faintly of disinfectant. There isn't a lot she can thank her father for, but at least he had the sense to pay in dollars for medical insurance with an American company that somehow has kept operating in Scotland.

At the nurse's station, she introduces herself and hands over the fudge and flowers. The nurse is young, smiley, bun-faced.

She tells Rhona he's doing well.

'He'll see me, will he?'

'He *asked* for you.' She adds cautiously, 'but he's still maybe not quite himself.'

Rhona smiles back blankly. *Say nothing.*

Roderick Ballantyne is in a room at the very end of the corridor. Rhona walks past several empty rooms. She can't blame the staff: you'd want to keep a bit of distance from him if you could.

Now she stands in his doorway. She looks at him and it's as if someone has just thrown her heart down a well.

One side of his face has slumped. His eyes are closed and he is on a drip and catheter – clear liquid in, yellow liquid out. His heart monitor chatters and bleeps, his hands hang huge on the counterpane. His left hand is curled and claw-like.

He is out of his coma but he can't, she is sure, be getting better. He always was a small man, but now, propped up by pillows, he seems miniature. His face is skeletal, mottled. There's a liver spot on his right temple, as if the grim reaper had lobbed him a blood paintball. This is fitting; over the years, so many people have wanted to hit him. Including her – especially her.

But he's ill now, and so frail. He surely can't hurt her any more. And, thank God, he's asleep.

His eyes snap open. He looks up at her and the good side of his face goes slack. His neck cranes forward, his scrawny arm reaching out, wobbling horribly. 'Maggie!' His voice is just a thread, 'Have you come for me, dearie?'

Rhona stands completely still. His speech is blurred as if coming from the inside of a bottle. But she can hear exactly what he says.

'Is it my time now?'

'No, Dad. It's *me*. It's *Rhona*.'

He slumps back down into his pillows.

'Oh, it's you.'

He shuts his eyes again. She knows that he'll make her pay for his mistake.

'Dad, she'd never come back to frighten you. Maggie wasn't like that.' Rhona opens the Irn Bru bottle and passes it to him. He gives her a lopsided crocodile smile and takes a swig.

'I suppose not,' he replies. His teeth seem enormous, far too big for his face. '*She* had a very giving nature.'

Rhona doesn't reply.

In his new, post stroke mumble he adds, 'I should've known. You always were that wee bit thinner.'

Maggie was a size 16, and I'm a 10.

'And she wore her hair up when she went out,' says Rhona.

'True enough,' concedes her father, and he looks out the window. Down below is the car park and beyond lies a blue lozenge of estuary. He gropes on the counterpane, finds his glasses, puts them on and looks out the window again. The spectacles have a gold and turquoise leopard skin design. She smiles – remembers his boxers with the banana pattern, the shirt with palm trees. The old bugger always had his flashes of whimsy.

She sits down in the visitor's chair on the side of the bed away from the window.

'How are you feeling?' she asks.

'How am I feeling?' He hawks up mucus into a tissue. 'Nice to know you care. I'd say not tip top. I'm recovering from a stroke. Do you really want to know?'

Not really.

'I've had a mild ischaemic right hemisphere stroke, with a touch of hemiplegia. This is a follow on from the first act. The good news is that my bowel cancer has been successfully operated on. They didn't get it first time – the bowel failed to join up, leading to abdominal sepsis, which the idiots failed to pick it up in time. Second operation and a few more weeks on I.C.U., with me ventilated and tubed up like a flat battery. I had some months in Inverness and then they shipped me down here.' His head gives a sudden sideways jerk like a bird. 'Are you listening, girl?'

'Yes, Dad.'

He is summoning his old powers of précis: 'Where was I? Yes. The stroke. And I've got other little companions: an on-off urinary tract infection, cardiomyopathy, arthritis in my hips and skin tags round my anus. Not that that matters. Because now I've got a bloody bag. You know what a bag is?'

She nods. She is surprised at how quickly he has recovered his poise. He may croak and slur but he has certainly regained his ferocious stamina

'And the bag's only the beginning. You get sores, you bubble and leak like an old radiator. And you *fart!* You fart into the bag! The indignity of it. All I can say is enjoy your arsehole while you still have it.'

'Thanks, Dad.'

'Shall I go on?'

She shakes her head.

He grins at her savagely, 'And you, why are you here?'

'I came to visit you.'

'You've taken your bloody time – it's been seven years.' For a moment he stares out the window.

'I couldn't come before. You know that. There was the shutdown.'

'The borders reopened two years ago.'

She doesn't reply.

'I never understood why you went chasing after that Italian. What was his name?'

'Sergio Verviani.'

'Byronic good looks, I daresay.'

She is mute – she can't think how to bat off this attack.

He has another go: 'I never expected you to fall for a foreigner.'

'I didn't fall for him. He was a criminal running a major racketeering empire. He had to be dealt with.'

'Far too clever for you.'

'I got him in the end. He's been put away.'

Her father is looking away from her, watching something down in the car park. He does that bird-like flick of his head again and now his eyes are on her.

'There's only the house left. The pension dies with me.'

She blinks.

Then he smiles. A new conversational tone: 'So how goes the life of crime? Tell me something interesting. The least you can do is occupy my mind.'

She leans back in the chair and tells him about Johnnie Fergusson's death and about meeting Will Henderson and his friends, and Arthur's visit to her at the morgue. She describes the bear attack and how something on the reserve is definitely not right. She mentions the drone. But, on a hunch which she doesn't entirely understand, she omits the pearls and the fingernails. Is she sparing a dying man? Or does she not trust him to be discreet? Maybe it's a bit of both.

Roderick Ballantyne listens. He doesn't ask questions – he's waiting for her to finish. That is what he always did. When he worked for the bank, customers would ask for a loan and he'd say, 'Talk me through your business plan.' He'd listen intently. Afterwards he'd grill them to a crisp.

So, she can see he's all alertness. She has set him something to think about: somebody else's terrible agony and death, not his own. It's a better gift than the whisky.

When she has finished, he swallows a couple of times.

Finally, he says, 'Do the bears get enough to eat? Does Henderson keep them hungry? He's always been too soft on his animals. The old laird used to starve his dogs. He said it sharpened their noses.'

'I don't know,' she says. 'There's plenty of deer.'

'You have to be quick to kill deer. Even the old hinds move fast. But to kill a drunken student? That's a different matter. Anyone could wipe out a student.'

'But Dad, the bear didn't eat much of the student. The guts and the big leg muscles were untouched.'

An unkind smile flits across his face. He winks at her with his good eye, 'Who'd want to eat a bum, eh? Even an ever-so-refined St Andrew's undergraduate's bum!'

She doesn't smile back – keep him on facts and figures. That, she knows, is what he's always been good at. And he is familiar with everything and everyone in the West Highlands. In the old days, if you'd said, 'I'm looking for a small to middling-sized mussel farm within 25 miles of Achiltibuie,' he'd name you three businesses and tell you their annual turnover.

'What do you know about Henderson's estate?' she asks.

'Can't you do your own work?'

'He says he used to hunt with you.'

'That was years ago. He's a good shot, and not a bad falconer. We had some good times together.'

He moves his mouth over his teeth. She waits.

Eventually he says, 'I always thought that rewilding was a mad idea. He came to the bank for funding. It was near the beginning and he had just brought back beavers. I think he called them "ecosystem engineers".' Roderick Ballantyne gives a little, strangled yelp of laughter.

'Did you give him the money?'

'Of course not. Don't be silly. Beavers aren't a business.

Nobody eats beaver steaks. Nobody wants beaver fur. Not nowadays. Not unless they're perverts.'

'Go on.' She wishes he wouldn't leer at her.

'And Henderson is no businessman. He's a romantic, a dreamer. We all know what happens to dreamers.'

'What happens to them?'

'They go bankrupt.'

'But he hasn't gone bankrupt. The estate is in really good nick. It's like a haven.' She looks at her father's pale, papery hands, at the river system of veins snaking their way round his metacarpals. His veins are the only plump bit of him.

The good hand, which a second ago was so still, suddenly moves. He's groping for the plastic glass of water on the side table.

She passes it to him. He takes a shaky sip. She reaches forward to hold the glass for him, but he tries to slap her away with his claw hand. The movement is pathetically weak, but it jolts the glass and half the water pours down his front.

Normally, she knows, he would shout at her. But because he wants to talk, he ignores the spill, regains his composure and continues: 'Have you seen his accounts? No, I thought not. The rates on the estate will be well over 300,000 merk a year. The Willies will probably want their cut too. And then there'll be the insurance premiums – his public liability will be off the scale with all those wild animals. *And* he'll be paying for the licenses.'

He leans back, glances out the window and then shuts his eyes for a few seconds. Then, his voice barely more than a scratch, he resumes, 'And there's the maintenance bills. The Big House has a right roof on it. There are the roads, and miles of that electric fence. And the staff. He's laid off half the old gamekeepers, but he still has a few odd jobbers. Who was that fellow you mentioned?'

'Matt Simpson.'

'Aye, him. And the housekeeper, and the checkpoint staff. They'll all need paying. They'll all have tied cottages with bad boilers.'

He goes on, 'Henderson doesn't have much private money. He's not a tobacco baron or a hedge fund millionaire. He's got a few iffy stocks and shares, a bit of property, but not nearly enough. And that Twiglet he married.' Her father waves his good hand vaguely, 'The ballerina? Marissa Something. She didn't bring him any money.'

'You know a lot.'

'Of course I do. It was my job. Bankers are as bad as fishwives. If some housewife wanted a loan for her knitting business, I'd visit her. I'd take a shufti at her spreadsheets, discuss her Fair Isle patterns. Heaven wept, I can't abide handicrafts, even Catriona's stuff.' He stops, expectorates into a tissue and wedges it under his pillow. '*Especially* Catriona's stuff. Anyway, I'd work out if this woman had half a brain. Then I'd say my goodbyes, drive off, and stop at the nearest pub and sit there nursing my pint. By the end of the night I'd know if she was a drinker, if her husband was a drinker, if her second cousins were drinkers...'

'I know, I know.' Rhona rolls her eyes. 'And you had the lowest rate of bad debts of any bank in Scotland. You've told me that a million times.'

'I'm merely making a point!' He gives a rich little cough. 'Know the balance sheet. But know the person too, and know the family.'

'And what do you know about Henderson himself?' she asks.

'He's a rum one. Not a drinker – not a *real* drinker. But

ask yourself this: how is he paying for that estate? Tell me that.'

'He said he made his money off wolf hunting.' She hates the way her father always seems to make her sound so naive.

His mouth clamps shut.

'What do you think?' she asks.

'What does it matter what I think?' He slumps back down into the pillows. 'I'm just an old man. Why should I do your work for you? But I suppose that's what you've come for.'

'I'd like to know, Dad.' She can see he's tired.

'Hunting wolves, that's what you're talking about, isn't it?'

'Yes.'

'The nearest equivalent would be deer stalking. That's the same sort of thing – big mammal hunting. You can charge a lot and it gives you some foreign currency. But it doesn't bring in *that* much.'

'You're sure?'

'This is basic stuff, girl. Highland estates charge anywhere between 5,000 and 10,000 merk a day per deerstalker. You can't offer it all year round, and you can't have more than half a dozen stalkers out at any one time. Now, for the love of God, do your sums. You'll see it doesn't come to much. He won't cover basic costs.'

'I think he gives talks too, and appears on forums.'

'Fora.'

'Okay, "fora".'

'It'll still only be chickenfeed. He's not a big enough name.'

'Maybe he's got a book deal?' She knows this sounds lame.

The old man gives a derisive snort.

113

There's a pause. He brings his good hand up to his mouth, as if in one-handed prayer. It's something she has seen him do so often when he's thinking. After a while he puts his hand back down on the bed and says, 'The wolves have wrecked any chance of him getting back the grouse shooting. There are no oil reserves under the peninsula, so he can't frack. And has he gone into hydro? No. Fish farms? No. Those are the only ways Highland estates really make money. So, why hasn't he done that? He's not a fool. Does he think hydroelectric power is too vulgar for him? Too modern? Or is it because no bank will lend him the money? Is that it?'

He looks at her, 'There'll be some special source of revenue. And it won't be good.'

'What do you mean?' She passes him the Irn Bru bottle.

He takes a drink, smiles at the taste, and returns to his subject. 'Think it through. What is the appeal to any respectable business in coming here? The "virus-free" line doesn't wash with anyone. And now that the rest of Europe is pretty clean, it's irrelevant. So why come? We're miles from anywhere. The weather is terrible, there's theocratic rule as bad as Iran, half the roads are single track with passing places every hundred miles. The infrastructure's still in bits, mobile reception is prehistoric, internet access is hyper-controlled, violent crime is through the roof, the people... Well, let's not even go there.'

'The people aren't so bad, not really.'

'May I continue? You're here to soak up advice, aren't you?'

'Actually, I came to see *you*.'

He ignores her, 'The real reason for anyone coming here must be that *no one comes here*. Welcome to sunny Scotland. And if you want to make one hundred per cent sure that nobody sees what you are up to, why not winch in a load of grizzly bears and put up a ten foot security fence?'

'I hadn't thought about it that way,' she replies. 'I thought he was a Romantic.'

'He may be a Romantic, but there's a steely side to him and he still has bills to pay. And you know what else makes me think that?' he adds with a crooked smirk.

'What?'

'Were you followed when you came here?'

'I don't think so.'

'You don't *think* so? Remind me, are you a trained police investigator? Or a bubble-headed girlie with a pickled onion for a brain?'

He's looking out the window again.

'Your car is that grey Ford Corsa, isn't it?' He recites the number plate to her.

'Why?' She stands up.

'Some fellow has been doing something underneath it. So either you've got a bomb there. Or a tracking device.'

A small blade of ice slides down her spine.

'What does he look like?'

'Can't say. Dark clothes – blue or black. And, of course, he had his hood up.'

She creeps over to the window, stands behind the curtain and looks down. But there is no one in the car park.

'Good thing I was watching, eh?' he says triumphantly. 'I thought by now you'd be more careful.'

'Where is he?'

Her father takes another sip at his Irn Bru bottle. 'He's long gone. He drove off in a little blue van. Q33 6XY. A nice proper van, not a welded-together job. Small dent in the left passenger side rear panel. My left eye can't be so bad after all.'

That, she is almost certain, is the number plate of the

blue van she saw from the tower in Ardnamurchan. She takes out her notebook and writes down the number plate, holding the notebook up high so that he won't see her shaking hand. She flicks back through the pages. Yes, it *is* the same van.

'Can't you memorise?' his voice drips scorn. 'Do you write your name down last thing at night so you have it in the morning?'

'It's part of my training,' she replies stonily. 'Everything, absolutely everything, goes in the notebook.'

'Oh, aye.'

She takes out her lipstick and that gives her a chance to turn away from him and look in the mirror above his wash basin. She slowly applies the makeup; her lips feel numb.

'That's put the wind up you, eh?' he says.

She can see him in the mirror, smiling horribly at her with those tombstone teeth.

'What do you usually do when people come after you?'

'It doesn't happen often.'

'It's happened before. Your sister paid the price, and so did I.'

She turns back to him, 'I've got to go now, Dad.'

'Don't get nervy with me, girl. I just thought it was good to warn you.'

'But do you have to do it with so much relish?'

'I always say you need pressure to make a diamond. A little bit of fright does everyone good. It peps you up, keeps you on your toes.'

'I'll be going now.'

'Do you think…?' His good hand reaches towards her, then the fight goes out of him and he lets the hand fall back down. He grimaces.

'Do I think *what*?' she asks, more gently.

'That this will be the last time?'

'I don't know. We never do know, do we?'

'What'll you wear to my funeral?'

She doesn't have to think, 'A black woollen jacket with leather trim.'

'Fair enough,' he says. 'Now go away and let me die.'

BEN RESIPOLE

Reading of the Day
'Blessed is the man that walketh not in the counsel of the
ungodly, nor standeth in the way of sinners, nor sitteth in
the seat of the scornful.'
Psalms 1.1

Rhona leaves the car in the hospital car park and spends the night at The Standard Hotel, where the Fort William police, in exchange for unspecified favours, have the permanent use of a suite on the top floor. The rooms are used for interviewing grasses and for illicit interrogations best held safely away from the station. Thankfully, the walls and carpet can't talk, but Rhona feels the suite always exudes a certain miasma of unhappiness.

She locks the door, showers, puts on a towelling dressing gown, lies down on the bed and drinks back the little bottles of spirits and wine in the minibar.

There's a holly leaf pattern on the wallpaper and she wills herself not to see the little red berries as eyes. She moves on to the beers and stares at the wall until the leaves merge into a wash of green.

By midnight she has emptied the entire minibar. Finally, oblivion beckons.

In the early morning her mobile rings. She answers, grunts hello. It's Archie Henderson and he sounds even more patrician on the phone. 'I'm going up Ben Resipole today. It'll be a good chance for you to get a feel for the land.'

'Uuhhh. Okay.'

'Rise and shine! I'll meet you on the shore at Resipole. Let's say 11.30.'

And with that he's gone.

She sits up in bed, quickly lies back down again and sits up much more carefully, letting the room settle. He shouldn't have her mobile number. And he certainly shouldn't be calling her. First Arthur is on her tail and now *him*. This really isn't right. Any normal self-respecting suspect – anyone remotely implicated in an untoward death – avoids the police and should be cowering at home, nestling into a can of lager. However entitled Henderson feels, he shouldn't be searching out detectives. Not if he is sane and sensible. Not unless he has some mad, murderous plan.

She calls Cat.

'Do you know what time it is?' says Cat.

'Sorry.'

'What now?'

'Just a little… a little *monitum.*'

'I wish you wouldn't use Latin.'

'It's probably nothing. But I just wanted you to know where I'm going today. Archie Henderson has invited me to go for a walk.'

'That's a good idea, is it? You're off swimming with the sharks.'

'This is just an insurance policy. I'd be a fool not to let someone know.'

'Blessed is the man that walketh not in the counsel of the ungodly,' quotes Cat.

'Spare me, please.'

'That was today's reading. Seems made for you, doesn't

it? Open your readings, Roo. Do it every day. I've told you before. You don't have to read them. Just *open* them.'

'Have the elders been onto you again?'

'They were at Gleneagles and gave me a "quiet word".'

'Sorry, Cat, not now. Please!' Rhona rings off.

But she does open her Reading Of the Day App. She shuts her eyes for the length of time she thinks it would take her to read the text. Then she closes the file again. Of course Cat is right. *Be more careful.*

She takes a shower and gets dressed. There's a faint smell of decay, which might just be the room and everything that has happened in it. She sniffs her fingers. There's still a slight odour of bear; at least that should see his dogs off.

She steals the bags of nibbles from the minibar, takes the lift down, totters through an empty reception and pushes the swing door open.

Outside, the sky is white, clouds clamped overhead like a pan lid. The air is cold and smells prebreathed, with the odours of Fort William's Friday night carousal still lingering. In the gutters lie dented cans and splashes of vomit. And, of course, the scally children are out on the street already. In the towns they're always out early, rifling through bins, hoovering up dropped chips, fighting it out with the seagulls.

As Rhona makes her way down the High Street, she hands out the bags of nibbles, one bag to each little posse of children that she meets. Mostly they say thank you. She notes, as she always does, how strangely old and careworn their little faces look.

Soon she has a trail of children behind her whining, 'Please miss, please miss.' She ignores them and opens the gates to the police headquarters. There's a vile, butcher's shop smell coming from the back of the car park. She ignores that too.

She takes the one spare patrol car that still has some petrol in it and heads out of town on the public road to the ferry. She is stiff-necked and feels at several removes from herself. She is driving badly, scraping the pavement, swerving away from obstacles at the last moment.

Her mouth tastes of old blood, but of course the hip flask is still in her own car, back in the hospital car park – if it hasn't been blown up. She is not in the mood to climb mountains; she doesn't even have her mints, and her smart little ankle boots are all wrong for hill walking. But at least she has told Cat where she's going; she has left a trace behind her.

At Resipole she parks in a disused driveway by some abandoned modern houses with cedar cladding, and atriums and huge boarded-up windows facing onto Loch Sunart. She walks down to the shore. Henderson is standing by the water's edge, dressed in green, the trousers, cap and jacket all matching like her father's avocado bathroom suite.

He has his back to her and is throwing sticks into the loch for his dogs. He casts hard and far. And the dogs, in high fettle, crash through the shallows and swim out after the sticks, their heads spearheading V-shaped ripples. They bound back to him, drop their sticks, and wait, tongues hanging out.

'Good morning! How are you, Mr Henderson?'

'Inspector,' he turns and gives her a quick smile. She notes the scoops under his eyes. He adds, 'I always need to get the dogs out. I always walk them. It's too easy to get stuck behind your desk.'

The dogs cower behind Henderson and eye Rhona narrowly. She eyes them narrowly back. They were ugly when dry. Now they're worse: black and Brylcreemed with wet, and monstrously skeletal. She's glad to be shunned.

121

'The dogs don't seem too keen on you this time. What have you been up to?'

'I dunno,' she says. Why is he asking? That drone must have been his.

'That's where we're going,' he points to the pinnacle of grey rock rising in the distance behind them. He adds, 'Put out your hand.'

Puzzled, she does as he asks and he takes a large round stone off the beach and places it in her palm. The stone, which is the weight of a heavy dish, has a jagged white line of quartz running through the middle. She looks down at it; the stone is riven to the core.

'What's this for?' she asks.

Henderson takes a second larger grey stone for himself, and says, 'We're starting a cairn for Johnnie.'

She follows him back across the road, the rock weighty in her jacket pocket, the dogs bounding ahead of them. Henderson opens his Range Rover, which is parked in a lay-by, and brings out two water bottles and a rifle from the boot.

'Follow me!' He sets off in long galumphing strides down a track towards the mountain. The dogs, familiar with the route, bound ahead. At times Rhona has to jog to keep up with him.

They pass another boarded-up house, ivy rampaging up the harling, a Yucca plant mouldering by the front door.

'It's a shame. All these empty houses,' she says.

'Those people weren't real Highlanders. They had no Gaelic. They were all retired policemen and civil servants from the south with their fat little pensions. They all wanted their bit of beauty and wildness. But they had to have it with underfloor heating.'

'I wish I had underfloor heating,' she says.

But he doesn't smile, and doesn't slow his pace. 'These

people couldn't hunt, they couldn't fish. They were absolutely pointless, and all they ever did was whine about their bad knees and their coronaries and how long it takes to get to the hospital in Inverness. When we started up the reserve they were all terrified of the animals. They couldn't hack it at all.'

'Did you offer them compensation?'

'More than I should have,' he gives an angry puff.

They cross a small weed-filled area of hard standing and then the path leads up into a wooded gully. The ground rises before them, the columns of pine high overhead, nettles and woodruff growing thick on the forest floor. She can hear the rush of a stream.

Henderson lopes ahead; again, she is jogging to keep up with him.

'I began with beavers,' he says, as if resuming an interrupted conversation. 'Beavers are really your starter mammal – cheap, easy, no safety issues, no need for fencing. It's all win, win, win with beavers. They prevent erosion, and they increase biodiversity. '

'They're cute too,' adds Rhona. *Just keep him going.* 'A lot of the landowners round here have beavers, don't they?'

'Exactly. So it's not that innovative or adventurous. Then I went on to lynx. I got a pair of them. We won a Green Globe Best Practice Award for our lynx. But you don't get much back with them. They just vanished into the land – it was like pouring water into a pond. Matt says he's seen paw prints up at Kentra. But the hunters never get any benefit from them.'

'The hunters?' she asks.

Why all this information?

'Yes, the hunters.' He stops, takes out a water bottle

from his jacket and swoops back a gulp. He passes the other bottle to Rhona.

'So how often do they come?' She packs the bottle into her jacket pocket. She knows she should drink, but the thought of water makes her feel queasy.

'Will you let me finish? First I got the wild boar, and then the wolves. I had to put up the fencing. That's 85 miles of high tensile steel fencing. The Scottish Executive didn't allow me any exemptions. And I thought those Glasgow Stalinists might like a few wild animals around, other than themselves!' He gives an angry laugh at his own old joke.

He continues, 'So I've had to fence every inch of the whole goddamned coastline – even where it's just rock. It's pay up, pay up and pay again.'

'Didn't you count the fence into your set up costs?'

Why do the privileged always feel so hard done by?

'Of course I did. But I had hoped for a little bit of understanding from the authorities. The wolves have been a *nightmare!* And it's damned hard to get a good wolf. Wildlife traders are like secondhand car dealers. You never know *what* you're getting! I brought my first pack in from Spain. Horrendous! Inbred, bad teeth, a couple of them even had blue eyes! And they were *tiny!* Some bloody chihuahua had got into the gene pool. And then, of course, they came down with flu in the winter, ate bracken, got distemper, you name it… In the end we had to put the whole pack down and start again. Back to square one. I got in a new pack from the Ukraine. Proper wolves – bigger, and meaner. They're hardier too.'

'And the bears?'

'The bears were okay,' he says heavily. 'Until now.'

They walk on up for about a mile. The path is steep and rocky. Her boots don't grip well and she rarely lifts her eyes from the ground. But eventually they come out onto a

124

grassy slope. And up ahead, on the crest of a small hillock, Rhona can see a round plantation of Scotch pine. On the rim of the wood, perched in the branches and straddling several of the trees, is a construction made of logs with one long, horizontal window.

Henderson follows her gaze.

'We call it Richard's Exhibition wood,' he says. 'It was planted as a rookery in 1851 by my great-great-great-great grandfather. He loved the Corvidae family. He admired their intelligence and used to speak German to them. He was convinced they understood.'

'Who put the treehouse in?'

'I did. It's not a treehouse. It's a hide.'

As they approach the rookery she notices a large metal trough at the foot of the trees. The ground beneath is muddy and churned up.

'It's for the bears,' says Henderson. 'We give them supplementary feed: pellets of protein concentrate covered in molasses. They can't get enough of them and it keeps their coats glossy. If you don't give them anything they get scraggy.'

She remembers Wilber's unglossy, deg-covered backside.

'So, if Wilber had all this food, why did he have to kill anyone? All he needed to do was come here and eat his pellets.'

'You're absolutely right,' replies Henderson with a quick flash of a smile. 'And that's why it was so out of order. I hope you'll stress that in your report.'

'I'll see,' she says vaguely. Then she adds, 'When did Wilber last visit?'

'He never came here. He had his own feeding station. This one is for God and Woly.'

'You called one of your bears God?'

'It's short for Godwin. William Godwin. And Woly is Wollstonecraft.'

'And the cub's called Shelley?'

He sounds pleased. 'Exactly. It's good to meet a well-read policeman.'

'Policewoman. I'm a *woman.*'

He doesn't reply, but sweeps the hair back off his face.

She looks up at the hide. One of the pine trees has steps jutting out from the trunk and spiraling upwards. There's also a handrail. All of it – the hide, the steps, the rail – is covered in moss.

'Can I have a look?' she asks.

'Be my guest.'

Rhona starts up the soft, slimy steps. She holds onto the wobbly hand rail and with her other hand she grasps the trunk.

At the top she pushes open a plank door fat with damp. It gives way and she comes into a narrow, mushroomy room, all curling plywood and with two tree trunks growing up through the middle. Light slants in from a long, horizontal window and the room has an air of sudden abandonment. The wooden viewing stools are upturned and there are still plastic cups and old biros on the ground. Some scraps of paper have sogged down into the floorboards.

Henderson follows her in.

'We don't use the hide now,' he says.

'I can see that.'

'It was just a waste of money.' In a sudden movement, he pulls a child's drawing of a bird off the wall.

'Don't people ever come and watch the bears?'

'They used to. We had "wild animal experience" weekends. We got in zoology students from Edinburgh University. They gave talks up at the house and we brought families down here to the hide before feeding time. We put a lot into those weekends. It was fun too. We used to hang apples from strings and tie mirrors onto the tree trunks. And we got in food that was tricky for the bears to eat: pineapples and coconuts and such like. Have you ever seen a bear cub try and eat a rambutan? They think it's alive and pounce on it.'

'So that's rewilding, is it? Teasing bears with tropical fruits?' she quipped.

He shrugs, 'It didn't last anyway.'

'What happened?'

'After the shutdown nobody came. Of course, in the dog days, all those middling sorts of people – the schoolteachers and engineers and what not – they were far too desperate to come bear watching.'

'Did you think of selling up?'

'Of course I didn't!' he says scornfully. 'I'm a Henderson. We've had this land for ten generations. It's my inheritance. What would my forefathers have said if I'd let it slip through my hands?'

'But your forefathers are dead and gone now.'

He ignores her, 'I needed to maintain the reserve, so I had to do *something*. It was a very difficult time. When the shutdown was lifted, the Scottish Executive hiked up all the costs and rates went through the roof. I needed something that would bring in *proper* money. I had to offer something unique. It had to be tailored to high-net-worth individuals.'

'You mean the rich?'

He breaks a piece of fungus off the tree trunk. He turns the little mushroom over – it's the size of a four merk piece, the ribbed underbelly pale and delicate. He drops it on the ground.

'I mean the *very, very* rich,' he says. 'Owners of oilfields, CEOs of multinationals, the new kings of the world.'

'So what do these kings want? Is it just hunting? Or birdwatching? Falconry?'

'Birdwatching?' he scoffs.

'But you've got sea eagles here, haven't you? I thought Arabs liked falconry.'

He replies nonchalantly, 'I've given up falconry. And birdwatching's not a proper business. Have you ever met a rich birdwatcher? Of course you haven't! Rich people don't want to *watch*. They're not passive. They're *active*. They want to engage with life, to wrestle with it. They want to feel its pulse. They want to hunt!'

'So do they go for the bears?'

He shakes his head, 'I don't have enough bears for hunting, and the Romanians have bagged that market anyway. They do it horribly – they use beaters to flush the bears out and then their clients just shoot them down from a high seat as if they were clay pigeons. You know Khrushchev once killed fifty bears in one day? The bastard! Just a *slaughter*.'

She wonders what exactly the difference is between killing and slaughtering. For Henderson, it doesn't seem to be a question of morality, but rather of aesthetics, of 'fair play'.

'So what do your rich people kill then?' she asks.

And Henderson gives a minuscule pause. He looks straight at her. 'Wolves,' he says. 'My people hunt wolves.'

She smiles. He said *his* people.

'We run wolf hunts. It's a small, exclusive operation. Just a handful of men against the elements. And it's serious stuff. The hunters are quite a challenge to work for. Sometimes we get almost no notice, and they have very high standards. I can't have any mistakes.'

'Could I come on a hunt then?'

'Certainly not!' he gives a bark of laughter. 'I'm afraid

this is very much a men-only sport. You wouldn't keep up. And they want complete privacy. We have to close up the gates and clear out everybody before they arrive.'

'So who looks after them on the reserve?'

'I do.'

'Just you?'

'Just me,' he says.

'And how much do you charge them?'

'I'm afraid that that,' he looks at her archly, 'is commercially sensitive information.'

'How often do they come?'

'Quite frequently. Maybe once a month. I often don't get much warning. They pay me to be "on call". A bit like a doctor.'

'I see,' she says. 'Do you provide accommodation?'

'Of course.'

'And alternative amusements?'

'What do you mean?'

'Girls?'

His head jerks back, 'I'm not a pimp.' He flings open the hide door and retreats down the steps. She follows him down.

They continue on up the mountain, the land stepping ahead of them in a series of rises. As the sun creeps round behind the clouds, they walk higher and higher and Rhona lags behind. The last part of the climb is the hardest – a cold breeze has come from the west and they're scrambling now between granite boulders. Again, the dogs run ahead, and she is so tired now and her boots rub. She no longer notices the wildflowers or the birds swerving overhead.

Henderson clambers up the rocks, quick as a spider. Whenever Rhona falters, he reaches back and clamps his hand on her arm and pulls her up. She knows she'll have bruises there tomorrow – little blue fingerprints belonging to Henderson.

At the summit, they clear a small patch of grass, place their stones there and then sit down in a dip in the rock where they are out of the wind.

'Well, we've made a start,' he says. 'I'll bring a stone each time I come. We'll have a small cairn here in no time. It's the best memorial a man can have.'

He pauses, 'Matt says you've taken Wilber's body away.'

'They're on a par, are they?'

'What do you mean?' He looks puzzled.

'Johnnie and Wilber. You mentioned them almost in the same breath.'

'So I did,' he doesn't sound surprised at himself. 'Matt wanted Wilber to be buried on the estate. He had marked out a rowan tree. We'd have put him there – Wilber loved rowan berries.'

She notes that Henderson is not asking for the body back. Thanks to the drone, he must know the bear has been chopped into bits.

'How old was Wilber when he came to you?' she asks.

'We got him at nine months from a Canadian reserve. It nearly bankrupted me.' Suddenly his chin jerks upwards, his eyes swivel across the sky, 'That was one of my sea eagles.'

She looks too but sees only a speck in the distance.

'So how big was Wilber then?'

Henderson holds his hands out a metre apart.

'So the size of a large dog?'

'More or less. Why do you ask?'

She ignores the question. 'Was he ever aggressive to humans?'

'He never even *saw* humans. Bears are reclusive.'

130

'So why are you carrying a gun now?'

'To protect you, young lady. To keep you safe from my reclusive bears and my nocturnal wolves. It's to put you at your ease. I'm carrying it out of *politeness*.'

'And I suppose if I got mauled, you really would lose your licence.'

'It wouldn't happen.'

'But Mr Henderson, it *did* happen, didn't it?'

He doesn't reply.

'And I am wondering if something else happened down in the dell before this young man died. Something that maybe wasn't to do with the bear.'

'What on earth are you getting at?'

'There are a few anomalies.' She isn't going to mention the pearls or the fingernails. Not now.

'Anomalies?'

'Yes. Some things don't quite add up.'

'What doesn't add up?'

'At the moment we're just trying to find out exactly what happened.' She always surprises herself at how good she is at the neutral reply.

'When you say "anomaly", that makes me think my initial theory, that the boy died and then the bear came upon him, must be true.'

He picks up a stone, flicks it down the hillside. But the dogs don't rouse.

Now he turns to her, 'Do you think I should send them all home? Not Will, of course, but the others.'

'Not till we've closed the case.'

'You know, I'm not sure about that Arthur.'

'In what way?' He must know they are lovers.

There's silence. She fixes her eyes on the rock she's sitting on. The colours are muted: tweedy shades of green and grey and brown.

Then, in a different, lighter tone Henderson says, 'Look! He's back.' He points to a huge, white-headed bird of prey, flying fast and loose-winged below them.

The sea eagle ploughs and slides through the air. It stills for a second and, with a couple of leisurely wingbeats, soars up and over their heads. The white wing tips merge into the cloudy sky. She can see the yellow feet tucked in under the belly.

'Magnificent, don't you think? He can take out animals three times his weight.'

'*And* he's colour coordinated.'

Henderson looks at her oddly.

'Yellow beak and yellow feet,' she explains. 'You know, matching – like an Italian fashionista and their motorino.'

He doesn't smile. 'I only freed him six months ago but look how well he's doing.'

'So, he was part of your falconry enterprise?'

'He was indeed. But when I stopped I let them all go.'

'And he has a name too?'

'Yes.'

'Kierkegaard?'

'No. Pete.'

Pete heads off into the clouds. 'It gives you an odd sense of longing, doesn't it?' Henderson has his hand up over his eyes like a visor. 'The way they *command* the air.'

'Do you feel that way about all birds?'

'Goodness, no! Birds of prey are fine flyers, but I can't be doing with all the little brown things. You know, the pipits and sparrows. I like corncrakes, though, they always make me think of my son.'

'Yes?' She glances at him in surprise.

'When William was born, he was tiny and he made this little creaking sound, just like a corncrake in the very far distance. I told Marissa we'd given birth to a bird.' He gives a short laugh, and then says, 'So, was it worth it, coming up here? At least you'll be able to tell Johnnie's parents that there's a cairn.'

'I'm very grateful to you – the walk has cleared my head. But there is something I still just don't get.'

'Oh dear! Not more questions!' he teases. 'Should I be nervous?'

She looks at him; he isn't at all nervous.

'It's just this,' she says. 'It's the wolves that make you your money, isn't it?'

'Yes, I do rely on the wolf hunts.'

'Then why on earth have grizzly bears? You're running a huge risk. If one hunter gets killed, that's your business done for.'

'You could be right. But the very rich are always looking for excitement, for wildness. And hunters always need an element of fear. In a good hunt you are yourself in danger. It adds to the experience.'

He turns his head towards her and his expression has softened. 'I wasn't this jaundiced when I started out, you know. I love wild animals, and that's really what this is all about. But I'm afraid the money is all in the killing.'

He gives her a bitter smile.

By early afternoon they have come down off the mountain and Rhona is heading home. When she is through the entrance checkpoint and the green metal fence is well behind her, she pulls the car over into a lay-by.

She texts Cat: 'I'm out!'

Then her mobile rings. It's an unknown number.

'Is that you?' slurs her father.

'I didn't know you had a phone.'

'I need some smoked trout,' he says.

'Need?'

133

'It's not too much to ask, is it? Your dying father asks you to bring him a wee bit of fish. You're living in his house, emptying his cellar, marking his laminate with your high heels…'

'You don't sound very dying to me.'

'Sorry to disappoint.'

'And I don't wear stilettoes anymore. I haven't worn them since I was in my twenties.'

'The old marks are still there.'

'I'll ask Cat what they've got in at the moment. She and Glenn have been diversifying.'

'Glenn owes me,' he says darkly. 'Bring 100 grams in tonight and keep the rest back in the fridge for me.'

'Do you want anything with it?' she says sourly. 'A slither of unwaxed lemon? A few fronds of dill?'

'Aye,' he says. 'And some more Irn Bru.'

THE CHURCH

Reading of the Day
'For the morning is to them even as the shadow of death:
if one know them, they are in the terrors of the shadow of
death.'
Job 24.17

It's another catatonic Sunday morning. The legal shops in Fort William are closed, the drinking booth grills are down, the Corran ferry rusts quietly at rest. Most drinkers and snivers are asleep or still stupefied from last night. Registered inhabitants, moving at prehistoric pace, prepare for church.

Rhona and Cat are in Cat's van, heading out of Fort William on the private road round the side of Loch Eil. Cat is in a cream dress, Rhona in a brown, two piece suit. It has been a long week and both women look pale and tired. In contrast, their Sunday hats, velvet and netting confections made by Cat, sit up bright and spry in the middle seat.

'Did your dad like the trout?' asks Cat.

'He loved it. That's how I'll be spending all my Saturday nights from now on. I'll be there, puffing up his pillows and being told off for failing to bring the pepper grinder. When I came onto the ward last night, there he was, propped up in the bed with his papers spread out all around him. And the first thing he said to me was, "You've aged."'

'So, back on form with a vengeance,' Cat smiles. 'And your car? Is it still there?'

'How did you know about my car?' Rhona is disconcerted.

'Everybody knows everything here. You should know that by now.'

At the head of the loch the road straightens out and a black stretch limousine glides effortlessly past them. A second limousine follows, and then a third one. The cars shrink away into the distance.

'That'll be a family heading to the Hogwarts theme park at Glenfinnan,' says Cat. 'It'll be Dad in one car. Mum in the next, kids and nanny in the third.'

'Yeah?'

'Extremely rich people never talk to each other. They are married to strangers. A few years ago I made some little books. *Who are you really married to? Twenty questions you need to ask.* It was jokey, but with a few home truths. Covers were gold brocade with heather gems on the front. Absolutely hideous. The punters loved them.'

'You are *so* cynical!'

'Cynics aren't born. They're made.'

Cat takes the turnoff to the Ardnamurchan peninsula. They pass through the automatic turnstile and come out on the public road.

A few miles further on they pass a van parked up in a lay-by. It's two vans really: the front is a very rusty Volkswagon beetle, welded to the back of a dented Blue Berlingo. The bumper is made from sawn-off strips of radiators and the solar panels on the roof are tied on with bungee cord. There's a strip of cardboard over the windscreen, signifying that the owner is closed for business.

'That's Peepers' van, isn't it?' says Cat.

'Yep.' Peepers is one of Rhona's informers. 'I wonder what he's doing up here.'

'He's probably just run out of power and has to wait till

the sun shines on his roof. These little solar cut-and-shuts are just like lizards – they need sunshine and warmth to get them going. And the West Highlands isn't quite the climate for lizards.'

'But he's usually down in Glencoe,' says Rhona. The prospect of Peepers, his many evasions and grubby bargains, makes her feel even more tired. She casts the thought of him aside.

After a few minutes Cat asks, 'Did you call the minister?'

'No. I didn't want to warn them. I just want to see what they're up to.'

'And what's my job going to be exactly?'

'You're my second pair of eyes. Having you with me might discourage them from murdering me and wrapping my entrails round a gorse bush and blaming it on some random, long-toothed otters.'

'Now you tell me!' Cat laughs.

Rhona looks out the side window. Years ago, in that exceptionally cold winter, this whole glen had frozen over. The ice on the end of the loch had been hard as glass and the long grass and gorse on the banks were laced with frosted cobwebs like tiny ghosts. She came skating here with Maggie and Cat and Cat's little sister, Susie, who they had bundled up in extra scarves and jumpers, and tied a cushion to her bottom, turning her into half child, half miniature armchair. They had skated back and forth across the loch with Maggie holding Susie's hand and wiping her nose and blowing hot potatoes onto her neck. Susie loved Maggie. Everybody loved Maggie.

'Do you remember?' says Rhona.

'The ice? Oh yeah! You know, I used to envy you and Maggie. All that closeness. But now I'm a bit relieved I wasn't a twin.'

'You never know. You could have been.'

'What do you mean?'

'Scientists think ten per cent of pregnancies start out as twins. Then, early on, one of the twins is miscarried, or just dies.' Rhona pauses. She can't *not* tell her. She lowers her voice, 'They never talk about the other alternative.'

'What's that?' Cat is wary now.

'That the other foetus might have murdered its twin.'

'Bloody hell! That's a terrible thing to say! Roo, how can you *think* like that?'

'It stands to reason – murders are usually committed by the victim's nearest and dearest. And twins are the ultimate enforced partnership, aren't they?'

'Sometimes I think…' Cat's voice trails away. She gives a resigned sigh.

'You think *what?* '

'Nothing. Just stop poisoning my mind.'

'Sorry, Cat.'

'So you should be.'

An uneasy silence settles on the car.

Rhona's thoughts drift. She rests her eyes on the loch, which is completely still, the water reflecting the mountains and sky with extraordinary precision. A thin white crease of shoreline marks the fold between this world and its double.

She takes a deep inbreath, 'I do sometimes wonder where I'll end up. Where we'll all end up.'

'I thought you were still a believer,' says Cat.

'I wouldn't put it that strongly. We're not close friends. He doesn't call, he doesn't answer prayers. Always seems to be staying in to wash his hair or something.'

'You'd better not make cracks like that in the office.'

Rhona splays her hand against the glass and looks out through the gaps between her fingers.

Eventually she says, 'You know the Romantic Poets talk

about us becoming one with the rocks and stones and trees. But that's not going to happen to me. My little particles will probably end up in a fence post, or a bollard. I quite fancy being a bollard in the next life.'

'Dogs piss on bollards.'

'And you'll be tiny particles of glue, or a rawlplug, or deep inside a pair of pliers.'

'It would be nice to be something useful.'

'And Maggie...' Rhona muses.

'Roo, don't go there!'

'Maggie is definitely a Tunnock's tea cake.'

Cat is silent.

'That was a joke,' says Rhona irritably.

'Is there anything you won't joke about?'

'All I've got left is jokes.'

'She'd never have said something like that about you.'

'Well, Maggie wasn't very witty, was she?'

'No, but she was *kind*.'

'Yeah, yeah.' Rhona reaches for the glove compartment where she put the hip flask. But Cat leans over and stays her hand.

'You never made life easy for her,' says Cat.

'She didn't make life easy for me. And I didn't have many choices. She was always the saint. Every time I got on the bus there would be some old lady pawing at my sleeve.' Rhona puts on a quavery, old lady voice, 'You've made all the difference, Miss Ballantyne.'

'You should be proud of what she did. She brought people a lot of happiness.'

'She brought them *cake*,' says Rhona bitterly.

After some time Cat says, 'Is that you finished now?'

'Mhmmn.' Rhona watches the pine trees shuffling past.

'You're so grumpy these days. So hormonal. You need

some joy in your life.' Cat turns and gives her a quick grin. 'Why don't you have a baby?'

'Why don't *you*?' retorts Rhona.

'I'm serious. I'd help you with it.'

'It's *you* that's gagging for a baby, not me. And if you did have one you'd have it tied to some workbench and gluing together picture frames before it could walk.'

'Well, I'm sure he or she would be neat-fingered. I couldn't bear a clumsy child.'

'Anyway, there aren't any men in my life.'

'You know there's a new start-up that's selling Highland semen,' says Cat.

'You're joking.'

'I'm not. It comes in something that looks like an ice cream maker. There's a screw top. When you undo it, it plays *Flower of Scotland*.' Cat's eyes slide sideways to Rhona, 'I could get you mate's rates.'

'It's not going to happen.'

Eventually they pass the road sign for Strontian and ahead of them lies the fence, and the entrance gate with the transparent, egg-shaped booth. Inside sits the guard, a fly in amber. A fly wearing a Sunday tie.

Rhona holds up her police ID and he opens the gates. As they drive away, she checks in the side mirror. The guard is on his mobile.

'They've been warned now,' she says.

The church, which is in the middle of Henderson's estate, is small, sturdy. It's set back from the road and surrounded by tall trees and an electric fence.

They drive over the cattle grid and press the metal buzzer. Eventually the gates open and they park beside Matt's Land Rover.

'It feels all wrong,' Cat stares grimly at the fence, 'It's like we're the ones behind bars, not the animals.'

They slip into the cool of the church. The service has already begun and they sit down at the very back.

The minister, young and shiny-faced, is reading from St Paul's Epistle to the Romans: 'He that is dead is freed from sin.' He looks up at them with round startled eyes, before returning to his bible.

Most of the congregation follow suit. Over the next few minutes, heads turn back to look at them. Rhona nods to Arthur, to Rachel and Zoë, to Mrs Collins, to Matt and his plain, plump wife, and to young Gordon. Only Henderson and Will, sitting at the very front of the church in the family box pew, do not turn.

Cat examines the prayer book, Rhona sucks at mints, wriggles in her pew and stares up at the vaulted ceiling, and at the carved roses on the joists. Each rose is different, with a slightly different configuration of petals. She knows this is thuddingly symbolic: we are all different, each of us with our own unique cocktail of failings.

She gazes out over the sloping shoulders of the congregation. The altar cloth has been sewn by hand: a dove dive-bombing into some badly appliqued flames. Each flame is labelled in wobbly cross stitch: patience, self-control, goodness, love, faithfulness, joy.

Why 'joy'? Joy has nothing to do with God.

Everyone gets to their feet to sing a hymn. They sit down again. They stand again, and sit yet again. More readings – The Book of Daniel, The Song of Songs.

The service continues for another three quarters of an hour. She wonders what on earth she is doing here. Why did she come all this way? What can she possibly learn from the back of everyone's heads? But, despite herself, she is moved by the old words. She absolutely hates church, hates the formality, the hats, the tedium, the reality-defying assertions, the way the past tugs at you.

Finally, it's all over and the minister walks down the aisle carrying his wooden cross. Rhona and Cat join the queue for the register. In front of them is Mrs Collins, a vision in lilac serge. She smiles dazzlingly at Rhona.

'How are you today, Miss Ballantyne? All the standing wasn't too much for you?'

'No, but thank you for your concern.' A sudden thought comes to Rhona, 'Where are your boys?'

Mrs Collins looks alarmed.

'Tom and er... Eddie?' prompts Rhona.

'Oh, the boys! No, no. The boys have gone home.'

'They have a home? I thought they were Henderson's wards.'

'They don't come often. Now, if you'll excuse me.'

Mrs Collins swivels round and hurriedly addresses another woman in the queue. Rhona looks at Cat, who grins back at her.

The ledger is large and leather-bound. Rhona scans the signatures. All are names she's seen on Matt's list. She turns back a page to last Sunday's congregation and runs her eye down the signatures. There's a new entry in a neat, backward slanting hand: James Andrew McCreal. She flicks back through the ledger: the signature appears repeatedly.

'Your little friend, the taxidermist,' she murmurs to Cat. 'He's a regular here.'

'How can that be? He lives in Oban.'

Rhona scrutinises the signature; now she knows why she came.

'It's an unusual hand,' she says. 'Backward tilters are normally introverts. Often hoarders too. Lots of internal suffering and intense possessive urges.'

'I didn't know you were a graphologist,' says Cat. 'Anyway, everyone is a hoarder now. You have to be.'

'McCreal is shy, isn't he?'

'He's more secretive, really. A bit odd, and a bit of a drinker. But basically sound.'

'Tormented?' asks Rhona.

'Of course, he's tormented! We're *all* tormented these days. It's not just you, Roo.'

'But why's he here on the reserve?'

'Exactly. He's always been a bit cagey about where he gets his animals.'

'He'll have a base here, won't he?'

Cat nods, 'Are you going to pick up that pen or not?'

They sit in the van watching the congregation disperse.

'Where's the tea and biscuits?' says Rhona. 'It's just each to their own car. Nobody's stopping for a chat. Everyone is busy, busy and yet it's a Sunday. What's all this about?'

'The minister looks like he's swallowed a frog.'

The minister, same startled eyes, is standing by the porch, smiling fit to burst.

'You heard him, didn't you?' continues Cat. 'He was asking God to deliver us from our enemies and "abate their pride, assuage their malice, and confound their devices". That's the old prayer for times of tumult and war.'

'So, he knows something's up,' says Rhona. 'They must all know.'

She watches Henderson. He's speaking to his son who looks so small at his side. Henderson's hand reaches out and holds Will by one shoulder for a moment. But Will's head remains bowed.

Archie Henderson must have sensed her gaze, for he looks over at Rhona, gives her an amused smile, and goes to his Range Rover.

Cat starts the engine and pulls the car out. 'That woman, the one with too much powder.'

'In purple? That's Mrs Collins.'

'What was all that about *boys*? She was lying, wasn't she?'

'Of course she was.'

'Are you going to arrest her?'

'How can I? I can't touch any of them. I haven't got enough to go on.'

They drive out of the churchyard gate.

'Go left,' says Rhona. 'We'll take the back road up by Kinlochmoidart,'

They cross the stone bridge and the road weaves along the bank of the loch. They pass more boarded-up houses along the shore and Rhona glimpses a tiny church hidden in the trees. Whatever Henderson claims, this land once belonged to others too.

As they head up through the woods, Rhona presses the window release, puts her head outside and breathes in. But the air is still heavy and unrefreshing.

'Put your window up,' says Cat.

'Why?'

'This is a game reserve full of wild animals.'

'They're not that wild, you know. The bears are fed on pellets. And I don't know why you've locked the doors. They can't use door handles – they don't have opposable thumbs.'

'A man was mauled to death here last week. Have you forgotten that?'

'I know, I know.'

'Think of it. What a terrible way to die. At least…' Cat glances at her friend. 'At least Maggie had a clean death.'

'A clean death,' says Rhona. 'Are you kidding me?'

'Well, it was quick. She wasn't ripped open. She wasn't *eaten.*'

'Being shot by a .45 in the chest at point blank range isn't a clean death.'

Rhona taps her fingers against the dashboard. 'It completely ripped her apart. There was only a tiny entrance hole, I grant you that. But the bullet smashed her breast bone and the right ventricle, and left a massive hole in her back. When Dimitri opened her up there were still pints of blood in the chest cavity, and he said he could have set up a black pudding factory. It soaked right through that tweed coat and it was all over the ground, too. So don't talk to me about a clean death!'

Another silence follows Rhona's outburst.

Eventually, Cat says, 'I know this may sound callous, but it was such a nice coat. I've never seen that Lovat twist again anywhere.'

'It was my best coat – far too tight for her.'

'You just said "at point blank range". So that means close, doesn't it?'

'Yep, close,' says Rhona.

'How close?'

'Probably two or three metres.'

'Hmm.'

'Don't "hmm" me. What do you mean?'

'Nothing.'

'You did mean something. I'm sick of the way you're always implying things.'

Cat stops the car, 'You are *so* snarky today!' she blurts. 'I've come all the way out here for you.'

'You wanted to come. You're nosy.'

'I was doing you a favour. I'm being a good *friend.*'

'You wanted to come. Life with the little moss men gets a bit boring, doesn't it?'

'For God's sake! I did you a favour! And the minute I say something, you bite my head off.'

Rhona sits hunched and smouldering.

Cat starts the van again. But the engine doesn't lock into gear. She turns the engine off, turns it on again. It still howls.

'And thanks for not getting my new gear box,' says Cat.

'That's it!' yells Rhona. 'You can drive back on your own.' She pulls up the lock and swings open the door.

'Roo!' Cat grabs her arm, but Rhona shakes free and jumps down onto the road.

She hits the ground with a thump that travels up from the soles of her feet and jolts her head back. She has never been more alive, more furious. Her voice blasts out, 'I'll walk back!'

'Get in,' says Cat tightly. She is looking into the woods beyond Rhona

'No, I'll walk!'

'There's something behind you,' says Cat.

Rhona turns. Low down, a few metres into the wood, something solid is moving. There's no outline and the shadow merges into the trees and the undergrowth. Now the movement has stopped, and the wood is utterly still and silent.

Rhona steps forward, grabs Cat's outstretched arm and lets herself be pulled back up into the van. Cat closes the door and Rhona buries her face in her hands. Cat puts her arm around her friend's shoulder.

In a shocked voice, Cat whispers, 'Look!'

Rhona lifts her head. Only a few feet in front of the van five wolves are crossing the road, heading for the trees on the far side. They're in their summer coats, looking lean and racy, their fur the pale yellow of dried grass, with a black undercoat showing through. The wolves trot quickly and silently on long white legs. Each wolf has its head down, tongue out, mouth red and open in a half smile. That's what makes them so frightening: the half smile.

The wolves move purposefully and don't even cast a glance at the van. But when they've crossed the road the last two wolves stop in the shade of the trees and look back at Cat and Rhona. Their faces are triangular, framed in white fur, the eyes very dark.

And then, in a moment, they're gone. Rhona gives a shudder.

Wolves stare just like men.

MAGGIE

Rhona arrives home to find a private ambulance parked by the front steps. The back is open and the ramp down. The driver is still sitting in the car and nods to the house.

Shit shitty shit, she thinks. He's back.

Roderick Ballantyne has got himself, in his wheelchair, up to the kitchen table. His place has been set: knife, fork, spoon, a bottle of brown vinegar, a side plate. He is dressed in a checked shirt and elasticated fawn slacks. A napkin is tucked into his shirt and he is taking kitchen scissors to a brown packet of Glenn's fish, resting on a plate.

'Where have you been?' He glides the scissor blades through the paper. She can see the pinky brown flesh of the smoked trout.

'Church.'

'Aye, of course. Which church?'

'Down in Acharacle.'

'You're still on that, are you?'

'I am.' She watches him balance a fillet on his knife, transfer it onto his plate, sprinkle it with the vinegar that will ruin it.

'Pity you didn't have any lemon,' he says.

She notes that he doesn't offer her any. This is his feast, his home. He slips a section of the fillet into his mouth, lowers his eyelids as he eats.

'How's the trout?' she asks.

'Good. The flesh is tender. But it's not as good as old Martindale's.'

Her father swallows. His neck is so scrawny now that she can see every movement of his throat.

'You know how he went? Did Catriona tell you?'

'Who?'

'Johnnie Martindale. He came down in the first wave. Keeled over in his smokehouse and wasn't found for hours. By then he was orange as a kipper and they could never get the smell out of him. Catriona had to pack the coffin with lavender.'

Rhona is glad she wasn't there, glad too that she isn't eating now.

'He was lucky to get a coffin. They ran out later on, you know.' Her father gives her a sideways look and forks in a second mouthful.

'I'm surprised you can still eat stuff from the smokery.'

'I've always had an *excellent* digestion.' He gives a thin snake of a smile. 'You've always been so pernickety!'

When he's finished the fish he pushes the empty packet away.

'You've been in the gun room,' he says.

'I have. I was looking for a bone saw. I needed it for that bear.' How did he know?

'Second bottom drawer,' he says.

'Exactly.'

'Which you left fractionally open.'

'You've got some very odd clothes in there,' she says.

'You been prying?'

'There are these two leather jerkins, clearly for children. They're covered in straps and little metal loops.'

Ballantyne looks up at the clothes pulley over the cooker.

'What are they?' she asks.

'Falconry jackets. I suppose there's no harm in you knowing that.'

'They're *child-sized.*'

'It was a long time ago. Is there a sweet? Have you got any tinned peaches from the export shop? I need building up.'

'No.' There are still some tins of peaches in the back cupboard of the larder, but she wants to keep him on track. 'What are the jerkins for?'

'I used to train birds of prey with Archie Henderson.'

'So he was a friend, then? The way you talked about him before, it didn't sound as if you knew him that well.'

'He was a *hunting friend.* So part of my circle, yes. And a good falconer. He was trying to train his sea eagles to hunt big mammals. So he had these little jackets made for his children: Will and his daughter. What's she called?'

'Lucy.'

'Lucy.' He pauses and takes a drink of water. His slurring is getting worse. She doesn't know if this is emotion or tiredness.

'I still don't understand,' she says.

'Will and Lucy were strapped into jackets and then he tied fox pelts on top of the leather and then had pieces of fox meat on top of that – that's why there are all those metal loops. The kids were sent up into the hills and the eagles would fly over and knock them down and grab the meat.'

'What a horrible idea!'

'It's a German thing. A chap called Remmler invented them in the 1940s. The Nazis were excellent falconers. They loved hunting.'

'So how old was Will at the time?'

'I can't remember. Work it out from the size of the jacket. Nine? Or ten? He was always small.'

'One of the jerkins is stained.'

'That would be right,' he says cryptically.

'The bigger jacket,' she adds.

He nods.

'Do I need thumbscrews? Why is it bloodstained? What happened?'

'One of the eagles footed the girl on the back of the neck, just above where the jerkin stopped. She got a scalp wound too and you know how they bleed. It was nothing serious, but she took fright.'

'And Will?'

'He just stared. All that boy ever does is stare.'

'And it didn't occur to you that this was cruel? That it's not normal to make your children bleed.'

'Of course I thought it was cruel. I'm not quite the heartless bastard you take me for. We stopped after that.' His head jerks up, he gazes round the room. 'What do you have for dessert?' He casts her a doe-eyed look. 'Your sister used to make a lovely crème caramel.'

He can't stop himself, she thinks. He always has to pluck at heartstrings.

'I don't cook. You know that. And why did you end up with the jerkins?'

'Can't remember. I just never got round to giving them back.'

'Really? Why?'

'They're handstitched. Nicely made. I like to keep things. I still have that bonnie wee box where your mother kept her hairpins.' He breathes in noisily through his nose. His eyes are wet. He adds, 'In fact, Henderson sent me a note asking for them back about a year ago. I think I told him I'd thrown them out.'

'Why on earth would he want them now?'

Ballantyne marries his knife and fork on the plate. 'I

can't say. But it might have a bearing on what you're looking into now.'

Once her father has left, Rhona staves off Sunday night misery with her usual sandwich of a glass of whisky, followed by a hot bath, followed by more whisky. She ends up taking the bottle upstairs with her. She lies on her bed, trying to read a magazine, but her mind is too skittish and jittery. Just after ten o'clock, she calls Cat and tells her about her father's visit, and about the leather jerkins.

Then she says, 'This morning in the car you went "hmm" at one point.'

'Did I?' says Cat.

'You know you did. We were talking about *him*. You know, about Verviani.'

'Is it really true that they've put a parquet floor in his cell?'

'Don't change the subject. You said "hmm". What were you thinking?'

'Me? I never *think*. I've just got clever fingers.'

'Come on! Tell me.'

Rhona waits.

'Will this get you off the phone?' says Cat.

'Might do.'

Rhona waits again.

'You said point blank range, didn't you?'

'I did.'

'So two to three metres.'

'Yes.'

'Then Verviani saw her properly and it wasn't an accident. He killed Maggie *on purpose*. He must have known it wasn't you. He knew this was better revenge than merely killing you.'

'Because once you're dead, you're dead. Whereas...'

152

'Exactly,' says Cat. 'He couldn't have been crueller. I don't know why we didn't think of it earlier.'

'So I got the short straw after all,' says Rhona.

'Ooh, Roo!'

Rhona takes a breath, 'It's a brilliant move – you have to hand it to him. His people wouldn't have been happy if they thought he'd done it on purpose – the Italians think it's poor form to take revenge on female relatives. They're always nice to mums and grannies.'

Cat pauses, 'But it's interesting how everybody was pretending, isn't it?'

'I don't follow you.' Rhona turns onto her back, wraps the coverlet around her. She wants to be swaddled up.

'Verviani was pretending to make a mistake. And Maggie, of course, was pretending to be you.'

Rhona pulls the blanket tighter. 'What do you mean?' she croaks.

'Oh God, Roo. Didn't you know? You of all people? I'm so sorry.'

'It was an accident,' says Rhona. 'Maggie just happened to borrow my coat that day. It was all a terrible mistake.'

'No! It *wasn't* a mistake,' says Cat.

Rhona tastes bile in her mouth and swallows. She resists the urge to put the phone down – there's no going back now.

Cat continues, speaking very quietly, 'Maggie did it on purpose. She dressed up as you. She'd read the death threats in your handbag. Think of what Maggie was like. Think of what happened. Of course she gave up her life for you.'

'It all sounds a bit contrived,' says Rhona. But this rings resoundingly true: so obvious, and so in character. And Maggie never normally borrowed her coat, never wore her hair loose outside. That fateful morning, before Rhona left for work, her sister had embraced her, kissed her on the cheek and had teared up when Rhona had, of course, bristled.

'Why on earth didn't you tell me?'

'Tell you *what* exactly?' Cat sounds riled. 'You wanted me to rub it in?'

'But how was I to know? Why didn't anyone say anything?'

'What could we say? It was excruciatingly, blindingly obvious. And then you just weren't here. You were hell bent on revenge and hotfooted it off to Italy.'

'Someone had to.'

'But not you, Roo. Not you.'

There's a pause. Rhona starts to cry.

'Maggie always knew more than you thought,' says Cat. 'You always underestimated her.'

Rhona doesn't bother to wipe her cheeks and just lets the tears spill down, into her hair and onto the pillow.

'That night I found a spray of crushed freesia under my pillow.'

'And you didn't think, even then?'

'Of course, I didn't. She was always doing things like that, sneaking into my flat in Glasgow and doing the ironing. Dropping little foil-wrapped brownies into my coat pockets.'

'Ah! She was so kind. She always said that she loved you more than you loved her, but that that was okay with her.'

'God, Cat! Do you want to break me? Have you any other mind-fuck, world-shattering truths that you'd like to just casually blurt out?'

'I thought you knew.'

Rhona can't answer.

'I'm coming over,' says Cat quickly.

'Don't. Leave me be. I need time alone. I'll be fine.'

Rhona rings off. She lets the mobile drop onto the bed beside her. She has cried her tears out now, but her hair and the pillow feel sodden. She stares at the flecks on the ceiling and everything falls away. She breathes in – always remember to breathe – and feels a soaring in her breast, a quite unexpected rush of love. For a moment, all her rage against her sister vanishes. Maggie had loved her more than she loved herself. She gave up her life for her.

She swallows the last drops of the bottle, shuts her eyes and sees her sister tidied up in her coffin, face made up, hair brushed, head resting on a little white satin pillow. Then, as always, she sees her again, lying on the road, Verviani's bloody thumb print on her forehead. Not tidy at all.

Rhona opens her eyes quickly. It'll be hours before she falls asleep.

THE MAPS

Reading of the Day
'Woe unto them that rise up early in the morning, that they may follow strong drink, that continue until night, till wine enflame them!'
Isaiah 5.11

In the morning the weather has turned cold and the air is muggy, waiting for rain. Rhona drives into the police car park where a pair of crows are grazing on the tarmac in the corner. Rhona toots the horn and a crow flies up and away with a red streamer of gore trailing in its beak.

She can smell that bear again.

In the office she hands Boyd her keys and tells him about her car. He goes off to the hospital with his own leather roll of tweezers and pliers and a tool that looks like a giant dentist's mirror for inspecting the underside of cars. She notes the spring in his step – he likes fiddling with engines.

She finds Cummings in the canteen and asks about the blue van.

'It's a charcuterie business based in Oban. I've got the name somewhere.'

'*Charcuterie?* That's a bit strange.'

'Why's it strange?'

She gives him a long look. Where is his brain? Did he leave it in one of his Tupperware boxes?

'Have you been to Oban recently? Housewives there get branded for stealing potatoes. If they don't have

156

enough money for potatoes, are they really going to want charcuterie?'

'It might just be a tax address.'

'Any names?'

'I'll get to that soon. I've had a lot of bludgeonings. We've brought in that woman from Corpach with the meat tenderiser.'

'And what about the "charcuterie"? Who exports to them?'

'Exports?' With every question Cummings' neck sinks further into his collar.

'Come on, Pinkie! Charcuterie comes from pigs, doesn't it? Apart from Henderson's wild boar, there aren't any pigs in Scotland. There haven't been pigs here for five years. They were all put down, if you recall. So, I am asking where the meat comes from.'

'Europe, I suppose…'

'*Suppose*?'

'That'll be my next line of enquiry.'

'Tell you what,' she says wearily. 'Just give me the address.'

At her desk she opens Google Maps. As the computer slowly cranks itself up she calls Ray, the missing student, on his mobile. When there's no answer, she tries his parents' landline. Still no answer – not even a recorded message.

Google Maps eventually appears and she puts in the charcuterie company address and opens the map of Oban. Areas of the town, including whole blocks of the seafront and the streets behind, which once housed the bed and breakfasts, have been entirely blacked out. What did the Scottish Executive give Google in exchange for having its more shameful zones censored?

She goes to the viewfinder and walks her cursor along

the gap-toothed esplanade. There are still some entirely respectable shopfronts. These include number 15, which is an ornate facade, painted burgundy and silver and with fancy lettering over the window. Rhona zooms in: *James McCreal, Purveyor of Charcuterie and Game, Est. 1998.'*

So, it was him. She stops, holds the edge of the desk to steady herself and takes a long inbreath. Maybe it was McCreal who operated that drone too. She wants to call Cat immediately but she knows that Colin Laidlaw, a pockmarked, darkly smiling presence at the far end of the office, will be listening.

Where is McCreal's place in Ardnamurchan?

She finds the Henderson's estate which is on Google Maps in its entirety of mountain, rock and forest. She moves the cursor quickly, striding, like Finn McCool, from one great boulder-shaped peak to the next. She comes down into the village of Acharacle, and finds the church and the graveyard. She moves along to Will's tower.

On the shore nearby lie a few ruined crofts and byres, presumably from before Henderson's rewilding project. The flat land still shows the faint lines of the old run-rig field system.

Rhona loves aerial photography – for it shows what's there now, and delineates what used to be there too. She also loves maps, especially ancient maps, for they recount what *might* be there: the mermaids, the sea monsters, the four fat-cheeked putti of the winds.

Sometimes, she has fantasies of making her own ancient crime map of Scotland. She'd draw in the pickpockets at the Highland Show, the sex workers on the waterfront at Aberdeen, the dodgy customs men in their kilts at Govan. For Glasgow and the West Highlands she'd have a light grey mist for Verviani's racketeering. Over Lanark – how she hated her time covering domestics in Lanark – she'd write 'wife beaters.' Over Milngavie and the Edinburgh New Town: 'embezzlers'.

And what of the Ardnamurchan and Sunart peninsula? What would she write? 'Here be...' Here be *what* exactly?

She sees that, behind the trees near Acharacle, there's a hangar with a square blue patch by the side. She zooms in. The middle of the tarmac is painted with a white dot: a helipad.

She takes the cursor inland from Will's tower, following the course of the river. She finds the little dell where Johnnie's body was found. She zooms out a fraction and notices a U-shaped building with a slate roof nearby. This must be the 'outbuildings' that Boyd mentioned so dismissively.

A drive loops round from this building to join up with the road. This was where McCreal was driving hell for leather on the morning after Johnnie's death. And this building, most probably, will be McCreal's base.

She notes something else: a small path leads from the U-shaped building to the dell and then beyond to another little clearing with a grey dot. This clearing is too small and too raggedy to be a helipad. She zooms in closer. No, the edges of the dot are a ring of stones and in the middle lies something grey.

A fire pit: the grey in the middle must be ashes.

This second clearing is only 150 metres from the dell where Johnnie died. Yet Boyd and Cummings never mentioned it.

She moves the cursor out. She can see now that the path leads eventually to the causeway. This could be where the students went that night. Maybe they still hang out there?

So they must know about McCreal, and McCreal must know about them.

She finds that she's smiling. She has a picture now. A

connection. She goes to the viewfinder to get a sideways look at the building. But Google Maps draws a blank.

Then a voice behind her says, 'Rhona! In my office!' The Bassett has come up behind her; despite his size he is surprisingly light on his feet.

She quickly reaches forward to turn off the screen, but he's already seen the map.

'I mean *now*!' he says.

She follows him down the passageway between the empty desks and into his office. The Bassett lumbers into his chair.

'Siddown.'

She sits down.

'What's going on? The car park smells like an abattoir.'

'It could have been worse. We didn't bring the bear inside, sir.'

'But get it cleaned up! A dirty car park causes reputational damage to the force.'

'It was worth doing. We found stuff inside the bear. We have two human fingernails. And some small seed pearls from a necklace.'

'So I hear. But you have *no body*. And, I assume, no missing person. You can't carry on an investigation with so little. And tell me, where is the public interest in all of this?'

This is new – The Bassett has never mentioned public interest before.

'I told you before how it all *felt* wrong,' she says. 'And it's clearly important. We seem to have upset somebody.'

'Yes, you have – *me*.'

'No, I'm serious. There was a drone watching over us when we cut up the bear.'

'Kids, probably.'

'No kid in Fort William could afford that kind of equipment.'

'You'd be amazed at the pester power of children. Anything else?'

'On Friday night somebody tampered with my car. Boyd is down seeing to it.'

'That could be any number of people. You're widely hated.'

She jerks her head back, as if batting the insult away. 'And Will Henderson and his friends know more than they're letting on.'

'What makes you say that?'

'I think they were there when Johnnie was killed. I had a talk with his friend – the older one, Arthur. He came into town on Friday to look me out. There's some strange dynamic going on there.'

'A *"strange dynamic"*. Is that all you've got?'

'Can I say something, sir?'

'What's ever stopped you?'

'With respect,' she pauses; *careful now!* 'I don't feel you're prepared to take this case seriously.' She doesn't need to say 'because you know the family' or 'because you lease a house at Kilchoan'. That's understood.

He looks at her closely, his hands cupping his chin, fingers sunk into his cheeks. She knows he has settled into himself, he has made up his mind.

He says, 'I don't take this case seriously because *there is no case.* You're a good instinctive detective, Rhona, but this is ridiculous. All you've got is a few fragments, some odd occurrences and now you're just going round and round in circles. And this business with chopping up the bear – I've already had the deputy chief constable on the phone. I'm tired of making excuses for you.'

He gives her one of his wise, kindly looks. 'I think you

should take a break. A few days off to recoup. It's been a tough time for you, what with your father.'

'I'm fine.'

'Take up a relaxing hobby. Jeanette found pottery classes helped with her psoriasis.'

Rhona nods stoically. If she isn't careful he'll be asking her to join him and the wife for Friday night bowls.

'It's just we're concerned.'

Who, she wonders, is 'we'?

'If you really want to help me, sir…'

'Yes?' he says heavily.

'You could widen the scope of the inquiry and get some funding from the Canadians.'

'*The Canadians*?'

'That's where the bear came from. Henderson imported it at vast expense.'

'What good will that do? If, aeons ago, some poor Canadian hiker took a wrong turn, then what's the point of going into it all now?'

'But there's been a fatality, sir. Probably a murder. And we're most probably talking of a child here.'

'A child?' He sits up.

'Yes,' she says.

'But a *Canadian* child.'

That slightly pedantic tone of his almost always leads to a 'no'. And he's already sinking back down into his chair. 'Maybe it *is* the death of a minor, but two little bits of fingernail still isn't much to go on, is it? You know that yourself, Rhona. If you had something more substantial you'd be beating a path to the magistrates for a search warrant.'

She says nothing. She can manage without him. All the really good work she's ever done has been in the teeth of her superiors.

'You can go now,' he says. 'But be a bit more careful. And get the car park cleaned up properly.'

'Sir?'

'What?'

'How's Joel?'

The Bassett gives her a sad smile, 'Thank you for calling in on him. He did make it through. They lifted him out yesterday morning. He was semi-conscious. I haven't seen him yet, but his mother says he's changed.'

The Bassett doesn't look at her. He just raises a hand as if to say 'that's enough'.

She's dismissed. She gets to her feet and, as she opens the door, she turns back to take one last look at his extraordinary face – the pendulous jowls, the rheumy eyes, the great blue-veined bags under his eyes. What drives him?

She goes out to the car park, Cummings trailing reluctantly behind her. The crows are still at work.

'I thought you'd be good at housework,' she says. 'You're always so particular.'

'I asked the cleaners to see to it, ma'am. We're supposed to be delegating non-essential tasks.'

'On a *Friday afternoon* you asked the cleaners? They collect their wages at 3 p.m. sharp.'

He shrugs.

'And what did you do with the bear?'

'Boyd took it home.'

'It's enormous!' She's interested now. 'Why did he do that?'

'You can ask him yourself, ma'am.'

Boyd is driving through the gates in her grey Corsa. He swerves the car into a parking bay and turns off the engine. He takes his time getting out. He stretches his arms, tucks his shirt back in. She waits, everything he does exudes attitude.

'Well?' she says.

He throws the keys hard at her, but she still catches them.

'There was a bug under the front bumper. A wee round listening device with a GPS tracker.'

'Can I see it?'

'You certainly can't. I put it on one of the ambulances – up near the siren. I thought that would blow the eardrums of anyone listening in.'

Rhona grins.

'And before you ask,' he adds. 'Yes, I checked for fingerprints. There was nothing there.'

'So, what do you think? The number plate of that van was Jim McCreal's.'

Boyd's eyes widen. For a moment he looks thoughtful. 'Was it him, though? Do we know for sure?'

'Who else would it be?'

'He doesn't seem the type.'

'When you and Pinkie were in the Dell...'

He stops her, 'I told you. There was nothing there.'

'We didn't see anything, ma'am,' adds Cummings.

'Tell me about the outbuildings. What did you find?'

'Just junk,' says Boyd. 'Some rusty old farm machinery. In every old farm there're always rooms full of rusty junk.' Boyd is always letting her know he was brought up on a farm and is a man of the soil.

'You fine-toothcombed it, did you?'

'I had a look,' he gives her a bald stare.

'I saw your fishing rods.'

Cummings sniggers.

Boyd gives her that stare again. Then a shrug. 'I had a few lobworm with me, so it seemed a waste not to give it a go. Nice temperature variants in the estuary. The sea trout rise well there.'

'Next time I hope you catch an electric barracuda and it pulls your eyeballs out with its fangs.'

He smiles at her. His teeth are improbably white.

'And the bear?' she asks. 'A headless bear is a funny kind of perk.'

'Marion does rugwork. I thought she could do something with it. I like a bit of fur on my feet first thing in the morning.'

'And the carcass?'

'I know a few street food vendors.'

Rhona can't think of a reply to that. She opens the car door and gets in.

'Are you back off to Ardnamurchan?' asks Boyd.

'Yes, and while I'm away get the car park cleaned properly. Or The Bassett will have another hissy fit. Then go and check out McCreal's shop in Oban – both of you go. And don't take fishing rods.'

'Be careful on the reserve,' says Boyd. 'There're more bears out there. And there's the wolves.'

'Don't sound so hopeful. Scrub the tarmac. Use Borax, or bleach, or drain unblocker. Just clean it good and proper.'

'Aye, aye. We're your cabin boys, Inspector.' Boyd gives a salute.

Again, Cummings sniggers.

She waits until the two men have headed inside, then her hand goes straight to the glove pocket. But both the hip flask and the bottle, goddammit, are empty. She walks back into the headquarters and takes the stairs down to the office dispensary in the basement. She knows that buying in-house allows the office to keep tabs on her drinking. But anything is better than the poison sold in the public off licenses.

The pug-nosed lad at the dispensary immediately puts a half bottle of Bells on the counter.

'634129,' she grasps the bottle.

'Inspector, I ken your payroll number.'

Rhona smiles wanly. One of the most intolerable aspects of ageing is the knowing air of callow young men.

THE NIGHTWALKERS

Rhona drives out of the police car park and along the public road out of Fort William. She passes the long queue of grubby-anoraked supplicants by St Mungo's soup dispensary and the hospital where the two ambulances are parked in their bays. Thanks to Boyd, one of them now has the tracker. How long will this keep them off the scent? Today is 24th June and the ambulances get their petrol ration at the beginning of the month. So there'll be no trips out today, or tomorrow, or the next day.

Three quarters of an hour later she reaches the checkpoint, and Henderson's guard waves her through. She heads to Acharacle and drives on past the dell. At the end of the road, by the estuary, she parks the car. She is going to leave the glove compartment alone but changes her mind and takes a little nip straight from the bottle. She takes several more nips, refills her hip flask and puts it and a tube of mints in her parka. Just in case. She feels the other pockets of the coat. Wilber's tracking device and the chip are still there.

She looks out over the estuary to the tower standing on its little island, with its green girdle of fence all but cutting it off from the loch. The sky above is white and sunless.

She walks slowly out onto the causeway, which is now merely a metre wide. There is time now for her to collect her thoughts. She isn't going to mention the fingernails, or the pearls – Will and his friends are already on their guard. But they're young, and more likely to crack than

167

McCreal. She'll let them lead her to the firepit and to the outbuildings. If all else fails, she'll send Boyd or Laidlaw out to Aberdeen to winkle out the missing Ray.

She climbs the path up to the tower and walks through the arch into the courtyard. She pushes at the latch and the great wooden door opens. She hears a murmur of voices and sweeps back the big velvet curtain.

'Hello, everyone!' she says.

Zoë, who is sitting in an armchair by the window, turns to look at her. But Rachel, who is lying wrapped up in a blanket on the sofa, just hunches her shoulders.

'Inspector! This is a surprise!' Arthur is standing with his back to the stove.

'I don't know why he said that,' says Zoë. 'I've been watching you cross the causeway for the last ten minutes.'

Rhona looks at Arthur questioningly and he smiles back at her, as if quite comfortable with his lie. She glances at Rachel whose face seems molten from lack of sleep.

'Where's Will?' she asks.

'I'm afraid he's still in bed,' says Arthur.

'Could you get him up, please?'

'He's not been well.'

'I could always take him up a cup of tea, but I'm sure he'd rather be woken by you.'

Arthur walks over to the stairs.

In the squalid little kitchen in the turret, Rhona watches Zoë light an ancient-looking stove. On a plate on the sideboard a magnificent rib of beef is defrosting.

Rhona finds herself staring at it. Nowadays, high quality meat never even gets near the grocery outlets.

'We're having a big dinner tonight,' says Zoë.

'Any particular reason?'

'You'll have to ask Arthur. He's the big chief.'

Zoë drains the puddle of dirty water in the sink and

washes three cups. Meanwhile Rhona takes a damp cloth to the sideboard.

'Sorry about this,' Zoë gestures to the dirty dishes.

'It's nothing. You should have seen the houses I lived in as a student.'

Zoë laughs.

'So, who does the housework here?' asks Rhona.

'Me. And Rachel. Arthur sometimes. Ray and Johnnie were completely useless and Will's mind is always on higher things. He doesn't *see* dirt. And he never eats unless reminded. In fact, we should make him something now. I'll butter him some soda bread. He likes that. It's what he eats most of the time.'

Rhona waits until both she and Zoë have hot mugs of tea cupped in their hands. Then she says, 'Were you close to Johnnie?'

Zoë blinks, 'We're all close. We spend loads of time together – not just here, but when we were back at uni too.'

'It must be a terrible shock.'

'Well, yes,' Zoë hesitates.

'You say that as if it *wasn't* a terrible shock.'

'This thing with the bear was, like, really random. But all the same...'

Rhona keeps her eyes fixed on her mug of tea.

'I know this might sound a bit odd,' Zoë continues. 'But Johnnie always *was* going to die.'

'How do you mean?'

'Of course, we are all going to die *at some point*. But Johnnie was kind of going to die *more than the rest of us*. If that makes any sense.'

There's a pause. Rhona, patient as a sniper, waits.

Zoë, shoulders slumped, continues, 'When I was growing up my mum had a photograph in one of her albums. It was of my great grandparents' wedding in 1915.

There was the bride and groom and all the extended family crowded round. Families were huge then and in the back row there were loads of soldiers in uniform, young men about to go to the front. Some of the faces looked a bit *blurry*. And, of course, most of those young men died. And, in a way, that was Johnnie for you. He was a bit like that, a bit indistinct. He was a great guy, but… I don't know. It's hard to explain.'

But you have explained; Johnnie was entirely expendable.

Will has come down and is sitting on the sofa. He's ruffled and pale, his neck thin as a stalk in the oversized jumper. Rhona thinks: stop taking drugs, wash, shave, buy a goddamned hairbrush.

Zoë brings Will a cup of tea and the slice of soda bread. She sits down.

'There are just a few things I need to clear up,' Rhona says in her official police automaton voice. She takes out her notebook and pen.

She checks Ray's contact details and tells them again that, as Johnnie's case has still not received an official verdict, they are not free to leave the area. This, she says, is now a formal caution; they are *not* to leave. Then she adds that she has met the Fergussons, and that they are staying in the Marriott hotel at Torcastle. They have asked if Johnnie's friends could come tomorrow to the hotel. Would tea time be fine? By then the colonel and his wife will have got through all the legal formalities.

There's a moment's silence.

'And obviously you should take Johnnie's bag and all his things with you,' says Rhona.

More silence. Will nibbles vaguely at his soda bread.

'Don't you think you owe it to his family?' Rhona looks

from one set of downcast eyes to another. 'If you were his parents you'd want to meet the people who'd been with your son when he died. No?'

Nobody corrects that 'when'. Nobody says, 'You mean *before* he died.'

'Okay,' says Arthur heavily. 'We'll go.'

Zoë and Rachel nod their agreement.

'We'd like him buried here,' says Will in a high voice. 'He loved it here.'

'That's a family matter, really,' Rhona looks questioningly at Arthur. Did he tell them of his visit to her? Clearly not, for he merely shrugs. She adds, 'It'll be a while before the body is released. So you've got time to work on the colonel and his wife.'

She doesn't rate their chances with the Fergussons.

Now she puts down her notebook. 'I've come here today about another matter. I want us to retrace your steps, for you to take me back to where you went on the night of Johnnie's death. Take me on exactly the same route. The walk should jog your memories. Even the most trivial facts may turn out to be important. Things you said, things you wished you'd said, things you'd thought and not said.' She takes a breath, 'And that's even if you were out of your tiny minds.'

Zoë gives a gasp of laughter. Arthur and Will exchange a look.

'So, let's get going,' Rhona stands up.

Arthur has still said nothing; he doesn't move.

'It's the wrong time of day. We walk in the dark,' says Zoë slowly. 'We're night walkers.'

'You'll have to make an exception. For once you can be a day walker.'

'Can't the girls take you?' says Arthur. 'Will's tired.'

'I want *all* of you there.'

'And if we say no?' Arthur gives her a heavy-lidded look – it's almost flirtatious. She wonders if he is being difficult again. It feels like a form of showing off.

'You don't want to go there. You'd be obstructing the course of justice and you'd get to try on my bracelets.'

His face is impassive.

She adds, 'I keep handcuffs in the car.'

'I did understand the reference. I know a threat when I hear one.'

'Good!' she replies. 'Then let's get moving. All of you. You've got five minutes to get ready.'

On her way out, Rhona stops by the coat rack in the front lobby and slips the bear's tracking chip into a small internal pocket in Arthur's greatcoat.

She waits for them by the stone arch. Eventually Zoë appears, dressed bizarrely in a flat tweed cap and with a blanket wrapped around her shoulders. Rachel follows in a blue poncho and a black floppy hat that dips down over her eyes. Arthur and Will arrive last. They are both in greatcoats, and Will's coat nearly reaches his ankles.

Arthur looks quickly in all directions, hides the huge iron key to the door behind a stone and they set off down the path. The air is still as glass. Ahead of them lies the black water of the estuary with the woods rising beyond.

Zoë leads the way silently along the causeway, her blanket rucked up round her waist. Rhona follows, and the others trail further behind. At the far side of the estuary, they head down the path into the woods. From Google Maps Rhona knows that the path leads to the clearing with the firepit: the students are taking exactly the route that she expected.

Nobody speaks. As they walk Rhona hears a faint clinking sound behind her. She turns and asks Will what it is. He takes his hand out of his greatcoat pocket and opens his fist. In his palm lie half a dozen pale limpet shells. 'I like to shuffle them when I'm thinking.'

'And what're you thinking about?' Now she sees his pale face close up for the first time. Cat is right; his eyes are most unusual; the white of one eye is much yellower than the other. He also has a slight cast which becomes more marked when he looks up or to the side.

He smiles vaguely, 'You know the kind of thing – how birds know where to fly to in the winter, whether you can eat sea urchins raw, what angels wear. After every thought I return to my shells. They're my relics of the sea. My rosary.'

'Inspector, shall we move on?' says Arthur.

After about half a mile, they come to the clearing. As she expected, it is a fire pit ringed with stones. The path on the far side leads on to the dell.

Logs have been arranged in a circle round the fire as seating. Nearby stands a neat triangular pile of firewood. There's even a small open-sided lean-to with chopped kindling, a pile of newspapers, matches and a can of paraffin. She is baffled: how on earth could Boyd and Cummings overlook this?

'Matt keeps it all stocked up for us,' says Arthur.

Rhona nods. If Arthur knows Matt, then Matt knows Arthur, and surely he'd have known Johnnie?

Zoë shifts a half burnt log with her foot. 'We get nannied over everything, don't we? We even get our wild woods curated.'

Arthur ignores her.

'Well?' he says dismissively, 'Where do we go from here?'

'Did you have a fire that night?' asks Rhona.

'Of course we did.'

'Then let's make one now,' she says. They all seem

173

so oddly passive. She brings over kindling, newspaper and matches from the lean-to. Zoë crumples up some newspaper and Rachel helps halfheartedly, but Arthur and Will don't even try. So it's Rhona who builds the little wigwam of kindling and lights the paper.

Soon they are sitting round a small spluttering fire. Will stretches out his long thin hands to warm them against the flames. Rhona takes out her hip flask and passes it round. They all drink from it, especially Arthur, who tilts his head back, his eyes staring out to the side like an angry horse.

He hands on the hip flask. 'I'm still not at all clear about this. Are you here in a private capacity?'

'Why do you ask?'

'Police officers don't normally light fires and drink when they're interrogating suspects.'

'You're not suspects. Johnnie was killed by a bear. And I'm not a normal police officer.'

'We can see that!'

Rhona lets it go. She mustn't get their backs up. Not yet.

'So, is this where you usually come?' she asks. *Always start softly.*

'Yes,' replies Arthur.

'And what else do you do once you're here?'

'We don't really *do*. We *are.*' says Will.

She waits.

'We drink, we eat, we talk,' says Zoë. 'Sometimes we eat yew berries.'

'Aren't they poisonous?'

'Only if you swallow the pips. Then they're deadly. But the pulp is quite sweet and there is something really cool about dangerous food. You make the slightest mistake and you're dead.'

Arthur's eyes narrow.

'Anything else?' asks Rhona.

'We just live very intensely,' says Zoë.

'Yes?'

Will prods a long branch into the fire. He says, 'It doesn't matter how long you live, that's a mere detail. It's how brightly you burn.'

He is *so* young, thinks Rhona. She says, 'There's something I wanted to ask you, Will. I've found these leather jerkins from when you and your sister were children. Is it true that your father sent you out covered in meat for the sea eagles?'

'Yes,' Will smiles at the recollection. 'Poor Lucy, she hated it.'

'And you? Didn't you hate it?

'It was a little gory. And terrifying. But also thrilling. I think it was the most vivid experience of my childhood. We always had at least half an hour before the eagles would come after us. And just before they were released, my father would blow the horn and it would echo through the hills. And that sound, when I hear it today, it still sends a thrill through me.'

Rachel and Zoë are sitting very still, eyes on the fire.

Will puts his hand over his chest, 'Just before the eagle swoops down on you, you hear the rush of air. And you are beyond fear. You see yourself from afar, as a bird of prey would see you. You are completely in that moment.' Will's voice cracks slightly, 'I think I've spent the rest of my life waiting for something from the heavens to land on my shoulders.'

He glances at Arthur, 'And maybe it has.'

Arthur looks uncomfortable. He gives a little half laugh, 'I wonder if Prometheus felt the same. Maybe he welcomed his daily visitation?'

Nobody smiles. *The women hate Arthur.*

Rhona says, 'Wasn't Lucy injured?'

175

Will just nods, his eyes faraway.

Rhona waits a few heartbeats, but still nobody speaks. Nobody has any questions. Talking to them feels like walking through dough.

'I'm going for a pee.' She stands up, walks away from the fire and stops at the edge of the clearing. She crouches down behind a tree, empties her bladder and then holds her breath and listens. Silence. If they didn't have something to hide, and if there hadn't been some kind of rift between Zoë and Arthur, they'd surely be talking now.

On the way back to the fire she passes the wood pile and bends over to pick up a couple more logs. Stuffed underneath the wood, at the foot of the pile, is a blue plastic bag. As she opens it the smell of old blood hits her. Inside are half a dozen empty plastic meat containers from foreign currency outlets, and there are more bits of that blue string. Something tells her to stop; she closes the bag and stuffs it back into the wood pile. She'll ask the girls later when she has them on their own. Not now.

As she stands up, she sees Zoë's head quickly turn away. The bag *is* important.

Rhona returns to the fire, to the silence. Everyone seems so dull and so stupid.

'So what exactly happened here on Johnnie's last night?' she asks.

Will goes on staring into the fire, Zoë gives a tired sigh.

Rhona is exasperated. 'Come on! You have to help us! If you won't tell me anything, you *will* be suspects.'

'Suspects for what exactly?' says Arthur coldly. 'You yourself just said he was killed by the bear.'

'The rule book is very big. I can always find something. *What happened?*'

'We just sat round the fire,' says Arthur. 'We drank a

bit and smoked. We looked at the flames. Will had a small drum which he played, and Rachel danced to it.'

'You did?' She looks across at Rachel, who's hunched in towards the flames. She hadn't noticed before but the young woman is really striking, with those heavy-lidded eyes and large mouth. Her hair hangs shining around her shoulders. She doesn't meet Rhona's gaze.

'Rach was at the Conservatoire in Glasgow before she got too big,' says Zoë. 'She's really good. She has an amazing dance where she uses scarves, and shawls and flaming branches. Sometimes she sings too.'

'So I'm a *"she"?'* murmurs Rachel.

'If you don't speak for yourself, then I have to,' says Zoë.

'So that night, Rachel danced. And the rest of you, what did you do?' asks Rhona. At least this little spat might liven them up a bit.

'Not much else, really. We just talked a bit,' says Arthur. 'Then we all went home.'

'All of you? Including Johnnie?'

'Yes,' says Arthur.

'Had you taken any drugs?'

'A few mushrooms,' he concedes.

'Did you talk about the bear?'

'Why would we?' he counters.

'Of course we did,' mutters Zoë.

'So you *did* talk about the bear?' Rhona looks at Zoë. 'Go on, tell me.'

'It was nothing, really. We just wondered where it went at night, and what it thought about. What *does* a wild animal think about? Does it think at all?'

'They live in the present,' says Will. Everyone again turns to him. His glasses shine in the firelight. 'For a wild animal, time must just be an endless series of nows. They're lucky that way.'

'You look terrible, Will,' says Zoë. 'You've gone blue round the lips.'

Will presses his hands to his cheeks. 'Rilke likened death to a bluish residue left in an old cup. It's not a bad description.'

'Come on, peewit, you should be back in bed.' Arthur stands up. He turns to Rhona, 'I'm sorry, Inspector, we are going to have to leave you.'

'Don't worry,' she says. 'The girls will keep me company.'

When Arthur and Will have left, Rhona goes over to the woodpile, retrieves the blue plastic bag and brings it back to the fire. She doesn't undo it – she doesn't need to. Rachel looks shocked, and Zoë draws herself up.

Rhona puts the bag down, 'What's all this about? Why the meat? And what's with this blue string?'

They don't answer.

'If it were the remains of a barbeque there'd be all sorts of other stuff – paper towels, plates, ketchup. But just this?' She picks out one of the strands of bloody string, dangles it in the air and looks at both of the women in turn. Rachel has her head down, Zoë is staring into the fire.

'You know I'll find out eventually.'

Rachel rubs her eyes.

'What do you think, Rach?' says Zoë.

'Well, what harm can it do now?' says Rachel.

'You must promise not to tell the Fergussons,' says Zoë.

'That all depends. If what you tell me results in criminal charges then it'll have to be public knowledge.'

'But we didn't kill him!' exclaims Zoë.

'Did you help him to kill himself?'

'Not quite.'

'Not *quite?* What does that mean?'

'The bear killed him, not us,' says Zoë. 'You know that.'

'Yes, I do,' replies Rhona. She can feel they're loosening up; soon they'll tell her. 'But, in some way that I don't fully understand, you contributed to his death. You helped let it happen.'

Rachel scrapes her hair back from her face, 'We tied the meat to him, that's what we did. Just like Henderson did to his kids. There. I've said it! Now you know.'

Rhona keeps her face completely expressionless. 'Why?'

'Don't you see?' says Zoë. 'The steaks were bait. Johnnie was tempting the bear, calling it to him. They come when they smell blood.'

'Was he trying to get himself killed?'

'Let's just say that Johnnie took off his clothes and we tied six steaks round his waist,' says Zoë. 'That's what we needed the string for.'

'This was Arthur's idea?'

'Of course it was,' says Zoë.

'And then what happened?'

'Then Johnnie did a dance round the fire.'

'Were you all high on drugs?'

'Not really. We'd had a few mushrooms but we weren't completely gone,' says Zoë. 'I think my mind was very clear.'

'Was it a punishment, then? Had Johnnie done something wrong?'

Zoë shakes her head.

'I knew she wouldn't understand,' says Rachel in a low voice.

'Then *make* me understand, Rachel!' says Rhona. 'Don't just hide behind your hair. One of your friends is dead. I thought you'd care about that.'

179

Rachel begins to cry.

'It's impossible for you to understand,' says Zoë with a shiver. 'Either you are inside this. Or you're not.'

'Inside *what*?'

Zoë looks into the fire, her features sharp with concentration. 'Ever since we met in first year, we have been searching for a higher truth – searching for the space between sleep and wakefulness. We've tried everything, but you never live more fiercely, more intensely than when you are on the very edge of life.'

'Go on,' coaxes Rhona.

'It's like flying. It's like going out into a storm or diving into a rough sea. You can't do it cushioned and cossetted. You have to put down your guard, risk everything. Feel *real* fear. *Real* danger. Stand on the edge of life where darkness gathers.'

Rachel has buried her face in her hands.

Zoë continues, 'The air was alive that night. I felt the earth turning under my feet. I felt the gods of the sky and the forest breathe down on me. The stars were at the very end of my fingertips. I have never been more excited, more awake. It was the same for all of us, for Johnnie too, I'm sure. Every particle of air around us was charged. We were one.'

She breaks off and shakes her head, 'I can't describe it.'

'And then what happened?' says Rhona. 'Did the bear come?'

'Not quite, not exactly. Johnnie saw something. He suddenly stopped dancing. He was looking into the wood, pointing. He cried, "That's her!" and he ran off.'

'When he said "her", who did he mean?'

'How do I know?' says Zoë.

'You're sure?' Rhona senses unease. 'You don't know who he could have seen?'

'I'm not a mind reader.'

So there was someone in the woods. Someone female. Was this what she and Gordon had heard in the dell?

'Where did Johnnie go?' she asks. 'Where did he run to?'

'He went that way.' Zoë points to the path towards the dell.

'Did you follow?'

'No, I was lying down at the time, looking up at the stars. I was in outer space. I didn't quite get what was happening.'

A minute ago she said she'd never seen things more clearly.

'Did anyone else follow him?'

'I did,' snuffles Rachel.

'And?'

'I got to the pond and there was Johnnie, standing with his arms stretched out. He was facing the bear. But I couldn't see the bear well. It was more of a dark shape, down on all fours, roaring. And Johnnie was just shouting, "Go! Go! Go!" And I ran back to the fire.' Rachel wipes her nose on her poncho, 'That's when he screamed.'

'The screaming went on and on and it was terrible,' says Zoë. 'And then it stopped. And that was even worse.'

'Did you go back to the dell?'

'Like fuck we did!' says Zoë. 'We ran the whole way home.'

'Then who folded up Johnnie's clothes and put them in the dell?'

'Were they folded up?' Zoë sounds bemused. She looks at Rachel who just shakes her head.

'Are you sure?' says Zoë.

'They were left in a neat pile near to his body, with a

flower on top and a playing card crumpled up inside the flower.'

'It certainly wasn't us,' says Zoë.

'The card was a Queen of Spades. What was all that about?' Rhona watches Rachel. For all her shyness, she is the one who tells more.

'We certainly didn't move his stuff,' Rachel looks at Zoë. 'Do you think it might have been that man?'

Zoë nods.

'Which man?' Rhona's heart gives a hitch.

'There's a man who works for Archie Henderson. He has a workshop near the clearing. A workshop and a kind of weird showroom thing. I think he sometimes sleeps there too.'

'What's his name?'

'Dunno.'

'How old is he? What does he look like?'

'Forties? Fifties? A bit paunchy, a bit balding. Red nose. Thick glasses,' says Zoë.

Rhona nods. Of course, it's McCreal.

'I'd like to see this workshop,' Rhona stands up.

'Be our guest,' says Zoë, not moving at all.

'No, both of you come with me.'

'Do we have to?' says Zoë. 'Arthur always said to leave him alone.'

So Arthur does know something. Everybody knows something – except her.

'Come on,' says Rhona briskly.

They walk past the dell, still muddy and churned up from Forensics. On the far side they find the overgrown path that leads to the old stone outbuildings. They still aren't far from the clearing; McCreal would have heard Johnnie's screams.

Rhona feels angry with herself. She should never have delegated the site inspection to a shirker (Boyd) and an idiot (Cummings). She should have raked the woods herself. And why had she let four days slip past before getting to look properly at the aerial maps?

She walks round the outbuildings with Zoë by her side and Rachel walking behind. There are no lights on, and no signs of anyone present. But a full cup of milk has been left by the front door. Rhona dips her finger in and tastes. The milk is still fresh.

Beside the cup lies an unopened packet of French chocolate brioche. Rhona knows that these days Scottish shops sell turnips and rock hard bakery and luminescent pink sausage meat. Nobody stocks French brioche.

She looks at Zoë who has stepped back from the building. 'Who is he trying to feed?'

'I don't know,' says Zoë stolidly. 'I don't know anything.'

Yes, you do.

Rhona knocks on the door, but nobody answers. She cups her hands around the window at the side of the door and looks in. At first glance the scene inside seems a picture of domestic normality: a scrubbed wooden table and a dresser with china plates laid out along the shelves, a standard lamp made of yellow material with fringes of brocade, two plush armchairs on either side of a fireplace.

There's an occupant in one of the armchairs.

He's sitting back with his legs crossed and a set expression on his face. He's very still, with prominent ears. It's strange that he's holding a pipe, strange too that he's wearing a tweed jacket and trousers. For he is a grey wolf.

Rhona jumps back from the window in fright.

'Don't worry. It's stuffed,' says Zoë. 'But it's strange, isn't it?'

Rhona feels a vibration at her hip and takes out her mobile. A text has come through from Boyd:

– We have him! Come NOW!

OBAN

Rhona calls Boyd, but he's not answering. She sends a text. A second later a new message pings in: McCreal's address in Oban and an emoji of flames.

She tells Zoë and Rachel that she has to leave urgently – she will catch up with them later. Then she sets off sprinting back down the path through the woods. When she reaches her car she bends over to catch her breath. The chrome of the bumper reflects back a horribly distorted version of her face, wide as a frog's.

She glances out at the estuary. There's a tiny figure on the roof of the tower. *It'll be Arthur.* She gets into the car and swerves off down the road.

It's only when she's driving back through the redwoods at Salen that the thawing rib of beef comes back to her. Why is she thinking of this now? Even for Will and his friends this joint is an extraordinary extravagance. They must be planning something for tonight.

Waiting for the ferry, Rhona watches an old woman with a hessian apron frying up fritters in a disused oil drum. For good measure, she has a pitchfork resting at her feet.

Rhona winds down the window and asks what's in the fritters.

'Gobbets,' the woman's mouth puckers.

'Gobbets of *what*?'

'Fillin',' says the woman, gimlet-eyed.

The fritters could be absolutely anything – street food

now is often cryptic and covered in batter. And Rhona has been caught out before. But she thinks, 'what the hell' and buys a 20 merk poke. She bites into a fritter and it releases a pungent, fishy discharge. She eats all the fritters anyway, takes a final gulp from the half bottle to clean out her mouth and drives up the ramp.

On the ferry Rhona tries again to call Boyd, but his signal is down. She phones the office and asks Jeanette for any news from Boyd and Cummings.

'They went off to Oban and we haven't heard back since. Ron has charged a new Tupperware box to expenses and says you'd approve it. You do approve, don't you?'

'Yes,' Rhona sighs. 'Has anyone else called?'

'The hospital, Dimitri, your friend Cat. And someone who called himself the red squirrel and wouldn't leave a number.'

She tells Jeanette that she's going straight to Oban and rings off.

As the ferry docks she watches a heron with a sprat in its beak flop slowly up into the air and fly away. The fish thrashes its tiny silver body for a moment and then suddenly it stops moving. It's dead, or has just given up. She shuts her eyes. There has to be a moment when you stop fighting back. And maybe it isn't just resignation and dread. Maybe there's relief in there too?

The hooter sounds. Rhona gets back into the car and bumps down the gangway.

The road winds round the coast of Appin; a well-known wild land. She keeps her police siren on to discourage ambushers and drives fast, dodging round the old tyres and rocks scattered across the tarmac. Before the Connel bridge she comes round a bend too fast and has to swerve suddenly to avoid a huge gap where a landslide has pulled away part of the road. Afterwards she drives more carefully.

As she comes down the hill into Oban she sees a column of smoke reaching up into the sky. She parks by the pier. As she steps out of the car she smells the fire. All around her ash has fallen like a black snow.

Rhona gives a 10 merk piece to the car watcher, a lumpy teenage boy sitting on a nearby wall. His left hand, red and swollen, hangs down like a joke shop limb.

She heads along the pavement towards a blackened building where a crowd has gathered. She hasn't been to Oban for a few months and the waterfront is worse than she remembered; more refuse silted up by the hoardings, more buildings burned out or boarded-up. Some of the fine old Victorian hotels still function as foreign currency shops. She passes a specialist sports retailer displaying Italian carabiners which cost more than a policeman's daily wage. Next door, a gentlemen's outfitters sells small, luridly-coloured tartan trousers for Japanese golfers. Nobody from Oban will set foot in these shops, and they're only usually open when the cruise ships dock. The real custom will be online, or wholesale to hotels.

A few doors down, the ornate façade of McCreal's charcuterie is now burnt away, with only patches of the original purple and gold still visible. The fire is over now, and the smoke has dwindled down to a thread of grey rising from the roof. But Oban has turned out in force. And, fires being an excellent looting opportunity, many of the onlookers have plastic shopping bags scrunched in their hands.

Rhona is easing her way through the crowd when she sees a familiar top knot of pale brown hair. She taps Cat on the shoulder.

'Hey, Roo!' Cat flings her arms around Rhona.

'This isn't your stamping ground.'

'Glenn saw the fire from his trawler. I had an awful feeling it might be Jim,' says Cat.

'Come with me,' says Rhona.

Sometimes – like right now – she can't quite believe what a shoestring operation the West Highland force has become. There are no fire engines, no ambulances, just Boyd's police car and a cordon of plastic tape, guarded by Cummings who wears his holster tucked under his paunch like a truss.

Rhona ducks under the cordon and then holds up the tape for Cat.

'This is a crime scene!' protests Cummings. 'The public can't enter.'

'Do you want your new Tupperware or not?'

Cummings stares at his shoes.

'That was a joke, Pinkie,' she says.

'Inspector, you won't be joking when you see what's inside.'

The front two rooms of the shop are a blackened hole, wet and smoky, still warm. The extension out the back, where Boyd is rifling through a desk, has only been lightly touched by the fire, but the air is thick with soot. Jim McCreal, in his shirt sleeves, is hanging from a beam in the ceiling. The chair he kicked away – or which was kicked away for him – lies on its side nearby. McCreal's face is plum-coloured, and the skin tight. His hands, in contrast, are white and the fingers are still slightly splayed from that final moment. It can't have been as fast as he'd hoped.

'Cut him down,' says Rhona.

'I just wanted you to see him how he was,' replies Boyd. 'We've taken the photos.'

Rhona reaches for Cat's hand, and squeezes it.

Cat bows her head, walks quickly over to the window

and stands facing away from the room, looking out onto the back yard.

Boyd rights the chair, steps onto the seat and starts to saw through the nylon rope with a hacksaw. The body, as if gaining a second life, sways under the momentum. Rhona grabs the man's legs and stills him.

'I never like a suicide,' observes Boyd.

'If it's a suicide,' cautions Rhona.

Boyd gives a derisive snort.

His saw gnaws on through the nylon cords and when the rope finally breaks the body drops into Rhona's arms. McCreal smells of scalp and chemicals. The weight of him makes her sway.

Boyd, taking his time, gazes up at the ceiling. 'They shouldn't let depressives live in houses with exposed rafters. Gives them ideas.'

'Get the body bag,' says Rhona.

Boyd grins at her, 'Inspector, you look like someone in one of those freeze-when-the-music-stops waltzes.'

'Get the bag,' she hisses.

There are no body bags. Instead, Boyd relieves her of the corpse, wraps it up tightly in an old sheet and ties the bundle together with string as if it were a parcel. As he works, he describes how he and Cummings arrived to find the shop already ablaze. The neighbours had been tackling the flames with garden hosepipes and buckets of water.

Rhona lets him talk on. She surveys the room – an armchair, a mahogany desk, some filing cabinets. She points to the empty can of paraffin.

'Is that the cause of the fire?'

'Looks like it,' Boyd shrugs.

'Did you find a note? Any letters?'

'Nothing,' says Boyd. 'And no sniv anywhere. The

bathroom cabinet had nothing interesting, no barbiturates, or reuptake inhibitors, or tricyclics.'

'I thought you only knew about sheep dips,' says Rhona.

Boyd smiles mirthlessly. He lowers his voice, 'But the freezer is quite another matter.'

'Eh?'

'With suicides you normally find bugger all in the fridge. There's nothing to take home. But this fella, he has a *zoo* in his freezer. Bags of squirrels and voles. Even a couple of tortoiseshell kittens.'

'Jim was a taxidermist,' says Cat, still staring out of the window.

'Was the charcuterie just a front?' asks Rhona.

'Not quite. But "charcuterie" would be a euphemism.'

'For what?'

'If you ever wanted cut price meat, Jim was your man. He had a shed out by Portnacroish where he sold rodents and road kill. Then he had his high end range too. Same meat, I think. He did the hotel shops – he wrapped squirrel fillets up in gold packaging and called them "Highland glove meat". He was clever like that.'

'Do you think he was the type to kill himself?'

'I don't think so. Jim was all right, really. Not a bundle of laughs, but okay. On the whole I don't care for taxidermists. Maybe the preserving chemicals get to them. But Jim, he was okay.'

'You're sure?'

'We worked together on some things. There was a big ferret craze ten years ago, and we did these ensembles together for the Marriott. You know the kind of thing: sword-fighting ferrets in doublet and hose, reeling ferrets in kilts. I did the props – all the clothes and miniature sporrans and sgian dubhs. Jim prepped the ferrets and mounted them. He was very good – the neatest fingers in the business. It's such a shame.'

'When did you last see him?'

'A while back. I think it was at the last Highland Show. That was a year ago. He told me then that he was going into a new line of work. He was a bit mysterious about it and said it was going to be serious money. Big pieces too, he said.'

'There's a stuffed wolf in his place in Ardnamurchan.'

Cat exhales loudly. She looks down at the parcel that was once McCreal. There's a slight rise in the middle where the sheet stretches over his paunch. 'It's such a shame. He kind of went out of circulation. I just assumed that, like he said, he'd hit the big time.' She adds bleakly, 'In a manner of speaking, I suppose he has.'

Rhona and Cat climb carefully up the blackened stairs to the first floor. The front bedroom has been gutted by the fire and the floor has collapsed. Rhona pushes open the door to the back bedroom, which once doubled as a storeroom. The smell of burnt hair is terrible and all the small stuffed animals stacked on the shelves have been frazzled, their pelts shrinking in the heat.

In one alcove lies a glass dome with a flock of siskin sitting on branches of silver birch. It was clearly once an exquisite thing, but now the birds' green feathers are brown and a heat crack like a lightning bolt zigzags down the glass.

In a nearby cage a badger lies on its back, eyes closed.

Cat puts a hand to her mouth and gives a little cry, 'Oh God! That's Gandalf.'

Rhona is puzzled. 'So, it's not stuffed?'

'Of course not. It's his pet badger. He's had Gandalf for years.'

'Odd sort of pet to keep.'

'Jim reared him from a cub. Gandalf was gorgeous! He kept him in his jacket pocket and you'd see his little black and white snout pocking out. SOOO cute! He fed him on condensed milk and little cubes of cheddar from the foreign currency shops.'

'So he loved Gandalf?'

'He *adored* Gandalf.'

'Then why would he set fire to the shop?' asks Rhona. 'He'd have known his pet would die, wouldn't he?'

'But suicides do that kind of thing, don't they? They take their children with them. So why not their pets?'

Rhona doesn't reply. She has a pulsing sensation in her forehead as if something – a blood clot, or a thought, maybe a premonition – were pressing in on her.

'Why do you think he did it?' asks Cat. 'Was he in debt? If Jim couldn't make a living with his fingers then we're all screwed.'

'I don't think this is about money. Was he married? Did he have children?'

'No. He liked women, especially young women. But not in a creepy way. Well, not in a *very* creepy way.'

Rhona pauses. It's an hour's drive from Fort William to Oban. The timing suggests McCreal might have known Boyd and Cumming were on their way. If so, who warned him?

'Of course, he had his demons.' Cat gives her a long look, 'But then we all have our demons. You know that.'

'What sort of demons?' Rhona gazes back into Cat's soft face. Her irises are blue, speckled as thrushes eggs.

'He drank.'

'But something else was going on. In Ardnamurchan, he was putting out food for someone.'

'Not for an animal?'

'You don't feed animals with chocolate brioche from a foreign currency shop. That's what he'd left by his door.'

'Good Lord!' Cat picks up a little stack of 5 merks on the mantelpiece and lets them fall through her fingers. 'I wonder if suicide really is a sin.'

'Oh, for goodness sake! I thought you were here to help! And why *did* you come? You can't have just been passing.'

'As I said, Glenn called me. He saw the fire from his trawler. He was sure it was Jim's place going up.'

'Yeah, but why did *you* come?'

'I thought you might need some help. But the fire was all but out by the time I got here and your little mates had cordoned off the property.'

'And then you stayed.' Rhona folds her arms.

'I thought you'd come along. Also…'

'Also *what*?'

'I know this sounds awful, but Jim had some excellent tools – lovely, high quality steel pliers and tweezers. You can't get these things nowadays.'

'Blimey, Cat! Are you some sort of fucking gannet?'

'That's not fair! I knew him personally.'

'So you're a personal looter then? I never thought you were so greedy.'

'We're all greedy about some things,' replies Cat.

Jim McCreal's workshop is in a long, narrow shed in the back yard. While Rhona unpicks the padlock, Cat leans against a wall.

Rhona opens the double doors and the stink of tanning billows out into the air.

'Come on,' she says, 'I thought you wanted some pliers.'

Rhona enters the workshop and Cat follows. There are several banks of tables, each with a dead animal at some stage of reconstruction. A wildcat head is waiting for its eyes. A mouse lies flattened on a wooden board.

Cat picks the mouse up by its tail. It has been slit open from chin to rectum and gutted.

'He didn't often use mice. He always preferred voles – the tails are so much easier.'

'Less to stuff?'

'You don't *stuff* in taxidermy. It's not like making soft toys.'

'Then what do you do?'

'You *stretch*.'

'That sounds even more revolting.'

'You carve a form out of polypropylene foam – it's quite precise work, you're making a perfect model – and then you pull the animal skin over it. It has to be dead tight, like a leotard two sizes too small. I might take this wee mousie home with me and give it a go.'

Cat wraps the mouse in some paper and slips it in her pocket.

Some of McCreal's finished works are arranged on the windowsill: a surfboarding mink on the crest of a blue resin wave, a wolf's leg cut off at the carpal joint and with the paw inserted into a stiletto shoe. A small silver ashtray is attached to the top of the wolf's leg.

Rhona picks up the wolf paw ashtray and turns it over in her hands, 'This is truly horrible.'

'There's real skill to that,' says Cat. 'You'd get good money for it.'

Rhona glances round the workshop. The surfaces are stacked with books and graph paper and paint pots. There are brushes, all neatly wrapped in rags, and Stanley knives and scalpels and hacksaws standing in flowerpots. In front of her is every type of tweezer and measuring caliper and set square. The arrangement of objects is so neat and orderly: glass eyes lie in little boxes organised by size and colour. She opens a drawer to find a dozen pairs of beautifully oiled pliers arranged largest to smallest, like the Von Trapp children.

No wonder Cat wanted to come.

Where is she now? Rhona looks up. There's no sign of her friend.

'Cat?' she calls. She opens the door to a small toilet. It's empty.

And then, Rhona spots her. At the far end of the shed, beyond the old armatures and piles of timber, there's a small area which has been cleared of debris. And sitting there, on a white plastic chair, is Cat. She's completely motionless, staring into space.

'Cat!'

Cat doesn't answer.

'What's up?' Rhona walks quickly to the far end of the shed.

Cat's mouth is a white line.

'What's the matter?'

'Just look around you,' says Cat bitterly.

Rhona's eyes glide over the ordered piles of hardboard and the old varnish containers. To the side of Cat's chair stand a group of statues made out of a yellow synthetic substance. There are life-sized stoats, rabbits, a couple of wolves, an enormous wild boar. There is the bust of a girl. The statues are strange and unearthly; the animals have no eyes or ears or teeth. The girl has hollows for eyes, and no hair.

She is young. She has large almond eyes, slanting and set far apart, and a broad face that tapers down to a neat clefted chin. The face is unusual, and also familiar. Rhona has seen that face before, seen it recently. But *where*? She feels on the very cusp of remembering.

'Do you know who this is?' says Rhona.

'No. But it's *someone,* isn't it?' says Cat. 'He didn't just carve her for the hell of it. This isn't a statue. Remember what I said about stretching pelts? He knows this girl, he must have sized her up, measured her. This is a taxidermy *form.*'

Rhona drops the wolf's paw.

PEEPERS

After Cat leaves, clutching a big bag of pliers, calipers, tweezers and threads, Rhona, Boyd and Cummings scour the building. They excavate the two chest freezers out in the boiler room, and the log pile, and the cupboards and the scorched chest at the foot of the stairs. They pull up the floors in the back room and the workshop. They bang the walls, listening for hidden hollows.

The search stretches into the evening and results in a plethora of furry corpses, big and small. They find skins and heads and paws and claws and bones and even a grey, purse-shaped wolf scrotum. But there are no human remains. The girl is nowhere. Maybe, Rhona hopes, he hadn't yet caught her. Maybe the chocolate brioche was for her?

At eight o'clock they finally close up the site and head back to Fort William. Boyd and Cummings load the boxes of McCreal's papers into their car. A small bag containing jack knives, nylon thread and the wolf scrotum is also slipped into the boot. Boyd always pilfers crime scenes, even if all he can find is an old blood sausage. His 'mementos' keep him sweet and she can't be bothered to waste a cold stare on him now.

Rhona heads back to Fort William. She drives slowly, headlights dipped for the landslides and the road clutter. The hills of Appin are a black mass above her, the sea stretches below. Her mind thrums.

As the road curves round the headland and turns east, she

recalls where she saw that girl before; it's the same face, those same eyes, that looked out at her from Mrs Collins' embroidery. So, the girl should be somewhere on that estate. Rhona knows she has to go back to Ardnamurchan. This time she'll go alone and on foot, avoiding the checkpoints. Her search will be secret and swift.

There has to be a way in. Who would know? She contemplates the motley local crims and low-lifers who make themselves available for police enquiries. She decides on Peepers, aka the red squirrel. Peepers is a part-time window cleaner and snatch thief who also sells unregistered wireless connections and dark web gateways from his amazing cobbled-together van. So he gets about and he knows a lot. And he is just about sane. He is hungry too; didn't Jeanette say he'd called?

It's late now and the grill will be down on the office shop. But she knows a grubby little tumbledown hut – she knows so many grubby little tumbledown huts, so many grubby little tumbledown vans.

She pulls over, takes the path down to the waterfront and finds the hut made of several sheets of corrugated iron, balanced together like a child's card game. She pulls the chain and waits. A slatternly woman emerges from the black mouth of the hut. She hands Rhona a plastic bottle of tea-coloured liquid with a stopper made from a scrunched up plastic bag.

The good angel of Rhona's better sense is, of course, screaming, 'Don't do it! Remember last time!' But it's been a long day and it'll be a longer night. She thinks, treat yourself! The liver can always regenerate.

She buys the bottle and wedges it in the boot beside the petrol can.

In Fort William, she unlocks the back door to the office and clatters down the metal stairs to the basement changing rooms. From her locker, she takes out a paper bag of crystallised ginger. Then she changes into her nightclub scruffs: tight, slashed jeans, a glittery top and a leather jacket with studs. In the toilets, she applies mascara, eyeliner, eyebrow marker and a vampy red lipstick. Then she rubs in styling gel and teases her hair into a just-out-of-bed look. Lastly, she puts on the winklepicker boots. Dear God, they hurt.

She gives herself a final check over in the mirror. Does she still look like a cop? Probably, but a very slutty one.

The Jacobite Inn is in the abandoned biscuit factory just north of the High Street. She enters the yard where the old warehouse stands, its roof open to the skies. A small metal door – the sign is spray-painted on the brickwork above – leads to steps down into the cellar. Leaning against the open door, cigarette cupped in his hand, is a young man in his early twenties. By his side stands a wooden crate.

'How are you, Archie?'

'Canna complain, Inspector.'

'Busy tonight?'

Archie jerks his chin towards the crate. Inside lies a jumble of broadswords, dirks, maces, a couple of spiked flails.

'It's a hairies' night?'

'Aye, they've been relegated tae Mondays.'

For Rhona, this is good news. Nobody will pay attention to her when the hairies are getting into fights at the bar. The hairies are always drunk. You can't really blame them; they spend all week locked away in their model village, bowing to the tourists and pretending to speak Gaelic. When they get out, with their merks burning a hole in their deerskin pouches, they go wild.

At the foot of the steps, she swings open the glass door.

The cellar is heaving with people – aging sex workers and hard, meaty-looking men with their even harder, meaty-looking dogs. And beyond, through the fug, she sees a dozen, bearded men in checkered bonnets crowded round the bar. The hairies are unbelievably filthy and very thin. For shoes they wear bags of leather tied at the ankles like clootie dumplings. None of them have trousers – their plaids loop around their hips and shoulders. Underneath, they wear coarse linen shirts and thick brown stockings made from the wool of blackface sheep. Even when very, very drunk, they never stop scratching.

Tonight they are well into their cups; three are already doubled over with drink.

Rhona approaches the bar, breathing carefully through her mouth. She orders a whisky and takes her drink over to a seat in a dark corner by the shove ha'penny board.

She doesn't have to wait long. Peepers, a little red-haired elf of a man, arrives looking even smaller than usual thanks to a new, black leather blouson jacket. She watches him appraisingly out of the corner of her eye. The jacket is too long in the arms and is slipping off his shoulders. He could have gone down three sizes. But thieves, like beggars, can't be choosers.

Peepers doesn't give her so much as a nod. At the bar he collects his drink – a small glass of pale liquid which he doesn't pay for. Then he comes over to the corner and sits down at the next table.

Rhona goes on watching two hairies who are flicking the nips from the bottom of their bags of chips at each other. Peepers, meanwhile, prepares the shove ha'penny board, sprinkling on talcum powder from a small shaker chained to the table. He smooths the talc into the wood, takes out his old pennies from a little pouch in his jeans and lines them up.

'I gather you called,' she murmurs.

He nods, juts the first old copper penny against the edge of the board, crouches down to eye it. From the bar no one can see his mouth.

'Ye got anything for me?' he asks.

She places the bag of crystalised ginger on the floor and then, with her foot, she edges it towards his chair.

'Ah!' his features warm slightly. 'Had a busy day down in Oban?'

She leans over, supposedly to look in her handbag. Her hair flops over her face, 'That's not why I'm here.'

'Ye got any bear steaks?' He flicks his first penny and grimaces; the coin goes too far and bounces back off the far rim of the board.

'Bear is very gamey. You wouldn't like it.'

'Find anything interesting?'

'Aren't I meant to be asking the questions?'

He looks up, 'Oh, no!'

One of the hairies is vomiting onto the footrest of the bar while his friend strokes his back tenderly.

'Ye know they're made to drink bull's blood?' says Peepers quietly. 'It's called "The Tacksman's Toast". They have to down a quaich in one.'

'No wonder they're so good at throwing up.'

In their model village the hairies eat nothing but porridge and venison jerky. So when they come into town they always gorge: a fritter supper, suet balls, maybe a rabbit kebab. At the end of the night, when the minibus comes to take them back, the barman hands out glasses of warm salty water and they retire to the latrines for a communal vomit. They have to get all the food and drink up in order to stay authentically thin; The Highland Experience weighs them once a week.

'They never last, ye know. The hovels are terrible,'

murmurs Peepers. 'Malcolm Brewer, from up the glen, managed two winters. He got bronchitis and then his kidneys packed in.'

'And where is he now?'

'Dead!' Peepers flicks another penny. It lands squarely between the lines.

'Tell me about Archie Henderson's estate.'

'Tell ye *what* about it?' Peepers carefully positions his next penny.

'I saw your van parked up near the estate on Sunday.'

'Aye.' He looks vague.

'If you had to sleep rough on the estate, where would you go?'

'Fort William.'

'Very funny. But if you had to stay there?'

He shrugs, 'Not in the boarded-up houses, that's for sure. Who are ye lookin' for?'

She ignores the question. 'Anywhere else?' she asks.

He leans down, takes a piece of crystallised ginger and places it in his mouth.

'Where else then?'

'Into the woods. Up the top of Ben Hiant. Maybe down the mines. But dinna stick your nose into the mines.'

'Why not?'

He lights a roll up. 'It's bad luck for women to go down the mines.'

'You expect me to believe that?'

'I suppose ye've had all yer bad luck already,' he muses.

She casts him a cold look. 'So what trade goes on there?'

'In the mines? The trade *was* lead.'

'And now?'

'How the hell do I know? And where's ma wee giftie?'

'Your "wee giftie"? Are sweets not enough? Let's just say that you won't be picked up for that raid last week in

Glencoe. There were fingerprints everywhere. You've got to sharpen up your act.'

He raises his eyebrows and his head sways from side to side as if to say, 'fair enough'. Glencoe is one of his domains. He parks his van there regularly and has a lucrative gig siphoning off heating oil and anti-freeze from the extreme sports adventure park. But he's a lazy thief, and getting lazier. Not wearing gloves was a sloppy mistake.

'So how do I get into the estate?' she says.

'Ye don't.'

'I do, Peepers. I do. Or your pelt will be hanging from the Caol gibbet.'

'Ardnamuchan is out of ma league.'

'Huh?'

'Dinnae go there. Nobody goes there.'

'You forget that I'm a police detective. I go where I'm not supposed to. How do I get in?'

'The fence is electric.'

'Take me for a fool? There's always a way in everywhere.'

'What makes ye so sure?' Peepers turns and writes his score up on the blackboard. It is curious, she thinks, that some people feel the need to compete over everything, even shove ha'penny.

'You can't seriously tell me that there is a Highland estate that you can't get into?' says Rhona. 'And I took you for a professional!'

He's bending over now, his gaze fixed on his next penny. His hands are white as a bakers. Thanks to the talc, he gives off a smell of stale Lily of the Valley.

'If ye want tae die, be ma guest.'

'I'm still waiting,' she says.

He hits a coin which goes too far. He sighs and crouches down again, and his eyes are level with the board. The words leak out the side of his mouth: 'There's a gunny where the river runs out.'

'So you have to go underwater?' She asks the question casually, but Peepers isn't fooled. He smirks as he taps his last penny into place.

'It's no bad. Ye'll no get stuck. The gunny is wide enough for barrels. Jim Sinclair kept a still runnen' up in the mines a few years back. He used the gunny week in, week out. There's a metal grid across the pipe but it's no wired up. And there's a gate in the metalwork. Use a master key.'

She nods – she always keeps master keys in the car. 'Why has Sinclair stopped using the mines?'

'Too risky,' says Peepers.

And now, at last, he looks at her. Wise eyes in his little ravaged face, 'Dinnae go there!'

'I have to.'

Peepers sighs, sprinkles the board again with talc and, as he smooths it into the wood, he gives her directions. Finally, he says, 'Ye'll see the fence and there's been plenty of rain so ye'll hear the river. Dinnae light a torch, mind the bog, and mind the cameras.'

'Any more advice? Shouldn't I be minding the bears, too? And the wolves?'

He shakes his head morosely, 'They'll be the least o' yer problems.'

'Don't look so gloomy!' She tries to sound cheerful, but her voice comes out high and brittle. 'I'll remember you in my will.'

But Peepers doesn't smile. He thrusts his hand back into the paper bag. 'Take a gun,' he says. 'Take a *good* gun.'

THE CULVERT

Rhona drives out of Fort William, swipes her police card on the toll and takes the private road which winds round by the hotels. After a plantation of rowan trees she pulls up in a lay-by, puts on a jumper and turns the car lights off. She gets the bottle of 'whisky' from the boot and sits in the dark, huddled and bug-eyed.

Half an hour seeps by. Occasionally the wind shuffles through the trees and once a Range Rover hums past. In the distance the slide tubes down Ben Nevis are lit up for late night rides; three thin glow-worms down the mountainside. But otherwise there's nothing; just the darkness and the bottle in her hand. If she gulps quickly the whisky really isn't so bad. And the burn of it in her stomach feels cleansing. She fills up the hipflask and then sees that there's only an inch left in the bottle.

For good measure, she drinks the rest, then moves onto the hipflask and finishes it too. That's failed restraint; she knows she's no better than a woman in a tearoom dividing a walnut butter cupcake in two and then eating each half.

But the time has served its purpose: she's now almost sure that nobody is following her. She munches her way through a tube of mints, starts up the car again and heads west, passing the head of the loch. She comes to the ruin of the Twa Corbies tackle shop – all that's left are two walls of moss – and takes a bumpy side road which rises and dips and swivels its way up into the woods, as if it too were feeling its way in the dark. The road becomes steeper and her wheels spin. She roars the engine and heaves on up the hill. Is this really a road? But then, ahead, she sees the old Angel Inn, boarded up now but with the sign still hanging outside. The angel, a leftover from a more optimistic age, is painted in flowing robes and seems to be wearing a push-up bra.

At the top of the hill Rhona passes a pair of white posts and turns onto an even smaller, rougher road. She drives more slowly now, and the engine judders. But she's okay. She is fueled, the engine is fueled. And the car is her diving bell – a warm, dry bubble in this wild land – and she follows the tunnel of light made by her own headlights in the darkness.

When she comes up onto the moor, she turns off the headlights. Now everything is reversed and it feels as if the outside, and whatever lies in the blackness beyond, is looking in on her. Hunched over the wheel, she snails forwards. She bumps and clangs over a cattle grid. Then she pulls over and turns off the engine.

She brings up the maps app on her mobile. Just as Peepers said, the culvert is about half a mile away.

To the right of the steering wheel, in a locked compartment, lies her lumpy little Glock 17. She opens the compartment and wriggles into the holster which is a length of thick black elastic that stretches around her waist. It's Italian – she bought it in the back streets of Naples – and looks like a cross between kinky underwear and a surgical truss, but it does the job better than anything else she's ever used. She loads the gun and slips it into its elastic pocket.

Of course, the gun isn't enough. The Bassett will say that she should have brought someone with her. And she should have pressed Peepers for a bit more detail. *Why* take a gun? What's there? Next time, if there is a next time, she'll ask.

For a moment she closes her eyes. It's a crazily small possibility that she can find something, yet she still has to try. She knows she isn't brave, but she is curious. And one day, as Cat has said a thousand times, it will be her undoing.

Time to go. She grabs her set of master keys from the boot, and puts on her Wellington boots and a green parka. In the pocket she has an infrared torch. She doesn't turn it on.

Then she steps out into the night.

Before her lies an eternity of dark moor, but the whisky has filled her head with an inner lightness. She doesn't mind the smatter of rain and happily breathes in the damp, cool air. Everywhere is alive with small sounds; when a branch cracks, she gently closes the car door.

The ground is sodden, covered in heather and bog myrtle. She goes slowly but still she stumbles. If only she had a full hip flask to hold her hand. She takes a step and her left foot sinks into a boghole, up to the ankle. She heaves her foot out and treads more carefully now. And every few feet she looks up, checking for lights. She can't see the cameras on the fence, but they'll be there.

She climbs uphill and reaches dryer ground, where the heather is taller and more brittle, maybe left unburnt for a decade. Now she has to lift her feet high like a dressage horse, and every few steps she stops and listens. After a while she hears a faint electrical humming.

Softly, she moves towards the sound. Her eyes have grown accustomed to the dark, but she can still see very little. If only she could turn on the torch.

The sound is getting louder. She stops, sways a little, finds her balance and peers. There's something, a bulky presence, very close to her. Startled, she steps back – this is the fence, of course, and it carries enough volts to knock her out cold.

Keeping the fence a few metres to her left she walks downhill and, at the foot of a steep bank, she finds the river. She can see glints of phosphorescence and it sounds as if it's moving fast. How deep is it? Carefully she places her left foot in and the water swooshes near the top of her Wellingtons.

She wades upstream. The culvert is a giant pipe, a metre and a half high. Nothing blocks the entrance, so Peeper's gate must be at the far end.

She stoops down and enters the tunnel. The noise of the water is astonishingly loud. There is nothing she can grasp hold of, and her hands slide against the slippery sides of the pipe. She takes small, firm steps and hopes that the tugging of the water won't get any worse. She's only breathing in little sips, and only thinking in little sips too. She mustn't dwell on what will happen if the current pulls her down.

The dark alters her measure of the world. She has no idea how long the tunnel is. But when she reaches the metal grid she grips it with both hands. At last she can be steady on her feet. She stretches out her right arm and feels along the length of the metal.

Eventually she finds the hinge – it turns out to be almost directly in front of her – and she traces round the edge of the door and reaches the handle. Underneath it lies the lock. She takes the clump of master keys from her pocket and starts working her way through the fob. The third key has the correct bore.

She gently turns and twists the key, lifts it just a fraction and feels the small, soft hitch as the first cog drops. Sometimes she can't get the knack of picking a lock. But tonight, maybe thanks to the drink, it comes easily to her.

She simply repeats the same motion with the key four more times, and the lock gives way.

She pulls open the gate. The hinges creak terribly, and she prays that the sound will be drowned out by the water. She steps out of the pipe, stands up properly, and leaves the gate ajar behind her.

Now she is on Henderson's land. She grabs a branch and climbs up onto the river bank. She leans her back against a thin tree trunk and tries to rest. She is in a wood, and that at least might give her some shelter from the cameras. When she looks up she can still see nothing: no moon now, no stars, only the darkness. But her other senses are sharp. She can hear branches above her, soughing slightly in the breeze. Peepers had said that the wild animals were the least of her problems. What did he mean?

Upstream, something plops heavily into the water. The sound makes her flinch. A beaver? What is it escaping from?

No, she mustn't get distracted. She'll start with the mines. They are up in the hills and, as mines are always near water, she'll just follow the course of the river. For a moment, she contemplates walking in the water itself – that way she will leave no scent. But wading is exhausting and she'll be too slow.

Instead, she sets out walking along the river bank. There is a light wind from the west – so her scent will not go before her, but will trail behind. And the sound of the river will cover her footsteps and keep her company.

The banks are thick with vegetation and all the time she's ducking under trees or climbing over clumps of bushes. She feels a dull, ulcerous burning in her stomach and wishes she'd brought some bread with her. When she burps, the backwash is so corrosive it makes her eyes water.

Everything here in the dark is guesswork. At any moment she could disturb a bear or one of the wolf packs. Or she could step on one of the clamp traps which Matt told her he sets for the mink.

But then she finds a path that runs alongside the river, about three metres above the bank. Maybe this was what Jim Sinclair had used to roll his barrels back to Fort William. Certainly the way is surprisingly wide, though not well tended – there are fallen trees and brambles have looped across the ground like tripwires.

With the walking getting easier, she starts to count her paces. She reaches a thousand steps. Now she must surely be out of sight from the boundary cameras.

The land begins to rise. She keeps up her pace, Wellingtons rubbing, belly burning, an arm stretched before her to ward off branches. Soon, she thinks, she'll be level with the mines.

She stops to rest and listens to the wood and the crack of twigs and the river. She can hear her own breathing too – she's more unfit than she thought – and the sound seems so loud, as if from two people.

She freezes. Someone else is here.

A faint sound comes from her left. But it isn't close – she can't feel any movement in the air.

The gun? No, not yet. Her hand creeps down into her pocket and she takes hold of the torch. In one movement, she swivels round, whips the torch from her pocket and shines it into the bushes.

A round pale face stares back at her. The girl is a skinny little thing – maybe nine or ten. Rhona takes in a tatty knee-length quilted coat, bare legs with trainers, straight dark hair. The eyes are very large, slightly slanted. And the chin is small and dimpled.

It's McCreal's girl.

As soon as the torchlight hits her, she runs off up the hillside.

Rhona calls and runs after her, galumphing in her Wellingtons and sliding on the dead leaves. But the girl is light-footed and quick.

Rhona stumbles on – she has lost sensation in her legs, but seems to be upright despite herself. She catches a glimpse of the girl's coat, a lick of bare calf disappearing behind a tree.

The girl moves fast and she is falling further and further behind. Eventually, Rhona breaks through some bushes and comes out in a clearing. Which way now? She arches the torchlight across the trees. Nothing.

Has the girl doubled back?

Again, Rhona swings the torch across the clearing and this time she sees that a sapling off to the side is still swaying faintly. She follows, diving between the trees. The slope steepens and after a short while Rhona comes out on a bare hillside. She shines the torch up ahead, raking back and forth across the slope.

At last Rhona finds the girl standing up on a ledge. She looks tiny, a will o' the wisp. And when the torchlight shines on her, she turns away and is suddenly gone.

Rhona climbs up after her. The path is narrow and slippery, and after a few metres it vanishes too, just like the girl did. Rhona holds the torch between her teeth; grasping at the rocks, she climbs on upwards.

Did she just blink at the wrong moment? How could the girl just vanish?

When Rhona reaches the ledge, the answer is obvious; behind the rocks lies the entrance to a cave about a metre high and twice as wide. She crouches down and shines the torch inside, but the light is swallowed in the darkness.

She sees a wooden buttress – it's a tunnel into the mines.

This is the moment when she should give up. You never follow fugitives into unknown, confined areas, especially not alone, especially not at night, especially not when your legs feel completely detached from you and your mouth is a bag of fumes. But she ignores her police training and crawls inside.

The air here is very cold. After the first couple of metres the roof rises and she is able to stand up. She is now in a long, winding passageway that threads its way into the hillside.

Underfoot it's sand and grit – nothing that will trip her up. She has to speed up. She walks faster, and when she comes to a long straight stretch in the tunnel, her legs do what they are meant to do and she breaks into a run.

Maybe she can catch up with the girl now? She does note a slight change in the air, but she doesn't react in time. She just keeps running and the tunnel curves round to her left. As she turns the corner, the ground beneath her drops away and she falls. The torch flies from her hand and she hurtles through the darkness.

The landing is hard – her feet smash down onto rock and her right ankle crumples and turns in on itself.

For a few minutes she lies holding her ankle. The pain makes her retch, but there's nothing in her stomach – just the bitter burning dregs of the whisky. If only she had a top-up. She breathes slowly, in and out. The pain slowly eases. This is just a sprain.

The thought comes to her in a pulse of white, alcoholic brightness. *This is no accident.* When the girl stood at the entrance to the tunnel she'd been *waiting*, wanting to be followed. She set a trap, and Rhona fell right into it.

Still holding her ankle, Rhona wonders if she will ever get out. She doesn't feel fear exactly – she is at some remove from herself which might be an effect of the whisky, or the pain in her ankle, or the absolute blackness of the air. Was this some bottle-shaped pit? What if this was the end? No one would ever find her here.

She pats her side and feels her mobile still in her pocket. There will be no reception in a hole in the middle of a hillside, but at least she can get some light.

She takes out her phone and turns on the torch setting.

The cave is maybe three metres wide and twice as high. Near the roof is the dark opening from which she fell. The walls are sheer granite and impossible to climb. But at ground level three other tunnels, each supported by wooden buttresses, lead off from this central hall of a cave. At least one tunnel will surely lead out onto the mountainside.

She lies back to rest for a moment. When she turns her head, she notices a clump of feathers lying on the ground nearby. With her good foot she carefully prods at the feathers. It isn't alive. And it isn't a bird either, for she can see a blue lining.

A hat?

Rhona reaches over, picks the thing up and shines the mobile on it. The feathers are long and brown with regular cream stripes. They lie in tapered rows just as they would on a hawk, or a hen pheasant.

She turns the thing over in her hands. One side is longer, with a small beak and eyeholes. So not a hat, but a *mask*. In two places, by the ear flaps, the silk lining is stained brown and crusted with small bits of skin.

She sniffs it: sweat, feathers, blood.

And now fear creeps up through her like sap. She drops the mask, wishing she had never touched it.

She looks up, and the dark walls of the cave stare back at her.

*

213

Rhona has to get out. She is not staying in this hole any longer. She tries to stand up, but her legs buckle. She tries again, and fails again. Now she is on all fours, breathing heavily, belly on fire, her mouth acrid. She wipes the snot off her nose with the back of her hand, loses her balance and topples back onto the wet ground. She lies there, eyes shut and in a foetal position. She draws in a deep breath and tries to muster some strength. She has to get out of here. She'll crawl all the way to the car if she has to. She'll bumshuffle till her arse is skinned. Anything.

Eventually she staggers to her feet. She grabs the mask and feels something small and hard inside. She tears at the silk lining with her teeth, turns the mask inside out and shines her mobile on a small GPS tracking chip, the same model as Wilber's one.

She's too tired to think what this means. Instead, she just stuffs the mask and the microchip in her coat pocket. Slowly, she limps down the nearest of the tunnels, bending over a few times to retch.

When she comes out of the tunnel into the cool night air she immediately feels better. She sits on a rock and shines her mobile around her; to her relief, she is on that same hillside as before – only this time she's lower down. The path to the culvert is in the wood up ahead of her. She tells herself that return journeys are always shorter, and that the wild animals will probably not touch her and, whatever the odds, she will make it because she always has made it.

She does make it. At first she hobbles, using a broken branch as a stick. But soon the pain eases, and at least the way is downhill and she finds again the broad path through the woods. She is pleasantly surprised by the speed of her recovery – by the time she reaches the culvert she can put her full weight on her bad ankle. And when she scrambles back through the pipe, she is less nervous of slipping and the tunnel feels shorter. She crosses the moor, walking almost normally.

But when she finally gets home and takes off her holster she realises that she has lost her gun.

THE LIGHTHOUSE

Reading of the Day
'While we look not at the things which are seen, but at the things which are not seen: for the things which are seen are temporal, but the things which are not seen are eternal.'
2 Corinthians 4.18

This morning it's the very lightest touch, just a hand cupping her chin. Rhona opens her eyes. She's too late. There is no one in her bedroom.

When she lay awake as a child, she'd creep across the landing and into Maggie's bed, and snuggle in. She'd run her finger across her own closed lips. Then she'd do the same to Maggie, and it would feel as if someone were stroking her own lips. Maggie would stretch a sleepy arm over her.

But these days, these years, their roles are reversed. It's Rhona who is woken by fingertips on her eyelids, or a cool palm on her forehead. And when she opens her eyes, it's always too late.

She rolls over. Her ankle throbs – it's still swollen from last night's fall. She gets out of bed and pulls back the curtain. A headachey pink wash has leaked over the sky, but the hills are still dark.

She swallows two paracetamol, wraps some ice cubes in a tea towel, makes milkless tea and takes it back to bed with her. She props herself up on the pillows, the tea towel round her ankle and the mug of tea on her knees.

She remembers again that she has lost her gun – it must have come out during the fall into the cave. And on her desk lies the clump of brown feathers. The mask surely belongs to the girl, to McCreal's girl. Who is she? She certainly knows the land, knows how to survive. And it's such an unusual face – those big, almond-shaped eyes.

Of course, there might be an innocent explanation. Maybe she lives locally? Maybe she can be accounted for?

At eight o'clock, Rhona calls Matt at the estate office.

'Good morning, Inspector!' He gives a little cough, but it doesn't hide the click of the recording device.

'Hello Matt!' She reminds herself to smile. 'I just wanted you to run through with me exactly who lives on the peninsula.'

'I sent you the list, didn't I?'

'Yes, but I'm just checking. It's for the Police Benefit's Board. I know this might sound strange in these times, but we're holding a fundraising disco in Ardgour for the young people. I thought you might have some local kids we could invite.'

'Well, there's my lad. And the Carmichael sisters up at Kilchoan. I think that's it.'

'How old are they?'

'The girls? Ailsa is 12 or 13. And I think the younger one is about 9. Maybe 10. The father is a dentist, they'll definitely be registered.'

'Do they ever come to Fort William?'

'I wouldn't know.'

'I just wonder if I've ever seen them?' she prompts.

'They're blonde. Long hair. I think the younger one is still in braces. They're boarding at the private school over in Tobermory.'

217

Matt's mobile rings.

'Answer it. I'll wait,' she says.

'Hello?' she hears him say. A pause follows.

'No!' Matt gasps. 'You're sure?'

She waits. Then she hears him again: 'I'll tell Mr Henderson, but he's still half an hour away. We'll just have to hope we get there before the wolves.'

Now he comes back to her on the landline. For a minute all she can hear is his breathing.

'What's up?'

'That was the air ambulance. There's another body. It's on the rocks, just under the lighthouse. They didn't lift it, they never stop for corpses.'

'Is it a man or a woman?'

'Jock said a woman, either drowned, or fallen from the lighthouse.'

Rhona rings off, scrambles into her clothes, wraps a bandage tightly round her ankle and goes to her car.

She drives steadily at 70 mph, with the siren blaring on the roof. It's early and the journey is glitch-free; no lumbering carts, no rock traps on the road, and the Corran ferry is docked in the pier as if waiting for her.

During the crossing she climbs up onto the quarterdeck. It could be a perfectly normal day: a light rain ripples over the surface of the loch, on the shore two young women with wild-haired toddlers are gathering seaweed into plastic buckets.

In her glove pocket she still has Wilber's tracking receiver. It takes a while to wake up, but then the screen glows green. Arthur, or at least Arthur's coat, is now at the tower. She scrolls back. Last night, at 1.25 a.m., the dot followed the road to the very tip of Ardnamurchan, where the lighthouse stands, where the body – either Zoë or Rachel – now lies. Arthur stayed there until about 4.30 a.m. and then made the journey back to the tower.

She calls The Bassett at home. He's in his kitchen – she can hear the burble of his coffee machine. He says he has just spoken to the office, and a car (he doesn't specify who) is on its way to Ardnamurchan.

'Don't tell me you're there already,' he says.

'I'm on the ferry.'

'You'll be the first to arrive then.'

'It will be another of Will Henderson's friends.'

'How do you know that?'

'I just do.'

He gives a tired sigh, 'Call me when you get there.'

At the checkpoint the guard opens the gates without looking at her. She drives straight through the estate and passes the stone pillars of the Big House at Glenborrodale. She is driving fast. The sooner she arrives, the sooner she'll know.

At the turning off to Kilchoan, the main road curves inland, following the old drove road. This is the very end of Henderson's wild land: rocks and mountains covered in grass and heather. It's mean pickings for the wolves, she thinks. No wonder Matt wanted to get to the corpse quickly.

At the very end of the road, she parks on the gravel in front of the lighthouse. Henderson's Range Rover is there already and so is one of the small estate pickups.

Matt appears from the far side of the lighthouse. He's carrying a rifle.

'Where's the body?' she asks.

He points to the rocks.

'It's one of Will Henderson's girls,' he says.

He's no longer claiming not to know the students.

'Is it the big, long-haired one?'

He nods.

So, it *is* Rachel. The flakier of the two women, the more vulnerable one.

She follows Matt round the side of the lighthouse to where the rocks fall away into the sea. This is the last spur of land before the ocean. The islands are set out before her: the low, grey lines of Coll and Tiree, the Sgurr of Eigg and the black shark's teeth of the Cuillins.

Rachel is on a small ledge of rock a few metres below. She's lying on her side, one arm doubled back, her lower legs pulped and her head unnaturally pivoted to one side. Even without a heat sensor the helicopter pilot would have known that she was dead.

Rhona climbs down to the ledge, but Matt hangs back. She notes that he seems far more uncomfortable than he was with Johnnie. But then this corpse is messier – from the knees down she is a tangle of blood and bone. Her white dress, made of a silky gauze, is covered in blood and has ridden up round her waist.

Rhona pulls the material down over Rachel's spattered thighs.

'She's decent now. You can look.'

But Matt is still staring out to sea.

'When you got here, was the lighthouse door open?'

Matt nods.

She looks up. The lighthouse is so high and so close that she has to crane her neck. A circular balcony with metal railings encircles the top of the tower. Rachel would have had to climb up and over.

Rhona crouches by the body. Blood has pooled behind Rachel's head and there's a smell of shit and of some expensive floral perfume. She catches sight of the woman's blue fingers and the delicate silver bracelet round her wrist.

Rachel's face, like all the faces of the dead, has an estranged, deserted quality. Her mascara is smudged down her cheeks and her eyes stare out, the whites still so white, the irises dark brown.

'I hope you don't mind, Inspector. I tried to close her eyes before you came, but I couldn't do it,' says Matt.

'You were probably too late. Rigor mortis always starts with the eyelids.' She looks at her mobile: 9.15 a.m. And Will and his friends had left four and a half hours earlier at 4.30 a.m. 'Thanks for trying. But she's been dead for a few hours.'

Rhona takes vinyl gloves from her jacket pocket. She puts them on and moves Rachel's long dark hair aside and touches the side of her cold neck. There are no tattoos, and no bruising on the neck.

When Matt walks away, she takes off her right glove, closes her eyes and gently brushes her forefinger along the young woman's lips. Nothing. No sensation. Her mind feels hollow and hard.

'Miss Ballantyne?' Rhona jerks her hand away and turns to see Henderson standing directly behind her. His approach had been completely silent.

'I just don't understand.'

'Nor do I,' she replies. 'We'll do toxicology reports and we'll want to talk to Will and his friends. I think they were here last night.'

'Here?'

'She couldn't have made the trip alone.' Rhona notes the creases round his eyes. The skin on his neck folds slightly over his collar. *He's a tired old lizard.* She adds, 'Have you heard from your son?'

'His mobile is off. I'm going round. He and his friends will have to leave. I can't be dealing with this – I'm very busy today. And it's not my responsibility. The viewing balcony was fenced in. We followed all the health and safety protocols. If someone is determined to kill themselves, there's not much I can do.'

'We'll want to cordon off the area.'

'*Cordon it off*? This was a suicide. Can't you just get her body collected?'

'We'll need to look at everything. Forensics will be on their way.'

His bony fingers comb through his hair, 'We're very busy. I've a lot on at the moment.'

She looks at him inquiringly. How can he be that busy? He has a little army of servants, and aren't wild animals meant to look after themselves?

'You'll need to get that body out soon,' he says. 'I'm closing the gates this evening.'

'Why?'

'It's for the wolf hunt. My clients have brought forward the date. We need everyone out.'

'I'm afraid they'll have to wait.'

'These aren't people who like to wait. Your man, Travers, will back me up on that. It's more than my life is worth.' His eyes slide across her face, 'More than your life is worth.'

'Are you threatening a police officer?'

He takes an angry breath, 'Of course I'm not! But, please conclude your business briskly, Inspector.' He turns and strides back up the path. A couple of minutes later she hears the churn of his wheels on the gravel.

The door into the lighthouse opens onto a stone spiral staircase, the interior cool and salty as a seashell. Rhona climbs up and up the steps and finally comes out onto the balcony where a west wind blows off the Atlantic.

The view is of sea and sky and rocks. Looking down, the pull is powerful.

Rhona walks the full circle of the balcony, her hand gripping the rail. Maybe they were all up here together? According to Wilber's tracker, they stayed for over two hours. Maybe they made a party of it. Yet there seem to be no traces of last night – no bottles, no cans, no joint stubs, no sniv wrappings. Did they preload? Rachel can't have jumped sober.

There is no such thing as a clean death scene; everyone leaves a trace behind. She walks slowly round the balcony once more. The metal floor, which is covered in tiny bumps like ostrich leather, is slightly muddier at the point looking straight out onto the ocean. This is directly above where Rachel's body now lies.

Rhona runs a paper tissue along the rail. Nothing. It can't have been an easy climb – the paint is anti-slip and there are no footholds. She must have hoisted herself up by her arms. Maybe she had help.

Rhona notices a slight outward bulge – the rail has been pulled out of true. And now she sees what happened: Rachel climbed over the rail, but she couldn't jump immediately. Instead, she leaned out, holding onto the metal with both hands, with that white dress fluttering, and her bosom into the wind like the figurehead on a ship's prow. And here she dithered, the weight of her bending the rail out of true. Rhona remembers the battered sign outside the Angel Inn.

Did Rachel climb the lighthouse alone? Or did Will and the others climb up with her? Did she jump? Or was she pushed? Pushed was unlikely. But encouraged, compelled? Maybe the others were down below, waiting. Maybe Rachel, in her floaty angel dress, thought she was jumping into air, becoming air.

She probably wasn't pushed, but she almost certainly did

it *for* them. In some way that Rhona still can't figure out, Will and his friends have brought about her death. They are dangerous, that group, toxic. She's known it from the very beginning and she should have trusted her instincts yesterday when she saw the joint of beef in their kitchen. A 'special supper' organised by Arthur was always going to end badly.

She looks down. The fall is 90 feet, maybe 100 feet; death was certain. If she'd had been young and drunk and stoned, would she have been tempted too? You could so easily give up everything for that moment of lightness.

On the rocks the men from Forensics are attending to the body. She watches Sandy tie back Rachel's hair, while Alex straightens out the young woman's limbs and places her arms by her side. At least this time there's a body bag, and they have vinyl gloves. They ease Rachel's feet and then her legs into it. They slip the bag under her bottom and begin pulling the material up round her body. There's a calm carefulness to how they work. Were it not for the gloves, you'd think they were tucking a child into bed.

THE GIRL

They know Rhona at the Sheriff Court, so she just smiles at the doorman and walks in. She pushes open the swing doors into the robing room. Margot, a sheriff in her fifties with her hair scraped into a little grey pony tail, is sitting on the wooden bench, taking off her high heels. Nearby, two young men are standing, talking intently with their arms propped against the lockers and their long black advocates' gowns falling widely from their shoulders. Rhona notes that Margot takes up such a modest Margot-sized space, while the young men are in full possession of the rest of the room.

Margot looks at her fondly. 'Hello, trouble. Coffee?'

'Sorry, not this time,' Rhona hates that we-little-women-together chumminess. 'I need a restraint order. Now. ASAP.'

'Tell me more.'

Rhona flicks her eyes at the men.

'In my room?' says Margot.

Half an hour later, Rhona leaves the court with a search warrant for the tower, another for Henderson's house and outbuildings, and a Restraint of a Minor Order for an unnamed girl, dark hair, age approximately 8 to10.

She drives to the police headquarters, walks down the stairs to the canteen, stops off at the drinks counter for a half bottle of whisky, picks up a sandwich too and eats it as she climbs the stairs two at a time. She knocks on The

Bassett's door, doesn't wait for a reply and walks in and places the papers from Margot on his desk.

'Sit down.' He fans the papers out across his desk like a pack of cards. His eyes stop on the restraint order.

'What's this?' His mouth sags. 'Who's this girl?'

'I saw her last night. I went onto Henderson's estate.'

'You'll ruin me. Ruin yourself too.'

'You know why I went. Those fingernails, and the pearls. Jim McCreal, the man who hanged himself – or was hanged – in Oban, he's tied up with all of this. And today's suicide? I was right. It was one of the students.'

'And this girl? How does she fit in?'

'I don't know yet. But she's living rough out there.'

'Where did you see her?'

'In the woods. But I followed her down into the mines.'

The Bassett takes off his glasses, squeezes the bridge of his nose between his thumb and forefinger. He speaks slowly, as if to a simpleton, 'We are being run ragged. Any minute now, we'll have a hotel takeover, or a murder raid on the highways. The scallies are out of control and you are worrying about *one girl.*' He looks over at her, pouchy-eyed, disbelieving. 'And going after Henderson of all people. What's possessed you? Don't you have *any* instinct for self-preservation?'

'I'll need a van, sir.'

'A van?'

'To get her out. I don't want the checkpoints seeing her.'

'And you thought it was okay just to go over my head to get your authorisation?'

'Had I asked you, sir, you'd have said…'

'I'd have said "no". Because it's a ridiculous idea.'

'Exactly. So, I didn't want to run the risk.'

There's a pause. She looks at the Victorian oil painting

on his wall: Bonnie Prince Charlie raising his standard by the blue mountains of Glenfinnan.

The Bassett shifts his weight in his chair, 'It never crossed your mind that I might be right?'

She continues gazing at the painting. Bonnie Prince Charlie is wearing a stupid little periwig, and his chest is wrapped in a blue sash as if he were a chocolate box. Little pouty lips, little pouty bottom. You never saw paintings of him when he was a jowly old drunk. Why did the Scots have to love such a loser?

'Rhona!'

She blinks back to him.

'There are thousands of feral children in Scotland these days, and we can't keep tabs on all of them. They're beyond hope. Remember that terrible little albino from Tyndrum that you brought in? He caused us nothing but trouble.'

She'd always thought of The Bassett as basically kind. But of course he's only kind by default: lazy-kind, compromise-kind. Like most people, really.

'Suffer the little children,' she says.

'Glad to see you sometimes open your Reading of the Day. I'd heard otherwise.'

She smiles at him bleakly and continues, 'The girl must be connected to all that other stuff: the pearls, the fingernails, Johnnie Fergusson. And somehow, Rachel's suicide at the lighthouse too.' She takes a breath and adds, 'I just want to get this girl out today. And I need to go soon. Henderson says he has his wolf hunt tonight.'

She hears The Bassett make a wheezy sound, as if expelling air from a secret pair of gills tucked in the folds of his neck. 'It was meant to be next week! He keeps chopping and changing things.'

'So, can I take a van, sir?'

Another sigh, which she decides to take as a 'yes'.

227

The Bassett adds, 'Take Boyd and Cummings too. And make sure you get out well before the hunt starts. These aren't people you mess with. They kill wolves with their bare hands.'

'You've seen that happen, sir?'

'Of course not. I never go there during the hunts. Nobody does.'

There's a pause.

'Rhona?'

'Yes?'

'How exactly are you going to catch this girl?'

'I suppose we'll corner her somehow,' she says. 'We'll put out something to lure her in. Maybe some sweets.'

'Take something she'll really want.'

'Like what? Chocolate?'

'Yes, chocolate. Maybe a doll too.' The Bassett eyes her carefully, 'Remember, children need something to love.'

Boyd and Cummings are at their desks. She tells them that they are to come with her to collect a girl living rough on the Ardnamurchan estate. Both men look dismayed.

'I was going to do some filing,' says Cummings.

'We aren't still on that bear case, are we?' says Boyd.

She puts her finger and thumb out and measures a centimetre. 'Jim, you're this near to being reported for negligence. You never searched those woods down in that dell. I found evidence in a woodpile that even an idiot would have seen. And you never told me about McCreal and his nasty little set up. Seems all you're good for is bludgeonings.'

'None of us is perfect.' Boyd moves his tongue round the inside of his mouth and watches her steadily. 'And at least you know where you are with a good bludgeoning.'

They take some meat paste sandwiches from the

canteen, requisition a van and fill it with petrol from one of Boyd's secret stores in the basement. Boyd gets into the driver's seat and Rhona sits beside him, with Cummings in the back. They drive out onto the public road and stop at a hut by the pier, where Rhona buys doughnuts and a bag of something vaguely resembling pick n mix. Someone in a garage somewhere is still manufacturing the sweets from her childhood; pink shrimps, coconut mushrooms, gummy lizards. The shrimps are just pink commas and the coconut mushrooms don't contain any coconut, but it's still sugar.

She climbs back into the van. The doughnuts are leaking grease into their newspaper wrapping. She quickly places the package on a tarpaulin in the back. Cummings winces.

'Now we need a doll,' says Rhona.

'You're out of luck there,' says Boyd. 'The nearest shop'll be one of the foreign currency outlets in Glasgow. Unless…'

Boyd and Rhona both turn and look at Cummings.

'You've got a daughter,' she says, 'Hasn't she got dolls?'

'I don't know,' says Cummings.

Rhona has seen the photograph on his desk: a crimped Jennifer Cummings, puffed sleeves, and a bracelet of tiny silver hearts. She is definitely a girl who has dolls.

'Come on, Pinkie. I know your auntie lives in St Andrews. You must have visited the currency shops there and bought her dolls. She'll probably have a Barbie hair styling set. Or Ken and his convertible.'

'Did you have a Barbie when you were young, Inspector?' asks Boyd.

'No, I didn't. And I didn't have a childhood either. I came out of the womb in a blue babygro with a truncheon and notebook in my hand.'

'You're very humorous today,' he says flatly.

They cross the River Lochy, and at the police and army

compound, they punch in a code and the gates open. Inside, Boyd parks in front of an arc of neat red brick houses, one of which belongs to Cummings. He disappears into his house.

'You could have a nice allocation here,' says Boyd as they wait. 'The officers' quarters have Juliet balconies and a secure room.'

'I'm fine at home.' She thinks of her father. She must start looking soon. *Very soon.* A week from now and he'll be wheeling his way round the drawing room taking a marker pen to the bottles of spirits.

'How do you know about this girl?' asks Boyd.

'Last night I snuck into the estate and I saw her.'

'You *snuck in?*' For once he looks impressed. 'How did you do it?'

'I crawled through a culvert up in the braes above Strontian.'

'You should be careful.'

'Don't you worry about me,' she replies. 'I'm well acquainted with the night.'

A few minutes later, Cummings returns with a pink wardrobe in his pink hand. He is also holding a Barbie doll upside down by the legs. The nylon hair sticks out stiffly sideways at an angle.

'I'll need to have this play equipment washed down afterwards in hot soapy water,' says Cummings.

'We'll *all* need to be washed down afterwards in hot soapy water.' She leans back in the seat and closes her eyes.

They take the ferry, and pass the gates into Henderson's estate. At Strontian, they turn onto the road up into the woods. Where, she wonders, are the wolves? From inside the car the land feels neutral, unimportant – as if it were just a picture.

Finally, about two miles inland, she glimpses the river through the trees and tells Boyd to pull over. She places the food in her jacket pockets and tucks the half bottle of whisky and the Barbie into the pink wardrobe. She gently closes the passenger door behind her.

'Stay in the van for now,' she says. If only she had her gun. 'Don't get out. I'll call on the walkie if I need you. But be ready to come quickly.'

'If I'd known, I'd have brought a magazine,' says Cummings in a wronged voice.

'We're not trapping elephants. She's not going to come out if she sees two big blokes in uniform.'

'We should have brought the sniffers,' says Boyd. Cummings nods and opens his thermos of tea.

'A cup of hot tea? Is that being ready to come quickly?'

'We're only human, Inspector,' says Cummings.

'And we all like a drink, don't we?' adds Boyd.

She turns away. Dislike has so many mansions. While she despises Cummings, she feels a hot bright loathing for Boyd.

In the wood she heads towards the river, treading on soft moss which slows her down and makes her body feel oddly weightless.

The bears or the wolves could be anywhere. She picks up two fist-sized stones and holds one in each hand. When she reaches the river, she joins the path she took last night.

The deeper recesses of the wood remain completely in shadow. A crow screeches up ahead: is it alarmed by the girl? Or by some animal? Rhona walks on, and the crow moves too and keeps on calling.

She comes to the clearing where last night she momentarily lost track of the girl. Now she takes the same way between the saplings and climbs on upwards. Beyond the treeline she comes out onto the bare hillside and ahead of her is the ledge where the girl stood.

At the ledge by the entrance to the mine, she stops; it's as good a place as any to wait. She glances into the passageway, but her gun is not there.

A fire is what she needs now. She gathers up branches and dead heather and old slices of pit props left in the undergrowth. She crumples up some pages from her police notebook and places them on the ground. She balances some heather and twigs on top. As she has no paraffin, she sprinkles on some whisky instead. She lights her tiny pyre.

The flames splutter. She takes a mouthful from the bottle and blows whisky droplets on the embers. The twigs crackle back at her. She feeds more wood onto the fire.

Now she has to slow down – that's the skill behind hunting: change your pace, copy the behaviour of your prey, *become* your prey. She must act like a child – she must play.

It was Maggie who'd loved dolls. Her father joked that she'd have six children by the time she was 25. And Maggie always said, 'No, Dad. I just want the two – a boy and a girl.'

Rhona thinks, playing with dolls can't be that hard: it's all dress, undress, dress, undress... She chews a coconut mushroom and takes hold of the Barbie doll. In the wardrobe, she finds a little pair of plastic skates and slips them onto the doll's feet.

She does up the poppers on Barbie's fiddly little skating dress and glides the doll across the ground. The Barbie is pretty limber despite her lack of knee joints. She skates backwards, on one leg, does pirouettes, even the splits.

Rhona changes the doll into different outfits and keeps glancing down the hillside. No one comes.

She knows this is a long game, a waiting game. So, at

first, she isn't discouraged, and the doll's interminable wardrobe just about keeps her occupied.

Scraps of clouds drift slowly by, a smattering of rain comes and goes. She knows she isn't safe. The wolf packs have their dens in the western, wilder part of the peninsula, but they cover vast tracts of land. And won't the other bears be taking over Wilber's territory?

Where is the girl? Boyd and Cummings would, of course, have brought dogs and possibly a stun gun. Maybe this 'soft approach' is a mistake. It seemed like a good idea, but it is taking so long, so very, very long.

Someone – she is suddenly sure of this – is watching her.

It's time to change tack. She puts the doll down, impales a marshmallow on a twig and huddles into the fire. The marshmallow doesn't seem to be roasting, but then it becomes a ball of fire and drops into the embers. She tries again, loses a second marshmallow, manages to catch the third marshmallow and eat it, but burns the roof of her mouth. She gives up on the marshmallows, slumps down into her parka and shuts her eyes.

Finally, someone comes and sits down silently by her side at the fire. Rhona waits, and keeps very still. Slowly, she opens her eyes. The girl is only about a foot away – her eyes fixed on the fire, pink, scraped knees tucked up against her chest. She is dressed just as she was before – the quilted coat done up to the chin, and trainers with no socks. Her legs are covered in scratches and her hair is matted at the back, ears sticking through at the sides.

Now that she is close – just touching distance away – Rhona can see just how filthy the girl is. She can smell her too.

Under each ear the girl has a patch of torn skin that is only partly scabbed over. The wounds are fresh, symmetrical: *the mask.*

'Hello,' says Rhona.

The girl doesn't answer. But she takes Rhona's gun from her coat pocket and places it by the fire.

'My name is Rhona.'

The girl just looks at her with those big, slanting eyes. Cleaned up, she'd be pretty.

Rhona smiles, takes her gun and slips it in her pocket. She holds out the sandwiches. The girl puts the packet in her lap and stretches her hand out again. Rhona gives her the pic n mix. The girl puts the sweets in her lap too. So Rhona hands over the Barbie doll which the girl also tucks into her lap.

What else can she possibly want? On the off chance, Rhona passes her the half bottle of whisky. The girl swivels open the screw top and drinks. She doesn't cough or splutter. Tipping the bottle right back, she takes a second gulp and finishes the whisky. She screws the top back on and hands the empty bottle back to Rhona.

With drink in her, the girl seems more settled. Rhona no longer feels that at any moment she will spring up and run away.

The girl starts on the sandwiches, eating quickly and wiping her mouth with the back of her hand. Rhona passes her the second packet. The girl eats more slowly. When she has finished, she moves on to the doughnuts and finally the pick n mix. She eats the shrimps and then the coconut mushrooms and last, the gummy snakes. During all of this, she keeps the Barbie doll in her lap.

Rhona feeds some bits of pit prop into the fire. She takes off her coat and places it round the girl's shoulders, and the girl doesn't resist.

Eventually the girl's eyelids start to droop. Rhona taps

her lap. 'Put your head down,' she says softly. 'You need to rest.'

The girl doesn't respond.

Rhona sings the *Mingulay Boat Song*, then sings it a second time more softly and lets her body sway faintly from side to side with the pull of the music. The girl sways a little too and, after a while, she rests her head on Rhona's lap.

Gradually her breathing deepens. Rhona puts yet more wood on the fire and rests a hand on the girl's shoulder.

At last, when she seems to be deeply asleep, Rhona gently lifts up her light little body and, as she does so, the girl reaches up and puts her arms around Rhona's neck. Rhona smiles to herself; *this child was once loved.*

Rhona carries her new charge down the hillside and through the woods.

THE MASKS

The girl sleeps for most of the journey back to Fort William. She only opens her eyes briefly when they are on the ferry and Rhona, who is sitting in the back of the van with her, strokes the girl's hair and tells her to go back to sleep. The girl shuts her eyes again.

At the headquarters, Boyd and Cummings open the van doors. When light floods the back of the van, the girl wakes, sees the two uniformed men and cowers in the corner of the van.

'Don't worry,' says Rhona.

The girl glares at her.

Rhona leads her to the basement shower room. She immobilises the lock and stands guard in the corridor outside. Jeanette brings down some jogging bottoms and a grey jumper from lost property. Rhona opens the shower room door a fraction and slips the clothes inside. She is relieved to hear the shower working – at least the girl isn't sitting mutely on the toilet seat.

When the girl emerges from the shower room, her hair is wet and flat against her head like an otter. The outsized clothes – she's rolled up the sleeves and jogging bottoms – make her look all the more tiny and gaunt.

Rhona takes her to the Beaumont Room where she sits perched on the edge of the armchair, her hands tucked under her thighs. She is too small for the furniture as well as the clothes.

In the main office, Rhona finds Boyd at his desk.

'Inspector,' he rummages in his desk drawer, 'Laidlaw picked up a wee scally in the Marriott kitchens and guess what he had in his trouser pocket?' Boyd opens his hand to reveal a small clump of bird's claws.

'Pigeons?'

Boyd nods, 'You've started an animal amputation craze.'

She smiles wearily, 'Can you go down to the canteen and get a fish supper for the girl?'

'On my tab?'

'Charge it to expenses.'

'But she had those sandwiches, didn't she?'

'You've seen her. She's famished, for God's sake.'

'There's girls like that everywhere. This one doesn't have any lipstick on yet. That's all.'

'So, exactly how hard and shrunken is your heart? Are we talking a walnut? Or a dried pea?'

'We're not her fairy godmother.'

'For Christ's sake, she's a child. Food is the only thing we *can* give her. Now get going. And bring up two hot chocolates too.'

A few minutes later Boyd returns with a tray which Rhona takes into the Beaumont Room. Tucked under her arm, she brings the Fort William mugshot folder.

The girl devours the food. She takes a cup of hot chocolate in both hands, blows on the surface and drinks quickly with a sound like a dentist's saliva vacuum. Afterwards, without wiping her mouth, she moves on to the second cup and sucks this up just as fast.

When she has finished, Rhona opens the mugshot folder on the coffee table.

The book gives each criminal a half page – a mug shot, a profile and a full length portrait. A few of the white collar crims and some of the pimps smirk at the camera. But mostly the faces are dead-eyed and wrecked; so many staved-in cheeks, skewed mouths, odd noses. There are several amputees, mostly men with stuffed gloves for a hand. But it's the women who seem particularly desperate: miniskirts over knobbly knees, greasy, badly dyed hair, crudely crayoned-in makeup.

Rhona has looked at this folder countless times. Every couple of weeks she puts it in front of some desperado. When she comes to their accomplices, it's always the same charade:

'Do you know this man?'

A shake of the head.

'Have you ever seen him before?'

Another shake of the head.

Yet only last week she'd seen the two of them, sitting side by side outside the hospital, sucking at alcohol wipes from the dispenser.

Now she asks the girl if she knows anyone from the book and she slowly turns the pages. The girl gazes dully at the photographs.

Rhona goes on silently turning the pages. When she gets to the middle of the folder, the plastic cover is sliding about on the glass top of the coffee table. Rhona flattens out the folder and turns another page. Here is V38965. A middle-aged man: swarthy, broken nose, monobrow. In place of his right foot he has an old mahogany table leg.

The girl is suddenly distracted, and stiffens.

'Do you know him?'

But the girl doesn't answer, doesn't even nod. Her eyes are no longer on the folder. She is staring up at the wall where there's a small framed photograph taken at an awards ceremony. Men and women in evening dress are standing by a podium with a gold banner: 'Highland Heroes'. They are holding up little glass trophies to the camera.

The photograph is from the old times, when there were

still businesses that funded civic beanos and newspapers and police forces would puff the event. Standing by the mayor in his gold chain Rhona spots a slimmer version of The Bassett – grinning and combed, and wearing an unfortunate tartan waistcoat. Next to him, in full highland dress, stands a more youthful Archie Henderson.

The girl goes over to the photograph. She jabs her forefinger at Archie Henderson and keeps her eyes fixed on him.

'You know him?'

She nods. So she does understand English, thinks Rhona.

'Is he the reason you're living wild?'

The girl nods again. Her eyes are still trained on the picture, watching it warily as if Henderson could slide out of the photograph at any moment.

'What did he do to you?'

The girl doesn't respond.

'Did he hurt you?'

The girl pulls back her long hair to show the two sores behind her ears. For just a moment she looks at Rhona, then her eyes turn back to the photograph.

I should hug her. Cat would wrap her arms around the girl and stroke her hair, and lie to her that everything was going to be okay. Why can't she do it too?

'Listen, kid,' says Rhona. 'You can't live in the police station. You're going to stay with a friend of mine. She's not police. Nobody will find you there.'

The girl gives a little nod, but continues to stare at the picture.

'If you do that any longer you'll wear your eyes out.'

Rhona finds The Bassett in the observation room where he's standing in front of the two way mirror, nursing a cup of tea. His profile descends in a series of soft scoops: the eyebags, the pendulous jowls, the chins, the paunch.

'You saw that, sir? You saw that she pointed to Henderson?'

'But she's not said a word, has she?'

'She understands, though. You saw her nod.'

'How old is she? Nine? Or ten? Probably doesn't even know herself.' He pauses, 'I'd have let her be.'

He prods at the teabag, making the little brown island bob on the surface. 'What do you think she's been living off? Birds' eggs? Seaweed?'

'I think chocolate brioche and pizza.'

'*Really?*'

'She stole food from the freezers at the tower and Jim McCreal was putting out food for her.'

At the mention of McCreal The Bassett's face creases with distaste, 'So where do we stand now with all of this?'

'We question Henderson. He's the reason she was there.'

'You don't know that for sure.'

'Sir, kids don't hang out in wild countryside all on their own. They form packs and congregate in towns and cities where there's food to be found. She must have been trapped in by that fence.'

'We still have the rule of law. You can't charge a man for two little wounds on her neck.'

'Margot gave me the restraint order, so I can always bring him in on abduction of a minor. At a stretch, I could go for procurement.'

'And your victim is a mute? That isn't going to wash.'

'But he's involved somehow. Remember the fingernails and the pearls. He has let his bear eat a child and kill an adult. And I wonder about two young boys that his housekeeper is looking after. What's going to happen to them? Really, it's time we brought him in. He needs to explain what's going on.'

'He'll not want to come in. Not now. He'll be busy preparing for the hunt. Can't it wait?'

'Can't the hunt wait?'

'Not now. I've had a call. The front gates close at 10 tonight.'

'Sir, when most people are needed in a police enquiry, we don't say, "I'll put it off because it's his birthday." Or "He may be up for armed robbery but it's his daughter's school play."'

'Granted. But you don't pull the tail of a tiger.'

'Especially when you have a burrow in his lair.'

The Bassett's face hardens, 'Don't forget that I could have you transferred with a click of my fingers.'

'But sir, it's still not normal.'

'I know it might not *seem* normal. But this is the West Highlands."

'That doesn't change anything.'

'Just go if you have to,' he says wearily. 'She's your requisition order so it's your business. But take Boyd with you. And get a move on – they'll be closing the gates soon.'

Back at her desk, Rhona calls Cat. 'I need a favour.'

'Uh-huh.'

'Can you look after a child for me?'

'Who've you found? Is it one of my Moldavians?'

'No. It's that girl – the one that McCreal had been making a form from.'

Cat swears under her breath, 'What am I supposed to do with her?'

'Feed her. Keep her safe. Care for her.' Rhona avoids the word 'love'.

'For how long?'

'Maybe just for a few days. Maybe forever.'

There's silence on the line.

'You always wanted a child,' adds Rhona.

'A bit of background might be helpful. What state is she in? Who is she?'

'We don't know yet. She's not talking.'

'Roo, you're asking an awful lot.'

'I know, but there's not much time. Yes or no?'

'And if I say "no"?'

'Laidlaw will have to take her to the Willies' seminary at Fassolich.'

'Then *yes*,' says Cat in a small, sullen voice.

After the call, Rhona arranges for Cat to collect the girl who will, in the meantime, be looked after by Jeanette who takes her knitting up to the Beaumont Room.

The rest of the office is packing up for the day and Boyd is closing down his computer. Remembering Henderson's dogs, Rhona takes two stun batons from her drawer. She stops by Boyd's desk.

'We have a job to do.' She hands him a stun baton.

'I was about to leave.'

'I need you. Get your little kitten heels down to the car park.'

'I'm not paid overtime.'

'The Bassett says you're to come with me. We're paying a visit to Archie Henderson.'

Boyd looks shocked. 'With batons? Are you going to string him up like a veal calf?'

'We're just going to bring him in for a few questions.'

'He won't want to come,' says Boyd. 'Not now.'

'Well, if push comes to shove...' she shrugs.

'You're not *arresting* him?'

Rhona gives him a flat smile.

BOYD

They arrive at the checkpoint to Henderson's reserve at 7 p.m. and the guard opens the gate but also comes out of his egg-shaped booth, gestures to his watch and holds up three fingers for the three hours before the gates close for the hunt.

Rhona nods to him and jerks the car forward. She jumps up through the gears: first to third to fifth. The chassis quivers, so she presses down harder on the accelerator. When she gets up to 70 mph the engine rights itself and the motion of the car smooths out. Never let yourself slow down, she thinks, never relax or you'll fall apart.

Boyd, quieter than usual, grips his seat belt.

The neatly boarded-up houses of Strontian whisk by. She remembers Peepers saying, 'not the boarded-up houses'. Why?

At Resipole Rhona takes the humpback bridge too fast and by the time she sees Arthur's green convertible coming up from the other side, she can't stop. She watches dispassionately as the two cars collide and Boyd's arms reach out for the dashboard. The impact jolts them both up into the air. The seat belt tightens across her chest and pulls her back down again.

The cars have stopped. Boyd sits tight-lipped, hunkered into himself. She breathes out slowly. No injuries. It isn't too bad – the airbags haven't even been activated

But Arthur's old convertible is a wreck; the bonnet is scrunched up, and steam rises from the buckled metal.

Zoë, carrying a duffel bag, gets out of the driver's seat and walks towards them.

'She hasn't even bothered to look at her own car,' murmurs Boyd.

Zoë comes to Rhona's window. 'Can you give me a lift to Fort William?'

'We've got a visit to make first. You can come with us or you can walk to Strontian.'

'I'm not walking.'

'Then get in. Quick!'

Zoë climbs into the back seat. She takes off her woolly hat and tilts her head back against the seat.

Rhona starts the engine again and drives steadily forward, ploughing the convertible back down the bridge and into the side ditch. Boyd opens a tube of mints and passes it round.

'You seem very eager to get away,' says Rhona. She takes six mints and crunches through them – she has never had the patience to suck.

'I am,' replies Zoë.

Now clear of the wreck, Rhona slams down on the accelerator.

'Where are we going?'

'Later. Got to concentrate,' says Rhona as the car jerks forward. Boyd remains silent.

The road weaves between the trees and the banks of Loch Sunart. She goes faster. That is the best thing the police ever taught her – how to drive a winding road at 70 miles an hour. Every few bends she feels Boyd's hand staying her arm. But she doesn't slow down.

She roars up the last hill to Glenborrodale House and turns in through the great stone columns. The gates are already open; *we're expected.*

'Oh God!' says Zoë. "You can't go in there!'

244

They both ignore her.

Boyd turns to Rhona, 'I'll bring the batons in for you. That'll keep your hands free.'

'Thanks, Jim,' she says.

The grounds of the house seem deserted. Rhona parks up by the front steps and, from the glove pocket, she takes her gun and puts it in her pocket. She and Boyd get out of the car.

'Don't leave me here on my own!' says Zoë.

'Then come with us.' says Rhona.

'We shouldn't go in. It's crazy!"

'Don't worry,' says Rhona. 'This is part of a police enquiry. You'll be fine.'

They walk up the steps, Boyd and Rhona, side by side, and Zoë following behind.

A pale-eyed man with a military bearing opens the front door before they have knocked.

'Is Mr Henderson here?' asks Rhona.

The man nods. He is dressed in a green fleece with the Henderson estate logo. On his hip, his corduroys stretch over a pocket gun in a holster and make a neat mound, like an extra groin.

Rhona and Zoë walk into the hall, followed by Boyd who is carrying the two batons.

'You must be one of Mr Henderson's men?' With McCreal, that makes two people missing from Matt's list.

The man doesn't reply. He is alert, watchful.

'Is he coming?' she asks.

The man gives another nod.

At last Henderson emerges from a servant's door under the stairs. His dogs pour into the hallway after him.

'Thank you, Kemp,' he says. The man in the fleece steps

back to the wall, where he stands with his legs apart, his arms behind his back.

'Good evening. How can I help you?' Henderson smiles at Rhona. He gives smaller smiles of acknowledgement to Zoë and then to Boyd.

'Mr Henderson, we'd like you to answer some questions back at the station,' says Rhona.

Zoë gives a gasp.

Henderson seems unsurprised, 'This isn't the *best* time. We're a little bit busy, as you know. The hunt is about to begin.'

Who told him? Rhona eyes up the dogs and Kemp. She'll probably lose in any show of force.

'Perhaps I could come later?' he says. 'I'll need to be in Fort William next week.'

'No,' she says. 'It'll have to be now.'

'I'm not so sure about that.' Henderson crosses his arms and this seems to be a signal, for the dogs move forward.

The grey-muzzled bitch is now behind Rhona, blocking off the front door. With one leap the dog could pull her down.

'I could arrest you for abduction and false imprisonment. We have picked up a minor on your land. She was in a terrible state.'

'This estate is 125 square miles. I can't be held responsible for every…' He pauses, looking for the word. 'For every *misdemeanor* that happens here.'

'Put off the hunt. You have to come with us.'

As she speaks, Henderson is flexing his fingers. The youngest, scrawniest dog bares its teeth.

'That's just not going to happen.' Henderson steps forward suddenly and grabs her wrist, pulling her arm up behind her back. With his free hand, he takes the gun from her pocket and throws it onto the stairs behind him.

She is pinioned. 'Boyd!' she cries. But he doesn't come to her aid. Instead, she watches in cold horror as the sergeant walks slowly forward and lays the stun batons down on the step beside her gun.

For a moment the shock leaves her speechless.

'You always were ambitious,' she says coldy.

Boyd cocks his head at her and grins.

With his free hand Henderson is patting at her body, searching for something. He plunges into her trouser pocket and removes her phone. Kemp, meanwhile, has taken Zoë's mobile.

'Boys, sort out her car,' says Henderson. 'And bring in the tray.'

Kemp and Boyd walk together to the back of the hall where a door in the paneling leads into a pale green corridor. As the door swings shut, Rhona catches a last glimpse of the backs of the two men. Both are walking at ease, side by side like colleagues, like friends.

Henderson lets go of her wrist.

Just for a moment Rhona wonders if she could do something. If she dived round him, maybe she could get to the stairs and grab the gun.

'Don't even think about it.' Henderson's eyes flick to the dogs.

'She's right about the girl,' says Zoë in a trembling voice. 'Johnnie and I saw her on the causeway. She was half starved.'

Henderson raises his eyebrows, 'Young lady, is this how you repay my hospitality? I thought you were better brought up.'

He draws back a pace, rests his hand on his chin and surveys Rhona and Zoë.

'You're both so young,' he says. 'So very young.'

Kemp and Boyd return. Kemp is carrying a silver tray.

'I've got a present for you.' Henderson beckons to Kemp who holds the tray out to them.

'Please,' says Henderson. 'Kindly take your pick.'

On the tray lie half a dozen animal and bird masks with the same blue lining as the mask Rhona found down the mine. There's a pine marten, a fawn, a hare with its ears tucked back, a cock pheasant, a couple of ducks.

Zoë lets out a whimper.

The truth, just like the masks, is neatly set out before her.

'Why these?' Rhona says, playing for time, hoping against hope that the masks might not be what they seemed.

'They're for the hunt,' replies Henderson blandly. He looks at Zoë, 'Do you want to explain to this clever detective. Or shall I?'

'It's *us* they'll hunt,' says Zoë.

'Perhaps it isn't quite what you expected,' says Henderson. 'It's wolves that do the hunting. And the wolves are men, of course. My clients dressed as wolves.' Henderson pauses, 'And Rhona, it's only fair. If you take away one of my players, you must provide a replacement. Or, better still, *replacements*. We were already short of prey.'

He nods to Kemp who edges the tray closer to them.

'Fine work, aren't they? Mrs Collins is a consummate craftswoman. Do please take one.'

Rhona doesn't move. Zoë is frozen too.

Then Kemp speaks: 'I don't know which ones will be big enough, sir. The pine marten has some stretch in it.'

Henderson puts the pine marten into Rhona's hand. The fur is slippery and soft.

He hands the fawn mask to Zoë who takes it with a shaky hand.

'Now, do please try your masks on,' says Henderson.

Rhona still doesn't move.

'Put them on!' says Henderson in the voice he uses with his dogs.

Zoë puts on her fawn mask.

'Rhona!' says Henderson.

Rhona squeezes the mask between her fingers and feels the tiny nub of a silicon chip tucked into the lining. She drops the mask.

'Do I have to?' Henderson brings out a pistol from his waistcoat and points it at Rhona's chest. 'Now, please. Let's not make this unpleasant.'

She stares at the gun and stands rigid, not moving at all until Kemp grabs her arms and pulls her down onto her knees. Boyd forces the mask onto her head.

She tries to shake it off, but the mask is a tight fit, and Boyd takes hold of the stem of her neck to keep her still.

She looks up. Henderson has his head at a slight tilt, admiring them as if they were women in new dresses. He says kindly, 'It suits you, Zoë. You're so fine boned, just like a fawn. Now all we have to do is sew you both in.'

He walks over to the wall and pushes the service button.

Mrs Collins appears immediately from the door under the stairs. Her face is flushed and she is carrying a small straw workbasket. She doesn't falter and walks straight across the hall and sets the basket down on the side table by the gong.

She takes out a bottle of spray from her tabard and approaches Zoë, 'Now, madam, if you could just lift up the ear flaps on your mask. You'll feel a moment of coldness. That's all.'

Zoë lifts the flaps and Mrs Collins sprays the patches of skin under her ears. Rhona can picture the identically placed sores on the girl's neck.

Mrs Collins then comes over to Rhona, avoiding her

eyes. Henderson still has his pistol pointing at her, 'It's just a local anaesthetic. We're not brutes.'

Boyd, with his hand clamped on her neck, pulls her to her feet. He lifts up the flaps of the mask and she shuts her eyes. She can smell the biscuity warmth of Mrs Collins and feels two short bursts of cold spray just below her ears.

'Now, madam,' Mrs Collins turns to Zoë. 'What colour of thread would you like? I know the children normally like to choose.'

'I don't care,' whispers Zoë.

Mrs Collins searches in her basket. 'Shall we say brown then?'

Zoë nods and Mrs Collins threads a curved leatherwork needle.

'Can you feel this?' Mrs Collins flicks her middle finger against the wet patch on Zoë's neck.

Zoë shakes her head. Mrs Collins smiles to herself and starts sewing. She is quick and nimble; just a few stitches on each side then she gives the fawn mask a tug to check that it is firmly in place. Zoë waits impassively, like a horse at the blacksmiths.

Then Mrs Collins says, 'Miss Ballantyne, what colour of thread would you like?'

'I don't give a fuck,' says Rhona.

Mrs Collins looks shocked.

'Ignore her, Marie.' Henderson gives Rhona a reproachful glance.

Rhona knows the needle is going in, but there's no pain.

When Mrs Collins has finished and snipped the thread, Boyd lets go of Rhona.

'Shall I, Mr Henderson?' asks Mrs Collins coyly.

'Why not?' he replies with a smile.

She takes out a paper bag from her tabard pocket, opens it and offers it to Rhona.

The sherbet lemons. Rhona shakes her head.

Mrs Collins offers the bag to Zoë, who refuses too.

'Do have one,' says Henderson. 'It's better if you get into the spirit of things. After all, we *are* playing a game.'

'Games are meant to be voluntary,' says Rhona.

'All of life is a series of games – you know that as well as I do. And nobody plays more games than the police. You've been on my tail for days now and you always would've nailed me sooner or later. So, I'm merely turning the tables. Now it's your turn to be hunted.'

'One more thing.' He puts his gun away and pauses. Rhona waits; she has to give him credit for his sense of theatre.

'We are proper sportsmen,' he says. 'We always give our prey a fighting chance. Don't we, Kemp?'

'Yes, sir.'

'My staff have seen to your car. You have two litres left in the tank. That should get you at least past Salen.'

'Who are the hunters?' she asks.

'You'll see soon enough. We have other prey too. A couple of young squirrels are out near Acharacle.'

'*Squirrels?*' Rhona is bemused.

'We're doing them a kindness, really,' replies Henderson. 'There are no long term prospects for these boys. And while they're here, they have an excellent quality of life and Mrs Collins gets their nutritrion up to scratch. Plenty of good food and fun and fresh air. She even reads *The Railway Children* to them at night. Don't you, Marie?'

Mrs Collins gives him a happy smile.

'So you fatten them up for the hunt?' asks Rhona.

Henderson shakes his head as if the question were too vulgar to merit an answer. 'Ask yourself this, Rhona. A month of perfect life and then a quick, thrilling death? Or just years and years of malnutrition and drudgery?'

It's a rhetorical question – she doesn't reply.

Henderson continues in the same reasonable tone, 'All in all, it's pretty fair. We like to keep things equal – four hunters, and so four prey. The siren will go off at ten o'clock. You'll know when it happens. Then you have 48 hours.'

'What happens when we're caught?'

'*When*?" he looks at her indulgently. 'You always have a chance, Rhona. Why not say *if*?'

'*If,*' she says wearily.

'Well, it depends. Some kill. Others wound – they're the ones that like to play with their prey.' He pauses, gives her a heavy-lidded look and adds, '*Then,* they kill.'

'And there are the wild animals out there too,' Zoë's voice is nearly a whisper.

'Quite right,' says Henderson. 'And that does make it a bit of an obstacle course.'

'I want my phone back.' She can see it lying on the bottom step of the stairs. *There's no harm in trying.*

'Dear girl, you won't need it, and we do.'

'Why do *you* need it?'

'For *eventualities.*'

He'll already have the cover-up planned.

'I'm interested. What do you have in mind for me?'

He shakes his head, 'You should get going now. You haven't long.'

Rhona stares at the hall. Everyone seems in their place, very still and outlined in the evening light. There is Henderson with the grand staircase lit by the red and blue panels of glass on the landing window behind him, Kemp is by the wall with Boyd at his side, Mrs Collins is still holding the paper bag of sherbet lemons in her hand. The dogs are arranged artfully around her and Zoë. Rhona stares down at Henderson's long boney shins in their

Shetland socks, his brogues of brown and cream leather with little holes arranged in decorative swirls across the uppers. She can hear her own heart beating.

Henderson's voice comes to her from far away. 'Get going! What are you waiting for? Surely you're not expecting sandwiches?'

THE WOODS

When Rhona starts the engine, the petrol warning light flashes. The clock on the dashboard says 8.45; they have an hour and a quarter until the hunt begins. She sets off in a whirl of gravel and races down the drive, scraping the undercarriage over the speed bumps.

She doesn't stop at the gate, but slams on the horn and swerves out onto the main road.

'How much do you know?'

'Nothing very useful,' says Zoë. 'Just that the hunters must be mad psychopaths. Part of some club.'

Rhona keeps her eyes on the road.

The mask is hot. Every time she moves her head the stitching pulls.

She stops the car abruptly at a humpback bridge on the far side of Glenborrodale.

'The masks are microchipped. We have to get them off,' says Rhona. 'You got a knife?'

Zoë shakes her head.

Rhona scrabbles in the glove pocket, but there's nothing sharp that would do. She tries to unpick the stitching on Zoë's ear flap with her fingers, but Mrs Collins' needlework is impossibly tight. When Rhona lifts up the side of the mask, Zoë gives a yell of pain – the anaesthetic is wearing off.

'It's just stitching. Let me try mine first,' says Rhona.

She holds down the skin under her left ear, takes hold of the earflap of the mask, and gives a brutal tug. A red starfish of pain tears into the side of her head. Quickly – or she'll never do it – she rips off the other side of the mask.

Blood pours warmly down the sides of her neck. She uses the mask to staunch the wounds, and soon it is covered in blood and resembles a furry sanitary pad. She throws it out of the window.

Zoë clenches her teeth and rips her mask off too. She gives a little grunt as each side comes free and then she too wipes up the rivulets of blood with her mask.

'You okay? We've got to hurry.'

Zoë nods and also throws her mask out.

Rhona sets off again. She drives at a crazy speed, swearing under her breath and thinking of the hunters, of what might happen if they are caught, of Jim McCreal's taxidermy forms. Faster, faster, faster, she tells herself.

They pass the empty houses at Resipole and the beach where Henderson gave her the stone with the vein of quartz. She skirts round the wreck of Arthur's convertible and flies over the humpback bridge. She is riding the corners like a racing driver, breaking sharp and hard just as she comes into the bend, and only turning the steering wheel at the very last moment. Each time, the car just, only just, holds the road.

Zoë is silent, her body swaying with the movement of the car. Eventually, when they come to a long straight stretch of road, she asks in a small voice, 'Do you think they're really going to kill us?'

'It's what happens *before* they kill us that worries me.'

Zoë gives a long sniff, 'It doesn't matter how fast you drive now. He'll have the checkpoint closed already.'

'I know that. But there's another way out.'

And she tells Zoë about the culvert.

The car runs out of petrol a couple of miles beyond

Salen. Rhona pulls into the verge. She opens the glove compartment and takes out the skeleton keys, the remaining four tubes of mints and the torch, stuffing them all into her jacket pockets. The clock on the dashboard says 9.20. That leaves them just 40 minutes to get to the culvert.

They set off running along the road. The sky and the mountains are darkening, the trees arch high above them and the rocks on the lochside are dipped in black shadow. All she can hear is her own panting breath and their feet hitting the ground.

They aren't pacing themselves; Rhona is running at full tilt; running through the damp, darkening air, and through the pain from her tender ankle. She must not stop. She knows that if she can't keep running she might as well be dead.

The road rises and dips and levels out and rises again. Passing earlier in the car, she barely registered these differences. But now every tiny gradient counts. Running uphill, her whole body strains as if harnessed to a huge boulder. And downhill is all release, with her legs gaining speed, her feet thumping on the road.

Halfway up a slope she does stop. She is bent double and fighting for air. Her knees shake.

Zoë is bent over too. 'I can't do this!' she gasps.

'You have to,' is all that Rhona can say.

They run on, and are reaching the outskirts of Strontian when she hears a faint thrumming. At first she assumes it's just the blood pounding in her ears and she keeps on running. But the noise grows louder, and then she sees red lights in the western sky.

They crouch behind the garden wall of an abandoned house and wait. Three helicopters are travelling westwards in a V formation. Where are they going? She tries to remember the aerial map in the office.

'There's a helipad at Salen,' says Zoë. 'And another one near the tower. How far is it to the culvert?'

'A mile and a half, maybe two.'

When the helicopters have gone, they run on. At Strontian, they take the turning off towards the mines. The road swerves to go up a hill, but they carry straight on, passing under a stone archway and into a wood of small, gnarled oaks.

Zoë is still close behind her, sometimes treading on her heels. Rhona hears another helicopter in the distance. Maybe the hunters are being dropped off across the peninsula.

At a turning in the path, she stops. She can't be sure in the poor light, but something has just moved, something to the side of the path and hidden in shade.

She shines the torch in an arc across the trees. Hanging from a branch, is a dead hare with a snare still round its neck.

'Matt often hangs up game,' says Zoë. 'It's to get the big predators moving around and to stop them from just lurking by the pellet dispensers.'

'Look!'

Rhona shines the torch again; there's a cluster of brown feathers on the hare's belly. The feathers shift, and an owl looks up from its feeding and stares at them. A moment later, it flies at them like a black bolt. In a wingbeat, it's gone, soaring up into the trees.

The pause has given them back their breath. Now they sprint on over ground blanketed in soft moss. Everything – rocks, branches, tree stumps – is covered in the moss, as if it were poured from some giant cauldron. Die here, Rhona thinks, and the moss would cover every trace of them and seal up their eyes and mouths.

She shakes off the thought. She mustn't think, mustn't think *ever*. Just run.

The path winds uphill. Their footfall is soft, almost soundless. The hunters' footsteps will be just as muffled too. And there is no sound of the river.

They are still climbing the slope when a hunting horn rings out. The sound, two notes played long and rising, echoes through the wood. It seems to come from far away to the west. *Our angels of death.*

'That's the start of the hunt,' says Rhona.

They fight their way through loops of bramble, the thorns tugging at their clothes. Finally they come to the river, and take the broad path that Rhona limped along last night on her way to the culvert. This is the last lap of their journey and the going is easy. *Too easy.*

When they turn a corner, she sees the fence up ahead in the twilight. Beyond lies the moor; in a few minutes they will be safe. Rhona stops. She looks out over the fence. There's no wind now, but one big gorse bush moves slightly.

She crouches behind a rock, pulling Zoë off the path after her. She watches the bush and waits. A minute passes and the memory of old Signora Riccone, the best store detective in Rome, comes back to her. The signora used to stay out on the pavement and pretend to be window shopping. Shoplifters never expected the store detectives to be watching from *outside.*

'What's up?' hisses Zoë.

'Wait!'

They wait. On the far side of the fence the land is completely still, as if holding its breath.

'Let's go,' hisses Zoë.

'I saw something move,' whispers Rhona and points. 'Over there, beyond the fence.'

'Deer.'

'Deer don't hide. It's something hiding. *Someone* hiding'.

'You're just imagining things. We're so strung out.'

'No. I saw it. And I can feel it too.'

Of course, Boyd will have told Henderson. She was a fool ever to mention that culvert.

'But the hunt is only on the reserve.'

'You think they care about that?'

A glimmer of light comes from behind the big gorse bush. She hears Zoë take a sharp inbreath – she has seen it too.

'Listen,' whispers Rhona. 'We creep back up the path a bit. Then we run like hell. There may be hunters coming from this side too. It could be a pincer operation.'

'Where do we go? There's no way out now.'

'We'll do what the girl did,' says Rhona. 'We'll go down the mines.'

THE MINES

Rhona and Zoë creep back up the path and then break into a run. Somewhere in the wood, they come off the path and find themselves out on the bare hillside above the trees.

The way gets steeper and rockier and now they are scrambling. Rhona heaves herself over a big boulder and comes to a dark gap between the rocks, the entrance supported above by a wooden lintel. She plunges in and Zoë follows her.

They are in a low-roofed tunnel, winding into the hillside. Rhona crawls along, her hands and knees on wet grit. She holds the torch in her mouth and this creates a circle of light to her side. Every couple of metres she passes wooden pit props – this is definitely part of the mines.

When she squirms round a corner she feels a new, colder draught. She stops, takes the torch in her hand and shines it in front of her – there is a hole so deep that the light vanishes in the darkness. She moves the torch across the walls of the shaft and sees a staircase of metal rungs stapled into the wall directly beneath her.

'Why've you stopped?' asks Zoë.

'We've come to a hole. There are steps down the side,' Rhona's voice reverberates against the walls.

She puts the torch back in her mouth, turns round, lies on her stomach and lowers herself into the hole. Her feet find the first rung and she takes a few steps down and stops. She waits until Zoë's legs appear, disembodied in the darkness. Rhona guides Zoë's feet to the rungs and they begin the long descent down the throat of the mine.

At the bottom of the shaft they come into a bigger, broader tunnel heading into the mountain. Stooping, they feel their way forward. After yesterday's fall, Rhona is careful. She has one hand resting on the wall of the tunnel and she tests out each foothold, always expecting the ground to give way beneath her.

The darkness here is absolute. If the torch gives out they have nothing and will be helpless. If the roof falls in then it's a living burial, a slow dark death. So it is good to have Zoë at her side muttering 'fuck, fuck, fuck'.

The tunnel is always changing. They squeeze through a crevice, then the space widens out, narrows again, tilts downhill and then upwards. At one point they are in a vast cavern as high and broad as a church, but then the air thickens and wet walls close in around them and they come down into a close, moist passage with a string of shallow puddles. When she hears a faint splash to the side, she shines the torch and Zoë gives a yelp as something small and white dives away into the darkness.

'What was that?' says Rhona.

'Dunno. A corpse gnawer.'

After the puddles, the tunnel heads gradually uphill. They walk along a much dryer passageway and Rhona is relieved to see a faint light up ahead. A few metres further on, the tunnel opens out into a low cavern, colonnaded with pit props. Everywhere there's clutter from the mines, piles of old tools, bent props, old ladders.

Moonlight shines in from a ventilation shaft near the roof of the cave and she sees a square of summer night sky; they have come out surprisingly near the surface. By the opening stand a couple of old wooden crates someone has used to hoist themselves up into the shaft. She feels that nobody could have followed them through every twist of these tunnels. She says, 'We are safe here for a while. And if they do come, at least we'll have an escape route.'

But Zoë isn't listening. She's crouching down at the back of the chamber. 'Look! There's some kind of nest here.'

Rhona walks over to her. The nest is a mass of shredded plastic – torn up shopping bags, bin liners, bubble wrap. This was once someone's bed, and the bedside light is a candle stub stuck to an old, imported pizza box. There are also some pieces of clothing, dried curls of orange peel, a plastic beaker, a couple of puzzle books. And permeating everything is a salty, unwashed body smell – the same smell that the girl had.

Zoë points to a tartan scarf. 'This was Rachel's. That girl must have nicked it.'

'Come on, let's get some rest,' Rhona spreads out a bin liner and sits down on it. She leans back against a boulder. If she shuts her eyes now she will be asleep in seconds. She want to remove the bandage on her ankle, but decides not to; she needs to be ready for whatever happens.

'Shouldn't we keep going?' Zoë hovers above her. 'It's as if we are just waiting for them to find us.'

'For God's sake, where can we go? It's pitch dark outside. This is the safest place we've found so far, so we might as well hole up for the night.'

'But…'

'Think of it this way,' says Rhona. 'We're both exhausted and we won't find anywhere safer tonight. Anyway, they'll find us sooner or later. But the longer we stay alive, the harder it'll be for Henderson to explain away our deaths.'

Zoë sits down at her side and wraps a length of plastic sheeting over her shoulders as if it were a blanket.

Rhona stares at the miserable pile of rags. 'At least we got her out. She's safe now. She's with a friend of mine.'

'Thank God for that,' Zoë pulls out some bubble wrap and places it over her legs. 'The girl changed everything for me.'

'Yeah?'

'When we first came here, I thought finally we were somewhere completely free and wild and kind of wonderful. You know, trees everywhere. Clean water. Money no object. All the food you wanted from the currency stores, brought in by Matt.'

'So what happened?'

'This scally girl showed up.'

There's a full bottle of water by the nest. Zoë opens it, wipes the top carefully and drinks, 'I thought the centre of the earth was meant to be molten? It's freezing here.'

'When did you find out about her?' Rhona takes the bottle. If only she had brought some whisky. She opens a tube of mints, but the sweets are a poor substitute.

'At first I didn't see her – things kept vanishing from the kitchen and I thought it must be some animal. I dunno – rats? Or a squirrel? But stuff went from the freezer too, so it had to be a person. And then there was that other thing of being *watched*. You might not believe in God, or elves, or whatever. But absolutely everybody, even the super, super dumb, knows that prickly feeling of being watched.'

'So you never saw her?'

'I caught a glimpse of her a couple of times. And then, one day, I was sitting on the divan by the window and I saw her properly. She was running over the causeway, back towards the woods. She was so small and pathetic-looking, in her little brown coat. She had two boxes of our pizzas under her arm. I called the others to the window, so they all saw her. But – get this – Will and Arthur were so *unsurprised!* Will did his dreamy-eyed thing and then you never know what he's thinking. And Arthur just reacted as if what I was showing him was basically a bit vulgar. Bothering to notice the girl made *me* vulgar. I was drawing him down to a lower level of being – as if I had made a crude joke.'

'So for him this was just another feral child?'

'I know they're everywhere, but you don't expect to find one *here*. Not on the estate. Not in our little Eden. That was a shock!'

'And you didn't think it could just have been a local kid messing about?'

'Not with that fence – how could she have got in? And certainly not with Archie Henderson prowling around. He's *such* a control freak. Haven't you noticed? The reserve may seem all green and wild, but it's all very carefully managed. There's not a blade of grass out of place. And it's all super tasteful. I sometimes think it's a bit surprising the wolves don't have central partings and trimmed claws. People don't just turn up here *by accident.*

'I couldn't work it out. Johnnie was worried about her too. He asked Arthur but didn't get much of an answer. We didn't know how she could survive on the reserve. It sort of gnawed away at me – made me begin to doubt everything. I suppose it was like when I got to St Andrews. I had all these grand ideas about becoming a doctor and saving lives. I was a sucker for that kind of thing and I'd spent all my summer holidays volunteering in a private clinic near home. But when I did my first uni placement, I saw how different things really were. I realised the public hospitals don't have proper drugs. You know there's no tamoxifen within 50 miles of Dundee?'

'I thought you'd be doing an arts subject.'

Zoë gives a little laugh, 'Can't afford to. I'll have to earn a living.'

Rhona sees that there are no signs of any fire – the girl must have eaten the pizzas raw. 'I wish I'd brought a hip flask. It would have warmed us up.'

'I wish you had too,' says Zoë. 'You always been a drinker?'

'Oh, yes. But you and I, we drink differently.'

'How do you mean?'

'You drink for adventure. I don't know – perhaps to access some other reality.'

'And you?'

'I just drink,' says Rhona.

Zoë laughs. Her hand reaches out to take Rachel's old scarf, and Rhona sees marks on the underside of her forearm. She grabs Zoë's other wrist, and pulls the arm towards her and shines the torchlight on her. All the way up to the elbow there's a cat's cradle of scars. Some of the cuts are deep, the skin rucked and puckered. Some are recent and still red.

'Scars,' Zoë shrugs.

Rhona can't count them. Hundreds of scars. 'Why?'

'I had stuff going on at home.'

'What stuff?' Rhona is still holding Zoë's left arm.

'My dad left. He had an affair, and then he left. I started cutting a few weeks after that. And then it just became a thing I did.'

'Oh Zoë!'

'I didn't ask for your sympathy,' she says coldly.

She's like me, thinks Rhona. Her rage is her armour.

Zoë pulls her arm free. 'I don't hide them, except when I'm in the hospital. I like the way the old scars have this sheen to them. It's a bit like wearing pearls.'

She reaches over and turns off the torch, 'When I went

to the Summer Ball last year, I wore a sleeveless jumpsuit. My scars are a sort of heraldry – they're my heritage. Rachel had a title and Will has that coat of arms with the eagle's head. But I've got *scars*.'

'And Arthur? What does he have?'

'Arthur's like me. He's a nobody.' Zoë pauses. 'And like all nobodies, he has to work all the harder.'

'What do you mean by that?'

'He's a puppet master really. He's full of tricks.'

'Tricks?' Rhona repeats in an undertone.

'You don't want to know. You really don't.'

'What happened between Arthur and you?'

'I found out what he was doing. I caught him out.'

'Caught him out at *what*?'

'We drew lots, you know, before Rachel died. Arthur brought out a pack and shuffled the cards and we all took one. We turned them over and Rachel got the Queen of Spades.'

'That's the card Johnnie picked too, isn't it?'

'Yes. And I'd always been suspicious. I felt somehow that I could predict who would go next. I just kind of *knew*.'

Rhona says carefully, 'Are you telling me that this was a suicide pact? That one of you was always going to jump?'

Zoë turns her head away.

'You might as well tell me. We're unlikely to survive this and nothing matters much any more.'

'At the time it didn't seem to matter either,' says Zoë mildly.

'How do you mean?' asks Rhona.

'We'd had this really special evening. We knew that later we would draw lots, but before that we would have a last time together. We sat on the roof. We were there all evening. We had had a lot to drink – I mean *a lot!* But it didn't seem to make us drunk – it just intensified

266

everything. I remember just feeling incredibly happy and clear-headed. At one point, I got the telescope and I looked down on the Scots pines and there, below me, was a little chaffinch with its feathers all fluffed up. And in my mind I could touch it, I could feel the softness of its feathers and hear the tiny beat of its heart.'

'And what about the others? What did they do?'

'Rachel and Arthur played chess. Rachel was losing and whenever one of her pieces was taken, or she took one of Arthur's, she flung it over the battlements. 'Here goes a castle!' she'd cry, or, 'Bye, bye, bishop!'

'Will and I just lay about on these big striped cushions. We had blankets as well. And it was one of those long dusks when the clouds are stacked up, dark underneath but shining above, with many different layers. You could see whole worlds there: palaces and temples and factories and shopping malls. I felt more content and excited by the world than I have since I was a kid, playing out on the street in the summer. There we were, on our cushions, staring up at the sky. Will pointed up to where a plane must have passed because there was a white line, like a seam, through the blue. He said, "If you peel back the sky, you'll come to the real world of dreams." And suddenly I could imagine that peeling back, and the world felt like a much greater, brighter place. He must have noticed some change in me – for he slipped his hand into mine.'

'Is Will some kind of a prophet to you?' Rhona glances at her.

'I still believe he's someone very, very special. He sees the world differently from you and me. He can make you see things and feel things that no one else can. We were always a bit in love with him, and kind of fighting over him.'

'So, what happened that night? Tell me, we've got all the time in the world.'

'It grew dark and Rachel and I brought up Tillie lamps and we laid them on the flagstones. Hundreds of moths – great big furry ones and tiny clothes moths – came to the lights and fluttered round them and of course they got too near the flames and were frazzled. We ate the beef and drank tequila and nobody said anything about the moths – it was too obvious. But we all watched them. And Will said he thought no creature was more beautiful, or more speckled. Why hadn't Gerald Manley Hopkins written about moths? And then Arthur said, surely Kafka should have had his character turn into a moth, not a beetle? A moth would have been more existential.'

Zoë's breathing is heavier now. But Rhona still says nothing and lets her talk on.

'You've got to remember how much we'd had to drink. This was a big night for us. Everything was on a knife edge. Time went really slow, like it had kind of darkened and softened, and then finally, at about eleven thirty, we went downstairs. We lit the stove and drank some black coffee. Arthur brought out the cards and at midnight we drew lots. Arthur presented the hand of cards to each of us in turn. He did it in a way that made one card stand out in the middle, one card that was easier to take than the others. He started with me – and I didn't take that card but one more to the side, because I already had a sense that things weren't what they seemed. Then it was Will's go, then Rachel's turn and Arthur took the last card. We didn't look at our cards until midnight chimed on the big clock.

'Rachel put her card straight down on the table, face up. And of course it was the Queen of Spades, the Black Maria. I remember – it's such a stupid thought – but I noticed that it was one of those packs where all the court cards are frowning. Rachel looked at the ceiling and then she said quietly, "I knew it was going to be me."'

'What did you do then? How did you comfort her?'

"I didn't say anything – I just couldn't. She went upstairs. She said she wanted a bit of time on her own. And she also said she wanted to go to the bathroom. "I have to have a shit. I want to be nice and clean for the pathologist." That is exactly what she said. She always did have this barbed, ironic take on life. It was something I really liked about her.

'So the rest of us stayed downstairs. Nobody said anything and we drank some more coffee. Eventually Arthur said, "I'll go and get her." But then they didn't come back down. And after a while I went upstairs. She had changed out of her jeans into one of her silk dresses. And she had her poncho on top. Arthur was holding her in his arms and I realised then, from just how he was holding her, that at some point they must have been lovers. That kind of fits, doesn't it? I couldn't hear what she said – her face was buried in his chest. And he was talking to her, stroking her hair. I heard him say very softly, "We'll be with you soon. So soon." Then he raised his head and gave me one of his turn-you-to-stone looks. So I quickly went back downstairs.

'A few minutes later they came down together. He was holding her hand. Then we drove to the lighthouse. It was all very strange. I was in the seat behind her. Arthur let her sit in the front, which is normally where Will sits – he gets car sick. So, I was directly behind her and I remember looking at her hair. She always had this fantastic dark, shiny hair. And as we were driving along, I was thinking. "Her hair is already dead. The rest of her will follow." It was an embarrassingly stupid thought – I can see that now. But you think strange thoughts at times like that.'

'And how was Rachel?'

'*Ever so quiet.* She always was a bit quiet, but now she was kind of wrapped head to toe in this silence. And no one else spoke – I think no one dared because every breath, every word, everything now seemed so charged, and so full of meaning. I was frightened – I even felt a bit frightened of Rachel, who was normally the most unfrightening of people. But, in some way, she had already crossed over. She had changed and become distant.'

'Didn't you feel frightened when Johnnie died?'

'I don't know. That was all weird and drugged up and sudden. Of course, I was less close to him.'

'And maybe you didn't see his body?'

Zoë just nods and continues, 'When we set off in the car, Rachel said, "I'm never going in a car again." Then when we left the woods behind and came to the mountains at the end of the peninsula, she said, "That's my last tree." I didn't know what to say, or how to comfort her. At one point I reached out to hold her shoulder, but she just shook me off. Then I handed her a packet of fruit gums. She took one and passed it back to me. She said, "That's my last fruit gum." in the same dirge-like tone. But then she laughed and we all laughed too. And then she started to cry.

'We got to the lighthouse and Arthur parked the car, and brought out a bottle of tequila. We passed it between us. I think that last drink helped massively. She looked ever so pale – beautiful, really, even though her mascara had run everywhere. We all hugged her and kissed her, and I wiped her eyes. At the end, Will gave her a little signet ring from his finger.'

'There was no signet ring on the body.'

'Arthur took it off her finger afterwards,' says Zoë tonelessly. 'He said it was really a family ring and should stay with Will.'

'And what did Will think of that?'

'He said nothing. He ignores a lot of stuff. He just leaves it up to Arthur.'

'Do you think there was a moment when Rachel might have changed her mind?'

'Not then. I don't think it was possible.'

'Why not? Everything is possible in life. She could've said, "To hell with this."'

'But don't you see? We'd been building up to this for months. Ever since the middle of Michaelmas term we'd been talking about it. You know, going on night walks together, taking mushrooms, reading, dreaming, preparing ourselves.'

Zoë pauses, 'And Arthur was there.'

'You think he forced her hand?'

'Well, not totally. But he was really fired up and he did go up the lighthouse steps with her. And when she was up at the top and climbing over the barrier, he was standing in the doorway. I don't know *what* he said, but he'd have made going back very hard.'

'We were down below. I wish I'd called to her. I wish I'd told her not to do it. But it was as if the decision had already been made. It didn't feel like I could stop things then. I shouted, "Love you, Rachel." But that sounded *so* lame and I doubt she heard it. She didn't wave or anything.'

'And then?'

'She let go of the railings and she fell. At first she was falling head first and her arms were spread out. But she must have changed her mind and wanted to live because suddenly her arms flailed and she turned in the air so that she was falling feet first. It must have all happened in an instant, but things like that slow down in your mind, don't they? And I can clearly picture it. She was about halfway down the lighthouse and the floaty dress she was wearing rode up over her head. So she looked like some giant seed pod. And all you really saw was her poor white legs. Maybe she hoped she'd hit the water. But she didn't. She came down on the rocks. And her legs just crumpled up. It was awful!' Rhona takes a deep breath. She knows she should comfort Zoë but she can't find the words. She says quietly, 'What happened next?'

'I ran to her,' says Zoë. 'I don't know how I thought she could still be alive. Her legs were completely mangled. And, Jesus Christ, one look at her face! Her eyes were still open. I'd known, of course, that she was going to her death. But I hadn't expected it to be so *squalid* and horrible.'

'But you're a medical student,' says Rhona. 'You've dissected bodies. You can't be that squeamish.'

'But don't you see? This was a *friend!* Arthur said we weren't to touch her. He herded us both back into the car and, like meek little lambs, we went. Will seemed a bit out of it. And Arthur kept going on about "letting the salt waters cleanse her."'

'In the car he said, "She's at peace now." God, he can be so fucking pious! But I'd seen her eyes and there's no way she looked as if she was "at peace". That just wasn't true. And then Will said, "I can feel her soul pulling at me now." I didn't know what to make of that!'

'So what do you think has happened to her soul?' asks Rhona.

'She's dead,' replies Zoë stonily. 'How the fuck do I know?'

'You must have some notion.'

Zoë picks up the torch and shines it on Rhona's face. Then she lets the beam flit across the cavern, over the old blackened machinery of the mine.

'Heaven? Or hell? Or limbo?' she says. 'Or some dark shithole like this?'

'I thought you'd have a clearer idea.'

'Arthur and Will have their own religion,' says Zoë bitterly. 'I suppose there's nothing wrong with that. All religions are made up, aren't they? It's just who tells the best beautiful lie.'

'But didn't you believe the beautiful lie?'

'I did. I suppose I was beguiled. But that all's over. This morning I found the playing cards – they were on a pile in the sitting room. And there was a small, crusty lump on the bottom of the Queen of Spades.'

Rhona nods. There had been that little lump on Johnnie's card too.

'I showed it to Arthur. You see they were *new* cards. He just shrugged and said it must be a bit of food or something that got lodged there. He picked it off with his fingernail. He said, "Look, it's fine now." He really thought I was that stupid.'

'Is that why you walked out on them? Because Arthur was cheating?'

'It was more than that. What happened after that was even worse. Henderson came to the tower and ordered us all off the estate. I was still kind of in shock over Rachel and then he just turned up and said that the hunters were on their way and we all had to leave. Will wasn't well enough to travel, and he refused to go to hospital, so then Henderson told us Matt would be round to nail up the front door from the outside. He said he couldn't trust us not to go out. And then – and this was the clincher – he ordered us not to go out on the roof.'

'Why was that so important?'

'Don't you see? He was hiding something. Why was the hunt so secret? Why couldn't we watch? And then – I can't believe it took me this long – I did the sums. There're only two packs of wolves on the reserve. So how many wolves?

Thirty at the most in each pack. The hunters come every couple of months. Each time they must kill a few wolves. Let's say they kill two or three wolves each time. That's 12 to 18 wolves a year. So that just doesn't work, does it? The numbers don't add up. They'd wipe out the packs in no time. So they had to be hunting something *different,* something they didn't want us to know about. And then I remembered the girl.'

'Well done. I hadn't worked it out,' says Rhona.

Zoë pauses, 'The amazing thing is how transparent the lie is. I can't be the only person who has worked that out, can I?'

'No you can't. What about Arthur and Will?'

'They *must* know. Or they half know and won't acknowledge it.'

'Did you ask them?'

'Yeah. Will wasn't well at all and had got very drowsy and out of it, so I didn't want to press him. But I asked Arthur and he got all shifty and just said, "I assume you're leaving."

'So I left. I nicked his car keys and crossed the causeway. On the road, I passed Matt driving a trailer with planks of wood. So now they'll be all boarded in.'

'And they'll be safe from the hunters, won't they?' says Rhona. 'So…'

And now it's Zoë who takes the torch and shines it on her, 'What are you driving at?'

'We could go there too. If we could only get in.'

'There's a fire escape rope ladder on the roof,' says Zoë. 'It's absolutely ancient.'

'Maybe they could let it down for us.'

'*Maybe,*' cautions Zoë.

'It's our best option. There's nothing better than hiding in plain sight.'

THE WOLVES

Reading of the Day
'Fear, and the pit, and the snare, are upon thee, O inhabitant of the Earth.'
Isaiah 24.17

Zoë is standing over her, shaking her awake, 'There's someone coming.'

Rhona opens her eyes. Light slants down into the cave from the hole in the roof. She can hear water dripping and a very faint scuttling, probably the feet of a tiny animal. And then comes something more purposeful: scrunching footsteps. She can't tell how far off; sound travels mysteriously underground.

She quickly gets to her feet. They dash for the skylight and, stepping on the crates, climb up into the shaft. After a short, dirty scrabble, they come out onto a steep-sided wood where the trees are lagged in mist and it feels like early morning.

'The tower?' says Zoë.

Rhona nods.

They run, heading west along the shoulder of the hill. The tree trunks whip past, and Rhona feels that her feet are flying. She keeps her mind on the question of exactly *how* Henderson will explain away their bodies. What kind of 'accident' would be feasible? A wolf or bear attack? No. Hard to believe, and there could be problems with the autopsy. It would have to be a car accident: the torched

Corsa with their burnt bodies inside was almost plausible, as long as the accident happened now, this morning. Of course The Bassett would know it was a cover up, but he'd be able to get it past his superiors.

They stop to catch their breath and listen. But mysteriously there's no sound – no one seems to be following.

'You don't think we'll make it, do you?' says Zoë. Yesterday's make-up has left a grubby residue on her face.

'We just have to keep going,' says Rhona. She opens a tube of peppermints, puts several in her mouth and passes the rest to Zoë. 'Eat them. You'll need the sugar.'

They set off running again.

At the far side of the wood Rhona and Zoë cross a field of tall grass. Ahead of them lies Ben Resipole, grey cloud crouching on its huge shoulders. To get to the tower they must cross the mountain ridge, come down through the woods and along the road to the causeway.

A narrow sheep track zigzags up the mountainside and then vanishes into nothing. They clamber as fast as they can: out here in the open they can be seen by anyone in the valley who has sharp eyes. Will the hunters have arrows? Binoculars? She remembers The Bassett saying that the hunters killed with their bare hands. If they don't carry guns, they'll surely have something else, something worse.

We must just keep going, just keep going.

When they reach the clouds the air suddenly becomes cooler and harder to breathe. The skin on Rhona's face feels tight and her fingers are numb. And now the climbing is up a rocky slope, going handhold to handhold.

Finally, they pull themselves up onto the plateau and try to walk through the fog with their arms outstretched, their hands splayed in front of them. There will be sheer drops and landslides here. Before each step Rhona taps out the ground in front of her.

But this is so slow. After a couple of metres, she gets down on all fours and crawls forwards. She shines the torch, but the light vanishes into the dense fog.

She switches it off. Zoë is behind her and crawling too. They've been reduced to moving like dogs.

'Any idea where we are?' Zoë's voice sounds muffled.

'No.' Rhona gropes her way forward again. She's getting more confident, picking up speed. She puts her hand down on something sharp and stops. There's a piece of glass stuck in the fleshy part of her palm. Her fingers are too cold and clumsy. Using her teeth as pincers, she pulls out a small triangle of glass and licks the wound clean.

A low rumbling sound comes from the west; a hunting horn playing one short note, tailed by echoes.

Rhona is rooted to the spot. She squeezes the wound on her hand, and waits

A second note rings out. Then, just as she fears, there comes the third note.

'Maybe it's a kind of dinner gong,' says Zoë. 'They're calling each other to lunch. I could do with lunch.'

'No. Three short blows is the mort call. They've made their first kill.'

It will be one of Henderson's squirrels, those two young boys. Rhona sees them again, sitting at Mrs Collins' table – innocent carefree children, completely engrossed in their game.

Zoë is binding Rhona's hand with a strip of cotton from her T-shirt when they first hear the wolves. The chorus of howls has a siren-like quality, starting low and climbing higher. Zoë freezes and looks up at her, and Rhona meets her terrified gaze.

They've smelt the kill.

'Are they're coming for us?' says Zoë. The sound is penetrating everything: the rocks, the mountains, even the fog.

'Not if they're howling like that.'

'I've never heard anything so frightening,' Zoë's shoulders unhunch slightly

'It's odd though, isn't it?' Rhona tucks in the end of the cotton on her neatly bandaged hand and thinks how lucky it is that she has ended up with Zoë, not any of the rest of the group. 'They should be running towards the kill, shouldn't they? Wolves don't howl when they are running, or when they're eating.'

'Yeah,' says Zoë thoughtfully. Then she adds, 'Are you always like this? Do you always dissect everything?'

'Don't you see? I think more when I'm frightened.'

'But are you never too frightened to think?'

'Almost never,' says Rhona. '*Almost.*'

And to stop Zoë from asking more, she points north and says, 'We have to keep going.'

Carefully, they make their way along the ridge. At first they are crawling, but as the cloud lifts they get to their feet and walk on. The wolves are still howling.

Rhona has nothing to drink, nothing to warm her, nothing to stiffen her resolve except fear. She feels hollowed out with hunger.

Bitter gusts of wind clear the last traces of fog. Now she can make out the steep cliffsides of the ridge and far below them, the forest and the blue frill of the coastline. In the distance, the dark mountains of Lochaber step away into the sky.

At the end of the ridge they come to a great knuckle of grey rock, braced by more cliffs. To the west the rock face has broken into a bank of steep black scree that ends down in the woods. Zoë, her face set, stares at the drop.

'You ever run scree before?' says Rhona.

'No. And I'm not doing it now.'

'Just keep your weight on the back of your heels. Whatever you do, don't stop or you'll go under.'

'The wolves are down there. I'm starving and I'm freezing cold. And now you're asking me to kill myself.'

'We can't stay here. The cloud has gone. Anyone with a pair of binoculars can see us.'

'Let's go back and find another way down.'

'We have to get to the tower. This'll be quick.'

'I can't do it.'

'And the sound will be covered by the wolves.'

'That's meant to encourage me, is it?'

'Come on,' she takes Zoë's hand. 'Don't look too far down,' she says. 'You can do it.'

Zoë sighs.

They take up their positions and stand side by side on the ledge, as if at the start point of a race.

'You're lighter, you go first,' says Rhona. The scree is a smooth, black crust; underneath lie the loose stones, ready to fall.

'No, let's go to our death together.' Zoë won't look at her. All Rhona sees is her profile, her sharp little nose pink from the cold.

They step out onto the scree. Rhona's foot sinks through the crust and she feels the stones pour away under her, pulling her down. She quickly puts her other foot down, trying to dig her heels into the sliding ground.

She takes another step, and another. The scree acts as if it has been roused from a long slumber; mini avalanches of stone and dust join a bigger fall of scree thundering down all around her. Zoë is ahead, her arms akimbo like a skateboarder.

The scree gains momentum and they are both sliding down, faster and faster. Soon it will overtake them.

Now she can't stop, and only metres ahead of her is the wood.

She sees Zoë crumple against a tree. Rhona puts out her arms to embrace the trunk of a pine. She slams into it and the stones pour on round her, walloping her calves. By the time the landslide stops, her ankles and calves have been battered with stones and she is buried up to her knees.

They pull themselves free of the scree and, treading quietly, they head along a path through the woods. The wolves, maybe shocked by the sound of the landslide, have quietened and they hear nothing but the movement of the trees. It doesn't feel as if they are being watched, but there are freshly broken branches along the way; someone, or some creature, has passed this way recently.

Gradually the path widens, becoming a driveway rutted with thick wheel marks from a quad bike or trailer. They keep close to the wood, ready to dive for cover at any moment.

They are coming round a bend in the path, and the afternoon sun has at last broken through and is shining down in bright slats through the tree canopy. Suddenly Rhona hears a metallic tapping sound. She smells wood smoke and stops. Zoë looks at her and nods.

They tiptoe forward a couple of metres. Up ahead is a clearing; the sound of men's voices drift towards them.

They creep into the trees and crouch in the undergrowth. They could skirt the clearing and loop round through the woods and out onto the road. But everything Rhona has risked has been for this moment. She must at least see who the hunters are.

She points to the clearing. Zoë, eyes huge, shakes her head. Rhona beckons to her again, but Zoë won't come.

So Rhona goes alone, crawling forward. It's slow work and every few minutes she hears the tapping sound again. Finally, when she reaches a thicket of dogwood about three metres from the edge of the clearing, she stops.

She sees the scene before her through the red bars of the dogwood branches. Maybe it's shock that makes her slow to understand. Separately, she takes in every component of the scene: the fire, the men, the body.

Firstly, the body. She sees the frame: two sets of tall wooden staves, crossed at shoulder height and tied together with leather cord. In happier days it was the kind of construction gardeners used for their runner beans. Only this frame is sturdier, less improvised. And the purpose is very different.

Between the two crossed staves lies a long metal pole. And hanging from the pole, tied neatly at the ankles and the wrist, is the body of one of Mrs Collins' boys. His head hangs down, the squirrel mask is pulled back from his freckly nose, the stitching under his ears has been cruelly ripped away. Rhona can see his red hair – his mouth is slit at the side, and bloody. His eyes are unseeing, open to the treetops and the sky above.

It wasn't a clean kill. The child's throat is ripped open, exposing the pale pink ridges of his windpipe. She can see that one hand has been mangled – he must have tried to protect his throat. There are also gashes to his arms and legs, and to his face. His belly has been split open from sternum to groin; he has been gralloched. Maybe it happened while he was still alive.

The tapping continues. She expected evil, but this is still a shock. Rhona shivers. Her diaphragm gives a tug and she pulls her gaze away.

To the side of the clearing she sees Kemp, who is standing with a heap of entrails at his feet and a rifle in his hand. Nearby, Boyd is at work. He has a pile of thin metal fence posts which he is hammering into the ground at regular intervals. He has a coil of electric cable looped around his shoulder and he threads the wire into the slots in each fence post as he goes. He works quickly and expertly; soon the fence will be up and running.

Inside the fenced-off area is a well prepared camp with neat piles of blankets, hampers with food and drink, and a small fire with trivets for kettles and pans. Three masked hunters, the centrepiece of this scene, are sitting round the fire on camp stools. They are short, full-chested men, their knees are splayed, and their forearms – they have all rolled up their sleeves – are corded with muscles. One man is blond, another has a luxurious brown beard which sticks out from under his wolf mask. The third man has lifted the front of his mask up, propping it on his forehead as if it were a pair of sunglasses. He has a most distinctive face: hooded eyes and a long, trowel-shaped jaw from which he's wiping sweat. He seems to be the leader and is the most decorated of the hunters; down the sleeve of his khaki shirt he has four round, embroidered badges with gold edging. She can't see clearly at this distance, but she feels sure that the badges must be Mrs Collins' work – miniature portraits of the prey. And the badges will be awards: each badge signifying a kill. These killers are just like boy scouts.

In front of the men, resting on a flat rock, is a heavy, square spirits bottle and a tangle of leather straps and shining metal blades. The contraptions look unusual: part orthopaedic brace, part armour.

Then she understands. The man with the badges was only using one hand to wipe his face. His other arm rests on the back of an empty camping chair, his hand dangling down with the metal brace still on. There are steel blades, about four inches long, attached to each finger; he is wearing a claw.

She watches the fireside group and feels oddly distanced from what she sees. They are all so relaxed: talking, and drinking. All is good with these men; they have had their hunt, made their kill, and now they are celebrating.

She feels that she has stared at this horrifying tableau for a long time. But only a minute has passed. The man who is wiping his face now passes round a Tupperware container. The two masked men each take a sandwich. It's white bread. She wonders numbly what the filling might be. Egg? Tuna? Some of McCreal's 'charcuterie'?

The man by the ice box, of course, eats his sandwich using only one hand. Rhona looks again at his claw. Now she sees why he has left it on; for while the braces belonging to the other hunters are still shiny and clean, the straps on this man's brace are stained, and the blades are brown with blood. He has done the killing and this claw is his trophy.

And he is gifted with a hunter's sense of presence. He looks up from his food and stares into the wood.

THE TOWER

Rhona slithers silently back through the undergrowth. She whispers to Zoë how the hunters have killed the boy. Zoë recoils, her face is contorted and she puts her hand to her mouth.

They cannot make any noise. As fast as they can, they move away from the camp and creep like shadows between the trees. When they come out on the road, they break into a run. Rhona is open-mouthed, tears streaming down her face.

The howling starts up again and grows louder and sharper as they run. Fear is making the wolves sound louder, she thinks. But no, they really are much closer, and seem somewhere up ahead. And then it becomes clear. They come to the lay-by with the big, slatted barn where Rhona parked when she and Matt went to kill the bear. At the time she'd noticed the terrible smell. Now the wolves are here, locked up in the barn. As Rhona and Zoë race by, the howling reaches a frenzy of excitement. Wolves are throwing themselves against the door and she can hear the cracking of wood.

Rhona pulls at Zoë's sleeve, urging her to run faster. This is the last lap. A mile more of this interminable road, with the woods to their right, where Matt shot the bear, and on the other side the dell and that round brown pond.

Finally, they are at the estuary.

It is high tide and the causeway is covered. But a few inches below the surface she can see the line of the shingle and she splashes out into the water with Zoë panting behind her. They are halfway across when she hears a faint whirring and spies a red and blue dragonfly with lights on its underbelly glimmering above them. She knows it's pointless – they must already have been seen – but Rhona gropes in the water for a stone and throws it at the drone, which jerks and flies off.

They scramble up the path to the tower and dash into the courtyard. Three thick planks have been nailed across the front door. Rhona glimpses a face looking out from one of the slit windows. It vanishes instantly.

'Arthur!' cries Zoë. She shouts again and again.

Arthur's head, small as a thumb, appears over the battlements.

'Get the fire ladder!' shouts Zoë.

For a few moments he just stares down at them.

'Please!' cries Rhona.

Then he vanishes.

She presses her back against the cold stone of the tower and, breathing heavily, she shuts her eyes. He won't help; there is nothing in it for him and he'll know that Zoë has told her everything.

But then she hears the clatter and thump of something falling. She opens her eyes to a wonderful sight: an old rope ladder with wooden treads is hanging down the side of the tower.

Rhona holds down the ladder while Zoë hoists herself onto the first step and climbs up, swiveling round so that she is using the side of the ladder. At the top Arthur reaches down to help her over the battlements.

Now Rhona takes a big breath and steps up onto the ladder. The treads are slimy with age and the old ropes creak under her weight.

'Hurry!' shouts Zoë.

But the climbing is harder than she expects; her arms feel so weak and the ladder swings back and forth. Eventually she does reach the top and Arthur takes her arm and helps her over the small wall. Exhausted, she slumps down on the roof and watches him pull up the ladder. At least for a while, they might be safe.

Arthur's face looks worse than usual: paler, lips crusted.

'Where's Zoë?' she asks.

'She's gone down to see Will,' he says in a hollow voice.

'What's wrong?'

'He's ill. Very ill.'

Rhona quickly gets to her feet and glances down at the estuary. But there's no sign yet of the hunters.

They head down the spiral stairs.

Will's bedroom is dark, the air warm and chemical from a paraffin heater. With a torch in one hand, Zoë is rifling through the bedside cabinet. Will lies on his back in the bed and from the slit window a narrow shaft of light falls on his pale chest and across his head which is tilted back, the chip of his Adam's apple jutting out. His skin is shiny with sweat and his breathing sounds as if he's sucking through a blocked vent.

'Will. It's me. Rhona Ballantyne. From the police.'

He turns his head a fraction towards her.

His face is white, his mouth agape, and where his right eye should be there's just a flat, sunken lid. His one eye opens and closes again.

Shocked, Rhona takes a step back. 'What happened?'

'Yesterday, he wasn't feeling well, and that was just the beginning.' Arthur is holding Will's hand, stroking the knuckles with his thumb. 'It's just got worse and worse. Yesterday he couldn't walk. Henderson wanted to call an ambulance, but Will wouldn't have it. He wouldn't budge.

In the end, his father had to let us stay. Then they boarded us in and took away the mobiles.'

'She means what happened to Will's eye,' says Zoë.

'His eye? Gave you a shock, did it? He always takes it out before he goes to bed.'

Zoë says, 'At some point he's had a tumour at the back of the eye removed. Probably a choroidal melanoma.'

'How do you know that?' says Arthur sharply. 'Did he tell you?'

'Of course, he didn't,' says Zoë with weary authority. 'And if I'd asked he would have made up a story about some green monkey disease from Borneo. But I spotted the prosthetic ages ago. The eyes never do move quite in sync, and since he's become jaundiced the whites haven't matched. The jaundice is a real worry. Arthur, are there metastases? Please don't tell me it's gone to his liver.'

Arthur looks up at the ceiling and doesn't reply. He is still stroking Will's hand.

Zoë puts two fingers to Will's throat and after a few seconds, she says, 'His pulse is really thready. And his colour is terrible. He may have a clot on the lung. That would explain things.' She glances at Arthur. 'There's no heparin here by any chance? Do you have any oxygen?'

'No,' he replies.

'We should let him sleep. You two go downstairs and make us something to eat. I'll watch him.'

'I want to stay with him,' says Arthur.

'Leave him be. He needs to sleep. You'll just fuss over him.'

'I should be here with him.'

'You only let us in because you thought I'd be able to help. So at least listen to what I have to say.'

Arthur turns away from her and moves the hair back from Will's forehead.

'Just do as I say,' says Zoë. 'Leave him be and go downstairs.'

In the kitchen Rhona opens a screw top bottle of Beaujolais, fills a glass and drinks it down like water. She pours a second glass and a glass for Arthur, who has opened the small fridge under the counter. He brings out half a pack of butter, some sweating cheddar and a couple of bags of kale.

Rhona opens all the cupboards. The idea of cooking at such a time seems ludicrous, like jumping over a muddy puddle on the way to the gibbet. And the food she finds – the *only* other food in the kitchen – is stupidly rarefied and impractical: antique orange breadcrumbs, sumac, Iranian black garlic, and several jars of salted capers. But there is also a bag of green lentils.

Rhona hands the lentils to Arthur. She pours a glass of wine for Zoë and carries it carefully up the spiral stairs. She stops at the slit window halfway up the steps and peers out – nobody is yet coming across the causeway. Again she tells herself that she is playing for time; the longer they stay alive, the harder it will be for Henderson.

In the bedroom, Zoë is holding Will's wrist lightly between her thumb and finger; she is checking his pulse again. Rhona notes how Zoë's careful impersonal touch contrasts with Arthur's needy pawing of his friend.

'How is he?'

Zoë shakes her head.

When Rhona returns downstairs the lentils are boiling and Arthur has turned on a CD of Rachmaninoff's *Prelude in G Minor*. He is chopping an onion, bringing the knife down in time with the big chords. His face is streaming with tears and his nose is running. Drops are landing on the wooden board. Rhona looks away. She was never going to eat anyway.

The lentils are slow to soften. Rhona leans against a sideboard and drinks a third, then a fourth glass. Arthur, she knows, is watching her. And she is watching Arthur, who, like so many men, is an impatient cook. She is sure he didn't wash his hands and he fries the onions at too high a heat. Then he tips in the kale, which also begins to burn. Rhona is too tired and too distracted and a little too drunk to interfere. She doesn't care anyway.

When the food – a terrible lentil gloop – is ready, Zoë comes down and the three of them sit round the stove with bowls on their knees. They eat silently like seminarians; Arthur and Zoë won't look at each other. Rhona eats her bowlful – she is surprised to find she has any appetite.

Zoë gets to her feet. 'I'd better go back and keep an eye on him.'

'Shouldn't I come?' says Arthur.

Zoë shakes her head, 'He needs to sleep. Every now and then he groans – I think it's chest pain.'

'Can't you do anything?'

'I've given him aspirin. I wish you had some decent painkillers.'

She puts down her empty bowl and stands up. 'He's sleeping. I'll call if anything changes.'

After Zoë leaves, they open another bottle and Arthur asks if she has seen the hunters. Rhona tells him about the dead boy, and how he had been killed and gutted and strung up like a dead deer. She tells him that even though she is a hardened detective, with countless murder investigations under her belt, she has never seen anything quite so grotesque. And the hunters had behaved as if stringing up a boy was nothing unusual – they'd been chatting and drinking and even eating sandwiches.

She lets out a great sigh and looks up at the ceiling. Arthur has his feet resting on the coffee table. He brings out his e-cigarette and takes a pull on it.

'You must have a feeling for children. You were a schoolmaster, weren't you?

'Sorry,' he replies 'I'm a little preoccupied.'

'You've always known about the hunt, haven't you? You knew about these men. You knew they were murderers, didn't you?'

'Let's say, I wasn't surprised.'

'So you *did* know? You knew about the children?'

Arthur keeps his eyes lowered. He sucks in the steam, 'How on earth did you *not* know, Inspector? All you needed to do was open your eyes.'

He's right.

'They're going to kill me and Zoë,' her voice is level. 'You'll be a witness, so they'll probably kill you too.'

'At least I'll die with Will.'

'If you'd only told me all this earlier, we could've stopped the hunt.'

'Don't blame me. It's Archie Henderson you should be getting at. Not me.'

'But those children. Don't you care?'

'In theory I care,' he says. 'But I don't have much room in my heart for extraneous people.' He gives a wry smile, 'I only really care about Will.' Another puff, 'It's still a shock. I've known it was coming and I thought I was prepared for everything. But watching him die will be unbearable. I've done the best I can, and at least he'll have company.'

'*Company?* What's that supposed to mean?'

'Anyone who lives well dies to join someone. You should know that.'

Arthur smiles into his steam. 'I suppose Johnnie will

be there holding the drinks tray, and Rachel will have plumped up the cushions.'

She looks at him uncertainly, but he doesn't seem to be joking. 'You can't really believe that.'

'It doesn't matter what I think. Will believes it, in a manner of speaking. He lives by myth and metaphor. He inhabits old tales. I think it's a measure of his greatness. And I'd say anything that makes his death easier is worth it. Wouldn't you agree?'

'So Zoë is right then. You're behind the suicides of Johnnie and Rachel. You inveigled them into it. You orchestrated everything, didn't you?'

He blows out another plume of vapour. 'You're never going to understand. Things were far more complex than you could possibly realise.'

'Were they really? I'm not so sure.'

'Helping Johnnie and Rachel out was an act of love. It was the most selfless thing I've ever done,' Arthur looks at her steadily. He says softly, 'And it was their fucking choice.'

Rhona turns to see Zoë standing silently at the foot of the stairs; her eyes are blazing.

'He's worse. His pulse is racing. You'd better go to him,' she says.

Arthur stands up. He strides across the room, passes Zoë without looking at her and races on up the stairs.

Rhona listens to the downdraft whining in the stove pipe. She rubs her eyes and tries to order her thoughts.

'I've been here a hundred times before,' says Zoë. 'It's going to be another sit back and watch your patient die for lack of meds.'

'There might be something in the stores.'

Zoë casts her a doubtful look.

'Well, we've got to do *something,*' says Rhona 'We

can't just sit and wait for him to die and for the hunters to descend on us. '

'There might just be some oxygen,' says Zoë. 'It's very unlikely, but Will once said that Henderson used to moor his yacht in the estuary. So he could have left behind some old diving canisters.'

Rhona nods. At least this will keep them busy. She feels oddly detached from what is happening around her. The search will be utterly futile. But so were most activities in life. And why should things be different at the end?

Play it with good grace.

They take the torch and go in search. In a low curved storeroom under the stairs they find firelighters, a fishing net, a couple of mouldering old tents, three luminous buoys. But no oxygen tanks. Then Zoë opens a tin chest and pulls out a couple of ancient Catherine Wheels leaking black powder. Underneath lie a bundle of rods tied with twine.

'They're nautical flares,' says Rhona, feeling the wrapping paper for damp. 'They may still work.'

Zoë gives a relieved smile.

'Don't get your hopes up,' adds Rhona. 'I don't know who would rescue us.'

'But the coastguard will, won't they?'

'The Lochaber coastguard probably won't. The chief officer, Colin Brodie, has a wife with lupus which requires imported drugs, so he'll be in Henderson's pocket. And by this time of night, the old supervisor, Tam what's-his-name, will be legless.'

'So there's no one?'

'We should still light them anyway. They could be hard for Henderson to explain away at our inquests.' She turns back to Zoë, 'There is another whole night and a day of the hunt to go. Will can't survive that long, can he?'

Zoë shakes her head.

Rhona leaves Zoë to search the cupboard in the lobby and she climbs the stairs, carrying the flares. She pauses outside Will's bedroom. Arthur is bent over Will, cradling his head.

She continues up the stairs and comes out onto the roof. The sky is mottled with rainclouds. Down in the estuary nothing moves, and the mountains and woods are dark, the treetops just a black silhouette.

There are six flares in the bundle. She undoes the twine and picks up a rod. She stretches her right arm out in front of her and pulls the small aluminium lever at the end of the shaft. The flare shoots up into the sky and with a soft 'woompf' it explodes, lighting the sky with an unnatural red.

Rhona pulls the lever on the second flare, which is a dud. She tries a third flare and it works.

There are three more flares. She doesn't trust herself to wait long enough, so she counts to two thousand. Then she sets off the fourth flare. With a burst, the sky is again lit up and Rhona sees, emblazoned in crimson, the woods and the estuary where a masked man is walking across the causeway.

Her eyes fix on the man's mask. It's different: brown and feline with tufted ears – a wild cat. The man is tall and gangly, and his hand braces are slung over one shoulder.

He walks with a familiar, loping gait. It's Henderson.

HENDERSON

R hona is slow to react. When Henderson's head gives a jerk and he looks up at the tower, she doesn't duck down under the battlements in time. She knows he's seen her, but she still stays crouched down while she tries to think. But her mind is blurred and the palms of her hands feel raw from all the crawling in the woods. If only she could have another drink.

One thought comes back to her repeatedly; her only hope, her only card to play, is Will.

In no time, or so it seems, Henderson reaches the foot of the tower.

'Rhona!' he shouts.

She doesn't answer. She thinks, he'll have something: a radio, a walkie talkie. He won't let his own son die.

'Rhona!' he shouts again.

'I've got news,' she shouts back. 'Important news.'

'What's that?'

It seems a such a strange thing to shout to someone, but she does so anyway: 'Will is very ill.'

'I know that,' he cries. He sounds annoyed, 'What kind of father do you think I am?'

'No, he's *dying!*'

For a moment she hears nothing back. She stands up, and feels a west wind breathing cold on her face.

'I'll come up,' he calls. 'Put down the rope ladder.'

'No!'

'For God's sake, Rhona.'

'Call an ambulance from where you are.'

'I need to see him! He's my son.'

'You'll kill us.'

'You have my word. Honestly. The game is over. I'll call off the hunt.'

She feels she has no choice. She cannot, of course, trust him. But she should surely let him see his dying son. If ever there was a time to be generous, it's now. She doesn't let herself think through the consequences. Instead she just swings the rope ladder back over the battlements and, as it falls, it clatters against the wall.

That was a mistake.

She grabs the twine from the flares, winds it between her hands to make a garrote and waits.

Henderson lands on the roof with a graceful, feline crouch. Rhona is ready, the twine between her fists, her weight on the balls of her feet. But he doesn't lunge at her. He stands up, pulls off his mask, folds it in half and stuffs it in his breast pocket as if it were an army beret. He nods to her and makes for the stairs down to Will's room. She drops the twine and follows him.

In the bedroom, Will is lying just as he was before, with his arms at his side, his head back, his hair flared out across the pillow. His chest heaves, his open mouth is a dark hole.

Henderson leans in the doorway, head slightly bowed. He watches his son for a moment and then enters the room and sits down carefully on the bed. He ignores Arthur and Zoë, who draw back to the fireplace.

A clicking noise comes from the back of Henderson's throat. 'Oh, Billy.' He takes his son's hand and holds it up to his cheek.

'Billy. It's me. Don't be frightened.'

Will's face barely flickers.

'You can hear me, can't you?' says Henderson. 'Billy?'
Will doesn't respond.

Rhona stares at the wall, which is as blemished as old skin, with cracks and dimples in the plaster and a scattering of mildew spots.

'If he doesn't get oxygen, this will be the end,' says Zoë.

Henderson doesn't look at Zoë, but he places his son's hand back down on the bed and stands

'I'll call an ambulance.' He takes a mobile from his trouser pocket. 'Just give me a minute,' he strides out of the bedroom and climbs up the stairs back to the roof.

Rhona goes downstairs, stepping carefully in the dark, one hand on the damp stonework. In the kitchen she lights a candle. The only drink left in the cupboard is half a bottle of port. She downs it straight from the bottle and climbs back up the stairs.

She finds Henderson standing on the roof, looking out to sea. He has his mobile in his hand and the glow shines upwards, giving him the eyebrows of a gargoyle.

'I got through,' he says bleakly. 'The coastguard are sending an air ambulance.'

'What about the hunt?'

'What about it? It's all over now. Everything is over.'

'But the hunters?'

'We'll see to them.' Henderson sits down on the wall of the battlements and puts away his mobile. He must be confident that she won't dive at him and push him over the side. Or maybe, she muses, that is precisely what he wants.

'You took your masks off.' He doesn't look at her. 'That wasn't very sporting of you.'

'It wasn't very sporting of you to put tracker chips in them.'

'I run a business. I can't afford wastage. A couple of children from one of our first batches just vanished. The hunters found that very frustrating and one time we nearly had a dry hunt.'

'Who were the kids? How did you get them? Were they Moldavian?'

'I don't know where they came from. It was Kemp who got them, so you'd have to ask him, or Marie Collins. I think he picked them up from one of those mobile vans with internet links. Young people don't seem to be able to do without that stuff.'

Peepers, she thinks. He was their procurer. And she had mistaken him for just an honest thief.

'How long has this been going on?'

'It all happened gradually. The reserve first got into trouble after the shutdown. But I told you that before, didn't I? We lost most of our customer base. Then things just got worse. And, after the separation, Marissa's lawyers were onto me. About the same time – I think that must have been about a year and a half ago – I got this offer I couldn't refuse.'

'You couldn't refuse an offer to kill children?'

'You don't understand. It was more complicated than that.'

She notices that, when pressed, he sounds like Arthur and adopts the same belittling tone.

'Of course, I wouldn't have agreed had I known,' continues Henderson. 'But it started out as just private hunting parties. They wanted a wild secluded space, and brought their girls and... and whatever.' With a wave of his hand he brushes away the rest of the sentence.

'At first the hunters tracked the wolves and killed them with rifles, but that was never going to be sustainable, even when we moved onto crossbows. Then we tried falconry. That's when we first got children in. It's by far the best way to train birds of prey.'

She nods; a year ago was when Henderson had asked her father for the bait jackets.

'When you say "training" do you mean what you did with Will and your daughter when they were children?'

'Oh, you know about that, do you? Well, it didn't do *them* any lasting harm.' He draws a breath, 'But I didn't realise then how dangerous baiting could be. We lost a girl – she died from the shock.'

'What did you do with the body?

'For God's sake, what do you *think* you do on a wild reserve?' Henderson looks at her scornfully. 'We used her as feed, of course. It's all part of good husbandry, giving back to the earth what it has given.'

Rhona bows her head. *The fingernails. The seed pearls.*

Henderson continues, 'But my clients soon got bored with the falconry. Very successful people are always pushing boundaries and they wanted something more hands-on. And we still had these kids knocking about. So, well, it was obvious, a natural progression... Of course, it wasn't me that first came up with the idea, but I couldn't very well say no. I suppose, after that accident they had a hold on me. And they are not people you say no to.'

'And where did McCreal fit into all of this?'

'He provided the trophies.'

'Trophies? You mean the children were stuffed?'

'That's why we needed all the planning, you see. We had to have the prey arrive at least a month beforehand. Mrs Collins got the children filled out a bit – their skin needed to look good. And McCreal had to take measurements.'

'It didn't occur to you that there was something terribly wrong with all of this?'

'It was only their heads,' says Henderson reasonably. 'And McCreal was a real master of his art. He could make the children look like they were laughing.'

298

Rhona swallows. *He really is mad.*

'Are these trophies still here?'

'Of course not. The hunters took them with them.'

'So, somewhere in the Carpathian mountains there's a log cabin with grinning children's heads all over the wall?'

He raises a finger to correct her. 'Not *grinning*. Grinning only happens if the skin is badly cured.'

'For fuck's sake!'

'You have to understand, my hunters need to get trophies. Whoever makes the kill must win something. They need a prize. It's a standard marketing procedure.'

Finally, she says in a robotic voice, 'So skinning people is a standard marketing procedure?'

He's exasperated: 'That's such a crude way of putting it! Rhona, vulgarity really doesn't become you.'

'And tell me something,' she says. 'I know McCreal used to cure meat. Did he cure this meat too?'

'No,' says Henderson heavily. 'That's where he drew the line. But I think he was pushed too far. He was definitely showing signs of stress. That girl on the loose seems to have got to him. He got too attached, too involved. Boyd says he was even putting out food for her. That was most unprofessional.'

'And that's why he had to die?'

'They didn't kill him. He did it himself. He knew they were coming back soon and I think he preferred not to leave the job up to them. I'd say that was rather a wise choice.'

'So, am I going to end up a trophy?' she says bitterly. 'Or do I get to be an ashtray instead!'

'You'd make a nice mounting.' He doesn't seem to be joking. 'You've got good teeth. And we could fill in the crow's feet.'

'Thanks,' she says. 'It's the ultimate chat-up line, isn't it?'

But Henderson doesn't answer. He looks out into the evening sky and says, 'They'll be here soon.' Then he adds, 'I should never have given way over Will. I should never have been so *weak.*'

'I wouldn't call you *weak*,' she says tiredly. She thinks, he's probably going to murder me, yet he still wants sympathy.

'I have just destroyed my life for one thing. Do you know what it is?' he says. 'It's *feeling.*'

'You didn't show much feeling for those children.'

'They were nothing. They'd have died anyway. I'm talking of Billy. In the greater scheme of things, I suppose he's nothing, too. He's always been sickly. He was premature and we should have just let him die. But Marissa and the hospital insisted and I stupidly gave way, and he went into an incubator for six weeks. Then, of course, he was never quite right – there's always been something not properly baked about him. All we've ever had is this drawn out agony.'

'Surely there have been good times too?'

Henderson shakes his head. 'You're meant to be grateful for what fate gives you. But I've always wanted more from life. And so has Billy.'

'He's quite like you really, isn't he? He's a hunter too, but just of a different sort. He and Arthur outdid you. There's nothing cleverer than getting your prey to do the work for you and kill themselves.'

He nods, thinking this through. She sees a small smile on his lips.

He says slowly, 'Every hunt is a form of seduction. And all prey are complicit, aren't they? Those little squirrels loved being fed on Mrs Collins' cakes and they were happy to scamper round the woods which was all about getting their fitness up. And you and Zoë, you didn't have to come to the big house, did you?'

'And you as well,' she replies. 'You're half in love with your "high net worth individuals".'

'What if I am?'

'You're prey, too.'

'Oh, I know, I know.' He pauses, turns to her and says miserably, 'Where does this leave the estate? Who am I going to leave all this to?'

'To your children?'

'Even if Billy pulls through this time, he won't see the year out.'

'Your daughter, Lucy?'

He shakes his head, as if the idea were unthinkable.

'How long till they get here?'

'Look below,' says Henderson.

She leans over the battlements and sees two hunters sitting on a low wall by the front door. They seem relaxed, they've rested their torches by their side and one of them is smoking a cigarette.

'I thought you'd called off the hunt!' cries Rhona.

He stretches out his arms, as if finishing a yawn. 'It's not you, it's me that'll pay the price. But there's nothing more honourable than self-sacrifice. It's the ultimate declaration of love.' He glances at her and adds sinuously, 'You, of all people, should know about self-sacrifice.'

Rhona looks away. *He knew about Maggie all along*

When Henderson stands up, she backs away from him, but he isn't coming for her. He's making for the metal rung on the side of the wall. Earlier, Henderson must have swung the ladder back down over the side of the tower. Now it's pulled taut. Someone is climbing up.

'So all that talk was just to distract me, was it?'

301

'Wait,' he says quietly 'Just wait.'

She dives for the rung. But Henderson grabs her arms and pulls her across to the edge of the roof. He thrusts her head over the side of the battlements. She tries to squirm free, but he clamps a hand round the back of her neck and has her pinned. She shuts her eyes. She can feel his forefinger and thumb pinching into the two soft dents at the stem of her neck. If he swivels his hand now, he can make a clean break of the vertebrae.

That would be quick, better than falling.

'You see down there?' he whispers, his mouth is close, his lips brushing her ear.

'No.'

'Open your eyes.' His fingers tighten on her neck. 'Open them!'

She opens her eyes. Henderson is shining his phone down over the side of the tower where the lead hunter, who has taken off his trophy claw, has climbed three quarters of the way up the rope ladder. The hunter looks up: that long, trowel-shaped face again. He locks eyes with her and gives her a terrifying smile.

Henderson pulls Rhona back, away from the wall. He's still holding her by the neck.

'Hunting is all about waiting quietly,' he murmurs. 'He's nearly at the third floor now. What's that? Fifty feet? Or sixty? I think that's enough.'

He pushes Rhona away and she falls forward on all fours. She turns to see him bend down by the metal rung, give a mighty tug on the rope ladder and detach the carabiner. He lets go and jumps back as the ropes whip away over the battlements. There's a short scream. She screws up her eyes. For a moment all she hears is the clatter of the falling rope ladder. When the thud comes it sounds soft, like a heavy fruit dropping on a stone floor. Henderson gives a yelp of excitement. His feet do an odd little dance and he keeps wiping his hands against the sides of his trousers.

Rhona slowly gets to her feet. In the southern sky, she can see two tiny boreholes of bright white light. She watches them grow. There's the faint whirl of an engine. The sound is quickly getting louder; a helicopter is juddering towards the tower.

Henderson walks over to the telescope. 'That'll be my men, or the coastguard. One or the other.' He bends down and peers into the eyepiece while swiveling the long tube up towards the helicopters. 'Now it's just a matter of who reaches us first.'

'We need to get Will up here,' she says.

But Henderson is busy adjusting the focus: 'Leave it to that little friend of his.'

Rhona heads down the stairs.

At first she thinks Will is already dead. He's lying swaddled tightly in a sheet with only his head showing. But his mouth is slightly open, and he is still breathing. Zoë and Arthur are putting a blanket round him – he's being packaged up for travel.

He's already in his winding sheet.

'What's happening?' says Zoë. 'We heard a scream.'

But Rhona just shakes her head. She can't even start to explain. Instead she says, 'The helicopter's here.'

Arthur climbs onto the bed and cradles Will's head and shoulders. Rhona takes Will's feet and Zoë holds up his middle. Arthur gives a nod and, very carefully, they lift him up. He is so light – there's nothing to him really – and, slowly as if he were something very fragile, they carry him up the spiral staircase. It's hard to negotiate the curve of the stairs and at times Will moans faintly.

At last they come out onto the roof and into a blaze of

headlights. The helicopter, its engine roaring and coughing, is hovering just a few metres from the tower. Henderson, with his shadow stretching long behind him, is beckoning the pilot to come forward.

They gently lay Will down. Zoë places another blanket over him and Arthur pulls off his neck scarf and places it as a cushion under Will's head.

But Rhona sees now that the helicopter isn't an air ambulance. The lights and markings on the bodywork are all wrong: no big red cross, no revolving red lights. This helicopter is longer, and thinner. It comes in over the top of the battlements, then backs away, dithers, edges forward again.

Eventually it comes juddering down, one landing skid hitting the flagstones before the other. The engine is still running, and a side door opens. Kemp, in ironed overalls, climbs down the metal steps onto the roof.

Henderson strides over to where Will is lying. He looks down on his son's white, cocooned face.

'How's he doing?'

'We need to get him out,' says Zoë.

'This helicopter is for me. But the air ambulance will be here soon.' Henderson crouches down and strokes his son's cheek. Rhona thinks it might be the effect of the helicopter's lights, but the lines on Henderson's face seemed to have deepened and he looks ravaged.

'Goodbye, Billy,' he says and he kisses Will on the forehead. Then he gets to his feet again, turns and walks to the helicopter. Rhona watches him go. He doesn't look back and he doesn't falter. His back is straight and he walks directly, as if pulled forward by an invisible cord, as if there were no other place to go.

He mounts the metal steps. Only at the top does he pause, but Kemp comes up behind him, puts his hand on the small of Henderson's back and both men duck their heads and disappear through the doorway into the helicopter.

The metal steps retract and, with the door still open, the helicopter lurches up into the air. In the windscreen Rhona glimpses Boyd's face, stern with concentration.

Rhona assumes the helicopter will fly off and away; Henderson will surely be making his escape. But instead Boyd veers back towards Ardnamurchan and heads low over the estuary.

She sees the reason; the downlights from the helicopter are shining on the causeway where the two surviving hunters are standing. They are no longer masked and appear composed, like men waiting for a taxi. One of them is talking on a mobile phone and the other one, with leisurely gestures, is beckoning the helicopter down. When it is a few metres from the ground, a thin ladder drops down, and the two men climb aboard.

The helicopter, with its downlights making a bright path on the estuary, rises again and flies out to sea. It clears the shallows and the tower. Over the deep water of Loch Moidart, it finally drops its load and Henderson, with his arms outstretched, plummets through the air. Over the roar of the helicopter, Rhona thinks she hears a tiny, high-pitched cry.

Henderson falls head first and doesn't try to right himself. There's no sound as he hits the water.

The helicopter moves off towards the open sea and the islands.

'Christ!' says Arthur. 'What do we do now?'

'We just wait,' says Rhona, scanning the night sky. She sees nothing but a pale paring of moon. 'We just wait. He called the air ambulance, I'm sure of that. They'll come.'

She looks down at Will's still pale face wrapped in the

white sheet. When had Henderson first realised that Boyd and Kemp had turned against him? Was it when he felt Kemp's hand on the small of his back? Or was it earlier?

Now the surface of the loch has smoothed over. But she knows Henderson will still be sinking, falling through the water, just as he fell through the air.

Soon he'll land on the seabed. She can foresee his flesh being nibbled away by the fish, seaweed and eels wrapping around his bones and threading through the girdle of his pelvis, maybe a spider crab setting up home in his rib-cage. A useful death, she thinks. And he'd far prefer that to a lifetime in Barlinnie prison or a chipboard coffin, courtesy of the Co-op.

EPILOGUE

Rhona stands at the side of the road, dressed in her black woollen jacket. She looks down on the bay below: a curve of white sand encircled by steep hillsides. The valley is small, just a small graveyard and two green fields divided by an avenue of trees beginning to lose their leaves. Out on the beach she can see a scattering of tiny people in dark clothes.

Rhona feels a slow, tight tearing inside her. All those months ago when Arthur showed her a picture of the bay on his phone, he was right. This *is* the perfect place to be buried.

Behind her the van doors slam shut, and she steps sharply back from the edge. But of course, it's only Cat and the girl coming towards her. The girl, who Cat has named Molly, is fuller-faced now, nearly plump. She still doesn't speak, or smile. But sometimes – such as now – she holds Cat's hand.

It is easy to get down to the bay since the fence meshing has been removed, and all that remains are the ugly concrete uprights which straddle the hillside. All along the coast they still mark the boundaries of Henderson's reserve.

The path they take leads in zigzags through rust-coloured bracken, down to the bay. Rhona and Cat walk slowly on account of their tidy shoes. Even Molly, who normally runs everywhere, goes carefully.

When they reach the foot of the slope, the air is very

still. Rhona enters the avenue of sycamores and walks down towards the sea. Cat and Molly are behind her, and other mourners straggle after them. No one speaks. And, as at all funerals, the mourners come with their own private retinue of the dead. Rhona feels Maggie by her side and the much vaguer presence of her mother slips in and out between the trees. It's pointless, she's always thought, to have a headstone, or an urn. The dead never do leave – they creep out at every fold and corner in your life, they pop up during pauses in the day, only to vanish again and spring back when you turn off the light at night.

At the end of the avenue of trees, where the path spills onto the beach, a small queue of mourners is forming. Rhona waits in turn and shakes hands with the priest, a man in the black robes and the pillbox hat of the Russian Orthodox Church. He looks painfully young and has an eager-to-please manner and a rash of pimples under his chin. Next to the priest, not young or smiling and not at all eager to please, stands Marissa Henderson in all her cadaverous elegance. Her face has the clawed look of the very thin.

Rhona nods to her and Marissa Henderson nods back. The queue moves along and Rhona is finally released from the obsequies. She finds herself at the top of the beach, near the enormous pyre. The base is broad as a house and cunningly built, with quick lighting gorse and driftwood at the base and larger branches of pine and larch above. On pallets on the top lie the bodies of Will and Arthur, in their winding sheets.

Marissa had wanted separate pyres, but Arthur and Will left a letter; their ashes were to be indistinguishable.

They had planned very carefully. Three days ago, on the autumn equinox, they held their banquet on the beach. They'd arranged a trestle table facing out to sea, covered

308

with red damask and laid out with decanters of claret, pâtés, cheeses, a silver salt cellar containing hundreds of Secobarbital capsules, a platter with pineapple, black Muscat grapes, kiwi, doughnut peaches – fruit that no ordinary Scot has seen in years.

When they'd eaten and drunk and swallowed some of the pills, they lay down together on the sand, and the tide and the barbiturates washed over them. Later, Dr Rabina put the time of death at just after midnight.

Rhona looks back up the hill. People are still coming down the path and along the avenue of sycamores. She spies Laidlaw, here no doubt to report back to the Kirk, with Cummings and Jeanette. Some way behind is The Bassett, wrapped in a great overcoat and plodding slowly down the hillside. Of course, he had to come; he has known the Hendersons for years, and he had attended that terrible scene. He'd been staying over in his cottage in Kilchoan when the coastguard called and, on his way into work, he met Forensics down on the beach and examined the wreckage: the bodies blue with cold, the damask tablecloth covered in crow shit and scattered pills.

A brown-haired young woman with a striking, beaky profile is now standing by Marissa's side. This is Lucy Henderson, whom Rhona met briefly in the hospital when her father was still being rehabilitated, and the young woman was at Will's bedside as he recovered from his embolism. Lucy, after three months of chaos, has taken over the running of the Henderson estate. Thanks to her, the wolves have been shot, and the bears are now caged and ready for export.

Rhona thinks again about how foolish she was and how very slow to understand. Normally, when you solve a crime, you find the culprit and put them away. But this time everything was so much messier, and she has no sense of accomplishment, or even of completion. All she can do now is recognise how she failed. The other 'squirrel' boy, Mrs Collins' other young charge, has never been found. No one has been called to account. Boyd and Kemp and the hunters made a clean getaway. She had the helicopter traced to a private airfield near Belfast and a flight, supposedly to Minsk, left later that night from the same runway. But all the paperwork has mysteriously disappeared. Mrs Collins also vanished, leaving behind a surprisingly squalid bedroom. Matt Simpkins is no longer at home and, for young Gordon's sake, Rhona hasn't asked too many questions. Anyway, what can she do? The law is such a blunt, crude tool. You can't have justice in a country like this, not these days.

She feels a tap on her shoulder and turns to see a petite young woman in a black trouser suit with a huge floppy black hat. The woman tilts up her chin and there is that familiar smile, those sharp little teeth.

'Zoë! I didn't recognise you!'

'Good to see you. Are you here in a professional capacity?'

'Of course not.' Zoë is carrying a large stick with a bulb of cloth wound around one end. 'What's that in your hand?'

'It's the torch. I'm to light the pyre. Arthur put it in the letter. It's a final peace gesture, I suppose.'

Zoë has rolled up her sleeve and on the underside of her arm and wrist, she now has a complex design of red roses which mostly cover her old razor scars.

'So how are you these days?' says Rhona, hoping she won't be asked the same question herself.

'I'm fine,' says Zoë. 'I'm finishing clinical work in a couple of months.'

'I like the roses.'

Stephanie Heaney and the late Michael Heaney, Mike Snow, Anna Husarska, Mandy Kidd, Beth Benker, Peter Clegg, Emma Whitlock, Cordelia Hall, Alison Joseph, Hilary Matthews, Philippa Milnes-Smith, Alison Sterling and Jenny Brown.

And lastly, my sincere thanks to Clare Cain and her colleagues at Fledgling Press.

'They're not perfect – scarred skin is hard to work with.' Zoë gives a grimace. 'But you know how it is. You make the best of it all. You keep breathing and just shuffle on.' She looks at Molly who is crouched on the beach gathering stones. 'Isn't that…?'

'Yes. She's called Molly now. She lives with my friend Cat.'

'How is she?'

'It's hard to say at the moment. It'll take time.'

After a pause, Zoë says, 'You know, I misjudged Arthur.'

'So did I. It seems I misjudge everyone these days.'

'When he was fiddling the cards, I thought he was just saving his own skin. I didn't realise it was because he wanted to make sure he was there at the end.'

'I didn't expect him to go, either,' says Rhona. 'Did he call you beforehand?'

'Only to ask if I knew where he could source real pecorino.'

'And what did you say?'

'I was busy – I had a test the next day. So I didn't reply. I should have guessed it was for a last supper.'

A hand bell sounds.

'I've got to go now,' says Zoë.

With the pyre in front of them, they stand in rows, almost as if the beach were divided into pews. The young minister says a prayer in Russian and the mourners bow their heads. A small crop-haired boy, who reminds Rhona of Henderson's squirrels, swings an incense burner.

After the prayer, they sing the *Te Deum*, their voices thin in the open air.

Zoë comes forward, dips the cloth end of her stick in a small bowl of paraffin, lights the torch with a long match and holds it against the pyre.

The fire starts slowly and smokily. Suddenly it flares into life, spitting and crackling and quickly growing very hot. The congregation steps back, and as the branches crash, the flames soar upwards, cupping around the pallets on the top of the pyre.

Rhona moves away. She doesn't want to see the pallets drop or the winding sheets unwind. She's seen enough bodies.

She walks back down to the shoreline and rests her eyes on the smooth water of the loch and the view over the water to the mountains of Appin. A little way down the beach stands Molly. The girl has taken off her shoes. Now, with her bare feet in the sand, she leans back, narrows her eyes, and with one skilful swing of her arm she throws a flat pebble flicking across the surface of the water. The stone heads towards the sun, skipping once, twice, thrice, four times, five times. On the sixth bounce it finally loses its spin and plummets down into the icy water.

Acknowledgements

This book has, in large part, been a family and friends' effort. I am enormously indebted (as always) to my sisters, Sally Mitchison and Harriet Mitchison, for their blue pencils and their medical expertise, and to my brother, Neil Mitchison, for all things Gaelic and for his faultless grasp of Scottish topography. I am also very grateful to Kate Hordern who has been such a generous friend and advisor throughout.

Other writers gave me enormous amounts of support. Huge thanks to Russel McLean for pulling the whole plot into shape, and to Val McDermid for pointing out elephant traps, and to Louise Welsh for fine early edits and handy warnings, and to Mark Cocker for telling me not to rush, and to Sara Maitland for general joyousness, and to my beloved companion writers/doulas: Rebecca Lisle, Christine Purkis and the late Shosh Copley (aka Margaret Tabor) who all so generously lent their eyes and ears, and of course to the warm and redoubtable crime writing posse from Moniack Mhor: Claire Wilson, Suzy Aspley, Tricia Golledge, Sandra Kohls, Gillian Duff, Sarah Turner, Sylvia Hehir, June Fettes, Lou Williamson and Edith Cormack.

For other help – from advice and moral support to climbing mountains with me, feeding me tea and biscuits and keeping the wolf from my door – I am indebted to: Nigel Leask, Evelyn Arizpe, Angus Robertson, Anna Raven, Norrie Maclaren, Suzy Kennard, David Solomons, Helen Grant, Dick and Jenny Haldane, Kona Macphee, Ronnie Brown, Grace and Gordon Brewer, Michaela Wrong, John Mcintyre, David Swinburne, Elda Boyle, Steve Cook,

Stephanie Heaney and the late Michael Heaney, Mike Snow, Anna Husarska, Mandy Kidd, Beth Benker, Peter Clegg, Emma Whitlock, Cordelia Hall, Alison Joseph, Hilary Matthews, Philippa Milnes-Smith, Alison Sterling and Jenny Brown.

And lastly, my sincere thanks to Clare Cain and her colleagues at Fledgling Press.